By eight he still hadn't arrived. She dialled the number at 23B Drake Mews and when no one answered called room service instead and ordered a Waldorf salad. Then she went to the mini-bar to get mineral water and maybe olives. She opened the wood-veneer outer door, found crisps on the shelf over the fridge and opened them, spilling the packet on to an enamel tray decorated with pictures of Burmese dancing women. She had to pull hard at the fridge door: something sticky like orange juice had leaked and then congealed on the rubber strip and it came open suddenly with a tearing sound. She made a mental note to mention it to the barman next time he came to replenish it, and swung it wide open.

At first she thought there must be some mistake because Renard's head was inside. The interior light glowed dimly through the lobes of his ears, which were white and bloodless.

She closed the door slowly, then opened it again.

Not only Renard's head. His hands and feet were neatly piled there too.

All the drinks had been taken away.

Also by Mark Jones in Vista

BLACK LIGHTNING

MARK JONES
CAVIAR

VISTA

First published in Great Britain 1996
by Victor Gollancz

This Vista edition published 1997
Vista is an imprint of the Cassell Group
Wellington House, 125 Strand, London WC2R 0BB

A catalogue record for this book is
available from the British Library.

ISBN 0 575 60058 6

Printed and bound in Great Britain
by Cox & Wyman Ltd, Reading, Berks

97 98 99   10 9 8 7 6 5 4 3 2 1

For my wife Natalya,
who is the best thing in my life.
And who showed me
the real Russia.

Chapter 1

July 1994. Baku, Azerbaijan

'No one can eavesdrop here,' Ferguson bellowed into the American's ear, grinning at him. They were on one of the rig's lower decks. Machinery twisting drills into the seabed roared and groaned through the steel plating under their feet.

The American, a corporate relations executive from Bison Oil's Houston headquarters named Fergal Halloran, nodded. 'It's ideal,' he agreed.

'And it's secure. I don't need to touch dry land much. Which suits me because Baku is one big poisonous brothel. A chopper takes me straight to the airport when it's time to fly home. Unless some jackass has messed the paperwork and I have to sit in the company compound for a day or two.'

Halloran looked around and wondered how anyone could prefer this to the amenities of a town like Baku. 'Let's go upstairs,' he shouted at Ferguson. 'Quieter on deck.'

They climbed through hatches and across gangways, coming out on to the helipad. Ferguson led the way over the whitewash circle, with its giant, beckoning letter H, to the shoreward side of the rig. They were two miles offshore. Leaning on the handrail, they surveyed the scene. From this vantage point it was possible to see the file of Soviet-era, shallow-water inshore rigs that marched past Baku's crowded waterfront like a parade of giant crabs. Nodding donkeys rose and fell. Flares guttered overhead – the unwanted gas which comes up with crude like bubbles in champagne.

'Tell me, Ferguson,' Halloran asked, 'why did the Russians never come out here?'

'They didn't have the technology. There's a lake of sweet light crude under us but it's too deep below the seabed for Soviet know-how.'

Through Ferguson's binoculars – Russian-made Tentos with

7

powerful 20×60 prismatics – it all sprang close. Halloran could see the beachfront behind the platforms. Girls swung along the promenade. People shopped at lines of kiosks. A launch cruised gently over the sunlit water towards them.

He focused on it. Two men paced up and down the fly-bridge. The Azeri flag fluttered from the pennant over its stern. The company logo – a silhouetted bison, head down to charge – was visible on the bow. The same device was emblazoned on the side of the rig, one of several exploring the Caspian Sea for Bison Oil.

'The glasses are good,' Halloran said, handing them back. 'That's the service boat – the one that brought me.'

'Dubok is on it,' Ferguson said.

Halloran turned and leant back against the handrail. It would be a while before the launch arrived. He watched a couple of Azeri roustabouts wrestle some tackle across a platform area near the revolving shaft of the drill. Other men appeared from crew quarters and made their way down to the landing stage, ready to receive the launch, which was also carrying relief crewmen and supplies. One of them, a swarthy, squat hard-hat with a big wrench over his shoulder and a mouth full of gold teeth, raised a hand to acknowledge Ferguson's presence on deck. Ferguson saluted briefly back, calling out the man's name: 'Nazeem!'

'How do you get on with these guys?' Halloran asked.

'I'm from Glasgow. I'm a Presbyterian. They're little dark fellas from Azerbaijan and they're Muslims. But I love them. You know why? They're oilmen. We speak the same language. Take Nazeem. He was the first local I took on, when we assembled this rig right here in Baku. He's my top foreman. He thinks he owes me because I fished him from the drink when he fell through an open grating in some squally weather and nearly drowned. But he'd do the same for me.' Ferguson mopped his brow with a big polka-dot kerchief. 'The same language. Odd how that melts the barriers.'

Halloran looked coldly at him. Sam Ferguson was Bison Oil's exploration-rig general manager in Azerbaijan. He was also, for reasons which now seemed to Ferguson himself little more than historical accident, an IRA sleeper, committed to provide one service for the Irish Republican cause whenever its leaders asked him for it.

Recently, he had been asked. And now Ferguson was growing nervous. It made him talkative.

'Odd how you can be a Presbyterian,' Halloran said.

'Why?' Ferguson was puzzled. Then he understood. 'You don't mean oil, do you? You mean the other thing – the thing you're here for.'

'Yes.'

'You think it's strange because I don't sympathize with the Orangemen?'

'It may not be strange for a Glaswegian from a Loyalist background to give up parading with the Orangemen each twelfth of July. That might just be growing up. But for someone like that to become an IRA gun-runner takes a tad more believing.'

'You'd have to know the history of my family.'

'I'm not sure I want to. I've been told you're OK. That's enough for me.'

In fact, Halloran already knew Ferguson's history. It was the kind of convoluted story typical of intercommunal conflicts. A man's daughter is tarred and feathered by a Loyalist gang because she innocently dates a Catholic boy. The father beats up gang members in reprisal. A week later he is shot through the kneecap on the way home from the pub. He dies in hospital of septicaemia. And a family that never bothered much with the conflict between Catholic and Protestant, which has plagued Scottish as well as Irish history, gets off the fence at last – on the opposite side. And doesn't tell anyone. Because one thing its members know is that you don't *ever* announce a decision like that. You wait, and you take your revenge coldly, in the best way of the vendetta.

It was sixteen years – most of Sam Ferguson's adult life – since his father's death and his sister's destruction. He'd had one meeting in all that time with one very senior officer in the Irish Republican Army. He'd sworn an oath to that man and promised to be ready whenever the day came to perform whatever service the Cause required, because that IRA man took it on himself to avenge his father's death.

And now the time had come. Unexpectedly, as it was bound to do. Nerve-rackingly so, because one day that same man had appeared right here in Azerbaijan, without warning and with a message from the leadership. Was Ferguson prepared to stand by his sworn pledge, or not?

He hadn't needed to think about it. The answer was yes. The doubts only began afterwards – for by this time Sam Ferguson himself had a family, a career, a future, and it could all go up in smoke for the sake of one promise made long ago.

But he had no choice; they'd found him, they knew where he was and they called him to account. After all, in exchange for that promise, three men had died – the ones who'd killed his father.

This was a blood-debt which had to be paid, he'd been waiting to pay it, and now the moment had arrived Ferguson felt release as well as gut-clenching fear.

He would try to do what was necessary, he'd told this strange, tough-looking American they'd sent. *Even if it means being party to trading in plutonium,* he said to himself, *because I have to believe what they say: the IRA would never use nuclear weapons in their war with the British, because they know that would be the end for them. It's for demonstration purposes, nothing more. To frighten the Brits into peace talks and the Loyalists into compromise. To bring the Troubles to an end at last.*

The so-frightening American didn't like Ferguson's hint of prevarication. He would *do* what was necessary, Halloran had told him, not just *try to*, and his fierce blue eyes and the set of his face told Ferguson that this man would be his executioner if he failed.

Both men turned back to the waterside and looked over to where the launch was inching up the floating jetty, its bow thrusters edging its nose sideways in, its big stern transom already obscuring half the jetty where various stores were being unloaded. The launch was big: there were two lower decks; separate berths for eight or nine at least.

'Play it like we talked it through, Ferguson. Don't vary the script. This is not a diplomatic mission. I collect the stuff and I'm out of here. I don't, and you pay the price.'

Halloran didn't want to push the other man too far. But Ferguson had to be frightened, of the right people and for the right reasons. They were about to meet professionals operating on their own territory. Ferguson was a guy who'd spent most of his life dealing with flow-charts, for whom machines were more dangerous than people. Halloran thought he was flaky, knew the others would seé it and use it if they could.

'Let's go and meet them,' Ferguson said, starting back over the helipad. Halloran didn't follow at once. Instead he leant over the side to look below where the launch was tied up. A couple of deckhands tidied ropes and secured moorings. A crane lifted out shrink-wrapped pallets of stores: drums of chemicals, frozen food, maintenance sundries. Oilworkers came and went, some waiting to board the boat for shore leave, newcomers crowding the stern gangway, ready to come on shift. They were all waiting for something.

Halloran could see the reason for the delay. Two men were still in the stern of the boat. They weren't seafarers or oilmen: Halloran knew at once what they were. His own kind. One was sprawled on a wide seat, smoking. The other was standing up, balancing awkwardly against the swell and looking intently around. Like his companion, he was probably a Russian – big, with slicked-back hair, dressed in a good suit with shoes shiny as a lick of oil. He caught Halloran's gaze and stared hard. He had a Samsonite case between his feet.

Halloran stepped back. He didn't want to be singled out, yet. He was supposed to be an oil engineer. He was dressed like one, even down to the clipboard. His own 9mm Beretta was stuffed down the waist of his pants, out of sight under a big sand-coloured safari jacket.

When he looked again the scene had changed. Two more men had come on deck. – they looked like bosses. One was fat and wore a big panama and a baggy grey suit that flapped in the breeze. The other was tall, thin, bald and wore a black suit, the jacket carried over his shoulder despite the wind. The waiting oilmen made way for them. The big Russian with the briefcase went ahead, running up a ladderway and turning at the top to help the fat man who was directly behind.

Halloran caught up with Ferguson at the top of a flight of metal steps leading down to a landing ten metres by eight in size, open to the elements and criss-crossed with slanted girders supporting the helipad overhead. Here pallets of solvents and lubricants, paints and other chemicals, jostled for space with fifty-gallon drums of fuel oil and aviation spirit.

'It's a temporary arrangement,' Ferguson said, seeing Halloran's surprise. 'We had a problem with the finish on the main storage tanks below. Frankly, it wouldn't pass muster in the UK, but Azerbaijani health and safety regs are looser.'

'Doesn't it worry you? It's you that lives here.'

'No. It's safe enough. The only thing that could go wrong would be a helicopter crashing straight through the deck.'

11

'Or sabotage.'

'That's something you can never insure against on a rig like this. But in practice the only real danger is the sea. The Caspian is an inland sea, but sometimes there are storms here which make the North Sea look like a fishpond.'

They passed down two more steel ladders and came out on an accommodation deck. Metal doors opened into Ferguson's quarters and the administration suite. He and Halloran arrived just as the group from the launch came up. The big Russian appeared first, holding the Samsonite briefcase as if it was an icon, and Halloran knew why. Behind him came the fat man and the second Russian, a shorter man, in his mid-thirties, stocky, wearing a neat short-sleeved shirt that showed his freckled arms. He had sandy hair and his face was freckled too. Last of all came the tall, sallow, unhealthy-looking man. Like the fat man he was in his fifties.

The fat man called joyfully: '*Mistair* Ferguson, *Mistair* Ferguson,' and barrelled over to them. His face creased with smiles, he offered his hand, decided it wasn't enough and embraced Ferguson instead.

Halloran watched this outpouring of synthetic warmth and waited for Ferguson to introduce them.

'Mr Dubok, this is Mr Halloran. I told you about him.' Dubok nodded politely. 'Mr Dubok is the representative of the metal combine,' Ferguson told Halloran.

The two men shook hands.

'And this is Mr Kaluzhny, also from Moscow,' Dubok said, motioning to the big Russian. 'And Mr Skonkin, his associate.'

Last of all was Manteyev, the tall middle-aged one. His eyes were set too deep and too close together, and he suffered from eczema.

Ferguson showed them all into his office. There was a big circular table at one end, cabinets and a bar with a coffee machine on top.

'Pardon this intrusion,' the fat man said conversationally to Halloran while Skonkin ran a hand-scanner over him and Ferguson. 'We have to be cautious.' Then Skonkin went slowly round the room, checking for bugs and cameras, and found none.

Dubok smiled and his strange blue eyes almost disappeared in rolls of fat. 'Actually, we were pretty confident about you from the start, Mr Halloran. We knew Mr Ferguson's connections, after all.

We have sold weapons to the Irish revolutionaries before. Mortars, RPGs, that kind of thing. AK-47s.'

'Now you know we're honest men, it's time to show us what you've got.'

'Agreed, let us not waste time on ceremony, Mr Halloran.' It sounded like a reproof. 'It is an Azeri bad habit. American tempo! That was what Stalin decreed. We never learnt it, unfortunately. Now. Ten kilos was spoken of, yes?'

'Yes. Ten kilos. And another ten to follow.'

'It is a large amount. Why do you need so much? Half that would be enough to frighten the British out of Ireland.'

'One kilo wrapped inside some Semtex and parked on top of Nelson's Column would get them talking, I don't doubt. But we need twenty to allow for possible losses. There must be a reserve.'

Dubok's smile was beatific. 'Like any nuclear power,' he joked. 'The IRA needs a strategic reserve.'

'Exactly. In any case, it's not your problem, is it? You just supply the stuff. All you have to worry about is if I can pay.'

'Very reasonable, Mr Halloran.'

'And the price?'

'As discussed. Twenty kilos, ten million dollars. In cash.'

'Delivery?'

'The first parcel, now. The second, in one week's time.'

'You have it with you?'

'It is in Baku, yes. And you have the money?'

'I do.'

'Then, why delay?' Dubok rubbed his hands together. 'Let us finalize the arrangements.' He gestured to Kaluzhny, who picked up the briefcase he'd been carrying, placed it on the table and opened it. The briefcase was lined with a pink plastic material. There was a small envelope of the same material inside, resting on a larger case crudely sewn from the same pink plastic. Kaluzhny lifted them both out.

'The protective material is Soviet technology,' Dubok said, picking up the small envelope. 'Invented originally to shield our missiles from Mr Reagan's X-ray lasers. Six times more resistant to radiation than lead. And it works, which the X-ray lasers didn't.' Dubok pulled on a pair of surgical gloves and unfolded the envelope, prising out a sliver of silver-grey metal, the size of a thumbnail. He pushed it out on the table in front of them.

13

'A sample. A small memento.' He passed another pair of gloves to Halloran who donned them and picked up the shaving, examining it closely.

'That's plutonium,' Ferguson breathed, backing away.

'Don't be alarmed,' Dubok said. 'It's much safer than you think.'

Halloran put the sample back in its small envelope and pushed it to one side. He looked curiously at the big oblong package. 'That's it? The ten kilos?'

'Yes.' Dubok opened the package. Inside was a metal oblong the size of a telephone directory. 'Is it acceptable?'

'If it's up to spec, then yes.'

'Well, then? Do we deal?'

Halloran produced a pocket Geiger counter and ran it over the plutonium. It clicked like angry crickets. 'Sure, why not?' He went behind the bar, pulling out a metal photographer's case and bringing it to the table. He opened it and took out a blue banker's money bag.

'Five hundred thousand-dollar bills.' He handed the two wads to Dubok, who passed them to Manteyev. Manteyev stripped the paper binding off and began to count, until Dubok told him sharply in English not to. 'We trust our partners, of course.' He smiled at Halloran and then at Ferguson. 'Mr Manteyev is a Chechen,' he informed them. 'Naturally, he does not understand good manners.'

The plutonium was packed away and put back in its case, except for the sample which Halloran pocketed. 'I've got some lab kit to test it with,' he explained to Ferguson. 'A pleasure to do business, sir,' he told Dubok.

'Indeed. We should celebrate.'

Ferguson took the hint, went to the bar and came back with Azeri cognac.

'You will be staying in Baku, Mr Halloran?' Dubok asked. 'It's unfortunate I was unable to acquire the whole amount at once for you.'

'I can wait, yes.' He pointed to the case of plutonium. 'We'll keep it in Mr Ferguson's safe. It might give him nightmares, but it'll be secure enough.'

Everyone except Manteyev laughed politely at Halloran's small joke.

'This shows that serious men with mutual interests can always make business,' Dubok told them. He proposed dinner, that evening. Halloran said no; it didn't seem wise.

'But there is nothing to fear,' Dubok protested. 'In Baku everyone keeps to their own business. It's common courtesy not to show curiosity. You are an oil trader, you have every right to be here.' He squeezed Halloran's arm. 'Come, let us be convivial.'

Halloran relented. 'Well, why not? Maybe there'll be details to iron out.'

'Toasts to be made!'

'Exactly.'

'We'll meet at the Karavanserai. I'll book a cabin. Mr Ferguson knows where the Karavanserai is?'

Ferguson nodded; he knew. But he didn't like the idea.

Dubok took his party back to the boat. Halloran walked with them, finding himself next to Manteyev, 'I knew another Manteyev,' he told him. 'In Chicago. He came from Chechnya, like you. Maybe he's a relative?'

'Maybe, who knows? Our people are scattered around the world, like the Scots and the Irish. What was his first name?'

'Ziman.'

The Checken shook his head. 'Don't know him, but why would I? I was never in Chicago.' Manteyev laughed for the first time. 'Too many gangsters in Chicago; much too dangerous.'

Halloran and Ferguson took the launch ashore that evening and walked the short distance to the Karavanserai, an ancient hostelry dating from Marco Polo's day, and used for centuries by merchants travelling the Silk Route. The place contained two large halls, each with a fountain. One hall served Indian, the other Persian, cuisine. Small stone cubicles, which were once stabling for horses and camels, lined the Persian hall, a separate one for each party of diners.

Azeri hospitality requires many meat and fish courses and much champagne and cognac, and Dubok wasn't the type to cut corners. Dinner went on till late. The only person who didn't enjoy it was Manteyev. When gypsies came in to dance and sing, he slipped a note to Halloran. Crude English letters spelt *We must talk now!*

When the evening was over, Dubok, ominously genial, offered to drive them in his limo back to the enclosed landing-stage, a

15

mile from the Karavanserai, where the rig's service boat was waiting.

Ferguson accepted at once. He was drunk, the way only off-duty shore-leave oilmen can be. Kaluzhny, who had lost most of his chill during the course of the evening and had even been singing along with Ferguson, opened the door and helped him in.

But Halloran wanted to walk, and Manteyev, the Chechen, offered to walk with him. It was a beautiful night. A warm breeze agitated the tops of Baku's palm trees; girls strolled arm in arm along the brightly lit promenade. Trams rattled up and down. The two men waved the limo on and walked slowly after it.

No business had been talked all evening. The Karavanserai was a well-known watering hole, frequented by Western oilworkers and business people, and top-heavy with Azeri as well as Russian secret servicemen. Now Manteyev wasted no time. 'Mr Halloran, I have something important to say to you,' he said melodramatically. He looked around carefully, suddenly bending to tie his shoe laces. Halloran looked around too; he'd already seen a little Azeri following them, but now he wanted him to know he'd seen him. The Azeri stopped, sauntered over to a kiosk, began to haggle for ice cream with the woman running it.

'That man is following us,' Halloran observed.

'I know, and I know who he is. Wait here please, Mr Halloran.' Manteyev walked slowly back to the kiosk. He spoke quietly at first to the Azeri, but within seconds a violent argument had flared; the two men began to push each other and onlookers gathered. Halloran walked over. Manteyev was screaming at the little man, calling him a pimp and similar insults. At first, the Azeri shouted back, but when he saw Halloran move he began to subside and when Manteyev pushed him a couple more times, he backed away into the growing crowd of spectators, and disappeared. His parting words were *Yuda-predatel*, Judas-traitor, a strong term of abuse in Russian.

The crowd moved on, and Halloran and Manteyev carried on down the promenade.

Manteyev was unnerved. He mumbled to himself in Chechen, which Halloran did not speak. It took a while for him to regain his poise. By then the landing-stage was in sight, so Halloran stopped and steered Manteyev to an outdoor beer-bar which was still open. The bar was empty, but the barkeeper was in no hurry to close.

16

More customers would drift along; two prostitutes, sleazy but glittering in the Levantine way of Baku, swaggered in and scrutinized Halloran, the obvious foreigner. He turned away, pressing Manteyev now, urgent, insistent.

'What's going on? We don't have time for this. Tell me what you know.'

'I know who you are, Mr Halloran,' Manteyev told him in his broken English. 'You are CIA. That I know, it does not matter; I knew anyway. It was my circle which hoped to tempt you here. But now Mr Dubok knows as well, and that is a different story. He found out this afternoon. Now he very angry. He even thought to poison you over dinner. I dissuaded. At least, I hope I dissuaded.' He looked anxiously at Halloran. 'How you feel now?'

'Fine. So far.'

'Good. I don't know anything. I am suspect too. This little man told me something very poor. Now I am shocked.' Manteyev seemed to be going into a panic attack. He'd begun to shake uncontrollably, and cold sweat glistened on his forehead. 'In this case, my life also – over.' He grimaced. 'I should like to call my wife, just now, but she in Moscow regrettably, because she too in serious trouble, because of me.'

He'd been talking fast, his poor English starting to unravel. Now his pale tongue wiped spittle from his lips. An extraordinary look appeared on his face – his mouth curled in a grin of terror, but his clenched, narrow eyes opened wide, and shone with what might as well be joy as fear.

'Manteyev, the turncoat, the Russian-lover; Manteyev the coward – that is what some of my people have called me.' He laughed, but his throat was too dry and it came out like paper rustling. He sipped beer and went on: 'These fools – stupid people – who call me spy. Imagine! And for them I did this thing. For them! So no one will say it again. No one.' He shook his head and groaned. 'What to do?'

Halloran said in Russian: 'Perhaps you should get straight to the point and save the melodrama for later. What's going on, Manteyev?'

'You are right, of course. They can come for us at any moment. The only problem is that the plutonium is on the rig. That is what makes Dubok really furious. It is his big problem. What the hell—'

The little Azeri had reappeared. There were others, shadows

17

moving in. The fat man had set everything up for the kill.

Halloran plotted the hit-team: there were four nearby, and certainly others in cars or further off.

A tram ground to a halt, stopping the traffic behind it, according to the local rules of the road.

'Let's fuck off out of here,' Halloran said, grabbing Manteyev's wrist and yanking him upright so that his eyes were on a level with his. 'Do whatever I say,' he hissed. 'I'm going to save you, OK?'

'OK,' Manteyev whispered.

Another oncoming tram grating noisily over points obscured the sound of Halloran's first two shots.

It didn't obscure the answering fire, however, or the screams and pandemonium erupting in the crowd as Halloran leapt from the tattered pavilion dragging Manteyev at a run behind. The doors of the stationary tram were sliding shut when he and the Chechen dashed through them. Bullets spattered over the outer skin, and windows shattered. But this was a Soviet-built tram, from the Chelyabinsk works which once also fabricated hull sections for nuclear submarines; it lurched unstoppably forward and the driver, a fat, sleepy woman, didn't hear the screams of the passengers and ignored the gunfire outside, which was not an unusual sound in Baku anyway.

They could see the two survivors of Dubok's team racing behind. A big white Mercedes swerved violently round and accelerated after the tram. Manteyev straightened up, saw the smile on Halloran's face as the tram slowed to its next stop. The driver had noticed something at last and was leering back at the saloon, where screaming passengers crouched on the floor. When the doors opened the two men leapt off and raced across the broad boulevard behind the tram, slaloming through roaring traffic, Manteyev leading this time.

Halloran followed him down a narrow passage between two houses, and almost immediately they entered the maze of narrow streets, courtyards and passages leading into the old town. They ran for several minutes until Manteyev had to stop at last. Now they were in a stone-dead, night-dark alley.

'We've lost them for sure,' Manteyev gasped, bent double and panting for breath.

'Maybe.' Halloran strained to listen, but there was no sound of running feet, no car engines. They waited five minutes, ten.

'I know Baku,' Manteyev grinned. 'And so do they. They know they've missed their chance. For now, anyway.'

'We need some help,' Halloran said. 'I can bring it here.'

'How long will it take?'

'Ten, fifteen minutes.'

'Too dangerous. We can't wait.'

'It's not only us. It's Ferguson.'

The Chechen grimaced. 'Too late for him already, my friend.'

They walked further into the old part of town, between white stuccoed houses braced around with verandas, mostly dark and closed, but some with the shutters thrown back and parties going on inside, often with girls parading.

They filtered through alleys and dodged old American cars that whirled like Wurlitzers, all chrome and lights, with wild Azeri cowboys whooping at the wheel, until finally they came to a quieter street of larger houses, turn of the century merchants' residences, and Manteyev led Halloran under an archway and into a circular courtyard, where a few cars were parked and an incongruous fountain played. Halloran checked the time; it was thirty minutes since the shoot-out.

Doors opened into the courtyard, and lights were on. They could hear girls talking. He followed Manteyev down a passage and into a kitchen, beyond which was a small, unkempt office with wicker furniture, a big ceiling fan and a Japanese air conditioner whirring cold air into the room from a corner. A blowsy Russian woman was talking on the phone, apparently to clients, discussing the prices of various girls, her feet up on a battered roll-top desk, smoking a cigarette while she talked. She nodded cursorily at Manteyev, looked at Halloran with more interest. Her haggling was all but done, and when she put the phone down Manteyev told her to bring them vodka and mineral water, and leave them alone. As she left the room she called him and he followed her out.

In a minute he came back. They sat down, and when she brought the drinks and a plate of salami and cut bread Manteyev slipped her a hundred-dollar bill. 'This is Rosa,' he told Halloran. The woman smiled at him and left without speaking. 'My kinswoman. Half-sister,' he added.

'How long before they come looking here?'

'They've already been. But they can't do much. There are three government ministers upstairs right now – and a deputy police

19

chief.' He grinned at Halloran. We'll be OK for a while.'

'Then it's time to call out the cavalry.' From his top pocket Halloran took the pen which also contained a Global Positioning Satellite location-fixer and radio beacon. He twisted the cap the three turns that triggered it. If it worked, a duty officer in the American embassy in Baku would hear the signal and with the aid of the GPS navigator work out within seconds where it was coming from, to within five metres. Then it would be a question of how long the back-up unit would take to find the place.

'Tell me about Dubok,' he said.

'Dubok is a big boss at Minatom. He thinks anyone who tries to buy his plutonium is a CIA plant. But he made an exception in your case. He is a very cautious old bureaucrat and would never have come here in person if he hadn't been so sure about you. It was a lesson for him. He decided that anyone who came on the personal recommendation of Sean McMahon, the legendary leader of the Irish Republican Army, had to be genuine. He was shocked to discover you weren't. At first he couldn't credit it – he told me he spent an hour on the phone to Moscow checking. But in the end he heard it from someone he just had to believe.' He glared reproachfully at Halloran. 'Someone betrayed you – us – and it wasn't our Irish friends.'

Halloran sipped water and let him talk.

'Dubok is important. Usually people who make these dime-store deals are not serious men. Simply shit. After all, a few measly million dollars! It is almost a joke. People of Dubok's rank don't normally interest themselves. So either he is too greedy, or this deal is a cover for something bigger. And I am sure that it is.'

'What bigger deal?'

'I'll tell you. This twenty kilos. You think this came from some depot, some barracks or silo-farm? It's another warhead, right?' He shook his head. 'Wrong. This is just a little something they stole from what was already stolen, long ago, in Soviet times. That's what no one knows about. That's why I say: test out the product. Find where it comes from.'

'I noticed that what Dubok had was just a lump of raw metal. It wasn't machined. I was expecting to see a spherical warhead component. So it could only have come from a stockpile. But how much is there?'

'A lot. One hell of a lot.' Manteyev gave him a sly look. 'Thirty tonnes. Surprised? Of course you are. I see it on your face. But it's true. At least that much! Maybe more.' He was swaying in his chair, drunk not so much with alcohol as with fatigue, with the endless pressure, with fear that never left him even when he slept.

'Thirty tonnes is impossible,' Halloran told him.

The Chechen grinned. 'Of course. Impossible. I know, your International Atomic Energy Agency tells you so, for one thing. The inspectors are crawling over every storage and reprocessing facility, every fast-breeder, every plutonium-capable reactor in the former Soviet Union. That's what you all think. What you are so sure of.'

'But how could a colossal amount like that slip through the net? It's enough to make thousands of warheads. There's been a complete audit of the Russian nuclear industry. They couldn't have missed it.'

Manteyev poured vodka, gave Halloran a glass and clinked it. 'Nevertheless, it exists.'

'Exists where?'

'The product comes from the Shevchenko fast-breeder plant. But it was long ago taken from there. We do not know where it is now.'

There was a faint shuffling in the corridor and Manteyev, who'd been slouching so deep he looked half asleep, surprised Halloran with the speed at which he came from his chair and rushed across the room, whipping open the door. Someone squealed, Manteyev's hand shot out, there was a yelp and a girl flew across the room and slammed into the roll-top desk opposite the door.

She was eighteen or twenty, brown-skinned, big-eyed and sulky. 'This is Dinara, my little chicken, my pet,' Manteyev said, his speech slurred and drawling.

Dinara turned round and Manteyev slouched to her, grabbed her arm and twisted her upright, then slapped her face, not playfully, but not cruelly either. She gasped but didn't speak or move, just hung limp. 'Why aren't you working, then, hey?'

'I was waiting for you,' Dinara lisped, all the time staring at Halloran, pouting at him, her great eyes full of curiosity. Manteyev shook her. 'Bring some sweets, chicken,' he told her, 'and bring a friend.' She flounced out, and he watched her go. 'They are like flies round a honeypot,' he said.

'Where is the stuff going?' Halloran asked Manteyev.

'Iran. All of it.'

'I still don't understand why you are telling me this, Manteyev. Just what is your angle?'

'When your friends arrive, I will tell you. Not here.'

They didn't have long to wait. The back-up unit – eight plainclothes marines in three civilian but specially modified vehicles – arrived in less than six minutes. The first was driven by Chuck Smith, Baku head of station.

There was no drama, apart from Dinara's vocal disappointment. As they pulled away in the second of the three vehicles, Halloran told Commander Murphy, the officer in charge, what he needed first: to get a helicopter out to the Bison rig, to bring back Ferguson and retrieve the contents of his office safe.

The marines did not find Ferguson and the safe was open and empty.

The rig manager's body was collected next morning from the underwater joists it had lodged in, beneath the Bison rig.

The cause of death was certified as accidental drowning. The coroner noted the high level of blood alcohol found in the body as a probable contributory cause.

Also discovered dumped in a Baku alley was a mutilated body. Stolen from Baku city morgue, the body would be identified as Dovlat Manteyev, a former particle physicist, by his wife who came from Moscow for the purpose.

Subsequently the Manteyevs were discreetly flown to the United States. After debriefing they began a new life with new identities, where Manteyev would not be at risk of jeopardizing an operation aimed at uncovering illegal Russian plutonium deliveries to Iran.

Halloran – whose identity in fact was CIA agent Douglas Renard – flew back to Washington at the same time.

Chapter 2

'I'm looking for the 1891 edition,' Douglas Renard said.

'We were told you might have it,' his wife Zidra added.

They were standing in a crowded, musty, over-humid book-shop, full of mouldering volumes and cagouled people most of whom had rushed from the street to shelter from a sudden downpour. There was an art festival in Burlaston, and the town was full of visitors.

'Really?' The bookseller looked uncertainly from one to the other. 'The second edition of *Stalky & Co.* This is a misery, isn't it? I am sorry.' He shook his head, disconsolate. 'But no.' His mournful, predatory eyes gazed at them. 'No, I can't think who might have said it. I haven't seen a copy for years.'

'A friend of mine told us about you. In Vermont.'

'Ah, I see. A friend from *Vermont*. That might explain it.'

'There's a Kipling society in Vermont. There's a market now for this kind of stuff.'

'Of course. A society. Kipling incunabula.' The bookseller had a round, pasty face, and his owlish eyes stared like lamps from behind thick lenses. 'And you are also from Vermont?'

'We're from Philadelphia. But we're members.'

'And you're in England on holiday?'

'Yes. And we're specially keen to find this book, now we're here. We were definitely told you were a Kipling collector.'

'I am. I have several first editions of *Stalky & Co*, and I even once had the 1891, complete with errata. But I disposed of it some years ago.'

Zidra looked crestfallen. 'You don't recall to whom?'

'It went to auction. I've no idea who bid for it.'

It was hard to talk because the bookseller was constantly distracted. An impatient, determined Englishwoman dragged him away to consult on a book about flower arranging. The Renards waited patiently until he came back to them.

'You'd still be interested, even if in the end you are unable to acquire it? If the collector refuses to part with it?'

'Exactly so. Just to see it would be great.'

'As I say, I don't have a copy myself,' he said. 'But I know of someone who might, though I'm sure he won't part with it. I'm wondering what the point is,' he said, his eyes round with sudden cupidity.

'Can you at least tell us where we can find him?' Renard said.

'He's not in Burlaston.' He gave a queer look. 'So there's a Kipling society now, in Vermont? A hundred years too late, I should say.'

'Better late than never!' Zidra said.

'Well, indeed.' The bookseller's mouth upturned in a gluey smile. He stuck a tubby hand out and shook each of theirs in turn. 'Loyard's my name, by the way. And you are?'

'Mr and Mrs Halloran.'

'Pleased to meet you. Yes, I know where there might be a copy. To tell you the truth I tried to acquire it myself, for twice what my own copy fetched at auction, and the chap refused point blank.'

Loyard was talking mostly to Zidra. She smiled encouragingly back.

'Who is this man?' she asked.

'Chap called Hitchens. He's got a little place in Eden Castle.'

'Eden Castle – where's that?'

'About fifty miles north of here. Got a map?'

'Of course.'

'You won't have any difficulty finding it. Hitchens' place is in the town's High Street.'

'Thanks.'

'I can call him if you like. Save you a wasted journey. Shall I?'

'That would be gracious of you,' Zidra said.

Loyard pulled a dog-eared notebook from the wooden drawer where he kept cash from sales, and slowly thumbed through it. 'You'll need someone to negotiate with him for you. He's a funny old fish. Here it is.' He picked up the phone and dialled the number.

The Eden Castle bookseller took a long time to answer, and, when he did, even longer to understand the point of the call. 'He's very old,' Loyard mouthed to Zidra, while the questions Hitchens fired at him buzzed in his ear like flies.

At last Loyard said goodbye and hung up. 'He's a jobbing printer as well, you know. Hot metal. *Lead*,' he said conspiratorially to Zidra, circling a fat forefinger at his own temple. 'But he's still got the book, and he'd be pleased to show it to you.'

They left at once for Eden Castle, driving through the scenic Welsh Borders.

Next morning Renard visited Hitchens alone, introducing himself as Fergal Halloran, an American oil executive. He thanked Hitchens for agreeing to show him the book.

And then the man began to talk.

What he said encouraged Renard enough to stay in the town for a few days. They booked the best suite at the Lamb and Lion and told the innkeeper's wife that Eden Castle was every American's dream.

'He's the one,' Renard told Zidra when he'd spent a few hours with Hitchens. 'There's no doubt about it. *Someone with a different kind of grudge against the British Establishment*, Sean McMahon said, *not the same as ours*. McMahon described him as in his late seventies, and a right-wing fanatic who met Adolf Hitler in his youth. Hitchens fits the profile.'

'Not the kind of person you'd expect to be supporting the Irish Republican cause,' Zidra said.

'Or providing a front for a renegade Active Service Unit which the leadership has lost control of. This was the only lead McMahon could give us as to its whereabouts.'

'That's the downside of operating through cut-outs.'

'They don't have any choice about that. If they knew where their own front-line troops were, they'd have to be in hiding themselves. Anyway, it's definitely him. He couldn't wait to tell me about himself. His parents were supporters of Oswald Mosley's British Union of Fascists. In 1937 they went on a touring holiday in Germany. He showed me the family snapshots. There's one of him dressed in a Hitler Youth outfit, shaking hands with Hitler at a Nuremberg rally. He was fourteen years old. He told me a lot about Hitler's eyes. Said if I'd been lucky enough to meet him, I would have understood a lot of things.'

They needed a base so they visited an estate agent in a crumbling lath-and-timber shop with oblique, rutted stairs and told him they wanted to rent a place. Maybe buy somewhere. He gave them a sheaf of prospectuses, and within a week they'd rented a farmhouse in a remote tract of land called Hawtree Fell.

Renard, correctly assuming that the agent was a conduit of gossip, explained confidentially that he and Mrs Halloran were touring Europe and would eventually go back to their New England life of quiet retirement.

They spent several weeks doing the obvious things: walking in the hills, viewing castles and battlefields, meeting the locals. They relaxed, read the papers, bought more books, few of them published in the twentieth century.

The farmhouse – built at the head of a valley overlooking pasture and woodland where nothing moved but sheep – was perfect. It had no electricity, a Victorian cast-iron range in the low-ceilinged kitchen, a Jacobean dresser downstairs and a four-poster bed above. Water came from the stream that tumbled noisily by the house, falling like a braid of light down into the valley.

The only road to the place followed the stream, so anyone approaching was visible for miles. Few did apart from locals and occasional opportunist climbers who wanted to assault the cliff which rose behind the house to the valley top.

If they wanted groceries they went into Eden Castle. Renard paid several visits to Hitchens, failed to persuade him to part with the second edition Kipling but acquired something he said he liked more: a Victorian vellum-lined bible. Solid, well made, it was the kind of bible that people inscribe with the genealogy of passing generations. Except this one was not foxed or worn with use and the dedication, scratched in spidery copperplate, read: *My beloved is mine, and I am his: he feedeth among the lilies. Until the day break and the shadows flee away.* It was signed *From Gwyneth to my Beloved.* The date was 21 July, 1886. Renard gave the book to Zidra.

'I heard from Bryce,' he told her one morning after a long session passing coded messages back and forward to the London station. 'And we can pack. The surveillance team won't be coming. The operation is off. McMahon has made contact with his people and called them in. It's over.'

'So they weren't break-aways?'

'No. Just incompetent, or unlucky. We can leave tomorrow or Sunday.'

'I have all these mushrooms to finish.'

'So I see.'

Zidra had spent the early morning mushrooming. She enjoyed walking, and mushrooming was a lifelong mania that also gave her a reason for exploring the countryside around Eden Castle. She'd had a successful outing and brought back kilos for pickling, commandeering every bucket, pail and bowl in the place, filling them with water to clean and detoxify the mounds of golden-brown honey mushrooms, their caps like umbrellas, the stalks thin and spindly; and the rarest treasure in English woods – *Boletus edulis*, smooth, heavy hemispheres stippled brown and shiny on top and with deep olive-green gills.

'It's a shame to go,' she told him while she worked. 'It was becoming a holiday. Maybe we'll rent the place a while longer anyway, and come back for a real vacation?'

'Why not? I'll call the agent. But we have to go to London first and finish up. The Broughtons are expecting us. And there's the Bison reception at the Foreign Office.'

'So this is our last evening here?'

'This is our last evening.'

'We should do something dark and obsessional, then. Like Gwyneth and her benighted lover.'

'I have the very thing.'

'What?'

'I bought you something else in Eden Castle.'

He gave her a little jewellery box. She brushed mulch and pine needles from her fingers, flipped the lid and looked inside. It was a pair of gold studs, set with ice-blue diamonds, a third or half a carat each. The posts screwed solidly into the butterfly back-plates.

'They're beautiful!' She held them up to the light. The diamonds glittered. 'But these are ear-studs,' she said, looking puzzled. 'Not very obsessional or anything.'

'No, they're not for your ears.' He held them next to her skin. 'Perfect.'

They drove to London the next day and booked in at the Mountbatten Hotel in Covent Garden as Mr and Mrs Davies. The following morning, Renard went along to the embassy. He was met by Frederick Bryce, who was the new CIA resident. Bryce was Ivy League, six-foot-two, blond, crew-cut, blue-eyed and charming. He was also ten years younger than Renard. Zidra had met him before.

'Bob Hill's flown in,' he told Renard as they walked the long corridor to his office. 'Something's come up. We've had word from Moscow.'

He showed Renard into a small white-walled secure room with a table for four, a coffee-maker and a PC with an OHP screen attached. Bob Hill was already waiting. While Bryce fixed coffee, Hill – the Texan freebooter, Renard's friend from way back – told Renard his news.

'While you two were vacationing in the English countryside, we continued to watch events in Baku. Everything Manteyev told us checks out. The Iran deal is on. And that's all we have to worry about, because there won't be any Irish deliveries. The IRA have got cold feet, and so have the Russians. They've all cried off, so we're folding our tents.'

Renard squinted at Hill. 'What happened? The White House lose interest?'

'On the contrary. The President is as interested as hell in Ireland. But the more State looked at it, the more nervous they got, until in the end they were hopping around like kittens on the outskirts of hell. And we could see their point – there are just two many balls to keep in the air at one time. It all sounds great in theory: let the IRA prove it can be a good international citizen by helping us entrap plutonium smugglers, and in return the Administration will prevail on the Brits to lean on the Ulster Unionists and get peace talks going; but in practice it's just too sensitive. Too many British bruised egos to worry about. Too much nervousness, frankly, about the IRA's real intentions. Though Sean McMahon looks impressive enough.'

'And McMahon is also paranoid about being set up, I suppose?'

'Totally. The President personally gave him his word that this operation was not CIA black arts and wouldn't be used to compromise the IRA in the future. But if his own front-line troops are starting to mutiny because they think he's sold out, then I can understand McMahon's getting cold feet.'

'If they have mutinied. Maybe the so-called renegades were acting under orders the whole time.'

'Why do you say so?' The smile on Hill's face faded as the implications of what Renard was suggesting sank home.

'Suppose the Active Service Unit has not gone to bush after all, but is still reacting to McMahon's orders? It makes a lot of sense for him to say that the IRA have lost control of events, in case something really does go wrong, or they are being set up after all. We'll be left holding the baby, and it won't help to argue that the Brits knew all along because *unofficially* you talk to Sir Derek Broughton. If it turns out that McMahon was suckering us to get his hands on the ultimate negotiating tool, then it will look as if the Brits are right when they say that these people are incorrigible terrorists and should be excluded for ever from the political process. The President will look more fatuous than unscrupulous, but enough of both to do him no good.'

'I think the British are much more ambivalent about Ireland than they show in public. McMahon, for instance, has never had any difficulty getting his views heard by British government ministers, however much they pretend in public that he's a pariah. And Broughton is very helpful, in fact. There's no way he'd be surprised by our working closely with the IRA on a security matter as sensitive as Russian nuclear smuggling. If they haven't done it themselves it's only because we thought of it first.'

'Yeah, fools rush in. I must tell you, Bob, that this kind of thinking worries me. The Brits and the Irish have been nasty to each other since the twelfth century. Now we've got an Irish-American President who wants to bring peace to Ireland and thinks this is a way. Even Ronald Reagan never had *that* fantasy. Doesn't it worry you?'

Bob Hill said, 'Forget it, Douglas. This is all academic because the whole deal is off, over, kaput. So let's get back to what we really know about – namely, Russia. That's what I came from Washington to talk to you about, not Ireland. Because a big piece of machinery has come adrift and it has to be put straight.'

Renard looked cynical. 'Don't tell me. Your Baku babies have fucked up again.'

'It's serious this time. Chuck Smith is dead. And he left a mess.'

Renard stalled, breathed in, exhaled slowly, and asked: 'How?'

'He was killed in a road accident, day before yesterday.'

'Where? In Baku?'

'Yes.'

Renard had the look of someone who has just been unexpectedly slapped in the face. More puzzled than hurt. 'How'd it happen?'

'A head-on collision. The other driver was also killed. you know how Azeris drive. The guy came round a bend much too wide. It wouldn't have made us feel anything more than upset, if Chuck hadn't been about to move against your pal Dubok.'

'Why? Because of the Iran deal?'

'He was certain that the thirty tonnes of plutonium is about to be shipped. Almost to the day when the Eden Castle thing was meant to happen. That's what we know, or what Chuck thought he knew, and told us. He didn't have time to tell us everything, though. We still don't know from where, or how, the stuff is going to be shipped. So we can't do anything to prevent it.'

Renard shook his head. 'I'm retired. Find someone else. I'm too visible in Baku, anyway. My own mission there was betrayed, and I hardly came out alive myself. And Zidra will kill me if I tell her I'm going straight back there. Be reasonable!'

'The leak might not have been there. Dubok heard something in Moscow; that's where you've got a problem, not Baku. Maybe it wasn't in Russia at all. Maybe it was right here, in England.'

'In that sense, it almost makes no difference, because it still comes down to this: in Moscow or Baku, I'm known, blown, and can't go back.'

'You can. You have to. No one else can make the connections in time.'

'What you mean is, you want me as cheese to put in your trap. But there are plenty of others who can go. You, for instance.'

'I am going, but I need you along. I can't do it alone. You know that.'

Renard was shaking his head, but Hill said: 'We're absolutely sure now that there's a link with the IRA deal-that-never-was. That makes the Iran delivery doubly sensitive. Because if things go wrong and it turns out we haven't kept our British allies informed and therefore able to stop us making the mistakes which permitted it to happen, it will be ten years in the living down. That, and a nuclear-capable Iran, will be too much for this presidency to bear. Morgan might not even finish his term.'

'How is it connected with the IRA non-deal? By the go-between?'

'Yes. You were right all along. The go-between is the same in both cases. That's one of the few things we know for sure. Harvey Goldman.'

'The British businessman?'

'Yes. Him. There's no doubt at all he's the link. He and his bosom pal and lifetime partner, Ernest Dubok. This is a story in the tradition of Dale Carnegie. Two guys who started small, just selling warheads out of suitcases. We know he's scouted the opportunities in Algeria. He's even been in Yugoslavia. Then as he and Dubok began to cosy up, they thought bigger. Dubok said he could lay hands on unlimited quantities of plutonium, which the Russian government had forgotten about and has never been declared. And Goldman thought of Iran.'

'If they plan to tranship the full amount that will be a big operation however it's done. It'll show up in lots of ways,' Renard mused. 'Why not just wait for the satellite images to tell us the story?'

'It'll be too late by then. We are not going to sit on our hands while Iran becomes the next nuclear power. With that amount of plutonium they would be second only to the US and Russia. That's why we need to find out what Goldman is up to.'

'Do you have anything useful to go on?'

'Yes. Goldman was the last person Chuck Smith met, just the day before he died. And he planned to meet him again. So we think it was Goldman who set him up.'

Renard made a face. 'That's awfully thin. Look, Goldman is a Brit. Have you talked to Broughton about him? At some point we have to level with them. Better sooner than later, in view of this escalating shite-ola all around.'

'Who is this Broughton character anyway?' Bryce asked as he handed out coffee.

'You're supposed to know that,' Hill told him.

'I mean, apart from the British ambassador to Moscow. I know he's that.'

'He's an MI6 Deputy Director and he's our direct link to 10 Downing Street.' Hill's look bordered on incredulity. 'Like I say, Bryce, you're supposed to know. He's also the only damn Limey I trust.' He did not hide the reproof. Bryce sat down abruptly and gripped his coffee cup in both of his big, very white hands.

'Well, *why* do we trust the Limey, then?' he asked.

Hill's look veered towards malice. 'Because I've known Sir Derek Broughton for more than twenty years. That do?'

'Not really.'

'Tell him, Bob,' Renard said and when Hill didn't answer, he told Bryce himself: 'In the first place, you trust someone because of the look in their eyes. Then because you work with them. The usual reasons, in other words. That's what Hill is afraid to say. Not because of Langley's bio-histories and profiles and test-scores. The files are mostly crap, in our specialty. The only ones any use are the KGB's, because they tell us what the enemy thought about us, who they respected and who among us they considered for sale. They helped. So it's down to that old subjective instinct thing. We're not proud of it. We get shouted at for it. But it's all we know.'

'Yeah, it's mainly because of the look in their eyes,' Hill said.

'You mentioned Manteyev,' Renard said, returning to the discussion. 'Does anyone in Langley believe him now?'

'That, of course, was the problem. Why are we so unprepared now? Because when Manteyev came along with the legend of the thirty tonnes it was generally assumed he was organizing his pension. No one believed a Chechen wild man.'

'That's been the trouble. The Irish have the same credibility problems. Family feuds, shoot-outs and vendettas – the only thing you can be sure of is that you can't trust any of the duplicitous SOBs. And whatever their leader says, there's always an extremist second cousin who says, *Fuck everybody, I'm going on with the war, and now I've got the ultimate weapon to do it with*.' Renard grinned at Hill. 'It was supposed to come from somewhere called Shevchenko, wasn't it? The thirty tonnes?'

'Yes. Bryce, where is Shevchenko?'

'Show him, Bryce,' Renard said.

'Sure.' Bryce fiddled with the OHP until a map of the former Soviet Union appeared on the screen. 'Here. On the eastern seaboard of the Caspian. The Soviets built a fast breeder there. They claimed it was a desalination plant. They were going to make the desert bloom. Actually they made the desert bigger and covered it with uranium dust.' He ran his finger round the Caspian, looking at God knows what, then sat down again.

'So who else will be involved, apart from us?' Renard asked.

Hill's smile was broad, frank, like a shark greeting its lunch. 'If you mean, is this going to be a three-person team, forget it. Zidra is *out*. The President himself told me to say so. Maybe he's fallen in love with her. Why not? Everyone else has. Whatever, she's forbidden to participate in this mission. You and I will go our own way to Baku and try to pick up the trail left by Dr Manteyev.'

'Ouch.' Renard looked rueful. 'But I can't disagree. She'd be too visible.' He shrugged. 'OK, forget it. So when do we leave?'

'Day after tomorrow. We'll go as business travellers on a scheduled flight to Baku.' He smiled at Renard. 'How will she take it?'

'Badly.'

'So don't tell her.'

'That's a lousy rotten trick. You know I never lie to her.'

'She doesn't know I'm in London. You could tell her you're going to Washington for a couple of days to meet me and the NSA.'

'Cheap. She'd never buy it.'

'We'll be back Thursday, Friday at the latest.'

'Don't worry, Bob,' he said in the end. 'I'll explain it to her.'

Hill said: 'Fine. One other thing. About Broughton. We need to update him.'

'Fortunately I have a dinner date with Broughton tonight,' Renard said. 'I'll meet him beforehand and find time to discuss what we're planning.'

They'd already finished when the phone rang: a receptionist called to tell Renard his wife was waiting in the lobby.

He said goodbye to Hill and went to met her with Bryce.

Zidra was sitting in an armchair reading a newspaper. It was a warm autumn day and she was wearing a short dress made of clingy peach-coloured silk and a big straw hat, and her legs. She stood up and shook Bryce by the hand, asking with dangerous politeness how everything was. Fine, he told her, compressing his lips in a thin smile. But Douglas would tell her the details.

Chapter 3

'I'll have to scrap lunch, Zidra,' he told her as they walked into the sunshine of Grosvenor Square. 'Do you mind?'

'No, of course not. Anyone I know?'

'John Reid. The *Financial Daily*'s man in Moscow. I want to lay hands on his archive. For my memoirs, before the Alzheimer's does me in.'

'I know him, and you're welcome to him.'

There were no taxis and they began walking in the direction of Mayfair to find one.

'What was the meeting?'

'Bryce pumping me for things I don't know or can't tell him.'

'A waste of time, then.'

'Not entirely. I spoke to Bob, in Washington.' He was in front, and he swung right round suddenly and walked backwards, watching her sashay along behind. The sunlight gleamed off her skin. 'I love you, Mrs Renard.' When she came close he grabbed her and kissed her. 'You're always the most beautiful woman in the room.'

'Which room?'

'Any room, it doesn't matter.'

A taxi hurtled past and he lunged for it. It didn't stop.

She folded her arms and watched him in silence.

'What's the matter?' he asked when he turned to her again.

She didn't answer.

He came right up to her. 'Look, I'll have to go.'

'To Washington?'

'Yes. I have to meet Bob Hill and the National Security Agency, just for a couple of days. Would you like to come?'

'You know I wouldn't.'

'I can't walk away now.'

'Your President needs you.'

'I can't help it; they just do.'

She looked doubtfully at him. 'Washington?'

'Yes, I said.'

'Couldn't you teleconference?''

'I need a couple of days there. It isn't the same. What will you do?'

'Go shopping.'

'Good. Take in a show.'

Renard was marching ahead. A taxi pulled over and he opened the door for her. 'I love you, Zidra,' he whispered as she went past. 'We have dinner with the Broughtons tonight, don't forget.'

'I remember. Be at the Mountbatten by six.'

'OK, darling.' The door slammed before she could say more, and he blew her a kiss. 'No more spooky meetings, please,' she shouted through the window. 'Have a nice lunch.'

'Sure, baby. Bob sends his love, I forgot.'

She turned and watched him as they pulled away. He had already hailed another cab.

'Stop a minute,' she told her driver.

Her cab swung into the kerb. 'Your old man told me Harrods, lady,' the cabby grumbled.

'Wait.' She looked behind. Renard was busy giving his driver orders; he didn't notice she'd stopped. His cab swept past them, then did a U-turn and set off the other way. 'Follow him.'

The cab lurched round in front of a bus and squealed off after Renard.

'He's having an affair with a woman,' Zidra said. 'I'm sure of it. Quickly, don't lose him.'

The driver looked her over in his mirror. 'He's either mad or more lucky than he has a right to be.'

'Don't let him see us. He's unbelievably tricky and deceitful.'

'OK, darling.' The car crawled along two cars behind Renard's. 'Heartless type, is he?'

'Yes, brutal.'

'I don't know why you stick with him.'

Renard's cab suddenly swung down an alley.

In two minutes they were back in Grosvenor Square. Renard's taxi drove past the embassy and swung into a narrow mews. As they slid past she had a glimpse of him lunging from the taxi, which was still in motion, and setting off at a run for the mews opposite.

'Stop, please,' Zidra said.

The driver turned and grinned at her. 'Now what?'

'Please, just go and ask his driver which number he went into.'

'Wouldn't normally, but for you, love . . .' The driver, who was overweight and in his fifties, heaved himself out of the cab and plodded over to the mews entrance, flagging Renard's taxi down as it emerged. He came back almost at once. '23B,' he told her.

'Wait here, please.'

'I can't wait here while you have a marital,' the driver wailed, but she was already out of the cab. He watched her run across the road and sighed. 'Women. They can break your heart.'

The mews was secluded, but not guarded, although a video camera was mounted on a wall. She put up the umbrella she'd brought with her and walked at a normal pace over the cobbles. The door of 23B was paned with beaded glass. She could just make out a hat-stand and behind it stairs leading to the flat, which was on the first floor. Renard's coat was hanging on the stand.

She walked past, turned slowly at the end and went back to her taxi.

'Have you got a mobile phone?' she asked the driver.

'Sure.' He passed the handset back to her, turning to watch her dial. She smiled acridly, and the cabby turned away.

The number answered after two rings. 'Henrietta? That you?'

'Zidra! Darling! How are you?'

'Fine. Wonderful. Renard told me we're meeting tonight, but I wanted to call.'

'How wonderful to hear your voice, dear. How is the Grand Tour going?'

'Great. Just flew in from Milan, actually,' Zidra lied. 'Henrietta, are you busy? Can we meet? Yes? Harrods? Wonderful. In half an hour, then. One more thing. Are you by yourself?'

'Yes. Derek is at the FO.'

'Can you find out a number for me? The address is 23B Drake Mews, W1.'

Lady Broughton repeated the address, slowly. No, Zidra didn't know who lived there.

Her friend went away. She was a long time coming back.

'You foreign?' the driver asked her while they waited.

'Yes. Czech.'

'Thought you was Czech. You an au pair?'

'Something like that.'

'You don't look like an au pair.'

'I keep house. It's the same thing.'

'No it ain't.'

Henrietta came back, sounding serious. 'Where are you calling from?'

'A taxi.'

'OK, we'll meet at Harrods food hall in thirty minutes? By the foie gras?'

They said goodbye and Zidra stabbed an arbitrary three numbers in to defeat the redial, then gave the phone back.

Henrietta Broughton was waiting for her at the game counter. Harrods was a ten-minute walk from the Broughtons' South Kensington *pied à terre*, the flat they used two or three weeks of the year and abandoned to their two daughters the rest of the time.

'That address you gave me, it's a CIA safe house,' Henrietta told her when they'd said hello. 'I don't know who's there now, obviously. I wrote down the number.' She was visibly unhappy.

Zidra didn't hide her surprise, shook her head at the piece of paper in wonderment. It was concrete evidence of Renard's double-dealing. 'Don't be concerned, Henrietta,' she said. 'I trust Renard, it's the company he keeps I'm not so sure about.'

'The Company indeed.' Lady Broughton spat the words. 'I'm so tired of these boys' games. My strong advice, my dear, is don't make a husband-and-wife cottage industry out of it. Take a back seat. He's the one on the payroll, let him get the ulcers. That's what I tell Derek.'

Zidra laughed. 'But how do you manage to take a back seat with him? You're totally involved. I mean in everything – ambassadoring, as well as all the cloak-and-dagger stuff.'

'No, I am not,' Lady Broughton said emphatically. 'I keep my nose out of it as much as I can. Of course, we talk, especially if the poor man is worried about something, although he never tells me sensitive stuff. We have our spheres of interest. They intersect, but they're not identical. We don't let it get incestuous and all jumbled together. That's important when you're living on the job, as we are. But all expats have that problem, you don't have to be a diplomat or a spy.'

'Yes, but what's the trick? I still don't see it. Either you share everything or you share nothing at all. That's how it seemed to us, anyway, at the start. So we decided to share everything. There are no secrets. And he told them at Langley that's how it would be. They had to accept it. They only half did, of course. They retired him and then found they couldn't do without him, and in the end it sort of made him more important not less. But I wouldn't have it different. I couldn't bear to know only half the story, and for him to suppress the most dangerous bits. That would only worry me more.'

'In my view that's what's sickening about the position they've put you in. Your roles aren't defined. You're like one of those fictional amateur detectives – glamorous but always outsiders somehow, and therefore unprotected. Where are the rules, the networks, the frameworks, in your lives? That lack of reference points would worry me enormously. I couldn't bear it, frankly. You have to make your life like a kind of Chinese puzzle. Otherwise you're exposed to everything he's doing, and he doesn't have a home to go to either. So you lose all the mystery of it.'

'I'm chagrined to admit that you're right, but you are. I wanted it like this – I mean, with no defined roles. I wanted that total one-on-one thing. But I hadn't reckoned with the umbilicus which keeps him attached to the Company.'

'Derek and I operate on a need-to-know basis. It's the only way, believe me, darling. I have no idea for example what he's doing with Douglas just now, although not being a halfwit I see the signs that something is up. And he certainly has no idea what I'm up to when I'm not with him, which is for as much of the time as I can manage.'

Zidra laughed. 'You're a tonic. But I know how you care for him, however cynical you pretend to be.'

'I am cynical. He could be sitting with two blondes in a Turkish bath. I wouldn't mind as long as he doesn't interfere with me when I do the same.'

'You've never been in a Turkish bath in your life, Henrietta,' Zidra laughed, 'unless it was a disagreeable diplomatic duty, and then you'd do it without complaint. And I'm sure that's true for Derek too.'

'Perhaps so.' Lady Broughton smiled back at her. 'I'm devoted to him, in truth. But I don't let him define me. Not totally.'

'I can tell you what they're up to, if you like,' Zidra said recklessly, blinded by sudden fury at Renard, and at the invidious need to lie even to her friends, as she had to Henrietta about where they'd spent the past two weeks. 'It's the goddamn IRA. That's what I'm sacrificing my vacation to this time. And I don't see what the hell it's got to do with us, frankly. I'm sure your MI5 or whatever is capable of dealing with it.'

'Good God, I had no idea. *That* business.' Lady Broughton looked truly angry now. 'They're like boys with train sets, aren't they? Can't leave well alone. I can understand Douglas wanting to help my husband. That's just professional *amour propre*. They all suffer from it. But why drag you in? That's what I would find hard to take, if it was me.'

'Not even the IRA, just some break-away bunch,' Zidra grumbled.

'For God's sake, don't tell me any more, Zidra. Let's do some shopping and talk about something else. Don't let it blight today.'

They were walking through the footwear department and Lady Broughton stopped opposite a pair of Gucci boots. 'What do you think?'

'Try them on.'

'Two hundred and fifty pounds, it's a lot.'

Zidra called a salesgirl over.

They began. Zidra jerked herself from depression, bought a dress, some shoes and a big straw hat, and her friend bought trinkets for Moscow. They had a *salade niçoise* in the restaurant, which cheered Zidra up; they gossiped about New England and how the Broughton girls were doing at university.

During the meal Zidra excused herself and went to the sports equipment floor where she found a payphone. She dialled the number Lady Broughton had given her. It answered on the second ring.

A man's voice, American, said 'Hullo?'

'I'd like to speak to Bob Hill, please.'

'Who's that calling?'

'Henrietta Broughton.'

Another voice came on the line. It was Bob Hill's.

She hung up.

What was Renard playing at?

She blazed with sudden anger.

After lunch, still scorched by Renard's treachery, Zidra walked arm in arm with Lady Broughton back to the flat. It was a warm September day. Knightsbridge was thronged with shoppers and sightseers. They pushed slowly through a crowded by-street, stopping for a gardener to lean a step-ladder by a hanging basket and water the tumbled mass of bright blue and red flowers.

'Of course, they will want to use Renard,' Lady Broughton said, catching Zidra's thoughts. 'And I'm sure he'll keep going back to Moscow. And you can't any more, of course. After last time.'

'But Douglas hasn't told me the truth.'

'Sometimes they just can't. You have to grin and bear it.'

'I'm not an English diplomat's wife, I'm afraid. I don't have the sang-froid.'

'Of course not.'

'I don't see why they need Renard.' Zidra said. 'He's too old for it.'

Henrietta laughed. 'Douglas is still in love with you, Zidra. He must desperately want to keep you out of it.'

'I thought I'd kept *him* out, of Russia anyway,' she said bitterly, 'but I failed.' She felt suddenly shop-worn and empty.

'Leave, that's my advice,' Lady Broughton went on. 'Go to Gstaad or the Camargue or charter a boat in the Caribbean. Have a change of scenery – but get him away.'

Zidra laughed and shook her head. 'I don't think I'm foxy enough to do it. Renard hauls his professionalism around like baggage but he's as tricky as hell for all that. He does what he wants.'

They arrived at the flat and Lady Broughton showed her friend into a front room awash with suitcases, carrier bags and tissue paper. 'Look at this, it's enough to make anyone feel like a refugee. I'll have to miss the reception at the Foreign Office tomorrow. It's my last chance to pack for Moscow.'

'I'll come afterwards and help, if you like.'

'Would you? That would be wonderful, Zidra.'

The Broughtons' Filipina, Maria, appeared, smiling as usual, helpless as usual. Lady Broughton sent her for sherry, and Scotch and water for Zidra.

'Is he merciless in bed? Henrietta asked abruptly.

Zidra laughed. 'What do you think?'

'Horribly. But he's done something for you – you're more

poised than before. Not so brittle.'

'Thanks. What have I done for him, do you think?'

'Oh, he's the same as ever.' She laughed. 'Sorry. I ought to shut up. Anyway, you are more devastating than ever, darling.'

They clinked glasses. 'How is Moscow?' Zidra asked.

'Bloody awful, as usual.' Lady Broughton sighed, changed the subject. 'Will Langan's do tonight? I know it's off everyone's list now, but that's why Derek likes it and I agree. You don't meet anyone there any more.'

'Of course.'

The phone rang. It was Sir Derek, calling from the FO.

Henrietta went to the kitchen to take the call. Zidra sat and stared at the Empire clock on the mantelpiece. Wondered again what Renard was up to.

'Derek says we'll come to the Mountbatten for you,' Henrietta said when she came back

'Then I'd better fly.' It was past four. Zidra wanted to try on a dress, get her hair fixed.

'Let me know how things develop with Renard. I really think you shouldn't let him get involved in this business with the CIA. If he's retired, they should let him alone.'

Zidra thought about that in the taxi.

Something was wrong with Lady Broughton. Zidra had no idea what. She still hadn't tuned her antennae to deal with the British. But something had come adrift in the social machinery. Henrietta had lost some of her sang-froid, the finesse of the English diplomat's wife.

She put it out of her mind, while the taxi crawled up a strangulated Oxford Street. She had started reading a novel by Mario Vargas Llosa, about torrid love between matronly dames and a manipulative, prepubescent but beautiful boy. She pulled the book out of her bag and opened it, imagining the deliquescent youth with those slightly flatulent, tending-to-corpulent, panting females as the taxi turned into Monmouth Street, pulled out of the shoals of traffic and unloaded her at the canopied entrance to the Mountbatten Hotel. A doorman appeared from nowhere, paid the driver, knew her name, ushered her inside.

The Mountbatten is the best hotel in London. It is a converted warehouse of some kind, higgledy-piggledy and inconvenient inside, like any old and good place, with rooms which triangulate into odd corners and are fitted with enormously thick and heavy curtains to drown out the roar from the traffic surging around Seven Dials. There is no car park. And it is expensive. But it is a real hotel. Portion control, pre-packs, dour porters and exhausted maids do not belong here. The Mountbatten has people, lots of them, who seem to care. And more important, it has oysters, the best in town, twenty-four hours a day.

Zidra and Renard were in the Burma suite. Zidra went there at once, threw off her clothes, called room service and ordered a dozen oysters and a bottle of Lanson Black Label for now, and more for later when her guests arrived. She went to the bathroom and ran the Jacuzzi.

She caught sight of herself in the mirror. She was scowling, two tiny vertical furrows etched over the bridge of her nose. Something was pricking at her, and she knew what it was.

The Burma suite was full of mirrors. She hated the sight of herself. She hated the cold feeling inside.

The hell with it. Zidra switched the whirlpool on full and threw in the bath foam.

Someone knocked at the door. She pulled on a bathrobe and admitted room service with the champagne and oysters. She tipped the boy, filleted the first two oysters from their shells, swallowed them, slipped off the robe and took the rest of the oysters, the champagne and the Mario Vargas Llosa novel into the bathroom. A mountain of foam had filled the bath and cascaded over the floor. She ignored it, turned the jets down low, checked the temperature and climbed in.

When Renard arrived just before six Zidra was sitting by the window and watching life revolve around Seven Dials. When he told her Sir Derek Broughton was delayed at the FO, so they would meet an hour later at Annabel's and not at Langan's, she threw the empty Lanson bottle at him.

'Wait a minute, Zidra. Let me give you a reason for violence first.'

'What reason? What's so special about the brothel at 23B Drake Mews?' She threw oyster shells one by one and they cracked on the wall and showered splinters over the room.

'We will have to do things a different way in the future, I know it. But I can't stop now. I have to finish what I started, you know that. But it's not a precedent.'

'There won't be a future if we go on in this self-deluding way, Douglas. If you're going to go on with the Company, then let me retire, at least. If this was going to be a business trip, then we should have dealt with it like that and not confused the issue by making it a kind of honeymoon. That's what makes me mad. And just because I'm mad at myself is no reason not to be mad at you.'

'I agree, Zidra. But I have to go on. I can't refuse.'

'You've got to go back, haven't you?'

'Yes.'

'Where? Moscow?'

'No. At least, I hope not. Baku.'

She threw the ice bucket. 'Where is Bob Hill? Here?'

'Yes. In London. I lied to you. I'm sorry.'

'What happened in Baku?'

'They didn't finish up properly. Chuck Smith's dead, in suspicious circumstances.'

'Fuck, and that's supposed to encourage me to endorse you going there?'

'Look, Zidra, after this I *will* retire, OK? Come on now; you were party to this whole deal. You *know* how it is.'

'When are you going?'

'Tomorrow.'

'Well,' she said, drawing a deep breath. 'Don't tell me any more about it. Is Bob going with you?'

'Yes.'

'Good.' She made a decision. 'I understand, Douglas. And we both dug the pit, it wasn't just you. I'm more to blame, if anything.'

'No, you aren't.'

'Well, let's not argue about that. If we're going to dinner, we need to get ready.'

'When I come back this time, we'll go somewhere there are no phones. A haven.'

'You know, Renard, I've been thinking that, too,' she said when they were dressed. She sat on his lap and her mass of flaxen hair fell round his face. 'There's a place called Bhutan where they have a thing called the Gross National Contentment. Nobody produces so there's nothing to steal. We could fly out next week. How about it?'

*

They were late arriving at Annabel's.

'I ordered a ton of oysters thinking you were coming to collect us,' Zidra told her hosts, 'but I've eaten them all, nearly.'

Sir Derek laughed. 'Then you have no appetite, I expect?'

'You're kidding. I could eat a horse.'

'Your wife is one of those remarkable women who can eat like a horse without ever looking like one,' Henrietta told Renard. 'Is that the Versace?' she whispered to Zidra. 'It's stunning.'

'Yes, these fragments of tissue paper stapled over Zidra are the Versace,' Renard answered. 'And it cost two thousand of your British pounds.'

'It's gorgeous,' Henrietta told her, 'and outrageous.'

'That's what I thought,' Renard said.

While the waiter brought small dishes of something dubious, Sir Derek told them of a recent trip to Azerbaijan, where British companies were negotiating huge contracts to take oil from the Caspian seabed. The ambassador looked tired, older than his years. His narrow face with its hawk-like nose was lined and each line told a story. But tonight he was on good form, describing how the Azeri oil minister had received them.

'Mr Suleimanov is not an Azeri – he comes from Bashkiria. He is a descendant of the Golden Horde and proud of it. He's had an annex built on to the oil ministry headquarters in Baku. It is round, with a dome on top. There is a *yurt* – a sort of tepee made of skins – inside. It smells rather like the players' changing room at Lord's. Mr Suleimanov sits on the floor like his nomadic forebears. He gave us dinner, Bashkirian-style. Edward Boningfield, the chairman of Bison Oil, was there and so was Hans Uhlaf, another member of the oil consortium. You'll meet them at the Foreign Office reception tomorrow, by the way. Young girls massaged honey from Mr Suleimanov's hives into our heads. That is an ancient Mongol remedy. We were offered roast horse flesh and *kumiss*, an aphrodisiac drink made from fermented mare's milk.' Sir Derek looked mournfully at Zidra. He shook his head. 'Baku is a wonderful place, but the water is very bad.'

'I was in Azerbaijan with Derek,' Henrietta told them. 'He had diarrhoea for three days. I had a wonderful time, and thank God I was not present at Mr Suleimanov's little do. I spent my time wandering around the *souk*, visiting the caviar factory, that sort of thing. To read the press you'd think there's a civil war going on, but it's not true at all. Baku is much more peaceful than Moscow.'

Fried cutlets thrown into a bowl of warm lettuce arrived.

'I cannot understand whoever told the French they could cook,' Renard muttered, prodding the lettuce.

'I've discovered a new Russian word,' Sir Derek told Zidra. '*Nakatilas*. The roll-over.'

Zidra laughed. '*Nakatilas* is just the fourth stage of the process by which the mafia destroys a legitimate business. Before *Nakatilas* come Entry, Fraternity and then the *Kompromat*. The mafia composes its crimes like the movements in a Beethoven symphony – the same themes are repeated and brought to a climax.'

'Let me see. Entry is the infiltration stage, that's easy enough,' Broughton said.

'Exactly. They bribe your most trusted staff, or scare them away and substitute their own, who are always provided with impeccable references. Anyone from a driver to a director.'

'Then begins Fraternity, when everybody is happy and the money is flowing in. The organization is on a roll. It is the phase before the crash, yes?'

'Yes,' Renard said. 'When the victim looks prosperous and clients are rushing to invest. Then – poof! The whole thing falls into dust and all the money has disappeared, God knows where.'

'Then comes the *Kompromat*, Zidra finished. The owners have a choice: be creatures of the mafia – put themselves and their families into mafia service – or be ruined. If they are honest enough to refuse, they will be horribly punished. Creditors will howl at their doors, they will lose their reputation, home, family, perhaps their freedom. And the nightmare is only beginning. They cannot fight back. They have been rolled over. *Nakatilas*.'

'Darlings, this is much too gloomy,' Henrietta said. 'You are too scrupulous, Derek. After all, Russians can be very civilized people. And life goes on, does it not?' She was trembling with barely concealed anger, Zidra noted with interest.

A waiter arrived to pour limp French wine.

Chapter 4

Earlier in the day and lower in the depths, in Henery's Oyster Bar in the City, another party was held. Henery's, a lunching place near Leadenhall, at the divide between merchant banking and more basic City functions, is the kind of frenzied eatery where sharp-faced, hungry young men from back offices and forfaiting departments jostle with the pot-bellies and red braces of the dealing floors.

There were only two guests at this lunch: Harvey Goldman, the British businessman who Sir Derek Broughton's sources incorrectly said was out of the country, and Julian Benderby, a respectable merchant banker. Goldman was the kind of Brit you can find in any British Airways executive lounge around the world – in his mid-fifties, florid, over-confident, sporting a solid gold Rolex, drinking vodka martinis so dry they squeak. The kind of businessman who favours Chester Barrie suits and vicuna coats and always has half an eye on something or someone else, wherever he is or whatever the context. Goldman was an elder statesman of the margin, never put down, always able to bale out from deals spiralling to disaster because of the interesting things he knew about surprising people. Goldman's charm was worn on his sleeve. His eye rheumy, his nose red, he would most likely die of a cardiac arrest on some long-haul flight between a gleam in the eye and a shady Bangkok hotel room. Bibulous, well-met and spiky with attitude, Goldman knew how to introduce eager backbench MPs and junior ministers to Russian 'entrepreneurs' or to minor Middle Eastern potentates and their avaricious, indolent nephews. Knew how to see the deals through to the end. He was a fixer, the lubricant at the rubbing edge between more or less straight business and the nether world of hard men with pocked faces who are the real owners of everything. Almost anything went in Goldman's world, where pariah countries swapped oil for hardware, and strange characters with vestigial South African accents, toothbrush-sized moustaches, and friends in the Ministry of Defence were on hand to help when things came unstuck.

Benderby liked to meet him from time to time and talk about gold and oil from Iran or Iraq, or about new opportunities like sugar futures – specially interesting just now, he mused aloud, when word on the London exchange was that the Russians were taking 100,000 tonnes of sugar a month into St Petersburg at a 15 per cent premium. So maybe they should take a position? Because Benderby knew a man with a take on the Brussels sugar-mountain . . .

No good, Goldman told him straight away. The Russians want *cane* sugar, not European beet. That's what carries the premium. And not because cane's better or because picky Russian housewives can tell the difference, but because cane is chemically distinguishable from beet sugar so it definitely won't be full of isotopes that make your jam glow in the dark. Because every Russian knows that all beet sugar comes from the radioactive Chernobyl-infested Ukraine and it makes no difference if the waybill, insurance certificate, quality certificate, authentication of origin and European Union export licence all say it's genuine European Union sugar. Because the St Petersburg sugar mafia forges everything. That's how the mafia has it both ways, Goldman explained: they make a thousand per cent mark-up on the Ukrainian stuff, which is rebagged at Odessa in Common Market bags and then sent on to Peter – and then they make another killing selling cane sugar to the panic-stricken consumers lucky enough to own Geiger counters.

'It's the Wild East out there, Jules. You got to cover yourself. Only last month the sugar mafia shot dead three traders in Peter and a broker in Vienna. Why? Because they thought they saw an opportunity and tried to bring in forty thousand tonnes of Caribbean cane. So my advice is, *forget it*.'

Benderby grinned, stuck several fingers into a bowl of rice crackers and confided through a mouthful that that was exactly why Goldman was so necessary. Because he was streetwise, and never let greed overcome judgement. 'Harvey,' he chomped, 'I trust you. If you'd said, *go for the sugar*, I'd've sorted you a back-to-back Letter-of-Credit at the speed of sound.'

'I know that, Jules. You've always played the white man.'

And that was also why Goldman needed Benderby. Without LCs confirmed on a prime bank the business fell, because there could not be consignment terms with the Russians. You needed cash up front, so you had to have a backer – someone like Benderby, with a line into deep pockets and flexibility about the fine print.

Younger than Goldman by at least ten years, Julian Benderby was different: a soft-spoken, self-contained Englishman who swapped his first Rolex for a Patek Philippe long ago but had not forgotten his origins now he was a banker who slipped smooth as oil through his client's accounts, elegant in a Hugo Boss suit and hand-lasted shoes as shiny as new tar. He was the kind of banker who would go on ascending, might one day get a gong for advising select committees on regulatory matters (no one knew more about the ducks and dives than he), but could equally well disappear suddenly and for ever down a pre-arranged bolt-hole, when the bank finds it is out by a million or a few hundred million and the grey men from Threadneedle Street are called in for late-night meetings.

Both men had business interests in Russia. On this day, they were celebrating.

'You know what it feels like, Harvey? Like the old days are back.' Benderby did a sedentary jig while two dozen oysters and cold Veuve Clicquot arrived.

'You mean, like when you churned the punters and got a bright red Porsche in every Christmas box?'

'Yeah. Those were the days, when you didn't have the fucking SFA, not to speak of the SFO, breathing down your neck.' Benderby swigged champagne; it tasted of seltzer and made him grimace. 'But that's all in the past, Harvey.' He leant forward and said conspiratorially: 'When the Ship's Master telegraphed us you could hear the cheers in the boardroom. Carter-Allis came out and slapped me on the back. *Well done Julian*, he said, *you'll be on to Stratstone for that Testarossa, now.*'

'Yeah, it's time for a few of the glittering prizes.'

Benderby grinned. 'I've already ordered the stationery. *Julian Benderby, Executive Director, Corporate Finance.* And at Palfrey & Griblock, the most respected merchant bank in the City with a client list of deepest blue.'

'Not bad for a lad from Stevenage. So tell me, what were the actual words on the telegram? I want to savour the moment.'

Benderby pulled the flimsy from his pocket and read aloud: '*Oil passed ship's flange at 0630 local time. Have signed Bill of Lading.* Thirteen words that are lucky for some. And the first of many such, I do hope.' His soft lips puckered into a moue. 'Five million tonnes of crude,' he whispered. 'Unbelievable.' He replaced the flimsy, pulled out a hand-exerciser – a kind of sprung-metal hot-dog – and squeezed it. In childhood, he'd contracted mild poliomyelitis, a result of his mother's resistance to 'them jabs'. It had left him with a weakened right arm and a slight stoop. The exerciser, emblem of an old fight, was always there, as some people carry worry beads or rosaries. 'Unbelievable,' he repeated, squeezing till it made a cracking noise.

'Oh, it's kosher, Julian. Deal of a lifetime.'

They clinked glasses. 'But all that aggro in Moscow you went through, Harvey.' They shook their heads in mock-horror.

'I got so sick of Club Europe you wouldn't believe, the plane always full of market researchers and washing-machine technicians on loan to joint ventures, all asking stupid questions, so I started to fly Aeroflot. Not bad service, either, if you don't look down.'

'Plenty of V and Ts.'

'You're not kidding. Even the pilot has a tipple while he's warming the engines. The stewardess takes him a bottle before they take off. On a little silver tray.' He paused. 'I met one stewardess. Her name was Irina.' He rolled his eyes. 'She had more acts than Moscow circus.' He upended an oyster and poured it into his mouth, revealing a row of gold-capped molars that gleamed in the dinner-table candlelight. 'First time I did it on a plane. I was knackered by the time we got to Sheremetyevo, and I'm sure Mikhail noticed.'

Benderby blinked. 'You did it on an Aeroflot plane?'

'Yeah. It was right after they spread their Airbus all over Siberia. There weren't many fare-paying passengers on Aeroflot after that for a while.' Goldman laughed. 'The flights were very exclusive.'

'You're a mad bugger, Harvey.' Benderby gazed in admiration.

'Talking of which, I called Mikhail this morning, and gave him the glad tidings. I'll bet the little lad is sitting in a dive somewhere in Moscow right now, celebrating.'

'It's well earned, for once.'

'I got ever so pissed off with old Mikhail at the time. I kept getting these faxes written in cockamamie English, and it was always the same story. *Come to Moscow quick dear Mr Goldman, I've met a man, and this time it's for real.* And every time I went over, it was the same thing: lunch a day late at the Restaurant Salmonellova to meet Mr Smelly-arse from Samara or somewhere who's got friends in high places and can fix anything. Export licence? No problem. Quota? No problem. Customs? Transport? Licensed export? And your actual oil? *No problem.* But then strange-strange there was never any sodding oil, and in a bit no Mr Smelly-arse either. Just Mikhail with his faxes.' He sprinkled Worcestershire sauce on an oyster, swallowed it and gritted his teeth. 'I don't doubt you were hacked off, too?'

'I was holding the ring. But that's corporate finance – taking the longer view, paying out some slack.'

Caviar arrived and Benderby stirred it with a teaspoon. 'Have you ever noticed how green this Iranian stuff is? But you can't get good Russian any more.' He grinned at Goldman. 'You know,' he said, 'I always knew we could do it. After all, *someone*'s buying the crude, so why not us? That's what I told Carter-Allis. And to give him credit, he let the deal stay on the books. Kept the dead hand of audit off me.' He spooned caviar on to a blini – a small pancake – shaking his head in astonishment. 'Strange, that – why old Carter-Allis believed so much in this deal.'

'I always thought he was Mr Sceptic Hardnose. How wrong can you be?' Goldman stuck the tip of his dinner knife into the mound of green, semi-transparent globules and shovelled some into his mouth, pressing them against the back of his teeth with his tongue until they exploded one by one and he felt the salty marine taste cascade down his throat. 'You know what Irina says this stuff tastes like?'

'Don't tell me.'

Goldman ate more caviar and they both gave silent thanks, Goldman for Carter-Allis's faith, that and the ten-million-dollar Performance Bond which had given the Russians confidence, Benderby for the tanker even now ploughing the briny somewhere off Novorossysk, bringing the first 80,000 tonnes of Urals blend to Rotterdam. In his mind's eye, Benderby could just see the ship wallowing like an untethered whale, bow-down with oil.

They talked about the shared hardships of the early days –

Benderby's meetings with snot-nosed single-handed accountants with licences from funny colonial universities and offices in the wrong postal district, north of Paddington; Goldman's encounters in Moscow with shady Russians in shellsuits from hell, who were all somehow related to Yeltsin's masseur or his personal bodyguard. The hassle of setting up offshore brassplates and Swiss accounts.

'And the sheer aggro of getting Barclays to confirm an LC drawn on a Cyprus pigeonhole,' Benderby complained. 'Especially when mention of Palfrey & Griblock was *verboten*. But that's the market – the hidden hand, the anonymous social actor. A man on his own, hacking a deal. That's what makes the wheels spin. Cavaliers of capitalism, that's what we are.'

Goldman reached for his glass and the 22-carat identity bracelet on his wrist clinked softly. 'You're a fucking poet, Julian.' And they began to laugh, silently at first, until a tide of mirth shook them and swept the whole of Henery's, where spirits were high anyway because it was Friday, when people come to the office in the Range Rover, wear Pringle sweaters and slacks and leave at three, maybe for the country.

'I've only got one worry,' Goldman said after a while. The words seemed to take him by surprise, and he blinked.

'What's that, old son?'

'Oh, you know.'

Benderby didn't know.

'Oh, about you-know-who.' He was reluctant to go on; he'd decided he'd made a mistake. But he couldn't stop now. He leant forward, whispered: 'You know. *Fallen Oak*. Him.'

'Aah. *Him*.' Benderby scowled. 'The ten million dollars, you mean. The Kerrygold deal?'

'Exactly.' For a moment, Goldman was taken aback. He'd launched on a forbidden topic, and saw at once that it was on Benderby's mind no less than his, and maybe the banker was glad to air it.

'That's been bothering me a hell of a lot, but unfortunately there's nothing we can do about it now,' Benderby said. He leant closer and said in a low voice, 'Even if Dubok changed his mind, we couldn't stop the deal now.' He tutted. '*Fuck*. It's a real nuisance.'

'And he won't stop, the old bastard. He'll do it his way—'

'Or not at all, and then that'll screw up the other thing. I know. He doesn't believe in numbers with more than seven or eight noughts.' Benderby shook his head disbelievingly. 'He wants a nice round figure, not too grand, but enough to retire to the Côte d'Azur or Argentina. I suppose he'd be left with, say, five million after he's taken out the pay-offs.'

'And that's enough. But I still don't understand why we had to go along with it.'

Benderby looked up at that. 'There was another reason. I shouldn't mention it, but I trust you.' Goldman leant forward to hear. 'That Performance Bond. You never wondered how we kept it off the books?'

Goldman thought for a moment and then a light came into his eyes. He sat back and blew air out noisily. 'Of course! It's the *Micks'* money! Well, you clever bastard! Of course, the amounts are the same! So you fed them Irish loot, but with Palfrey & Griblock's name on it! In all my life I've never worked out how to get such a bloody big bank guarantee organized. I wondered how you did it. It's clever, Julian. But it does keep us under the duvet with them after the passion has waned. That's the drawback.'

'I know. It's sodding inconvenient. But leave it to me. Better not to trouble yourself about that business. It wasn't your fault. You had to get the ball rolling. Anyway, it's out of your hands now, for better or worse. The only plus is that I think I might have worked out how to push the whole problem away, and maybe even keep some of the lolly. I can't discuss the details, even with you. But I'll tell you this much – if it all comes good then we'll grab the dosh and blame the Micks for everything – and what's more we'll get the Yanks to help us, as long as they've foolishly stuck their noses in.'

Goldman looked stunned. 'Well done, that man. If the Micks will buy off on it,' he breathed, 'then you're a genius. A real genius. You'll have stuffed the IRA and the Yanks in one move.'

'Shush!' Benderby's smile was sardonic. 'Walls have ears, especially in this dump.'

Goldman regarded him in silence for a while. It really would be a coup. Benderby sat oblivious, immobile, like some archaic predator. The thought suddenly came to Goldman, who was not drunk but, as the Irish say, *having drink taken*, that in some earlier incarnation Benderby must have been a scorpion, rattling under rocks in hot sand, waiting patiently for passing prey.

'OK,' he said. 'Done. I agree. I leave everything to you. That leaves me free to go back to Moscow and carry on there.'

The matter was closed and they called it a day. Outside in the roar of Leadenhall they promised each other to go down to Tottenham like the old days and eat jellied eels, drink beer and lose a few quid on the dogs. They embraced and parted like brothers.

'I'll call you when I get back from Russia.'

'I might see you there myself.'

Goldman stuck his big red hand out and a cab lurched to the kerb. He clambered in and left with a wave. The smile on Benderby's face disappeared with him. He stared after the taxi until it was swallowed by traffic.

Hill would not complete arrangements for their flight to Baku until the next evening, which made it possible for Renard to attend a presentation by Bison Oil's Global Risk Analysis Team at the Foreign Office in the morning. The subject was the future of Caspian Sea oil. There was one person present whom Renard wanted to meet: a Russian environmentalist called Minakov. In their private discussion after dinner at Annabel's, Sir Derek had reminded him that Minakov, amongst other things, was an expert on the Shevchenko fast-breeder reactor. It was pure luck Minakov was in London. Few people knew more about the history of plutonium production at the Shevchenko plant than he did.

The King Charles Street headquarters of Her Majesty's Foreign and Commonwealth Office is the finest ministerial premises in London. It is a gothic pile whose ornate carvings, cheery porters, poor fare and seedy officials give it the unpromising air of a British public school. Zidra took Renard there by taxi, planning to meet for lunch and return for a reception for the Azerbaijan/Bison Oil guests in the afternoon.

The presentation was given by GRAT director James Humphries. Humphries was an oil industry planner with gold in his head: twenty years' experience in the field and five years fronting GRAT. He told the meeting, attended by Bison main board members and Azerbaijan government ministers, about GRAT's unique *Nostradamus* software matrix, so secret it could not be patented, so precious that the security team created to protect it carried out lifetime surveillance of employees. Preventing unauthorized access to the system was a nightmare since *Nostradamus* had to be open in order to receive tidal waves of data from thousands of sources.

The system contained 'genetic evolution' software whose self-replicating program elements evolved spontaneously as they adapted to the changing data environment. After thousands of generations of software evolution, no one really understood how *Nostradamus* worked. They only knew it did and in so doing made Bison, the world's third largest oil major, also the most profitable.

Humphries told them frankly that he was unhappy about giving a briefing on *Nostradamus* at all, even to a gathering which had the highest security clearance. But these were the movers and shakers who needed to know *something*, he'd been told when the order came down. So he would give them an insight.

Flawless GRAT-inspired forecasting of market trends guided its decisions. If this software fell into the wrong hands Bison's dealing floors in London and New York would overnight lose their market advantage in spotting price trends. And within a few months or a year, anyone with the will and money to replicate Bison's database would have taken from Bison its unique strategic planning capability.

That was a reason why the Russians were so interested in joining the Azeri oil consortium, as well as their strategic interests in the Caspian region. Because at stake was more even than the strategic question of control over world energy supplies. Bison and other oil majors (all British or American owned), were near the heart of the West's geopolitical planning. Their time horizon was not less than fifty years, because the task was to ensure the permanent supremacy of American leadership. Access to this hidden heart of Western planning, sharing its knowledge-basis, perhaps gaining control of it, Humphries told them, was the task set themselves by some brilliant and dangerous young Russians in leading positions in the worlds of Russian banking and finance. It signified a Russian ambition to re-emerge as a superpower, an ambition which was certain to fail, however.

'Information, not ideology, is the real key to power. That's the main lesson the Russians have learnt from their defeat in the Cold War. But the oil dimension remains at the heart as well.' Humphries used a laser pen to point to a map of the old Soviet

Union. 'Look here: Tengiz and Karachaganak in Kazakhstan, together with the Caspian Sea territories of Azerbaijan, constitute a vast energy reserve. Without developing these former Soviet resources, the free world would eventually have been destroyed. That is the stark fact of the matter. The Soviet Union, if it had survived just fifteen more years, would have won the Cold War because of our growing energy deficit. Look at these predictions.'

The map disappeared and a slide flashed two bell curves up on the screen.

'The first bell shows world economic growth to 2050 without the benefit of Soviet oil. At first there is dramatic growth, mainly in Asian countries and the Pacific Rim. The world's vehicle park doubles and trebles to more than two billion. Then shortages of oil begin to become chronic, destroying economic growth. The second bell curve shows economic growth taking off again in the second half of the next century, as new technologies – fusion fuel, hydrogen engines and so on – combine to overcome hydrocarbon shortages. Soviet oil was always necessary in order to bridge the gap. Without it, energy shortages would have led in time to inflationary crises and finally to war and revolution.'

He clicked a button. The two bells came together.

'If the downward line of the first bell and the upward line of the second bell intersect around the year 2020, then the world could look forward to continued market-driven, capitalist-style growth. But the *conditio sine qua non* of this is that we got our hands on Soviet oil.'

The two bells opened out again, this time connected at their peaks by a line.

'The line represents crisis-free stable growth. Achieving this requires development of Caucasian oil and gas. That means Azerbaijan. That is why the new consortium is so important. It will make Azerbaijan the Kuwait of the next century and it will transform the Caspian region. It will also lessen our dependency on Mid-East oil and weaken the power of the Islamic countries.'

The projector was doused and the lights came up. 'A final point. Nothing must stand in the way of our exploiting Azeri oil. If China or Russia makes the running, then in the end we may be eclipsed, annihilated. *Azeri oil is our future. Without it, the West may die.*'

Humphries sat down to applause.

55

Sir James Wilshman, the British Foreign Secretary, stood up and invited questions. Someone asked about GRAT's methodology.

'Our approach to crisis-prediction,' Humphries answered, 'is the kind of secret which – to paraphrase Winston Churchill – is so important that it must be surrounded by a bodyguard of lies. But I can reveal that *Nostradamus* is based upon Kondratiev's theory that long waves of approximately fifty years' duration are evident in history. Our database for the two oil shocks of 1973 and 1979, for instance, includes more than fifty million separate items. To process this amount of data we deploy parallel-processing machines whose neural networks have evolved to a point where we don't fully understand them ourselves. But for the first time we have succeeded in capturing empirically the dynamics of major crises which at the time could not be resolved and led to serious international conflicts. We have similar databases for historical events which include both world wars, the Russian revolution, and the rise of American capitalism. This is just icing on the cake, of course; our main work is predicting trends in the hydrocarbons and energy industries. But it means that we are in a position to predict processes which might lead to unwelcome historical outcomes such as war and revolution.'

Humphries was a remarkable intuitive statistician and knew what he was talking about. His role was to tell the GRAT story. He was used to being called in at crisis meetings and to briefing the often irascible, overloaded and overstressed leaders of industry and government. He could read his audience, and he knew how to mix theory with the plain boiled-down assessment of the facts which was all his listeners really wanted.

In his early fifties, Humphries was a man of personal modesty, capable of drawing the best from others. GRAT boasted the roughest diamonds from Bison's drilling crews, men who were more at home on a North Sea rig or in frozen Siberia than in Bison's steel-and-glass headquarters ('the most hostile environment known to man,' Humphries joked). They worked alongside computer nerds, social scientists and economists. Humphries had welded them into a team which produced some of the best forecasts of any think-tank.

Questions flowed into general discussion. Having mentioned *Nostradamus*, Humphries told them that subject was off-limits;

but nothing else was.

Fred Jenkins, British ambassador to Azerbaijan, the oil-rich former Soviet republic, asked about Russian involvement in the new consortium.

'The Russian government have tried to block western participation in the Caspian, as they do in Siberia. They continue Soviet politics, without Soviet capability,' Humphries said.

'But there is now a Russian member of the consortium, isn't there?' Jimmy Wilshman, the Foreign Secretary, asked.

'Eddie?' Humphries gave the floor to Sir Edward Boningfield, chairman of Bison Oil.

'We have given ten per cent of the consortium to a Russian oil company, yes,' Boningfield said. 'The company is called Arctic Star, based in Perm, a defence-industry centre in the Urals. Its president, Sergei Ivanov, will be attending the reception this afternoon. Getting Arctic Star on side is an achievement that we hope will be enough to get the Russian government off our backs.'

'What's he like, this Ivanov?' Wilshman asked. 'Another Siberian wild man?'

'Ivanov put together Arctic Star from bits of Urals defence industry grafted on to a geological survey institute and an oil industry design bureau, both Moscow-based,' Boningfield said. 'There are Russian banks involved, and the Russian oil ministry of course.'

Wilshman said: 'Fine in theory, but useless unless there's some money, and there never is with the Russians.'

'There is this time.' Boningfield riffled through papers. 'Bison are stumping up a billion dollars for phase one, which is feasibility studies and the Environmental Impact Assessment. Arctic Star are committed to another billion.'

There was a silence, looks were exchanged around the room.

'Where've they got that kind of brass from, I wonder?' Wilshman mused.

'That is a lot of environmental money by anyone's standards,' Sir Derek Broughton said. 'Just how serious are the problems?' he asked Humphries.

'Very. The Caspian is shallow and extremely polluted. We are working closely with Professor Minakov, Yeltsin's environment adviser and Director of the Astrakhan Limnological Institute.'

Jimmy Wilshman looked puzzled.

'Limnology – the study of life in water bodies. Minakov has won the Nobel prize for his work in the Volga river and Caspian Sea. He's Yeltsin's main environmental adviser so if he supports the Bison Oil consortium it's good news. Makes it harder for the Russians to refuse. Everyone knows what disasters they created in the Caspian when they had the chance.'

'Mr Humphries is right about the politics,' Wilshman said. 'We need to resolve this with the Russian government. It conditions the whole future path of our relations with them. We received a note from the Russian Foreign Ministry last week, warning us that they will not permit development in the Caspian unless they agree to it. Naturally we reject their diktat. Unfortunately they're still not house-trained. We don't object to them having ambitions, but they must learn to play by the rules.'

Humphries spoke. 'The Russians have never accepted Azeri independence. They think the Caucasus is theirs. We should support Arctic Star's involvement because the alternative is that the Russians will destabilize the Azeri government.'

Sir Derek Broughton said: 'Frankly, the whole region is a tinderbox. The Caspian is seven thousand kilometres in circumference and it is surrounded by people who hate each other. There are many flashpoints: Iran, with a million Azeris living there, hated by the Farsi majority and just ripe for a spot of ethnic cleansing. Turkey with its Kurds; Afghanistan to the east and the Balkans on the west. Not to speak of the mess in Georgia. It will require the utmost diligence to control the Caspian region in the future.'

Chapter 5

The reception at King Charles Street that afternoon was impressive even by the standards of the Foreign Office. Hans Uhlaf, Chairman of the Plate River Corporation, another Azeri Oil consortium founder, had laid on the food, which was therefore not the usual FO fare. He had flown in a slew of chefs and waiters from his Hanseatic Hotel, thought by many to be Moscow's finest.

The men from the Hanseatic had buried a long table under Caucasus cuisine – fragrant pies, consommé, pilaff, fish and poultry terrines, gigantic heaps of tiny, intensely flavoured wild strawberries from the Causcasus mountains. Pride of place was a gigantic sturgeon, six feet long. It had been stuffed with herbs and steamed. Waiters dressed in the crimson cummerbund and long white apron of the *traktirshik* carried it in on a silver platter. They placed it between gleaming, charcoal-fired samovars and surrounded it with solid silver buckets filled with caviar from the twenty-eight kilograms, worth sixty thousand dollars, which the fish had yielded. The caviar had been sieved and salted by Uhlaf's own chefs.

Hans Uhlaf said that no one knew more about the preparation of caviar than his people at the Hanseatic, and invited them to judge for themselves. And in an odd inversion of protocol he invited the British Foreign Secretary to speak.

Wilshman stood, raised a glass of the Crimean champagne flown in from Uhlaf's estates, reminded them of George Gilbert Scott's words when he built the Foreign Office a century ago to be not just an office but 'a drawing room for the nation'.

'In my tenure here,' Wilshman said, 'the fare has more often resembled the refectory at my old school. We are indebted to Mr Uhlaf for suggesting to us what Scott had in mind'. He bowed towards Uhlaf. 'Fortunately I shall not have to answer to the Treasury for today's hospitality.'

Uhlaf bowed back in his stiff Bavarian manner.

Caviar, like Treasury funds, was more plentiful a hundred years ago than today, Wilshman said. Mr Uhlaf was doing much to restore the sturgeon fisheries of the Volga and the Caspian after the ecological disasters of Bolshevism. Mr Uhlaf was a model entrepreneur. He understood that creating wealth went with conserving the environment.

'We are only temporary trustees of our world,' he told them. 'We have to use wealth rationally. Some people have still not grasped that private consumption should not be conspicuous, or it becomes socially destabilizing. But that is part of the learning curve for nations newly freed of communist tyranny.'

Zidra, who had left piles of bags at the porter's lodge and infiltrated the reception, yawned, looked around at the other guests. Saw the biologist, Minakov, who was staring scornfully at Uhlaf.

The speeches and toasts continued for an hour. When they were over she followed Minakov to the table. He stood in front of the giant sturgeon, shaking his head, muttering the Russian word which means disgrace: '*Pozor.*'

'What is disgraceful? Eating fish?'

He turned about. 'Of course not. It is very healthy meat. But you were eavesdropping!'

Zidra laughed. 'I didn't mean to frighten you.'

'I was not frightened, of course.' He looked doubtfully at her. 'But I am sure it is not Mr Uhlaf's fault. These rascals' – he motioned at the two fat and genial chefs from the Moscow Hanseatic who were moving slowly through the throng receiving compliments – 'have sold the real thing to some more valued client. The mayor of Moscow or some other chieftain is eating Mr Uhlaf's fish, I expect.'

'Is there something wrong with the sturgeon?' she asked, astonished. 'It looks quite beautiful.'

'Oh, it's *edible*. But it is not from northern Caspian waters,' he said. 'It has nothing in common with Azerbaijan. This is *Acipenser guldenstaedti persius*. It is from Iran. I expect it was purchased at your Billingsgate market. The caviar is also commercial, and quite poor quality.'

'How embarrassing for Mr Uhlaf! I suppose someone ought to mention it to him?'

'I am not sure what the point would be.' He frowned at her.

60

'Who are you?'

'Zidra Renard. I'm just tagging along behind my husband,' she told him. 'He's with RAND.'

'He's an American? But you speak Russian?'

'My father was Russian.'

Minakov nodded, took his card from the pocket of his ancient, shabby waistcoat. It described him as Peter Minakov, Lenin Laureate, Nobel Prizewinner, Astrakhan Limnological Institute.

'Thanks.' She studied the card. They studied each other. Zidra was wearing purple suede high heels, a belted and buttoned dress in purple silk which fitted like a glove, and a raw silk jacket in faded beige. She wore a floppy straw boater on her head. It was embellished with a purple ribbon and a bunch of purple silk grapes.

Minakov had strange eyes and slender, cruel, hands which felt and probed and knew. And they were expressive too. The gestures they made were confident, impatient, self-assured, full of intellectual arrogance. They were the hands of a maker who was restless enough to unmake everything.

'My institute is based in Astrakhan,' he told her, but I spend half my time in Moscow.'

She turned the card over. It gave his Moscow address: *Astrakhan Limnological Institute. Moscow Branch. 5/9 Varvarka Street*. There were two numbers. 'I have a flat there. I also have an office in the Kremlin. Are you ever in Moscow?'

'From time to time,' Zidra said.

'Perhaps we shall meet there. Or better still, in Astrakhan.'

'Perhaps we shall. But tell me, professor, how you knew this sturgeon was wrong?'

'Mr Uhlaf thinks this is beluga – *Acipenser stellatus stellatus* – but it obviously is not. Look—' He pointed a silver dinner knife at the head of the fish. 'Its snout is too short for one thing. And beluga is much more impressive, perhaps fifty per cent bigger.'

She inspected the snout. It seemed long enough for any purpose she could imagine. 'You poor thing, you are here on false pretences, and the good professor has found you out,' she told the fish. 'But where is its mouth?' she asked Minakov.

'Underneath. Like a shark's. The sturgeon is a member of the same family, but evolved differently. Sixty-five million years ago the Caspian Sea was part of the World Ocean, but then it became divided off. After that, all the species within it went their own evolutionary way.'

She touched the great fish's nose with her finger. 'Is it dangerous? Does it have teeth?'

'No, it's a bottom dweller.' He made a sinuous, planing movement with his hand. 'It swims through the ooze, sucking up whatever it can eat.'

Two waiters pushed past them to carve the fish. They stepped aside, but almost at once an apologetic Assistant Under Secretary from the FO's Far East department led Zidra away, promising to return her to Minakov.

The AUS led her to where her husband was talking to Sir James Wilshman and another man whom Renard introduced as Henry Carter-Allis, chairman of City bankers Palfrey & Griblock, who were organizing the finances of the new Azeri oil consortium.

Wilshman liked women. They energized him, brightened the tedium of a political life overgrown with doubt and drawing to its close. Wilshman's face was florid, his back stooped, his eyebrows white and bushy. But he still held himself well, with a raffish charm. He belonged to the class of Tory politicians who are as at home on the grouse moor as in the Palace of Westminster, for whom politics is one hobby amongst others, who live comfortable lives in comfortable bodies and are at ease with themselves and the world. Wilshman was a born predator of women. He had noticed Zidra and he wanted to meet her.

Carter-Allis was different. He was deferential, calculating, he had Jewish blood and he came from a family of moneylenders.

The four made small talk for a few minutes and then Carter-Allis came to the point: he was having a house party in two weeks' time. The Wilshmans would be present, and so would Sir Edward Boningfield, the chairman of Bison Oil and a friend of Wilshman's since Eton. Perhaps the Renards would attend?

With great pleasure they would.

Wilshman was the kind of man who can overwhelm women with a combination of frank lust and overpowering politeness. He scarcely disguised his intentions towards Zidra, even in Renard's presence. He made Zidra laugh, either with him or at him; she wasn't sure which. In a few minutes more she made an excuse and went back to where Peter Minakov stood talking to Hans Uhlaf and Sergei Ivanov, president of Arctic Star.

Uhlaf's pale blue eyes with their sawdust-size flecks fixed on her. 'I was waiting for you,' he told her, making a ponderous compliment. 'You are like a lighthouse; all eyes are on you, but all are in darkness unless you choose to shine upon them.'

Zidra laughed.

'We were discussing the scandal of the sturgeon that got away,' he said, looking balefully at Minakov. 'Unfortunately, the Russian mafia has tentacles everywhere. But at least the fish is fresh and it is a sturgeon.'

'Is it really so valuable?' she asked.

'Yes. The caviar alone from this fish is worth fifty or sixty thousand dollars. It is the world's most precious food! So you see, anyone can have an interest in, let me say, diverting it. Anyone.' He glowered at Minakov. 'This was supposed to come from your institute's fishery, was it not?'

'I hope you are not suggesting that my staff stole your sturgeon?'

'Of course not.' Uhlaf gave Minakov a watery smile. The professor didn't look angry, just puzzled. The idea that Uhlaf might be suggesting he stole it himself was too ludicrous even to occur to him.

Zidra warmed to him. For all his hard analytical mind and hard analytical hands, he was frail, vulnerable.

After the reception, Renard went for a private meeting with Minakov, promising to meet Zidra at the Mountbatten at six. Hill had called; he wanted to see him too, if possible. They would leave for Baku first flight in the morning.

Zidra kept the promise she'd made and went to help Lady Broughton pack for Moscow.

Henrietta Broughton was distracted, her movements birdlike, anxious. She told Zidra to take no notice – she was flying back to Moscow. That was reason enough to be nervous.

They stared in silence at the piles of boxes and bulging Harrods carrier bags which covered the floor.

'And how was the reception?' Henrietta asked.

'Mr Uhlaf brought a team from his Moscow Hanseatic for the occasion. I was interested to meet Uhlaf because I've had dinner at the Hanseatic. It's an awful place. Germanic. Pompous. It's a folly, the architectural equivalent of a Nuremberg rally, with

63

twenty-metre-long German flags draped outside the entrance.'

Henrietta laughed. 'And it's only fifty paces round the corner from the British embassy. It quite makes us look like poor second cousins. Which we are, of course, nowadays. I even spoke to Hans about the flags.'

'What did he say? He's such a strange man!'

'Why do you say so? Well, never mind. Personally I rather like the Hanseatic. I think Hans has style. When the Treasury inspectors sent a memo round forbidding us to put our people up at the place, because it's too expensive, Hans smiled like a wolf and said *Next time have them send the bills to me, dear Lady Broughton.* Henrietta smiled indulgently at her friend. 'Derek says he has a true business cosmopolitanism, and that his deals are astounding. Anyway, he's certainly arrived.'

'He's a bit mercurial, I agree. Is he a womanizer, like they say?'

Henrietta nodded absent-mindedly. She was weighing up the chances of getting another Harrods bag into a bulging suitcase. 'Yes, he is,' she said. 'But that's because he knows how to make himself interesting. I think he's the rare kind of man that even other men think is sexy, yet don't see as a threat.'

'Well, he's not my type. He's brilliant on the surface, but his eyes are metering the responses he gets, so it's all an act. Which means you don't know what he's really like underneath, but it's probably not very nice. I wouldn't want to wake up to that in the mornings.'

'Well, he's phenomenally eligible. He's charming, only forty-three and already chairman of the Plate River Corporation. It means he'll be around for donkey's years so all his City chums had better beware. As Derek says,' she said mockingly, 'even his rivals seek his counsel.'

'Poor Sir Derek. You are very cruel to him, Henrietta.'

'Not a bit of it. I tease him because he's secretly envious of Hans and that makes him tiresomely pompous.'

'I can't imagine Derek envying anybody. He's much too clever.'

'Of course, and that's the point. It's not in the brains department that he has to suffer comparison, is it?' She was suddenly dismissive, savagely so. 'But I don't doubt that Derek will end up as chairman of Mr Uhlaf's board if he ever gets tired of ambassadoring. Which he never will, of course.' She sighed slowly. 'I do just wonder what is happening to us. Derek is a good man, but when I look at the Service nowadays . . .' Her voice trailed away, her gaze wandering over the pile of pink-and-silver striped gift boxes on the decorative French table beside her; at last she chose one and handed it to Zidra, 'to go in the Escada bag on the left'.

'I've never seen you in Escada stuff,' Zidra said wonderingly.

'You never will, believe me. It's much too garish for my taste, but Escada is very popular with Moscow's *nouveaux riches*.' She half disappeared under a tide of tissue paper on the floor. 'Sort of a step up from Lurex tights and leather miniskirts and all that kind of thing, I suppose.' She picked up the roll of pink-and-grey ribbon for binding the presents. 'Darling, hand me the scissors.'

Zidra passed them over, and had a fleeting image of Lady Broughton tutoring assorted Muscovite tarts, the wives and mistresses of Russian entrepreneurs, in the basics of taste. Did the Know-How Fund organize short courses in dress and deportment? Did Sir Derek give equivalent classes to the bankers and businessmen, the big boys in loud dogtooth jackets, with their ill-concealed shoulder-holsters and Rolexes like solid gold golf balls on their wrists? She didn't ask.

'Tell me what you thought about Professor Minakov?' Henrietta was enquiring.

'I had a conversation with him. A very odd one. He's got strange eyes. They don't just undress you, they leave you naked like an embryo. And there is such *pain* behind them, you feel you are talking to the King Lear of ecologists.'

Henrietta brushed her hands together, shaking shreds of tissue paper on to the floor. 'His colleagues in the Russian government call him the Ayatollah. Come to think of it, I'm told that one is apt to discover the odd dead mullah lying around in the Foreign Office cellars, so he wouldn't look out of place. Really, a very dislikable man. He's a constant thorn in Hans's side. But unfortunately he's too honest and too highly placed for Hans to get at.'

'Too honest for what?' Zidra looked puzzled.

'Life, my dear.' Henrietta sighed. 'How tiresome these Dali scarves are. No one understands what they're worth.' She put on one side a small heap of hand-printed silk scarves with liquid pocket watch motifs from Dali's posthumous period – perhaps the surrealist master's most productive in terms of output – when his assistants embarked on a frenzy of necessarily short-lived but profitable inventiveness. 'I thought they'd go with all the Escada horological stuff, but they don't. They look washed out, that's all.'

Lady Broughton emerged like Amphitrite from the mounds of tissue paper. She looked at the ormolu clock on the mantelpiece. 'I'll never do it in time, will I?'

'You will, we've nearly finished.'

It was getting late. Lady Broughton stood in front of Zidra and the sunlight gilded her English beauty like a manuscript. Hers was the face on a thousand portraits of statesmen's wives. She had always been there, would ever be, through war and crisis, boom and disaster. She was silent duty and unremitting care, the warden of the home fire, the blessing of motherhood, the civilizing mission amongst the nations. She stood till death for England, and never complained.

'I'm terribly grateful for your friendship,' Zidra told her. They kissed each other's cheeks.

There was no more time to talk; they had twenty minutes of frantic suitcase-stuffing, of jumping up and down on bulging lids, of frayed zippers and fraying tempers, before Sir Derek Broughton suddenly arrived from King Charles Street, shouting that they were impossibly, hopelessly late, he would have to ring BA and get them to hold the plane, which was unforgivable, and that two taxis were waiting with meters ticking outside in the mews.

And then they were gone, and Zidra was left alone in the place, with just Maria the Filipina to mutter embarrassment at her. She took a taxi and headed back to the Mountbatten.

Renard was late getting back but she expected that. He had planned a meeting with Bob Hill. She would hear the outcome when he returned – if he wanted to talk. In the meantime she lay in the bath until she finished the Mario Vargas Llosa novel. By then the water was cold.

The book wasn't so interesting, in fact. You had to believe it was possible to screw impotent boys. Zidra threw it aside, grabbed a towel and rubbed herself down. She had been so long in the bath she had goose-bumps. She put on her bathrobe and walked through to the mini-bar, was on the point of opening it when the phone rang. She expected Renard. It was room service. Did madam want her ironing now or later? She told the woman, later.

She picked up the remote control from its slot by the phone and turned the TV on. The channel was set to a cartoon network. Donald Duck was doing something unspeakable to Mickey Mouse. She watched for a while without knowing why and then shook her head and flipped channels. Cowboys were doing something unspeakable to Alan Ladd. She switched off, unwrapped the towel from around her head and pushed between the sofa and the mini-bar to the window. It was early evening. Passers-by were strolling around Seven Dials and on up Shaftesbury Avenue. She watched for a while, wondering if she would see Renard.

By eight he still hadn't arrived. She dialled the number at 23B Drake Mews and when no one answered called room service instead and ordered a Waldorf salad. Then she went to the mini-bar to get mineral water and maybe olives. She opened the wood-veneer outer door, found crisps on the shelf over the fridge and opened them, spilling the packet on to an enamel tray decorated with pictures of Burmese dancing women. She had to pull hard at the fridge door: something sticky like orange juice had leaked and then congealed on the rubber strip and it came open suddenly with a tearing sound. She made a mental note to mention it to the barman next time he came to replenish it and swung it wide open.

At first she thought there must be some mistake because Renard's head was inside. The interior light glowed dimly through the lobes of his ears, which were white and bloodless.

She closed the door slowly, then opened it again.

Not only Renard's head. His hands and feet were neatly piled there too.

All the drinks had been taken away.

The door creaked shut. Zidra sat on the bed and looked at her hands. There was blood on them. Her eyes swivelled back to the mini-bar.

She started noticing things. Like, for instance, she had stopped breathing. The silence was uncanny. All your life you live with the sound of your own breathing. Now silence poured out of her. Then the silence became a scream that started not with her or even in the room but somewhere a long way off. It rose in a crescendo and then the scream was really inside her, and it did not come out. It was still there after she stopped.

She was glad she had stopped. Screaming was not professional.

Professionalism, they had taught her at IMEMO's school for spies, was exactly about situations like this. The unexpected. Because that is how the running dogs entrap reconnaissance officers.

She thought that was funny and now laughter spilled out; seized her and shook her as a cat shakes a mouse, until her teeth rattled and stars flashed behind her eyes.

Laughter was harder than screaming. It annihilated her. She laughed and tears poured down her face even when she knew the phone was ringing; until she bit her lip and saw the blood spurt. The laughter swept past her like a shock wave leaving strange flat land behind. She picked up the phone.

'Reception, madam. Porter's lodge. Peter here.'

Zidra listened in silence. She could hear noises in the background. Reception was busy. A door slammed, someone shouted for towels. A porter outside in the street hailed a taxi. Theatregoers talked and laughed. Then Peter spoke again. She tried to focus. Heard the sounds, but could not form words from them.

'Sorry?'

'I said, is everything all right, madam? The waiter is outside your door with your salad. He heard someone scream. Could you answer the door now? I can send security if—'

'No. No, thank you. I also heard a scream, but it wasn't me. It was two doors down, actually.'

'Ah! The honeymooners.'

'Exactly.'

'I'm sure that was it, madam.'

'Thank you, Peter. I'll open the door now. I was in the bathroom. Good night.'

'Of course. Good evening, madam.'

She put down the phone.

Good night, life.

Goodbye – she wanted to say her husband's name but it had disappeared into a black hole. She could not remember it.

She went to the door and let the waiter in, put the salad on top of the mini-bar. She gave him five pounds for his trouble.

Then she went to the bathroom and cleaned her teeth.

Perhaps it wasn't Renard after all. Renard's hair was brown, and there was a small scar on his chin which ran into the lower lip: a scratch from a playful cat he'd owned as a child. She did not recall a scar on the head in the fridge, but then she no longer recalled anything. Perhaps there was no head in the fridge. If she opened the door again she would see a lot of esoteric makes of beer, and five minutes later Renard would be here.

There was whisky on the sideboard.

She picked up the bottle and poured, noticing the blood beside it. In fact, there were traces of blood everywhere. Funny how she hadn't seen it before. She drank the whisky, poured another and drank that too.

Life was *inconvenient*, was it not? That was what Henrietta Broughton liked to say. *Inconvenient.*

Life, in her case, was retching, screaming, hysteria.

She knew she would have to get the body parts out and look at them, there was no other way.

Strange, how a life can implode, leaving nothing behind. She would not even have a place to live.

She would be arrested, imprisoned probably for murdering her husband. That was OK, she had not saved him anyway, but first she had to kill his killers.

Where was the body?

What had happened to the rest of the blood? The place must have been like an abattoir.

They must have bled him to death in the bath tub.

Zidra decided to check the wardrobe, because the torso had to be somewhere. Her feet did not work so she crawled on hands and knees to the place, slid back the door, and a zip-up dry cleaner's bag crashed to the floor beside her. That was it. She unzipped the bag. The body was inside.

It was wearing the suit which Renard had on that morning.

This was still not identification, but it took her a while to do more. And then it occurred to her that she knew how to settle the question without going back to the fridge. She heaved the corpse half out of the bag. The bag was full of blood. The stench was overpowering. As she pulled the legs free, a Sabatier carving knife fell out, tarry with blood.

Zidra's shaking hands peeled the trousers down. She expected to see more mutilation, but they had not touched that place and she saw at once that, whoever it was, it was after all not Renard.

69

She collapsed on the floor. It took another half-hour to find the courage to open the fridge. First she removed the hands, which were crossed neatly in front of the head. The tips of the fingers had been sliced away.

It is hard to tell anything much with dead meat, and the left hand wore Renard's wedding ring. But she did not think it was Renard's hand.

She took out the head, carefully. It was ravaged, one eye was missing and part of the nose, as if he had been shot at close range with a large-calibre weapon. So why no blood? The other eye stared dully at her.

But she knew now whose body it was. The head did bear a resemblance to Renard and she knew why. She had once joked that they must be brothers.

It was Bob Hill's head.

Zidra went to the bathroom to wash away the blood. Then she went round the suite and opened all the windows. Fresh air scoured the room and brought the sounds of the city with it.

She threw blankets over the headless corpse and a couple of towels over Bob Hill's head. Then she sat down on the sofa and tried to think.

Chapter 6

After they took him, they ferried Renard to a big house in a fashionable part of Hampstead. They stripped him and hung him on the wall of what looked like a heavily soundproofed garage. Not that he was observing much. His head ached from when someone had bent metal over it.

After they hung him they brought him a big video monitor and left him alone for a while. The video they played had been filmed in this same place. It showed an attractive young girl who soon turned out to be of Russian origin. At first, everything was normal. The girl was shown around the house, almost as if she was a prospective purchaser, by one of the men who took Renard. Or perhaps she was just a casual date. From his voice, the person behind the viewfinder was the other of the two men, the smaller one with a stoop and a disability of the right hand.

The girl is brought to the garage and seated on a sofa. The man with her arranges one or two cameras on tripods. By now the girl is showing signs of anxiety, but it is too late. He goes away and reappears wearing a balaclava. He is powerfully built, strong and extremely violent. The girl, who looks to be in her twenties, is quickly subdued and stripped and chains are attached to her feet, hands and waist (all this equipment was in the room and visible to Renard). The system of hoists and pulleys is ingenious, because although the subject can be raised or lowered the chains to the feet and hands are horizontal. The arms and legs are stretched wide apart, to the point where her screams suddenly become muted, presumably because she is suffocating, and it is possible to hear her joints cracking.

The girl is raised slightly by the waist, the head hanging down. The man now undresses and then rapes her twice, first with a stick, the second time himself.

The rest of the film, which lasts an hour, shows the dismantling of the girl, using a variety of tools starting with a soldering iron

71

and progressing to knives, hacksaws and finally a hook. By this time the girl has gone mad and it is a only a relief when the man at last cuts her throat. Then the man bows to the camera and the film ends.

Renard had not noticed that the two men had re-entered the room. They approached and stood in front of him. 'How do you like Pete's home video?' the shorter one asked Renard. 'I find it ghoulish myself, but his methods are unquestionably effective.' The speaker was squat, walked with a limp, wore a silk business suit.

'Your friend is a twat,' Renard said, 'and so are you.'

The man hit Renard in the stomach, hard, his fist balled round a hand-exerciser. 'You need to be more respectful,' he said. He giggled, pleased with his efforts. 'Your colleague is dead, because he didn't want to show respect. We asked him for his help and he very discourteously refused. I hope you will be more sensible.'

'What do you want?' Renard said with difficulty.

'Some merchandise is being sold to some people.' He cocked his head this way and that, as if working out how much to tell Renard. 'To the paddies, actually. We need a cut-out. A go-between. You're it. You've already involved yourself, poking about in Eden Castle, where you shouldn't have. Now you can make yourself useful and help the deal happen.'

'Why do you need a cut-out?'

Renard squirmed a little. He felt as if something had snapped inside, and he knew it was going to be a long night. It was hard to ask the proper questions without feeling it was just a waste of time. Especially if it was true that Bob was really dead. He'd still been alive when they'd hauled him off.

But mostly, he felt surprise. These people could only be IRA leader Sean McMahon's. No one else knew about his stay in the Welsh Borders, let alone in Eden Castle.

So McMahon was the traitor, but it was hard to know why he'd moved against the CIA, and just now, on the eve of the warhead delivery.

Unless it meant the IRA intended to use the plutonium after all, as a blackmail tool if not for real.

'You're CIA. You can take the blame. No one will come looking for the CIA afterwards, will they? Not even the British police.' He looked pleased by this thought. 'You'll take the rap, but you'll walk away from it too, because you'll have a reason. And because you'll be doing us all a service. So everyone'll be happy.'

'What service?'

'You'll be screwing the IRA. Showing the world just what bastards they are. Probably you'll get a medal.'

Renard looked at him for a while. 'And what other reason, apart from the medal?' he asked.

'To save a life, maybe.'

'Whose?'

'Your wife's? That do?'

'No, I'm not going to be interested,' Renard told him after a few moments' thought. 'Besides, I don't know what you're talking about. And I hate mysteries.'

The man looked disappointed. He called the other over.

'Please yourself. I've given Pete a list of questions for you to answer.' Frost scaled the man's face. 'I'm sure you'll want to assist him.' He snapped round and, without another word, left.

Pete went out with him and when he came back he had undressed, apart from the balaclava and some kind of genital thong. He snapped the thong's strings. 'Like it?' he asked Renard. 'I made it myself. Got it from that Russian girl you were just watching.'

Renard looked more closely and saw what the thing was made of.

'I got the idea from *The Silence of the Lambs*, but that book is crap. It doesn't tell you properly how to tan a skin.' He walked around Renard, sizing him up. 'I ruined a few good ones before I learnt the knack.' He stood for a while, watching him, then went away. When he came back he was pushing a roll of barbed wire on a little trolley. 'I got this idea from another book, called *American Psycho*.' He began to wind the wire round Renard's feet, which were tethered loosely to the floor. The tethering seemed to be in the way, so he stopped partway through, stood up and hit Renard in the stomach, where the other man had; but Pete was in training, he was big, and the effect was different. Renard began to convulse. Pete unloosed the tetherings, one foot first, then the other. When Renard tried to kick back, Pete tutted and hit him again in the diaphragm. Then Renard didn't kick back any more.

'Of course, I'm not wholly derivative,' he told his captive. 'I have a few ideas of my own. I'll show you some, if you have the time.'

Renard couldn't refuse. He was gagging.

'I'm sorry? I didn't quite get that. But I expect you're tired of hanging around,' Pete said, and lowered Renard enough for his feet to rest upon the floor. They looked like balls of barbed wire. Blood dripped out, slowly at first, then more rapidly. 'You've got a nice-looking tart, as well. I've seen a piccy of her. Nice hair – sort of flaxen-coloured. I like it long, like that.' While he spoke he beat another tattoo on Renard's abdomen. 'That's what we have in common – we both like Russian girls. Better tits than Brits have, I think.' He lowered Renard to the floor, watched him writhe and gag. 'I like that, too.'

The man went away and when he came back he carried a big mug of tea, white except for black letters and a red heart, which read: 'I love London.' He watched Renard slowly quieten down.

'Another good point is that no one cares what happens to them. I wanted to find your tart today, but someone screwed up and didn't deliver her on time. Pity. I would have preferred her to you. But I left a nice present anyway.' He snickered. '*Presents*, I should say.' He picked up a baseball bat and began to prod Renard in the kidneys. 'Pieces of a pal of yours.'

Now he wrapped chains tightly around Renard's ankles, then switched on the hoist and hung him up by his feet. 'I need to slow the blood flow,' he observed. When Renard was at eye level he said, 'You shouldn't mock an artist like me. Sure, I'm still a beginner. But I'm learning all the time. For instance, that Russian kid. I've had a lot more practice since then. I don't make that mistake now. I get them to co-operate, it's much more fun. I'll do that with your girl, when we collect her.' He picked up the list of questions, ignoring the strange noises Renard was making. 'This is strictly business. And as you've already been sold I can't damage you too much, unfortunately, so make it easy on both of us by answering these questions now and then I can let you down. First question: who are you liaising with on the British side?'

Renard was passing out. His last thought was to wonder why the man should expect Zidra to sit quietly waiting, if they'd left parts of Bob Hill lying around the hotel room.

In her suite in the Mountbatten Hotel, Zidra was sitting quietly. She had started to think.

One question could be answered at once, with luck. She called the porter's lodge. She recognized the voice which answered – it belonged to a handsome Scottish lad, a medical student called Clive. 'My husband is quite late,' she told him. 'Can you or any of your colleagues remember when he left? He's the tall American.'

'The guy who looks like the young John Wayne, in *Stagecoach*?'

The words seemed to emerge like black worms out of some hole in the wall. She braced herself to answer. 'I'm sure he'd be pleased to know you think so,' she said, which seemed creditable.

'I wasn't here, ma'am, but if you wait a minute I'll find out.'

He put the phone down and the next person to pick it up was the head porter. 'Your husband came back about four this afternoon. No one saw him leave again,' he told her. 'But he received three visitors late in the morning.'

Renard hadn't been in the room in the morning.

'What time?'

'Logged in at eleven-thirty, madam.'

'When'd they leave?'

'There's no note in the book, madam. I do apologize.' He said it with a finality. 'Is there anything I can do?'

'No, I don't think so.'

'Don't be concerned, madam. We'll keep an eye out for him.'

'Oh, he's having an evening on the tiles, I expect.' She thanked him and hung up.

They'd taken Renard out by some service access, that was all.

It meant only one thing.

Someone with a pass key had entered the room, or been admitted by Hill. A guest booked into a different room. Or someone familiar enough to the porters for his presence not to be noteworthy.

She watched her fists clenching and unclenching, even felt pain from where fingernails bit deep. That was good; pain meant life. She tried to shake the numbness out of her head.

Think!

What did they expect her to do? What *should* she do?

She might involve the British authorities. They most likely expected that, counted on it. While officialdom enfolded her in its process, the trail to Renard would go cold. And if Renard had been shipped out, the British could not help.

It would end with her collecting a flag-draped coffin from some godforsaken place and ceremonially installing it at Arlington.

There was a shuffling sound in the corridor. She stared blankly at the door. The sound receded; another guest leaving their room.

Most likely, the killer was still on the premises, watching events. If so, he would return. Would expect her to be waiting for him.

Hill's body had been mutilated to make recognition difficult. What had the killer expected her to do? Everything had been arranged so as to produce shock and hysteria. She might have been expected to mistake the remains for her own husband. The fingertips had been removed so the only sure means of identification would be by dental examination and DNA testing, all of which takes time. Especially when the victim is a foreign national whose records are held in a different country.

Another thing: why kill Bob Hill but take Renard alive?

Perhaps because they knew who Renard was but did not know Hill, who on the face of it was a still greater catch. Killing Hill had certainly been a mistake. Perhaps he'd fought back and been killed for that.

But they *knew* Renard. That conclusion was inescapable.

Someone had betrayed him. First in Baku. Now here in London.

She thought again about Bryce. About his recent and ill-prepared move to London station, replacing a close personal friend of Renard's in one of Langley's recent purges.

If not him, who?

No one in England knew of Renard's mission here, not counting the unimpeachable Broughtons, now on their way to Moscow. It was Henrietta's packing frenzy which had made her late and so saved her. Even then, Broughton had not known that she and Renard had already been in Eden Castle for weeks.

The only certain thing was that whoever started this had done so in Moscow. The answer had to be there.

And, Zidra thought, whoever killed Hill and took Renard would have to come for her.

Even while she was thinking it she heard a knock at the door. Gentle, unintrusive, a servant's knock.

She went to the door, switched off the lights and swivelled the peephole cover.

A waiter in a white jacket stood outside. He was small, Filipino-looking, and he carried a silver tray with a champagne bottle in an ice bucket.

It had to be the man. Come to kill her, or take her.

'Who is it?' she called.

'Room service, madam.' The waiter turned to the door and smiled. 'Compliments of the management.'

'I didn't order anything.'

'I said, compliments of the house. You good customer.' His accent was thick, but that didn't prove anything.

The suite was at the end of a corridor. There were no corners for a second assailant to hide round. The man was alone.

She opened the door.

The man came in, walked ahead of her to the sitting room. Hill's carcass was on the floor in the bedroom; his head was in the mini-bar. The man put the tray down next to it, asked her if she'd like the bottle opened. It was Lanson, a vintage brut.

'Why not?' she said.

He smiled at her, put the bottle down and peeled the foil off the cork. 'Nice weather for time of year,' he announced.

'I suppose it is.'

His smile set in a line while he struggled with the cork, which was stuck. He didn't want to concentrate on it. She was too close. At last it squeaked out and he poured champagne for her.

She had been studying him. He was not, she saw, a Filipino. He studied her in return. 'I take you to him,' he said as he handed her the glass, holding it at arm's length. 'You want to join him?' He watched her take the glass. Her hand was steady. Then he stood back a little more. 'He want to see you, madam. Waiting for you.'

'What's the point?' she said.

'You lovers. Not just a team.' He sounded reproachful.

'If I don't go?'

'What choice you got? It's your man.'

'I can call the police. Have them arrest you.'

'Then I kill you,' he said quietly. 'It would make like suicide. First murder, then suicide.' He shook his head. 'No loose ends.'

'Where is he?'

'I told you, I take you there. Drink, please. It's only way you see him. Drink, then we go, quick.'

She could not reach him. If she moved, he stepped politely back. Kept out of range.

He looked Chinese. Perhaps he was a Kalmyk. She spoke a few words of Russian to find out. Told him his mother was a camel. The face remained impassive but the eyes said something.

'You better dress,' he told her. She looked down at herself, suddenly surprised. She was still wearing the bathrobe. The hem was stained with blood that was already blackening. She had not noticed before.

'I suppose so.' She straightened up and looked at the man, He was nearly a head shorter than her. His eyes were black, darting like a bird's. His hands hung loose at his sides. He was relaxed, but coiled underneath.

Zidra breathed out, slowly. She looked resigned, as if many things had just decided themselves. She stepped out of the robe.

The man's eyes tightened.

'Perhaps you'd like to help me,' she said quietly. 'There's a body in the way of my wardrobe door. I need to move it.'

She turned and walked through to the bedroom. The little man trotted after her. She went to the big mirror, switched on the vanity lamp and stood with her back to him, brushing her hair, watching him in the mirror while he towed Hill's remains aside.

When he finished he rubbed his palms together twice then stood watching her. She put the brush down and stared back at him in the mirror.

'I go bring your drink,' he told her at last. There was a catch in his voice. 'Now you dress, please. Don't want to catch a cold.'

Zidra pulled on pants. He came back with the champagne, watched her snaffle stockings up her legs. They were white and sheer with fancy elastic tops. She turned to face him. 'You got nice jewellery,' he told her, looking at the stud Renard had set in her.

'Yeah.' She reached for the champagne and the stud glittered. This time he brought it to her, sniffing the air round her like a tomcat, watching her sip it. She put the glass aside, turning back to face the mirror. The after-taste was obvious. 'Good vintage,' she told his reflection. Her hands were resting on the shelf below the mirror, gripping the edge.

'Give you good night sleep,' the man joked. His eye trailed down her back to her legs, but he never saw them punching back at him. The Kalmyk had one gold incisor. When her heel hit his face he lost it and several teeth besides.

He crashed back against the wardrobe, slumping into a silent heap. She decided not to take chances, took the bottle and smashed it over his head.

Maybe it was extreme, but you never could tell with Kalmyks. Especially ones who didn't care what you called their mother. And after what had happened, Zidra was jumpy.

She tied him up with scotch tape, went through his pockets, found nothing except car keys, poured herself a whisky and waited.

She had hit him too hard. It looked as though he wasn't going to come round at all. After a while it was obvious he was sliding into a coma. His breath came in rasping pants, and blood leaked from an ear.

'Fucking shit,' she muttered. She looked at the car keys. There was a Hertz rental docket on the ring, and a registration number.

Zidra finished dressing, putting a track suit and sneakers over the silk stockings. She placed a few essentials in a small hold-all and left. The Kalmyk's breathing was stertorous. He seemed to be dying. 'What a fucking mess,' she said as she closed the door. It was eleven-fifteen in the evening.

She smiled brightly at Peter the head porter and said she was going to find her old man and kill him. And she did not need a taxi; she wanted some air.

'Be careful, madam,' Peter said. 'There are some strange people around.'

'Don't worry, I've dressed down.'

She scoured the streets around Seven Dials. It was difficult; cars were double parked, squashed nose to tail, as tens of thousands of Londoners and their guests partied in the clubs and eateries of theatreland and nearby Chinatown. Twice she got propositioned, and then a policeman offered to arrest her for loitering. She smiled sweetly, said she'd lost a ring somewhere, walked on.

Then she saw the number plate. The car was a new Ford. She clicked the remote and its lights flashed. Inside, she found nothing at all to identify the man. There was an A–Z street atlas, but it was brand new. She went through it page by page looking for markings. Nothing. Not even a dog-ear.

Zidra walked slowly back to the hotel and returned to her room. Perhaps the man was alive still. Perhaps there was something she'd missed.

Not only was he alive, he was halfway to consciouness.

She propped him, filled a glass with cold water and gave him a few sips. His eyes opened blearily and closed again. He was pale, and he'd been sick.

'Where is the American?' she asked him in Russian.

'Which American?' he mumbled.

She gave him a few more sips. It seemed to bring him round. The eyes opened again. A rictus of a smile stiffened on his lips. He glared at her, his tongue clicking against broken teeth as he tried to speak. She knelt close to listen, and at last heard the words: 'Nice jewellery. Very nice jewellery.' There was a rattling laugh and this time he was dead.

'Fuck.'

She went through his clothes again, this time more carefully. Cut the tape from his hands to pull the jacket off. Took off the shirt and examined it minutely. It was cheap, Hong Kong made. The label bore a laundry mark, which might be a telephone number: 9230397. She walked to the phone and dialled it; a metallic upper-class English voice told her she'd made a mistake. She ripped out the label anyway.

There was nothing else to go on.

She left the hotel, went back to the car to check it again. She pressed the redial on its mobile phone, cycling through the last four numbers. One did not answer, the second was an angry, sleepy officer worker who was the previous renter. The third was information. The fourth was Pizza Hut take-away.

She slammed the phone back down, then had another thought, pulled out the shirt label and dialled it, this time with the Moscow prefix: 007-095-9230397. Another metallic voice told her this phone did not have international dialling and she should contact her airtime supplier.

There was a Mercury pay-phone a few yards down the street. She went to it, swiped a card and dialled the number again. There came the usual agonizing series of clicks and buzzes, half-heard conversations in Russian, blizzards howling. Then the number rang.

'Yes? I'm listening.' A man's voice, hard, sober.

'You've got Renard, the American,' she said. 'I want him back.'

'Wait a minute.'

Long silence. She looked up and down the street. Some lads were knocking on car windows. She watched them progress along the alley, testing out doors, never once triggering an alarm.

Another voice came on the line, rich with aggression, suspiciousness: 'Who is this speaking? Who is calling?'

'I know you've picked up the American, Renard,' she repeated.

'You're crazy, you've dialled a wrong number. Where are you calling from?'

'Where have you taken him?' she asked. 'Release him at once. Tell me now where he's being held. Is he still alive?'

'Who are you?'

'How much for the American?' she asked. The lads had reached the hired Ford. One of them looked across at her.

'You're crazy. I don't know anything about any Americans.' The man covered the handset, spoke to someone else. 'Who are you?' he said again. 'I don't see any numbers here, where are you calling from?'

So he was using a caller-recognition device. They work only on internal Russian lines; the display remains blank if the call originates from another country.

'You want to deal?' she asked. 'We'll give a hundred thousand dollars for him. But you must deal now.'

Silence. Then: 'This is not a telephone talk,' the voice said. It was wary, cold, hard. 'Where are you? We can send someone, anywhere.'

'I'll come to you,' she said, watching as one of the lads opened the door of a car further down the street, yelped at the others to come.

The line had gone dead. She dialled again, and this time there was no answer. Even though they could not tell who was calling, they could tell that it was international. Local calls ring differently in Russia; the signal is shorter.

The lads drove past, giving her clenched fist salutes.

There was no answer, but it didn't matter. Because those guys knew all about it, that was sure.

Besides, it was her only lead. She'd never find Renard looking for him in England. She would go to Moscow, knock on their door. Tomorrow.

She went back to her hotel room, doused the lights and sat by the window, watching. London had died at last. It was well after five. There was fog on Seven Dials. A street cleaning machine rattled by.

Without planning it, she fell asleep. She came to fighting off panic. It was six-fifteen.

She grabbed her hold-all, put the Do Not Disturb sign on the door and left.

She drove to Heathrow in the Kalmyk's car. From there she took the early flight to Moscow.

The answers were there. They always were.

Chapter 7

Moscow hits you like a door slamming.

Dirt, smells, bright snow, black earth, ostentation jostling despair in the streets, seething rumour, coup plots, currency scams, cholera, corruption, icon-smuggling, busted messiahs, the shortage of carrots, the abundance of carrots, the phenol in the water, the bankruptcy of Gorky Park, the plan to build a new Gorky Park, the shoot-outs in steel-and-chrome boardrooms.

Dazzling women for sale. Plundered women cast aside.

Vast, shuffling, angry crowds. The brazen clangour of Orthodox bells, the quiet of Red Square, the bustle of Chinatown. Dacha parties, sour Slavonic cooking, biting cold outside, stuffy heat indoors. Tedium, loneliness, inconvenience. Artistry and wonder. Sex. Bribes that start with a Rolex and end with an island off Mauritius. Or a coffin.

Zidra had no time to notice. She hired a car at the airport, drove downtown and booked in at the Hanseatic, registering under the name Sandra Davies and leaving a British passport.

She would work alone. Not touch any of the old school, who were either at peace in retirement or hiding or living abroad. To use them would be to advertise her presence.

She went to the Mezh, that concrete skull of a building thrown up near the White House by Armand Hammer a generation ago, to please his friend Brezhnev. Booked another room in another name – Katya Springels – using a Latvian passport, which she had thought was just a souvenir from the old *Sobor* days.

The Mezh is modelled on a suburban mid-western, mid-1970s shopping mall. Its heart is huge empty space. Tiers of walkways open on one side into this space, on the other into the termite-warren of rooms. Pick the right room and you have a good view of all the comings and goings.

Italian businessmen and gangsters like the Mezh. There is an Italian bar and ice-cream parlour. The first historic contacts between Sicilians and their Moscow counterparts took place here in the mid-1980s. The Mezh – the word is an encapsulation meaning International Trade Centre – louche, cockroach-ridden, full of girls, was a good place for Zidra to work from.

She went down to the concourse and called the number of a KGB *spravka* – a kind of private information service for authorized users. It was a long shot. Maybe such services no longer even existed, in the new era of wonders like telephone directories.

A bored woman asked her what she wanted and who she was.

Zidra said she was the secretary of a Colonel Martov in the Kremlin garrison. She wanted an address to go with a number. She told the woman the number from the Kalmyk's shirt label: 9230397.

No, she did not have confirmation of Martov's ID, but she promised the woman she would get it next morning in the form of dismissal from her post if she didn't co-operate.

Zidra sounded right – arrogant, over-confident. The woman caved in. She gave an address: Entrance 3, Flat 14/7 Chaussee Entusiastov. The name of the addressee? The operator snorted. How was it possible she did not even know whom she or this Martov was calling? *The name of the addressee*. The woman caved in again. She told Zidra that the number was listed under one Ilya Almazov.

Zidra rang off.

Chaussee Entusiastov. That was an address near the centre, but not too near. There were good, old-fashioned blocks in that part of town, traditionally given to tenants from Moscow's artistic community: members of the famous operas and theatre companies, or the circus.

Zidra went to the German boutique on the mezzanine floor. She bought a red fox hat and quilted coat, a big handbag, high-heel boots, a pair of red stilettos and one of real crocodile-skin court shoes, a business suit in blue, a black cocktail dress, two jumpers, a tracksuit, jeans and some quilted flat-heeled boots, and a huge overnight bag to put them all in.

She went to her room, showered, changed into jumper and jeans, put on the quilted overcoat and left the hotel.

A chill wind was blowing up the nearby Moskva river, and snow was falling. She wandered around the huge car park for a while until she saw what she wanted: two big S-class Mercedes side by side with number plates separated by one digit. Both drivers were sitting in one of them, smoking, chatting, waiting for their boss – a Moscow banker or some such.

She tapped on the window. They ignored her. She tapped again. The driver wound it down, looked her over, asked her what she wanted. 'But if it's trade, we're not interested.'

'It's not trade, it's business,' Zidra told him. 'I want to buy a gun.'

The two men exchanged looks, laughed.

'Piss off, girlie,' the driver said and wound the window back up.

She tapped again, until he suddenly threw the door open. 'I told you to clear off. We're not arms traders.'

'You can lose your gun and get another. You have a licence.'

'Yes, I have licence, and that is what I can lose, talking to you.' The man was big, young, fit-looking. 'I sell you my gun, you go inside and poop off a client you don't like, and I get done for being your pimp. Even I am not that stupid, girlie. Piss off.'

'One thousand dollars.'

'Don't crucify me with humour.'

'Cash. Now.'

'Where's the cash?'

'Where's the hardware?'

They looked each other over. 'What's it for?' he said at last.

'Insurance. I don't plan to use it.'

He grinned cynically. 'No one's going to hurt *you*, baby. Where you from, Voronezh, somewhere like that? Find yourself a pimp. Don't waste your money. You'll shoot yourself.'

'That's not your problem. A thousand, take it or leave it.'

'Sell her the Makarov, Sasha,' the other man said from inside the car. 'It's a fifty-buck cannon. Let her have it.'

The driver snorted. 'OK,' he told her, 'but this gun is not licensed and maybe it's not in good condition. Maybe it's already been used too often.'

'Show me.'

Sasha shook his head, reached for the boot lever. The boot came up and he went to the rear of the car and began rooting in his tool box.

'What you called, kid?' the other man asked her.

'Lydia.'

'What you doing when you've finished killing someone, Lydichka?'

'I'll have a hole in my life, obviously.' She returned his look. It was full of calculation. 'What's your name?' she asked him.

'Benito. After Mussolini.'

'Hah-hah. Funny.'

'Come here,' Sasha called to her from the back.

She went to him and he showed her the Makarov. The first thing she looked at was the date of manufacture on the butt. 1953 9mm. 'A vintage model.'

'It was in store for a while. It's OK, if fires bullets.' He moved to take it back. 'If you're not interested—'

'I didn't say that.'

He watched her break it open, look down the barrel, check its parts.

'You know what it's for, then,' he said.

'More or less.' She smiled encouragement. 'It'll do. But only with ammunition.'

'Don't pull my leg. It's got my prints all over it. Get your own ammo. Use it tomorrow when I'm not around.'

She handed it back. 'Clean it, then.'

'Jesus fuck. OK, baby.' He slammed the boot lid. 'What are you, undercover police?' He looked sarcastic. 'Get in the car. It's too fucking cold out here.'

Sasha opened the back door and she climbed in, smiling at the other man who leaned back to look.

'It's rude to stare, Benny,' she told him. He touched her knee and she slapped his hand. Hard.

'Be careful,' Sasha said mockingly. 'She's a soldier too.'

While the driver cleaned the gun, Benito and Zidra made small talk. His name really was Benito. His mother had studied Italian at college and had an affair with an Italian diplomat while working as a translator for the government. He was the result. 'I got lots of jokes at school about my name. That's when I learned how to scrap.'

Sasha finished with the gun. 'I got twenty shells, that's all. You want more, go to Rizhki Rinok and get some. Now – one thousand bucks, lady, as agreed.'

Zidra opened the door, climbed out. 'Let's do it outside,' she told him. 'The money's already counted.'

That was not Sasha's plan. He meant to take the money and keep the gun. She saw the look on his face, saw Benito put a warning hand on his, whisper something to him. There was a moment of hesitation, then the big driver hauled himself out of the car. He didn't look cheerful.

'OK, lady. Stop kidding around. You want it or not?' He held the ancient Makarov out to her and took the money, counted it, then passed her the shells.

Benito climbed from the car. He was the senior of the two. Now he told Sasha to get back in and wait.

'I'll walk you to the entrance,' he told Zidra.

'You like your boss?' she asked him when they were out of earshot.

'He's a pearl of a fellow. He's a banker.' Benito spat in the snow.

'Where can I contact you?' she asked him. She saw the look on his face, added, 'Strictly for business. Don't make any plans.'

'I'm half Italian, what do you expect?'

'I expect you to keep your mitts off. If I decide to use you I'll pay well. It won't be risk-free but it won't be dirty, either.'

'Who are you, anyway?'

'A businesswoman.'

They were at the door. He stopped to look at her. 'You want a number?' he asked.

'I already said.'

'You want to write it down?'

'I don't need to.'

'OK, OK. It's 7389887. Evenings only. I can do the odd day, if it pays.'

'I'll be in touch. I don't keep regular hours.'

They shook hands and Zidra went back in the hotel, the Makarov weighing heavy in the German leather bag she'd bought.

It was seven-thirty. Pain for Renard stung her guts, but that didn't stop her being hungry. She wandered into the Continental restaurant on the ground floor of the hotel.

She would find a few people, this way or that.

You can never tell who will help and who will hinder.

She was too tired to hike over to the Hanseatic so she spent the night at the Mezh. At first it was quiet, but parties began in the early hours and at two-thirty someone knocked at her door. She grabbed the Makarov and looked through the peephole. She could see a woman's face, which didn't say much, but she put the brass chain on its hook and opened the door anyway.

The women was naked except for a cigarette.

'You want a good time?' she asked.

'Wrong gender,' Zidra told the whore. She could see along the corridor which curved away on either side. The girl was alone, so she slipped the chain and swung the door open.

The woman shrugged. She was young, cheap-looking, but her body was still fresh. 'Makes no difference. I can still give you a good time.'

Zidra thought for a minute, then told her to come in. The girl grabbed her synthetic fur coat from the walkway rail and wandered in.

'Put the coat on,' Zidra told her. 'I don't want sex. Just to talk.'

The girl pouted, lit a cigarette, sprawled on the cheap sofa. 'You want me to talk dirty?'

'No, I can look at you and imagine.' Zidra opened a window. 'I want to talk to you.'

'Fifty bucks for fifteen minutes.'

Zidra laughed. 'Nobody ever told me my conversation was boring before.'

The girl didn't get the point. Zidra asked her her name.

'Zizi,' she said.

'That's your trade name. What's your given name?'

'Masha.'

'Who do you work for, Masha? Who's your minder?'

Masha looked suspicious. 'You the fucking cops?'

'No. I'm a sociologist. Doing research.'

The girl's face twisted in a sneer.

'For the Rockefeller Foundation.'

'You're strange,' Masha told her.

'So, who do you work for?'

'You here all by yourself?' the girl asked.

'I have this for a friend.' Zidra laid the Makarov on the bed.

Masha stopped lolling and her expression changed.

'Which gang runs you?' Zidra asked.

'Lyubertsi,' Masha whispered.

It was Zidra's turn to look mocking. 'You're cheap shit. They don't use creeps like you.'

Masha flashed indignation. 'You're crazy, I'm one of the best in the Mezh. I cost five hundred dollars a night. She stood and bent over, showing her backside to Zidra. 'Look,' she commanded, pointing a maroon-painted nail at the tattoo of a snake curling over the left cheek. 'See it?' she asked proudly. 'The Lyubertsi symbol.'

Zidra knew the symbol and what it meant. The girl really was the property of the most feared street gang in the Moscow region.

'OK, I believe you. Take it away, please.'

The girl sat down, looking triumphant. 'You can photograph it if you like.'

'Thanks. Maybe I will. So, what's your line? Straight sex, or what?'

'That. And . . .' She opened her mouth to go on, stopped, traced circles on her leg instead. She pouted all the time; it was just a reflex, Zidra decided.

'You roll on the punters?'

'Sometimes.'

'How?'

'Oh, you know, all the usual. Put something in their drink. Or take them to a flat and then the boys roll them. We don't do it in the Mezh any more, though. They don't like it because it's bad publicity. So we've got a deal with the hotel administration. Some of them are also Lyubertsi. Now we're the only firm that works the Mezh.'

Zidra relaxed a little. She could believe this, and it meant that the girl was only providing sex. There would be no follow-up visits by gang members in the next half-hour or so.

'You could organize a party for me? In the pool?'

Masha perked up. Parties meant opportunities. 'Sure. How many guys? How many girls you want?'

'I'll let you know. Tell you what, Masha. Give me the name of someone I can talk to.'

Masha thought for a bit. She smelt money. She had been watching Zidra and forming her impressions. She didn't want to be excluded so soon.

'Trust me, Masha. We'll work together. I'll look after you.'

Masha grinned, flopped forward in the seat. 'Thanks,' she said. Her body was all elastic, without dignity. 'There's a man called Vinogradov. Volodya Vinogradov. He's head of hotel security.

He's Lyubertsi. He's here during the day. There's another guy I can find right now if you want—'

'No, that'll do fine.' Zidra went to her hold-all and came back with two hundred dollars in small notes. 'Thanks for the chat.'

'That's all you want?' Masha looked almost disappointed. 'It's not worth two hundred greens. I can give you a massage if you like. You look tired.'

'No thanks, Masha. I *am* tired, and you woke me up.'

'I'm sorry – I came to the wrong room. There's a fat German in room 414, but this is . . . ?'

'Room 441. Don't worry. I'm glad we met. Masha, do you have a number?'

'I don't but my friend Tanya does.' She wrote it down.

Zidra looked at it, threw the paper away. The girl looked hurt, so she told her the number. 'I have a photographic memory, and I filed it, OK? So don't worry.'

Masha gawped at her. 'Sure you won't change your mind? I like women.'

'Thanks, I won't, today.'

The girl pulled her coat around her to go. Zidra stroked her cheek. 'How old are you?'

'Twenty-two.'

Zidra pressed another fifty dollars into her hand. Masha began to protest. 'It's OK, really, I don't need it.'

Zidra laughed, made her take the money, showed her out. 'Take care, Masha,' she called after her.

She went back to bed and fell asleep at once. She slept later than she meant to – it was past eight when she woke. She showered, put on the blue business suit, which fitted where it touched but would do, and left.

After a breakfast of greasy coffee and rock-hard buns she went to find Vinogradov, head of security and Lyubertsi gang member, according to Masha. He was in a private office at the back of a big open-plan administration floor, all bright lights, pot plants and humming terminals.

She explained what she wanted: in a couple of days she would hire the hotel's pool, and the three saunas and gymnasium that went with it, for a private function. Siberians would be there, and Moscow businessmen. She was their administrative assistant. She knew their tastes: they liked a good time. That, of course, was not listed as an available service, but maybe he could help anyway.

Vinogradov was about her own age, brisk, businesslike, wore a short-sleeved white shirt and Levi Evaprest slacks and knew what she wanted.

The girls would have to be clean. Vinogradov raised his eyebrows. They were both serious people, weren't they? Of course the girls would be clean. There would be seven or eight guests, so five girls at least would be needed. There was one girl called Zizi she had been told to ask for.

No problem.

Everything would be arranged, but he would like twenty-four hours' notice and five hundred dollars up front, please.

She peeled off five bills, thanked him and left. He watched her go halfway through the administration floor, turn round and come back.

'One more thing.' She came back into his office and waited while he closed the door. Then she peeled off two more bills. He took them without waiting to learn why. 'My boss wants to find out who someone is. I don't know how to do it. Maybe you can help?'

'Who is your boss?'

'He's respectable.'

'I need a name. Before the big party, anyway.'

'OK, I'll call you later.' She pushed a slip of paper across the desk to him. 'This is the guy I want a feed on.'

He picked it up, read aloud: 'Ilya Almazov. Moscow 9230397. Entrance 3, Flat 14/7 Chaussee Entusiastov.' He glanced at Zidra. 'Never heard of him. What do you need to know?'

'Just who he is.' She smiled at him. 'Anything that's easy to come by.'

He looked at her in silence. She peeled off another two hundred dollars.

'OK. What room are you in?'

'441.'

'Give me the morning. I'll be in touch.'

They shook hands and she left, driving downtown through a snowstorm to the Hanseatic, transferring her new wardrobe to her room there.

She dialled a number which answered after two rings. 'Tatiana Ivanovna?'

'Yes.'

'Don't be surprised. It's Zidra. Zidra Latsis.'

There was a silence, a slight expulsion of breath, and the woman said, 'It can't be. You're in America.'

'I'm here for a few days. Tanya, I can't talk now. Are you busy?'

'As usual. We're mounting a big exhibition, of artworks stolen in the war.'

'I want to see you.'

'I'd love to, Zidra, but—'

'Today. It's important.'

The woman paused. Then she said: 'OK. Come at six. I'll be waiting.'

'I'll look forward to that,' Zidra told her. 'And there's something I want you to do . . .'

Her conversation with Tatiana completed, Zidra wondered whether to call Theo Thomson, the CIA contact in Moscow and another old friend of Renard's. She decided not to. If the rot started where she now thought it did, she would only be making trouble for Thomson.

There was one person she could call at once: the biologist, Minakov. When they'd met at the Foreign Office reception Minakov had told her of his intention to return at once to Moscow. She would see if she could find him. There was a question he might be able to help her with. When Renard had talked about the smuggled plutonium shown to the British by the IRA, he had mentioned Shevchenko as one probable source. Renard never used words in vain. She had looked at a map afterwards. Shevchenko was just two hundred kilometres by sea from Astrakhan, across the northern neck of the Caspian. Minakov lived and worked and had his roots there. He was involved in environmental campaigns so he must know all about the Shevchenko fast-breeder reactor. Maybe he knew something specific about the thirty tonnes of plutonium which Renard said he had gone missing. It was a thin chance but there was almost nothing else. She called him now, at his Varvarka Street office. The phone rang for a long time, and when it was answered an indifferent-sounding woman said only: 'He's at the Kremlin,' and hung up.

She dialled again. 'I don't have that number,' she told the woman.

'You must be unique, then,' she said, and gave it.

Zidra dialled the number and Minakov himself answered. At

first he could not remember her. When he did he agreed to meet her and suggested his office later that afternoon. He was flying to Astrakhan the next day and would not be back in Moscow for a week.

She agreed at once.

When they had finished she made coffee and decided she had given Vinogradov enough time. She dialled his number at the Mezh.

'You were right to call. I've found out who your pal Ilya Almazov is,' he told her.

'You were quick.'

'It was easy. He's a banker. Head of the international department at Mosinterbank. I've got his office number.' He read it out. 'Anything else you need to know?'

'There is one more thing, actually. I have a car registration number and a couple of names for you. I'd like to know who they are.'

'OK, tell me.' She gave him details and they said goodbye.

Zidra dialled Almazov's number at once.

'Ilya Almazov,' a voice said. She introduced herself as Katya Springels, told him she was a Latvian entrepreneur with Baltic dried milk to sell in the Moscow market. She wanted Mosinterbank to arrange the payment procedures. He'd been recommended by a Latvian associate. Would he help?

Zidra did not disguise her voice. She was sure she sounded different now. She was no longer in shock. Almazov listened patiently, then told her that while the bank could process this kind of routine transaction, it wasn't very interesting and certainly not a sufficient reason for them to meet. He had staff to deal with such matters.

She had recognized Almazov's voice at once: she'd heard it from a pay-phone outside the Mountbatten Hotel two days previously, except that this time there was no wariness, no ice. Just a bored bureaucrat trying to fob off a customer who had too little to offer.

Zidra sat down on the bed and depression swamped her. She had been tired before she started, and all this activity seemed like treading water. Renard was in pain; somewhere people were torturing the life from him, and she knew it and felt it. She was powerless, helpless. In the dark, groping blindly.

Chapter 8

At one-thirty she drove to Varvarka Street for her meeting with Minakov. The building was gloomy, old-fashioned Soviet-style. The sign on the door said *Russian Academy of Sciences. Astrakhan Limnological Institute. Moscow Branch.* She collected a pass from the uninterested militiaman on duty at the door, and followed his directions to Minakov's third-floor office.

She entered the secretarial anteroom. It was deserted. A radio played dance music, almost inaudibly. Trailing pot plants pushed leached-out, dried fronds here and there. Dust was everywhere.

She walked over the creaking parquet and opened the door to his private office. There was an inner door, which swung open when she knocked on it. The room inside was deserted. She walked in anyway.

The room was spacious and high-ceilinged, but deep in shadow. A long mahogany dining table was placed by high French windows which led out on to a balcony. Not much light penetrated – a taller building opposite obscured the view.

The table was piled high with books, reports, papers in different-coloured folders and mostly thick with dust. Bookshelves covered two walls from floor to ceiling and they too were crammed with the results of a quarter of a century's research into the flora and fauna of the lower Volga. A gigantic German dresser stood against the wall opposite her, its glass doors opaque with grime. Perched on top of it was a stuffed sturgeon more than two metres long. It looked down on the head of Siberian white wolf, mounted opposite.

The floor, like the table and almost every other horizontal surface, was also piled high with books and papers. But it did not seem likely that this was Minakov's principal working place; the air in the room was stuffy, thick with the acrid smell of old books.

'You are impressed with my disorder?'

Zidra swung round. Minakov had entered through a doorway

opposite the entrance from the reception area. Presumably it led to his private quarters. He came over to her and shook her hand.

'I am ashamed of it, really.' He dropped his hands in a gesture of hopelessness. 'Perhaps it looks picturesque, but it is a disaster. There's a year or two of cataloguing which needs to be done, but I cannot find time to do it and I have no responsible graduate students left, unfortunately.'

'Is that why you spend so much time travelling? To escape all this?'

'Am I a refugee from my own life?' He laughed. 'Of course. But so is every Russian. I see the same thing in every campus, university and scientific institute. Empty halls, abandoned libraries, collapsed research programmes and an intelligentsia which has been blown to the winds. The lucky ones have got contracts to work abroad. The rest have become *ko-operativshiki*, selling anything they can.'

They sat down.

'I sympathize with your difficulties, Professor, but right now I am facing one of my own and I have come to ask for your help.'

'I am surprised that someone in your position could possibly need the help of someone in mine.'

'My husband has disappeared. He has been abducted and brought here, to Moscow. And I am trying to find him.'

'Why? Who would do such a thing?'

'There are people. Douglas's speciality was nuclear proliferation.'

Minakov nodded. He scrutinized her in silence for a while, weighing it up. Finally he said: 'I spoke to him when I was in London.'

'I know. It happened the same day.' She met his gaze levelly. 'What did he tell you he was interested in?'

'Shevchenko fast-breeder plant. He had many questions. I don't think I helped him much.'

'What kind of questions?'

'Background, mostly. He told me he worked for an institute in Washington – one of the backroom boys, analysing our nuclear industry and preparing reports for the American government.'

'He was doing more than that, actually.'

Minakov smiled gently. 'Why don't you tell the authorities about this? It's very dangerous for you to be here.'

'I want him back. Telling the authorities would sign his death warrant.' She stared him out.

'I don't know where your husband is,' he said abruptly. 'I hope you don't suppose that I do. I am not involved. I don't wish to be, either.'

'My husband is a CIA agent,' she said in a low voice. 'He was part of an undercover operation directed against plutonium smuggling from the former Soviet Union. He must have found out too much. I know very little about the matter, except that the American authorities are concerned that a huge amount of plutonium has been stolen and is in mafia hands.'

Minakov raised his brows. 'Do you think it advisable to discuss this matter with me, bearing in mind my position in the Russian government?'

'I do not know if it's advisable, but I mean to get my husband back. That's all I care about.'

'I can understand that. But I cannot see why you are telling me and not your own government, or the British police. How can I help?'

'Because you might know something about the missing plutonium.'

Minakov burst out laughing. 'I am an ecologist,' he protested. 'I don't know anything about missing plutonium. This is pure fantasy, madam.'

'The plutonium was stolen from Shevchenko. You do know about that.'

'You are very direct,' Minakov snapped. 'Yes, I know what everyone knows about Shevchenko. Not more.'

'Well, what does everyone know?'

'That a vast uranium mine was built there at Lavrentii Beria's behest. It has long ceased production, but not before contaminating the eastern seaboard of the Caspian with low-level isotopes.'

'And this is what concerned you? The uranium mines?'

Minakov's bushy eyebrows came together. 'Is this to be an interrogation?'

'Of course not. I am seeking your help, and I don't have much time.'

He stared at her, considering something. Finally he made up his mind. 'There was a great secret about Shevchenko. Officially, the place was supposed to be a desalination plant, turning Caspian sea water into fresh water which could make the Kazakh desert bloom. Of course Western intelligence knew from the beginning that the real purpose was plutonium production. What they may not have understood was that Shevchenko turned out to be the most successful fast-breeder the Soviet Union ever installed. For the plant's directors, that was a problem. In Soviet times plant directors commonly under-reported their successes. Otherwise their plan targets just got increased. Shevchenko exceeded its plutonium output target by forty per cent every year. But the managers never let on. They just stockpiled the stuff in the backyard. There was always enough for the needs of the Soviet armed forces, anyway.'

'How do you know all this?'

Minakov smiled bleakly. 'I am the senior governmental adviser on ecological questions. Naturally, I made a point of understanding what was going on at Shevchenko.'

'OK, then. You were in the magic circle of provincial bosses, so you just knew. Probably the story was just a joke at dacha parties – all this goddamn plutonium which no one knew what to do with.'

'Of course it was. At one time it was common knowledge. And thousands of people worked at the plant. They also knew. For one thing, it takes big storage facilities to keep that amount of plutonium safely.'

'Then I don't understand you. Either the existence of the plutonium was a secret or it wasn't. What happened?' She frowned. His story seemed to make no sense. 'If it was all just a kind of half-secret then the West must have known about it.'

'For a while a blind eye was turned. The management's consistent under-reporting of production was officially accepted. Then something happened which changed everything. In 1988 there were ethnic riots in Sumgait. The immediate result was the halting of production at Shevchenko.'

'But Sumgait is on the opposite shore of the Caspian. It's in Azerbaijan, not Kazakhstan.'

'Indeed it is. But thousands of Shevchenko employees lived there. Shevchenko itself is just desert and uranium mines; it's impossible to raise a family there. So the workers commuted, by ferry or helicopter. These were mostly Russian nationals, and when the Sumgait rising happened very many of them were slaughtered by Azeris, just at the time that the conflict in Nagorno-Karabakh reached its height. It was a devastating massacre. Shevchenko was finished after that. And in the midst of this disaster the half-secret thirty tonnes of plutonium fell out of sight and mind. The authorities had more urgent problems to deal with. Then there were more political convulsions, and the authorities disappeared too. New people came along, nationalists who never knew the whole story. But someone remembered, of course. Someone always makes money out of disaster.'

Zidra stared at Minakov, digesting this information.

'This is what happens when you build dangerous, high-technology defence facilities in the midst of volatile, backward peoples,' he said. 'And now the West had begun to panic because the stolen thirty tonnes – enough to blow up the planet earth – had started to turn up in the hands of terrorist groups. The plutonium mafia is selling it, parcel by parcel. The CIA should have thought about what might happen earlier, when they sent their agents into the Caucasus and stirred up ethnic risings in places like Azerbaijan.'

Zidra boggled. 'Did they do that?'

'Don't be naive. Of course they were behind many of the unexplained risings and massacres which marked the final collapse of the Soviet Union.'

Zidra shook her head in disbelief. 'But tell me this – how did the mafia manage to steal the plutonium? I mean, physically remove it?'

For answer Minakov moved aside so she could study the huge map of the Soviet Union which almost filled the wall behind him. The S-shaped splash of blue in the lower left corner of the map was the Caspian.

She came over to look more closely, her finger tracing the line of the Volga estuary where it enters the Caspian, halfway along the top of the S. The ancient Silk Route town of Astrakhan, from where merchants had once taken caviar, gold and furs to Asia and Europe, stands at the mouth of the estuary. Dotted lines sprouted south over the Caspian from here. They indicated ferry routes, to Makhachkala and Baku on the western seaboard and Krasnovodsk to the east. The town of Shevchenko was marked on the Prikaspiy promontory sticking out from the eastern coast, midway between Astrakhan and Krasnovodsk.

There was a port, but there were no ferry routes indicated.

Sometimes the truth is so obvious it is banal.

'Shevchenko isn't Russian territory,' Zidra said. 'It's in Kazakhstan. Right?'

Minakov sat back in his chair, looking at her. 'You've worked it out, I see. After the Soviet Union collapsed in 1991, everything on Kazakh territory officially belonged to the new Republic of Kazakhstan. But the thirty tonnes of plutonium didn't exist on any inventory. The only people who still knew about it were the people from Minatom who managed the plant, and they were Russians. So in the general confusion they had the bright idea of taking it to Russia – for "safekeeping". And they didn't have to go far. They just popped it on a couple of barges and shipped it a few hundred kilometres north. To Astrakhan. And that's where it is now. Hidden somewhere.'

'You knew all along,' she told him. 'Didn't you? And you being you, you didn't like it. No doubt the plutonium is stored in highly dangerous conditions, right in your own Astrakhan backyard. With no effective supervision, it's fallen straight into the hands of the mafia.'

Minakov gave her his chlorine smile. 'People will go on forgetting, of course. Nothing human is permanent. History is just the blink of a sturgeon's eye.' He pressed his fingertips together, making an arch. 'There will be new political convulsions. Nothing can stop them. Meanwhile the orphaned plutonium will rot into the soil, until it kills the Caspian.'

She went back to her seat. 'You have to help me. Because this has got to stop, you know it and I know it. And you can appease your environmental conscience by nagging on about oil wells under the Caspian Sea if you want, but it doesn't help you sleep at nights any more, does it? Not with *this* staring you in the face.' She looked puzzled. 'You knew but you didn't tell anyone.' Minakov laughed, and then she understood something else. 'But of course – *you* did do something. You warned the CIA. But you did it through a third party. Probably the Company didn't listen to you at first . . .'

He shrugged. 'We warned them years ago. They weren't interested. There was a love-in going on at the time. The Americans believed whatever the Russians told them. After all, our side had opened the books! We were taking stunned

Americans on guided tours of missile bases and defence plants. But neither the Russian nor the Kazakh government has ever conceded that any plutonium was missing from Shevchenko.'

She looked at Minakov in silence, thinking. 'You know where the stuff is, don't you?'

'Not exactly. That has been the problem. I haven't been able to prove that it's there. And remember there has been so much time to permit the relocation of the plutonium. I can tell you this, though. There is a big defence plant in Astrakhan, the Raketa factory. It used to make missile electronics. In Soviet times it was operated by the Ministry of Radio Production. Later it was sold off and privatized. The plant is big, well equipped. At first, the plutonium was stored there. Recently it was moved again, I don't know where.' His face was a mask. 'Now maybe only one or two persons know exactly where it is.'

'But I don't understand one thing. Once the DIA or the CIA began to believe that the missing plutonium really was stored at Astrakhan, why didn't they insist that the Russian government make its own investigation? Why have no inspectors been sent to the Raketa plant?'

'A whole alphabet soup of agencies has gone to look. The International Atomic Energy Agency, which has mandatory powers of inspection, was the most recent. They found nothing, and when they asked the Russian government for more help they were politely but firmly told to go away.'

Zidra nodded. 'I can guess. They left it all too late; by now the whole business is covered by hundreds of corrupt and lying bureaucrats.'

'Of course. And if you don't care about elementary safety considerations, you can store it anywhere. The containers could have been shunted into a railway tunnel. Anything is possible.'

She stood and went behind him again to the map. The southern seaboard of the Caspian is Iranian territory. 'In any case,' she said, 'it seems clear that if things got too hot in Astrakhan, it would be easy to ship it to Iran. All you'd have to do would be to put it on a barge and take it south over the Caspian.'

'If they did send it to Iran,' he told her, 'it would go to a secret Iranian nuclear missile centre quite near the coast, at a place called Moallem Kelaieh. Some has undoubtedly been sent there already.'

While he spoke, Minakov reached for the phone.

'Who are you calling?' Zidra asked, picking up her big leather bag from the floor. She trusted him, but this was Moscow.

Minakov understood the gesture, put the phone down and said with irritation in his voice, 'I have fought all the great environmental campaigns, from Lake Baikal to the Volga. And I have survived. I think it is important to live to fight another day, don't you? But this is a more dangerous business than any of those. The CIA's operation to locate the missing Shevchenko plutonium has already been smashed. You are certainly being hunted down, and if I was not connected with you and your husband before I certainly am now.' He watched her unzip the bag. 'We cannot survive, let alone stop this thing, by ourselves. We have to have help.'

Zidra's hand was on the butt of the Makarov. She saw how Minakov uttered the word *Shevchenko*, as if it burnt his tongue. Saw his fear – and suspicion even of her.

The safety catch came off the Makarov and the click was audible in the room.

'What is the point of that?' he asked. 'If you kill me now you cannot help your husband or save yourself. You have to trust me. And you have to trust someone else whom we need to involve – the person who is the third party.'

'Who is he?'

'A KGB officer. Former diplomat, retired or semi-retired, whatever happens to them these days.'

She shook her head. 'I don't want anyone from the KGB.'

'You must consider it from my point of view. You are only interested in finding your husband. You may succeed in that, you may not. But you will certainly change things in the process. My concerns are different, and I have to protect them. We are only allies of convenience, after all. I need this man. I cannot work with you otherwise. Besides, he has proved his reliability in the past.'

She was silent. He let her think it over for a while, then said, 'Mrs Renard, we must begin to work together. I am prepared to believe in you, if only because of your mad bravery. Choose.'

She decided. 'Make your call.'

Minakov dialled. 'Misha, it's me. How are you? . . . Good . . . Good. Misha, listen – there is someone you should meet. Who knows about the caviar . . . yes, *that* caviar . . . OK . . . OK, I'll send her to you. Her name is . . .' He looked at her.

She said, 'Katya Springels.'

Minakov repeated it, offered to send her at once, but Zidra interrupted him: 'Make it tomorrow, early in the morning, say ten o'clock.'

He replaced the receiver. 'Even if some plutonium has been sent to Moallem Kelaieh, at the moment it is still mostly in storage in Astrakhan. Let's start with finding that. Whoever is physically controlling the stuff can lead you to your husband.' He shook his head mournfully. 'Personally I think you are involving me in a suicide pact. I know these people. Yes, if you can get close to them, of course you can do whatever you want. But I know how it will be. You might as well hope to walk into Buckingham Palace without an invitation and ask for a cup of tea with the Queen of England. Except there they will only send you to a mad-house. Here, no one will even find your bones afterwards.'

Zidra left Varvarka Street and went back to her room at the Hanseatic. She had an hour to spare. She made coffee, threw her shoes off and rubbed her toes. The new shoes were uncomfortable, they crimped her feet.

Minakov was a survivor, which meant he knew how and when to trim, to compromise, maybe betray. But she had met this type of Soviet ecologist before. He was in love with his subject. In the end he didn't care about anything else. She'd watched him climb off the fence that afternoon. He would see it through to the end. Because the stakes were high enough, for him too.

But she was in despair. It felt more like a wild-goose chase, now. Minakov had infected her with his own lack of hope. During their meeting the thought had come to her that the whole plutonium thing was a scam, which meant that Renard was already dead and the scamsters had scuttled off under the rocks.

The story of hidden over-production and forgotten plutonium stockpiles was plausible enough. It was the kind of fantasy Russian crooks could invent over a bottle of vodka. They would do it to frighten people, to get bribes, to blackmail the West. Minakov said that US experts had failed to find anything untoward in Astrakhan, although that didn't signify, either. They'd been fooled before. Perhaps what started as a scam had grown teeth, assumed a life of its own. It was a bubble which many people had begun to feed on. Everyone wanted to get something for their story. Suppose, she thought, the mafia had found a British businessman to help them unload their alleged hoard of plutonium. They might have twenty or thirty kilos of the stuff to show as a 'sample'. It would be a spectacularly clever move to pass this on to the Iranians, and even encourage them to hand it to the IRA. That would make the Iranian state a party to a massive blackmail hoax. Billions of dollars could be wrung from the West that way, if you could believe such a thing possible. Just now she couldn't.

Billions of dollars – enough to finance Russian participation in the Azeri oil project, for example. She would check up on Arctic Star. In particular, she would find out if connections existed between that company and the Raketa enterprise in Astrakhan. Cross-shareholding, common directors, anything like that.

Taking the speculation a stage further, she imagined that the British had invited the German investor, Hans Uhlaf, to join the Azeri-Bison Oil consortium when he had shown how to placate Russian fears and to find a solvent Russian partner. But if it emerged that Arctic Star's dollars had come from a plutonium scam, then Uhlaf's Plate River Corporation would be finished, maybe the whole consortium as well.

In short, vital Western strategic interests could get snared up in the burgeoning plutonium black market.

Was that why the CIA was working in England on these matters?

Because the British government had discovered the scam too late to do anything but *support* it, because the damage from losing the Azeri deal would be too great?

In other words – as Sir Derek Broughton had hinted in London during their dinner at Annabel's – an unholy alliance between bent City financiers, a crooked German businessman and a bunch of mafia guys was holding the British to ransom, making them party to a scandal so gigantic that any attempt to suppress it would have to be crushed *even if that meant killing and abducting CIA men in the process.*

Zidra's head began to go round in slow, lazy circles, like a shark in the water. Were there circumstances in which the British might let the Iranians get hold of plutonium? She could think of none, but still . . .

Some speculations are just too vast to think through. And she

103

was handicapped by her lack of insight into the overall picture. It was so hard to make progress when you never heard the whole story, never got enough to mosaic it all together and see the big picture.

One thing nagged at her: the man Almazov, who had answered the phone number she found on the Kalmyk's collar, was clearly involved, but he was a banker. In Russia, a banker's primary task is providing financial services to organized crime. Normal banking activities come a distant second. But it didn't tell her anything about how Almazov was involved with plutonium smuggling, unless his bank was assisting in the money-laundering side of the business. If it was Almazov's people who had lifted Renard, then Renard had presumably been chasing that end of the affair – not the physical location of the plutonium, which was more his forte.

Nothing made sense, but she knew one thing: Mosinterbank was involved.

She picked up the phone and dialled Vinogradov's number again. It answered at once; the Lyubertsi gangster who doubled as head of security at Moscow's prestigious International Trade Centre was still at his desk.

She asked him when he went off duty, because she wanted to discuss with him certain questions, in particular about Mosinterbank.

Vinogradov sounded dull, bored, a little hostile. He agreed to meet her that evening – he was on late shift. But he told her he knew very little.

His tone worried her. Vinogradov looked the type who would be loyally yours until the moment your worst enemy gave him fifty bucks more than you had. He had certainly been interested in her, not enough to do any serious digging, but enough to ask questions. And if the questions had been asked of people around Almazov, who had taken Renard and knew her physical description, then Vinogradov's prying could have set alarm bells ringing.

On an impulse, she picked up the phone again and called the number which the bodyguard, Benito, had given her.

There was no answer.

She finished her coffee, grabbed her things and left. It was time for her appointment with Tatiana Ivanovna, an old friend who was also Director of the Pushkin museum.

Chapter 9

In London, Pete was unhappy. He had gone too far again, and now Renard had had to be installed in a foreign-owned clinic in a quiet Surrey suburb. And he still hadn't answered the questions which Pete had been given, and which mostly came down to who was his British operational controller.

It was all a hassle. A twenty-four guard had to be arranged, and Benderby asked a lot of questions about how the mistake had occurred. Personally, Pete thought it was down to Renard being physically weak. He had been hung upside down for too long, was all. Pete didn't think that the loss of blood was so serious.

To console himself, he called a woman he'd met on one of his trawls around singles bars. The woman had often comforted him after experiments which did not work out – experiments which she knew nothing about, of course. She was intelligent, half Austrian, and spent one week in four in London. The rest of the time she was posted abroad. They didn't discuss the details – that was part of the deal between them. The woman was in her early thirties, brunette, too thin but not unattractive, despite a somewhat pronounced nose. The main thing about her was not that she was a masochist but that she was clever, inventive. He'd told her he had little experience. Maybe she believed him. In any case she taught him a lot about women and about himself. Mostly she taught him where the limits lie. That was something which Pete had always had difficulty understanding, partly because when he got excited he worked himself into an uncontrollable frenzy and that always ended the same way – the partner was just meat which screamed, and then meat which stopped screaming. And that was frustrating. It made him depressed afterwards. But as he usually could not remember much of what happened it was hard to learn where to draw the line.

And partly he had difficulty understanding the limits because he had never found out how to visualize the victim as a person. The

Austrian woman showed him that self-control was the key to power.

She taught him so much. One day, he would certainly kill her. They both knew it. She was always waiting for it. In fact, if she hadn't secretly desired it so much he would already have done it, maybe.

But now she still showed him things. Still comforted him.

She was in town for a day or so, and yes, they could meet. He invited her over, but she declined. She'd made a few innovations at her place. She wanted him to see them. He took the night off, grabbed his Nikon with the zoom/macro lens and some lighting gear, some Ilford 400 ASA black and white, an Olympus voice-activated microcassette recorder, and left.

The woman – he called her Heidi – had acquired a new scourge on some jaunt to central Asia. Had fitted various mechanisms to the walls around her king-size bed. The scourge was thickly plaited, stiff horse leather, useless unless you wanted a flayed corpse after ten strokes. He unbraided it and cut away all but two of the strands.

That night when she lay braced to the bedframe and he tightened and loosened a silk cord about her neck and lashed her and photographed her, he also made her tell him – for the first time – who she was and what she did.

She said she was a financial journalist, well known in the City, who worked in the Moscow Bureau of the *Financial Daily*. Under his more or less controlled pressure she told him names, dates, places, some of the unpublished scandals that could blow London apart. Told him about Russia, the stories of governmental corruption which the paper would not publish. When she'd finished he quietly swore to her that he would use the information, would destroy her name and then destroy her. He made her list the members of her family and while he brought her repeatedly to a climax he explained how he would ruin them as well, one by one.

Afterwards, he had her make ham and eggs while he told her about his own current problem. About the American he could not break. She was a journalist, she knew how to pry, he permitted her to question him and then said more than he meant to. Then she gave her some advice. Strong men, she said, are focused. Women are diffuse, orgasmic, lacking one centre. But men are penile, concentrated. She laughed when she pronounced this; it was pop Freud. But no less true for that. All men have a weak link. Snap it, and you have the man. That is never true of women. You could crush a woman utterly and she could still turn round and kill you in the end.

He, also, had laughed at that. Had wondered aloud what Renard's weakness might be.

If he was such a superman, she told him, the weak link would be sentimentality. It was banal, but generally true. Torture his wife and he'd crack.

'And what is the best way to torture a woman?'

'*You* are asking me?' She thought for a moment, then said: 'Make her orgasm in front of him.'

Zidra drove down Volkhonsky Street to where the great Pushkin museum was locked in darkness. She went through a rutted way to the rear and entered by a gate leading to a small compound where recent snow dusted a jumble of twisted metal and builders' debris. She came to a battered wooden door with a feeble bulb glimmering overhead. It opened on to an echoing, ill-lit corridor which twisted and doubled back, at one point ascending a ramp which led to a landing. Zidra stamped the last snow from her feet and pushed through another door. She entered a homely office, decorated and furnished like a living room. A man and a small, plump woman sat close together in two chairs, examining something spread on a table before them. When the woman saw Zidra she rose to her feet to greet her, arms outstretched. 'Zidra! Come in, darling!'

Tatiana was in her late forties or early fifties, wearing a thick cardigan, heavy black skirt and strong calf-high boots. She had a grey shawl on her head and she wore glasses with thick acrylic frames. She rushed to embrace Zidra, kissed her cheeks and then turned back to her companion. 'And here is the friend you wanted to surprise. Sir Derek – you know my dear Zidra? Say hello!' she commanded.

'I came to look at a beautiful thing,' Broughton said gallantly, 'but I had no idea it was to be you.' He was pale and his hand trembled when she took it. The shock was genuine.

'Tatiana Ivanovna is my oldest friend in Moscow. She's told me all about your passion for Pushkin,' Zidra told Sir Derek. 'But she swore me to secrecy. She said you don't allow anyone to know of your many acts of generosity to the museum.'

Broughton smiled at Tatiana and said, 'You cannot imagine

how very pleased I am to see this lady. You could not have done me a better service. Thank you.' He bowed.

The curator relaxed, offered tea and bustled to where a samovar hissed in a corner. Broughton immediately raised his finger to his lips, but his eyes were burning with curiosity. Zidra smiled reassuringly and squeezed his arm. 'Later,' he breathed. She nodded. First there was her social duty to Tatiana.

'You're cold, Zidra,' Tatiana said while they sipped tea. 'This weather is the worst time for pneumonia. Rain, wind, snow, God knows what. But soon we'll get a real Russian frost.' Eventually she took away the cups. 'Now, I have something special to show Sir Derek.'

She led them into a small, warm room used as both storeroom and office. Tables were piled with paintings, icons, statuettes and other objets d'art. In the heart of this tumult were two small sofas, torn and old with horsehair hanging from their leather coverings, placed at right angles to each other. A tiny electric fire stood between them, next to another samovar.

'I have found a folio manuscript of Pushkin's *The Bronze Horseman*,' Tatiana Ivanovna said, pushing them to a sofa. 'It is great good fortune.' She opened the doors of an oak chest, pulling out some dusty tubes. 'Sir Derek is such a friend, such a lover of Pushkin, and he *understands* him,' she said to Zidra.

She laid down a heavy, leather-bound tube with brass inserts at either end, and pulled a bottle of Moldovan sweet wine from under the table, pouring it into small crystal glasses. They sipped and then she opened the tube and drew out a manuscript.

Sir Derek thanked her for the remarkable gift and the director bowed.

'I have to attend to something,' she told them, smiling conspiratorially. 'I shall be gone for at least thirty minutes.'

She left, closing the door firmly behind her.

'She thinks we're having an affair,' Zidra said. 'Poor Tanya.'

'Never mind that.' Broughton rounded on her, gripping her wrists, his eyes blazing. 'What on earth are you doing here? Tell me what's going on. I know that Douglas is missing and Hill was found in your room at the Mountbatten. What happened?'

'I'll tell you what little I know, Derek.' She wriggled free from his grip. 'I came here for your help. There is no one else I trust now, because I'm sure the leak is in Washington.'

' 'You may be right. I had a long talk with Douglas about that the other night. He still wasn't sure. He thinks it's probably on our side. But who? No one knew about his mission except myself, the Foreign Secretary and the PM. And two civil servants that one absolutely has to trust, and whom I *do* trust implicitly. So who? It's incomprehensible.'

'Derek, you can understand that at the moment everything is secondary to getting Douglas back in one piece. I'm frightened they are keeping him for a purpose, and it's connected with this delivery of plutonium to Iran. And . . . I can't see why they'll need him after that.'

'You think he's a hostage?'

'I don't know what he is. I don't know why Hill was killed and he wasn't. I don't even know for sure he's still alive. The only thing I have to go on is what I found on the guy they sent to collect me.'

'You mean the second body? The waiter?'

'Yes. I killed him.'

He nodded. 'That explains why his time of death was put later than Hill's.' He gave her a long look. 'Poor Zidra, I am sorry for this. You are afraid to go to his people?'

'Yes, I am.'

'Where are you staying in Moscow?'

'The Hanseatic. I wanted to see you partly because if anything happens to me as well, then someone should know at least that I was here. I believe that Douglas was brought here. That's what I gleaned from the waiter.'

'Are you sure?'

'No, but it's the only lead I had and it brought me here.'

'But it could have been the Irish who—'

'I don't think so,' she said brusquely. 'They have no current interest in a war with the CIA. Someone might want to provoke such a war' — she glanced at him — 'that's what Douglas was wondering. MI5, for example. People who hate the sight of the Irish terrorists being hailed as freedom-fighters by a new President. That was why he wanted to keep the list of people on your side who knew what was happening as short as possible.'

'Yes, but if Douglas suspected the British secret service of being capable of such a thing, then he shouldn't have told anyone at all, not even the PM. There's no way such a thing could be kept from MI5, not the way Downing Street works.'

'Look, Derek, I don't think it was the IRA or MI5. Maybe he is still in England. The point is that wherever he is, the *answer* is here. That's what I *am* sure about.' She stared hard at him. 'I'm sorry to press you like this, Sir Derek. But I'm sure you can help me more than this.'

Sir Derek picked up the wine glass, drank it to the bottom. He sighed. 'We did our best.' His voice was almost invisible, like the edge of a sharp knife. 'One cannot do more.'

What did that mean? She didn't ask.

He held the glass to the light, peered at it. Small purple crystals were left in the bottom. He took the bottle, offered some to her and gingerly poured himself another. 'One ought to decant it, of course.' He sighed. 'Life is refractory, especially in Russia. Nothing works as it ought. Even when it's something worthwhile, like this. Or like Pushkin.'

She shook her head. 'Pushkin?' She was puzzled.

'He didn't work, no: not if he really was meant to be their Shakespeare.' He emptied the glass and placed it on the table. Now he was leaden, weary, somehow occluded. Not just the usual reserve, but something else: a malign indifference had settled on him. 'Shakespeare, Racine, Goethe. They were nation-builders. Creators of a nation's most potent weapon, its language. Pushkin was the greatest poet of all, but Russian is a failed tongue. Perhaps the country is just too big. It breaks everyone, in the end. *Duraki, duraki, duraki*, as Ilyich said: *Fools, fools, fools, all around me.* Even the great Lenin was broken. In the end.'

It was said without irony. It was all just words-on-duty, she suddenly realized. Conversation filler, the stuff diplomats dish up with the canapés. And she saw why. There was something important he wanted to tell her, but he was afraid to, and he was using the time to think through all the angles. Somewhere in the back of his mind she'd dropped one small pebble, and now a few tiny stones were starting to shower down. Soon a million tonnes of rock was going to flatten everything, and he knew it.

She waited quietly. At last Broughton sighed, pursed his lips. 'There is someone. His name is Julian Benderby. He's our operative. He too is looking for that legendary thirty tonnes of plutonium. He doesn't know everything; for instance, he's unaware of Douglas's involvement. I'll speak to him. Perhaps you can help him too. I wish you would.'

'Where is he now?'

'He works in a London merchant bank, Palfrey & Griblock.'

'There was a representative of that bank at the FO reception, wasn't there?' she asked.

'Yes, there was – Henry Carter-Allis. He's the bank's chairman.'

'And?'

'Until recently Benderby has been working on fraudulent trade matters. Specifically, on aluminium export from Russia. Latterly he has become involved in investigating oil – commercial investigations related to fraud or Iraqi sanctions-busting, that kind of thing. He is new to the plutonium black market. He backed into it, rather. It wasn't a conscious decision, not at first anyway. One of his chaps made friends with someone at Minatom, the Russian nuclear energy ministry. He found the Russians were blatantly selling nuclear technology and material. His name is Goldman.'

'Goldman is also based in the UK?'

'As far as I know. He may have an office of sorts in Moscow. He is a thoroughly disreputable sort of person. I believe he runs a Dubai-based offshore outfit. Probably has something in Cyprus too.'

'And you wouldn't know his Minatom contacts?'

'There's a man called Dubok. We know very little about it. Apart from their meeting, they seem to have met only in Moscow. Dubok was head of a department at Minatom which dealt with the fabrication of large structures. Civil engineers, with an emphasis on pipework.'

Zidra studied his face. He wanted to help her, but it was over. He was drained, now. She stood up, saying, 'Thank you.'

'I hope you find Renard. I should hate anything to happen to him.'

'It already has,' she said.

Chapter 10

The City of London. No other financial centre in the world could handle business as big and as dirty as this. Nowhere else combines faceless criminality and genteel respectability to such a degree. Broughton had been pointing them at it from the start. Zidra remembered how he'd *insisted* on Renard attending the FO reception. Carter-Allis, the banker he'd now directly implicated, had been there. She'd met him with Sir James Wilshman, the Foreign Secretary.

Minakov had been there.

Hans Uhlaf had been there. His Plate River Corporation had set up the oil deal, together with Bison – and with Palfrey & Griblock.

And there was Arctic Star, a Russian firm. Based on a defence industry town, Perm, with deep roots in the nuclear business.

What were the connections?

How to find out? She did not know, and it made her want to cry.

After leaving Sir Derek, Zidra went to the Mezh to meet Vinogradov. She took the lift to the administration floor and pushed through the swing doors past a protesting guard in horn-rims, waving to Vinogradov through three or four glass screens. He was still at his desk, every inch a sobersided executive working late in his own time. Strange to think that somewhere he bore the tattoo which said he was a Lyubertsi who had killed for the gang, taken a life as a *rite de passage*, just to show he could.

Vinogradov made her welcome, pulled up one of his flashy Bauhaus chrome-and-velvet chairs, poured her coffee, sat down next to her, asked how was her day.

'Busy,' she told him. 'Yours?'

He grinned. 'Another day, another dollar. I found out more about Almazov.'

'Tell me.' She eyed him. He was tall, rangy, strong. Stronger than her. And he was an *aikido* master. He had shown her his trophies.

He looked her over in return. She was wearing the short silk skirt, black tights, crocodile skin high heels – dressing down for Moscow. But she knew she was good, and she was proud. Too proud. He had been checking her out all day, with scant result. 'You don't live in Russia, do you?' he asked. 'You a business tourist? In from the States, or are you from Latvia like your passport says?' He flipped her the document which, according to the rules, she'd left with the hotel administration when she checked in. 'You've got US visas, that's why I ask.'

'You checked my passport, and I suppose you checked my Amex card and a few other things, so now you know all about me, right?'

'Wrong. All I know is, your identity is phoney as fuck. I haven't yet worked out who you are. Interpol? FBI? Some kind of Cosa Nostra thing? Colombian?' He grinned. 'All I know is you're a blonde from Latvia. Maybe.'

'It's flaxen. Not blonde.' She put her coffee down, picked up her shoulder bag. 'You've been a busy lad. Too busy. I can't say I took the same trouble with you. It's enough to know you're Lyubertsi. That took me all of three minutes to find out.'

The grin faded from Vinogradov's face.

'Don't mess with me,' she said gently. 'You want to know who I am, you ask me and I'll give you an answer that's good enough for you. OK?' She watched his eyes open wide. 'I didn't pay you to check on me.'

She had to say something, but that was a mistake. '*Nobody* talks to me like that,' Vinogradov told her quietly. 'Just saying that word' – he meant *Lyubertsi* – 'is already a fatal error, lady.'

She could have bitten her tongue. Zizi, of course, had been loaded with dope when she came and knocked on Zidra's door. Life had already given up on the girl. She could say *Lyubertsi* and not worry because she was just a suicide no one had yet bothered to kill.

Zidra wondered how to claw back some ground, but it didn't look promising. 'Cool off, Vinogradov. It's no secret round here who you are.'

'You're alone, I guess on the run. You know what can happen to people like you?' He picked at her skirt. Zidra stiffened. 'You know what? People disappear at this time of year, right outside their own front door,' he told her. 'You know how? They slip, because they're drunk or they get a heart attack, the snow falls on

113

them, and they stay in the gutter until the municipality digs them out next spring and tries to match them to its list of missing persons.' His voice slashed at her. 'Disappearing is the easiest thing to do.'

She knew that was true, saw Vinogradov was not going to be mollified, and went for broke. 'Grow up, Junior,' she shouted, loudly enough for the guard three rooms away to hear her voice. 'Don't try to frighten me. I'm not fresh from kindergarten. You think you're talking to one of your girls? Don't pimp me. Don't ply me with your cheap threats.'

Vinogradov's mouth opened wide but nothing came out. Actually, his frothing was mostly acting and he didn't want to hurt her. But the matter could not just be left.

She sensed him tense. He leant towards her. 'You're right, talking's too good for you.' His voice was a hoarse whisper. 'I need to show you discipline.'

Zidra laughed in his face. 'It's a good thing we're alone here, so no one can see you show such low class. Are all you Lyubertsi slobs so *unfinished*? I thought you believed in some kind of private *bushido*?'

She was sitting less than a metre away and he rose to slap her, his hands whipping up like breaking springs, but she catapulted from the chair and he found the barrel of the Makarov pointing at his nose.

Vinogradov froze, crouched in what looked like the *aikido* prayer posture, only the prayerful hands had meant to smash her to the floor.

'Was I too quick for you?' she whispered. 'I can do it again, if you didn't catch it the first time.'

Vinogradov was like an ice block in spring. Silent but melting.

'OK, sit down, Vinogradov.'

He sat. They looked at each other for a few moments. He pulled out a big red silk handkerchief and wiped his brow. 'What now?'

'Let's get serious,' Zidra told him. 'You made a mistake with me—'

'So I see—'

'—but it makes no difference, because I still need your help. So here's the deal: you don't pry in my affairs. *You don't check up on me.*' She stood in front of him, still holding the Makarov. 'You hear me?'

'OK,' he said, shrugging. 'I was out of line, but what did you expect?'

Zidra didn't hesitate. She put the gun away and sat next to him. She even pulled his cuffs straight. 'We were both just kidding around. But we're busy people, Vinogradov. Now we've made each other's acquaintance, we've made up, so now we can talk, right?'

The Lyubertsi nodded, breathing heavily.

'So let's move along. I'll make you a proposal. While I'm in this shit-hole town, I won't use anyone's services but yours, for the things I know you're best at. If you can't do it for me, I won't try to do it. I think that shows respect.'

He took the point at once, and nodded.

'It means I know there's no one better, yeah? It means that I won't go around you, won't go behind your back or set you up or screw you down.'

She looked at him, waiting.

Vinogradov had to be satisfied. 'OK,' he repeated, 'I'm listening.'

'But as long as we're going to work together, and you're going to get an insight into my business, understand this. It's *still* my business, and if you try to go around *me*, Vinogradov, I will kill you. Clear?'

'Yeah, but—'

'No buts. Those are the rules. The Lyubertsi are not bankers or condom-manufacturers, you're a street gang. If I need a condom or a loan I know where to go. When I need help on the street, I'll come to you and only you. That might mean my life is in your hands one day. So don't but me buts. Yes or no? That's all. Or do you have to ask someone else first?' She did not sneer. Just gave him the words.

Vinogradov had relaxed a little. He studied her. 'OK,' he said at last. 'The answer is yes.' He stood and offered his hand. She rose too, and they shook on it.

'Good.' She put the gun away, zipped the bag up, put it aside. She sat straight in her seat and when she spoke to him again it was a consultation with a colleague. 'Volodya, I want to ask you again about this Almazov. You have time to talk, or is this inconvenient?'

'It's convenient.' Vinogradov straightened his tie. Grinned, sheepishly.

'I don't want your trade secrets,' she told him. 'I want Almazov.'

'But how come you don't know Almazov?' he asked her. 'When I found out who he is, that's when I decided to check you out. You're messing with big boys.'

'Tell me. First, how you checked on me.'

He pointed to the terminal on his desk. 'We have Dunn & Bradstreet on line. Usually that's enough. If it isn't, like with you, I can call someone at the Central Bank or the KGB. Usually *that's* enough.' He grinned again. 'Not with you, though. They drew a blank. That's when I got curious. The FBI have opened an office in Mosow, and naturally we've cultivated someone there, so tomorrow I was going to get a line into Washington on you.'

'Ingenious. Remember our deal, though.'

'Sure, I mean to.'

She inspected his face, decided that really he meant to – or that he would find some much more circumspect way to check her out than through their bought person in the FBI.

'So who is Almazov?'

'Sonofabitch. No friend of ours. He and another guy, Kadarov, run Mosinterbank. They have big offices in Gorky Street and a lot of guys running around with fancy titles and fancy suits, but it's just those two who control it. And before you ask, I'll tell you. Mosinterbank got its start-up capital by robbing the old Komsomol, the Young Communist League, of around twenty million dollars. Kadarov and Almazov were both big Komsomol leaders. Their daddies were politburo creeps. You know the type – they got all the breaks, foreign education, everything on a plate.'

Zidra nodded. She did know the type. The most unpleasant kind of New Russian – arrogant, self-serving and generally parasitic. The clever ones, like Almazov and Kadarov, had emerged from the collapse of the Soviet Union with their hands on large chunks of stolen assets.

'I want to bring him down,' she said, looking into Vinogradov's eyes. 'Will you help?'

'Jesus, you frighten me, lady. They might be sonsofbitches, but they're strong. Unless you know something we don't you won't do it. We'd love it if you did, but I'm not interested in dying out of bed with my boots on just because of your shining eyes.' He spat into an ashtray. 'Excuse me.'

'OK, so you want a long life, a pension and grandchildren to sweeten your dotage. But the answer is yes, I know how to do it. In the meantime, what I want to do is to get Almazov on neutral ground. I have a date with him tomorrow but I don't want to meet him inside some private fortress which I might never get out of again.'

'Not so easy. They don't believe in neutral ground. They've got too many enemies already. They have more guards than Boris Nikolaevich, and all they do is commute between their armed compound in dachaville and their bank fortress, as you rightly call it.'

'Volodya, let's think about it, you and I. But over a meal.'

'Sure. No problem. Where do you want to eat?'

'The English pub on the first floor – the Red Lion. I like English beer. Let's try there.'

'By the way, I got some news on those other names you gave me.'

'Tell me while we eat.'

The conviction was growing in Zidra that she would have to visit Astrakhan. Her talk with Vinogradov confirmed it, even though any provincial city was more dangerous for a highly visible foreigner than Moscow.

As far as organized crime went, Moscow was Russia's heart of darkness, a city steeped from head to foot in lawlessness. It occurred to Zidra that a crucial difference between Prohibition Chicago and contemporary Moscow was that although Al Capone bribed half the public officials in the Windy City, at least they never made him mayor and promised to make him the country's next president. But Moscow offered the protection of visibility. In the provinces everything could be done in silence. And Zidra knew that in a few days, at most, she would be a target, no longer able to leave a building without fear of being 'flashed' by the two high-velocity shells which hit the target's head a few inches apart, vaporizing it.

So she decided to take some visibility with her to Astrakhan. After her supper with Vinogradov she went back to room 441 and called the only journalist she knew in Moscow, who also happened to be the doyen of the British press corps, the famed *Financial Daily* writer John Reid.

The call was taken by the other journalist at the *FD*'s Moscow bureau, Inessa Almond.

Zidra could hear a noisy conversation in the background, but Inessa's voice was just an indistinct croak. 'I've got a sore throat,' the Viennese-born reporter explained. 'I caught it in London – just got back, actually. And we're a bit frantic because a Duma story is breaking. Can you call in the morning, Zidra? Jack's tied up right now.'

'Tell him who it is,' Zidra instructed Inessa, who put the phone down without another word. Inessa, she thought, alternated between supine docility and unrestrained aggression. She and Jack were a strange pair. Perhaps lovers. Perhaps not. Renard said people in the British government thought Reid was a 'closet pinko', but in fact he'd been recruited by MI5 to spy on the left while still a student. At the time he'd been the secretary of the university Friends of the Young Hegel Society. Whoever recruited him – actually a respected academic on the campus – had decided that Reid combined some necessary qualities; modest to the point of invisibility, the Scot had a chip on his shoulder about his working class origins, which a little judicious massaging, a little flattery, a few weekends at nice houses in the Borders and introductions to obliging lasses with cut-glass Highlands elocution, had smoothed into something more amenable to service.

And he was good at names, details, circumstances; kept orderly files. Ideal material, in short. Soon he was launched as the industrial correspondent of a respected northern daily, someone who in time came to be accepted and even respected by union bosses and employers alike.

There was a long delay. Then Reid picked up the phone. 'Yes?'

'Jack? It's Zidra.'

'Hullo.'

'How are you, Jack?'

'Not bad.' He stopped. She waited. 'How's yourself?' he said at last.

'So-so.'

'What can I do for you?'

'I've got a story for you.'

'Oh?' He didn't radiate interest.

'Can we meet?'

'Tell me about it.'

She sighed. Reid was uncouth, but this wasn't the time to tell him. 'I found an honest politician.'

118

'Where?'

'In Moscow.'

Pause. 'If it's serious, you can come round. Only, we're working late.'

'OK.'

He hung up.

She dialled the number of Benito, the guard. A woman answered.

'Benito, please.'

'Leave him alone, fucking whore, you.'

The line disconnected. Zidra waited for a second, then redialled. This time a man's voice answered, thick with sleep. Benito.

'Remember me? Your pal sold me something at the Mezh. Remember?'

Benito remembered. 'You want me now?'

'Yes.'

'For how long?'

'Hour or two.'

'OK. You're in room 441, yeah?' Benito asked.

'Yes.' She put the phone down. She didn't remember telling him her room number.

She went and showered and changed into the tracksuit she'd bought. While she dressed she thought about Vinogradov. He was a hustler, but likeable. But it would be risky to use him. He was completely rotten.

When Benito arrived, she invited him in, told him to sit down. He looked solid, more serious than Vinogradov. She knew it meant nothing. You couldn't tell.

'Want a drink?' she asked.

'No, thanks, I'm loaded enough if I'm driving.'

'I have to go to Sad Sam for an hour. You know where it is?'

'Sadovo-Samotyochnaya? Certainly I know. Foreign journalists' place.'

'Benito, you're a nice boy. Who do you work for? Bankers?'

'I told you.'

'Which bankers?'

'Christ, you want to know? OK, it's called Chic-bank. You must have heard the commercial: *Your most reliable, most experienced friend.*' He sang the well-known tuneless jingle. 'Ever heard of them?'

'Maybe. Sounds crap, frankly.'

'It is crap.'

'Who's your boss?'

'Kadarov. The Big Boy. That's what we call him.'

'I thought Kadarov was head of Mosinterbank.'

Benito said: 'Fine, if you know. Me, I didn't hear that. I don't hear much of anything. They grow us like mushrooms: keep us in the dark, then take us out and shit on us from time to time.'

'You sound disillusioned, but you're doing well.'

'Nah, not disillusioned exactly. I'm not doing well exactly, either.' Benito grinned. 'You know, I don't do much moonlighting any more. It's frowned upon. Times have changed. You have to love your boss and worship the bank.'

'Why do you do it, then? You don't need the money.'

'Who said?' He looked surprised. 'Everybody needs the money. I'm building a house, I had to borrow from the bank, I got a wife and kids and a mortgage.'

'You know a guy called Almazov? He's another of your bosses.'

That wiped the smile off Benito's face. 'How long you going to need me for, lady? I got to go home early, I forgot to feed the cat.'

'You don't like Almazov?'

'It's not a question of that. It's just that he's a different side of the business, that's all. Look, lady, why're you so sure you're safe with me?' He scowled. 'I'm OK, I'm reliable, but you didn't take up references on me. Maybe you're too reckless. I don't work with careless people, because it's not worth it whatever they offer.'

'I already know who you are, Benny. I know you live in Pervomaiskii, your wife is called Nina and you have a kid, Dima, and a baby girl, Natashinka.'

Benito swung round, glared at her. He was big, beefy, with hands like shovels. 'Who the fuck are you?' he asked her. 'You from the bank? Checking up on me?'

'Relax, take it easy. No, I'm not checking up on you. I have a proposition for you. And if you agree I'd like you to meet some of my friends. You ever hear of the Lyubertsi?'

Benito repeated mockingly, '*I ever hear of the Lyubertsi.*' He grinned. 'Funny lady.'

Chapter 11

Sadovo-Samotyochnaya – Sad Sam to its inhabitants, who are mostly foreign journalists and businessmen – is a big ugly apartment block on the Garden Ring.

John Reid, Moscow's *Financial Daily* Head of Bureau, lived and worked there. A freeze-dried Scot, Reid lived for his work. He relaxed by listening to opera through five-hundred-dollar Beyer headphones while drinking ice-cold vodka straight. If he was working he sometimes piped the sound through massive Celestion speakers.

Benito knew the place, as everyone did. It took less than fifteen minutes to take Zidra there from the Mezh.

She went to the *FD*'s first-floor flat and rang the bell. It took a few minutes to throw the tumblers and slide the bolts on the armoured Finnish-made door. When it swung open in a blaze of *Madame Butterfly* she faced Reid himself: a tall, thin man wearing a vest, unshaven, his black hair tousled.

He said 'Zidra' in tones of irritation and turned back inside. She followed him down the passage and to her surprise found herself in the bathroom. Reid looked nonplussed, waved feebly at the giant cast-iron bath, which was just then filling with the brackish water from Moscow's communal system.

'Coffee?' he said over his shoulder. 'Inessa's in the kitchen.'

'OK.' Zidra left him, went back down the passage and threw her coat on the hat-rack by the front door. Then she went to find the second member of the *FD* team.

Zidra knew Inessa Almond only slightly. She and Reid formed an impenetrable, dark union. If anything, Almond was more disconcerting than he. Intense, tall, thin, she walked with a slight stoop, generally wore black, and chain-smoked Sobranie cigarettes. She had dark eyes with heavy circles underneath. Her nose was too large, but it counterbalanced the eyes.

That evening she wore a black sweater and ankle-length skirt, and a silk paisley bandanna wrapped round her neck. She looked ill. Zidra wondered if they'd been fighting – she had a black eye, and when the bandanna slipped down a little Zidra saw bruises like thumb prints on her neck.

She could still barely speak, her voice just a sibilant croak. She closed the passage door, to shut out the sound of Madam Butterfly's torment, and told Zidra again that she'd caught a cold in London, where the weather was warmer and wetter.

Zidra was not much interested in her problems, but she knew she would have to listen anyway, because Inessa loved to talk about herself. Maybe she would garner something useful. She braced herself for half an hour of emotional kitsch, all the time burning with an impatient desire to move on, to find Renard, to free him.

'I told the bastard,' Inessa said, referring to Jack Reid: '*You are the carrion crow of history, Jack, scavenging the dead flesh off the corpses of political causes*. He makes me completely sick and I shall be forced to leave the *FD*.' She waved a recent copy of the pink newspaper in the air. 'He's degenerating, of course. Listen.' She read aloud. '*In Russia, privatization has been the triumph of greed over fear, of despair over experience. Yet the shops are full and living standards are rising. We are all learning to love the "New Russians"*.' She threw the paper down. 'See what I mean? Rubbish written to order. The mewlings of a Scotch cop-out. Find me an *honest* Russian. *That* would be news. Meanwhile he brown-noses the money. Yesterday it was the new oil minister. Tomorrow it's the turn of the Germans.' She stopped to light another cigarette. 'Are you going to Uhlaf's breakfast, by the way?'

'Which breakfast?' Zidra asked.

'At the Hanseatic tomorrow. I thought you might be.'

There was no reason why she should be going, but she immediately decided she would.

'Yes, I will. What about you?'

Inessa gave a sneering laugh. 'Not fucking likely. I'm not interested in Uhlaf. Let Reid whitewash the ordure for once. I'm off to Vienna. It's my Jewish aunt's eightieth birthday. I want to be there; there aren't many of us left.'

'I've met Uhlaf. He seemed OK.'

Inessa exhaled smoke in rings, smiled like a hyena. 'Good for you, my sweet child.' She got up to pour more coffee, wincing as she did so. 'I fell over at the airport. I'm covered in bruises,' she mumbled. She told Zidra a story about the latest scandal at Moscow City Hall. The mayor had taken a twenty-million-dollar public works loan from the World Bank, granted to build an incinerator to help deal with the city's horrifying waste disposal problem, and was using the money to rebuild the rides at Gorky Park instead. 'He wants to rename it *Miracle Park*. That it certainly will be.'

Inessa offered to put Zidra up for the night. At first she refused but the rangy Austrian was insistent so in the end she agreed. In any case, it made sense if she planned to go with Reid to Uhlaf's breakfast the next morning, so Zidra went downstairs and told Benito to go home. She gave him one thousand dollars – 'seed capital', he called it.

Eventually Reid appeared from his bath. He ignored Zidra. 'You'll be back Monday, then, Inessa?'

She glared at him. 'Don't worry, Jack. I'll see to the Duma thing. I'll be on the morning flight.'

'Good. I'll send Sasha to meet you.'

'By the way,' Inessa sneered, 'Zidra is going to your breakfast with Uhlaf.'

Reid looked staggered, then stared at Zidra. 'Why? Were you invited?'

'Maybe I can contribute.'

He looked suspicious; then a thought occurred to him. He remembered Zidra's connections, smelt a story. 'Do you know something, through your people . . . ?'

'Maybe.'

'Interesting.' He paused. 'You must have contacts on the aluminium side. It all seems to happen in Latvia . . . Yes, great idea.'

Inessa looked disappointed. 'I'm going to have an aspirin and a nightcap and then I'm off to bed,' she announced. 'Good night, Zidra.' She shook Zidra's hand, nodded to Reid. 'John.'

Reid nodded silently back.

'Who is Hans Uhlaf, actually?' Zidra asked Reid when Inessa had left.

'Nobody really knows.' Reid twitched on his seat, tried to look polite, but he hated questions which weren't his own. 'He's a Bavarian. No one's quite sure where his money comes from. He was an accountant who made good in the 1980s property boom.

But his growth in the past two or three years has been quite spectacular.'

'I know. I looked in the file yesterday. He's got lots of fingers in Russian pies, hasn't he? Gold in Kazakhstan, diamonds in Yakutia. Hotels. Oil.'

'Had the run of the place. Bought more than a few Russian politicos. Anything about that in the files?' Reid blinked at her; it was the first time he'd made eye contact.

'Not the ones I've seen. I know he's involved in the caviar trade and wants to help sturgeon conservation in the Volga.'

'There's a Know-How Fund project, paid for by the British government, to set up a new fisheries protection service, because they've got massive problems with the caviar mafia and the existing militia is hopelessly corrupted. Uhlaf's invited me to go and look at what his Plate River Corporation is involved in, as a matter of fact.'

'When are you going?' Zidra asked.

'In a couple of days, with a party Uhlaf's taking.'

She asked him if he knew the city.

'No. I've never been further south than Volgograd. Astrakhan used to be a closed city. It's still hard to get to, so I'm lucky. It still has some kind of secret facility. But Uhlaf has bought a fish factory there. I think he plans to take over the whole caviar business.'

'Well, he has the flashest hotels. I suppose it makes sense to supply his own caviar.'

'Riddled with mafia, though, that business.'

'Hotels or caviar?'

'Both. Do you know the Hanseatic's history, for instance? The hotel was German-owned before the 1917 revolution. It was one of the best in Moscow, but in the Soviet era it was used as offices, then allowed to fall derelict. A few years ago a company called Balt-Polak-Rus Property bought it for a few thousand rubles from the Moscow municipality and immediately resold it for millions of dollars to Uhlaf's Hanse group. Which was fine except for the fact that Balt-Polak-Rus Property is actually controlled by none other than Yura Pryapov – the mayor of Moscow. That deal founded Pryapov's empire.' He grinned cynically at her. 'Now there's a property boom and Moscow rents have outstripped London. Drink?'

'Why not? Vodka, please. I rather like the Hanseatic, actually – all that north German solidity and grandness. The style is quite Baltic. Makes me feel at home.'

'I forgot – you're a Latvian?'

'Yes.'

'Uhlaf's headquarters are in Bremen, which is an old Hanseatic League city. Uhlaf is a great one for historical continuities.' Reid laughed. Underneath the glacial exterior there lived allegedly the sharpest journalistic mind in Moscow. He watched her, wondering how to extract the real reasons why she'd come to Russia. 'What I don't know is how relations between Pryapov and Uhlaf developed subsequently.'

'How did he start in life, Pryapov? I mean, what sort of honest socialist labour did he do in the bad old days?'

'Hah! Sewage engineer in Moscow's water department. He made friends with Chechen street-fighters. That was his first step on the road to becoming a great democratic leader in the new Russia. Nowadays he's surrounded with clever lawyers and accountants, mostly British. He's becoming one of the world's great property speculators, a sort of Russian Donald Trump. He's buying up British property. I know he's connected to Uhlaf, but I haven't worked out all the ways yet.'

'Dangerous business, Jack. One day he'll send some Chechens round to talk to you, if he hears this kind of stuff.'

Reid looked dubiously at her, unsure whether she was mocking. His thin lips, from which small bitterness-lines spoked out, made a moue. 'Why so? This is just everyday Moscow rumour-mill. Obviously, we don't publish it.'

'So Yura Pryapov has nothing to fear from the *Financial Daily*, then.'

'Hardly.' His mouth formed a smile. 'More vodka?'

'Why not?' She watched him pour. His fingers were stained with nicotine – Reid chain-smoked, like Inessa. 'And now Uhlaf has joined up with Bison Oil?'

'Looks like. And that is another story which history is labouring to deliver.'

It was late and Zidra was tired. She had a lot to think through. Reid showed her to a makeshift divan in the office part of the flat, handed her a blanket and left her to it.

She went to the bathroom and heard Inessa still moving about, so she knocked on her door and asked for more blankets and a pillow. Inessa shoved them at her without speaking. She'd been crying.

Zidra curled on the divan and immediately fell asleep. Three hours later she was woken by an insistent tapping on her shoulder, a tapping which found its way into her dream. She was swimming in slow circles around a large tank of warm salt water, and someone was watching her – there was a man's face, indistinct above the rippling surface. She saw his lips mouthing a word: it looked like *Moonbeam*. The man prodded her with a stick, as though training her. It was Minakov. Somehow he had turned her into a big silver carp . . .

She jerked up, looked around. Inessa Almond was lying on the floor at the end of the bed, one arm resting on Zidra's feet, sobbing gently. Zidra leant down, stroked her hair, wanted to say: *I need sleep, Inessa, like a drowning woman needs air*.

Instead she asked what was the matter.

Inessa had a story to tell. She was wearing a black lace, full-length nightgown, very décolleté, and she threw it off dramatically and had Zidra inspect her wounds. She'd been whipped, front and back. Where the weals criss-crossed the skin had come apart. There were cigarette burns, black thumb and finger bruises on her neck, rope-weals on her wrists and ankles.

She told Zidra it was a man she'd met in a bar. But this was no one-nighter which had gone wrong. As the story unfolded, Zidra understood that Inessa had formed a relationship. It was not the first time she'd been tortured, in fact. Haltingly, the story came out. It sounded torrid, but Zidra was hard put not to yawn. Inessa told her how at first she'd encouraged her lover, but the last time he'd been a wild beast.

Zidra was more than surprised.

'It's not the physical pain,' Inessa explained. 'I can deal with that. It's the humiliation.'

'Who is this man?'

Inessa pulled her lank black hair distractedly. 'I don't know, some kind of gangster, I think.' She sat on the bed with her head in her hands and sobbed uncontrollably.

Zidra wanted to sleep. She tried to comfort Inessa; there seemed no other way to be rid of this predatory woman. In the end she poured a tumbler of vodka and two sleeping tablets into her, let it take effect and shunted her back to bed.

She was sickened. Sometimes the perverse masochism of women outshone anything which men did to them. Inessa could not explain how it had happened. The last time she'd been with the man it had been involuntary sex. Rape. Inessa had shuddered when she talked about it. The man had made her ˙climax repeatedly while he violated her. The more profound the violation, the deeper the climax.

And it would happen again, any time he wanted her.

It was Reid who dragged her from sleep next morning. Uhlaf's car had arrived. They would leave as soon as she was dressed.

'Big limo,' Reid told the driver as they climbed into the Mercedes.

'Bigger than the German ambassador's,' the chauffeur said complacently.

'Mr Uhlaf is a big man. You worked for him for long?'

'Only six months. Before that, I was *Spetsnaz*.'

'Does he spend much time in Moscow?'

'Sometimes.' The driver glanced round at them. His smile was cynical. 'You journalists,' he joked. 'All the same.' He slid the smoked-glass window shut.

The manager of the Hanseatic, a German named Fischer, greeted them in the foyer of the hotel when they arrived, leading them over an acre of marble to a private lift which swept them up to Hans Uhlaf's penthouse. They were ushered into a reception room that was overloaded with gold finials, with nymphs and cherubs peeking coyly from behind gigantic pot plants. An inner door opened and they were ushered through to a small parlour. Inside it, Hans Uhlaf stood up to greet them, raising both arms in welcome. He was wearing a quilted green-and-gold smoking jacket, dress trousers and patent crocodile-skin shoes. He seemed to have modelled himself on an old print of Glubb Pasha. It made Zidra want to laugh.

'Jack! Zidra! My dear friends! Please come in! Welcome!' Uhlaf strode across the room, seizing Zidra's hand in both of his and leading her across to a window which overlooked the River Moskva. Next to it a delicate Regency table, entirely out of keeping with the rest of the decor, had been laid for breakfast.

'Uhlaf.' Reid extended a reluctant hand.

They sat down and a waiter materialized from the foliage.

127

While he fiddled with crockery a pianist sitting at a baby grand at the far end of the room began to play, very *doloroso*, the *andante* of Tchaikovsky's 'Autumn Song'.

'Will it be a Diary piece, Jack, or something more substantial?' Uhlaf asked, eyes shining. 'Profile, perhaps?'

Reid's own eyes were glazed. He shrugged. 'I don't know, Hans. My editors decide.'

Uhlaf's laugh was nervous. He pulled blini from a tray, using a pair of silver tongs, and gave one to Zidra. The waiter pushed a bowl containing half a litre of black caviar at her, and a jug of sour cream.

Reid wasted no time on ceremony. 'What's this about Plate River building pipelines?' he asked at once, stabbing a blini with a three-tined, sold gold replica Alexander III fork. 'That's a new departure, isn't it? Sure you can handle it?'

'You mean the pipeline from Azerbaijan? Of course we can. The consortium includes Bison Oil.'

'Isn't there a big argument going on about the route it will take?'

'We can rebuild the existing pipeline that runs through Russia. Or we can build a new one, either through Georgia and Turkey, or south through Iran.'

'But it's right through bandit country.'

'That's the drawback, of course. Personally, I favour going through Russia.'

'But then you will be in their hands, won't you?'

'That's the Foreign Office view. It isn't mine. The FO live in the last century. But the age of Great Power rivalry is over. I'm only interested in looking at it commercially.'

'But we need to keep the Russians happy, don't we? And they've been objecting pretty strenuously. They think the Caucasus is their sphere of influence.'

'Maybe they do.'

'So what's your solution, then?' Reid asked.

'To involve them by making them partners in the Caspian.'

'Is that Wilshman's approach?' While they talked Reid had made a kind of sandwich out of two blinis, instead of rolling them into tubes and drenching them in sour cream as custom required. Now he shoved the sandwich into his mouth.

'Yes, it is,' Uhlaf said. 'Wilshman is more on side than his advisers.'

'So how is it going to be financed, this pipeline through Russia? It'll cost at least ten billion dollars, won't it?'

Zidra sat in silence, watching them talk. It was Reid's breakfast. But she could feel Uhlaf's interest in her. The man's body language showed his slight but growing irritation with Reid's style.

Uhlaf clicked his fingers. A waiter appeared and filled their champagne glasses. 'We're ignoring our charming guest,' he said, smiling somewhat acridly at Zidra. He really did not like Reid, but he needed him. They needed each other.

'This is the black gold which really interests me,' Uhlaf said to her, pointing at the caviar. 'Beluga. Osetrina. Oil doesn't compare with these gifts of nature. This is the true history of Russian wealth. Oil is just a means to an end. *This*' – he spooned himself more caviar – 'is the end.'

'No money in it, though, is there?' Reid crashed on. 'From what I hear, it's just a headache.'

'That's where you're wrong, Jack. It's big business by any standards – worth at least two billion dollars, and that's just the legitimate trade. Today, the Caspian fisheries are merely an overhead taken out of the oil business bottom line. We'll be investing in caviar for years to come before we see a return. But it's a way of saying we're serious about environmental issues, and about supporting the local economy. We're good corporate citizens; naturally we want to play our part. And in the end, it'll pay back.'

'So who will decide the pipeline issue? You? Or the British government?'

'The Caspian pipeline is a matter for the consortium to decide. We are only one of its members. But it makes no real difference to me whether the pipeline runs through Iran or Russia as long as the decision is a hard-headed commercial one. We're simply the facilitators – we and the World Bank, the Know-How Fund and similar bodies.'

'But if the pipeline deal collapses, Plate River Corporation might get egg on its face – you've backed the Russian alternative, haven't you? So you stand to lose money on the deal.'

'Nonsense. PRC is totally guaranteed and totally secure.' Uhlaf's lips pursed. 'You already know that, Jack,' he said quietly. 'All of which means that Hanse, as a major PRC stockholder, is and will be more than solvent. We're big players, Jack, and talking down the credibility of PRC could damage others as well as us. Including bankers and City institutions. No one wants that – especially your employers, who also own PRC stock.'

'Do they?'

'Yes, Jack, they do. I checked yesterday.'

Reid grinned sourly.

Zidra now knew why she had not been able to remember Uhlaf's face. It was featureless, blank. His eyes kept their secrets behind their watery blueness. She began to drift, half listening to them talk about business, then about Britain's future in Europe, which seemed to preoccupy Uhlaf. She wondered if there was one single solid truth behind this man's exfoliation of images, this wheedling, ingratiating, cozening style of his. Uhlaf wanted to be all things to everyone, everyone that is who might be useful. That was why his relentless appeasement was so grating – because it was inverted megalomania. His very kindness, so superficial, so transparently self-serving, only underlined his cynicism. He was a chameleon, taking the colour which flattered whoever he was with. It was a quality he used in the calculating way of the born businessman, but its origin was self-hatred.

She was thinking about that when she heard Uhlaf say he was proud of being an Anglophile.

'But Britain,' he said, 'is like a big cruiseliner – this is how I see it – sliding away into the mists, with its lights blazing and bands playing. That worries me. We need to anchor the dear old place to Europe. To the future.'

'Very touching,' Reid sneered. 'But maybe that *is* the future – a theme park called *Titanic*. What do you think about that? Do we have any other role? Want to give me a quote?' he said with malice.

Uhlaf twitched nervously, thinking about tomorrow's headlines. 'I'd rather not say, except that England must learn to listen to her friends more,' he murmured.

He turned to Zidra and asked her why she was in Moscow. 'It's a dangerous town for a beautiful woman,' he joked. 'Where is your husband?'

'He's got business in Washington,' she told him.

'And you prefer Moscow? That's whimsical. He is a diplomat, I believe?'

'Sort of. Jack says you're taking him to Astrakhan soon. Perhaps I'll come too, if you invite me? I've never seen the lower Volga in the autumn floods.'

Uhlaf would be delighted. He was intrigued by the idea. 'But we are leaving tomorrow. Can you be ready?'

'Sure. I like adventures.'

Reid ignored this exchange, pressing on with his questions, asking Uhlaf about his known friendship with Jimmy Wilshman, the Foreign Secretary.

'We share the same club. That's all,' Uhlaf told him.

'Oh, come on, it's more than that.'

'I have had dinner with him. He has been my guest, I have been his. Our children know each other. But these are private matters, they're not connected with business.' Uhlaf drank his coffee. 'I am allowed friends, Mr Reid.'

'OK. And Sir Edward Boningfield?'

'The chairman of Bison Oil is both a friend and a business associate.'

Reid wanted to discuss the Azeri oil deal more but Zidra had got what she wanted: an invitation to Astrakhan.

Chapter 12

Misha Benin was a thin, short, wiry man with a red face and a jerky, marionette-like energy. He reminded Zidra of someone, she could not recall who. She guessed he was in his early fifties; in fact he told her he was sixty-one. Benin did not own a car. He walked everywhere at speed or hailed taxis with suicidal recklessness, practically throwing himself at them.

His office was in the Russian Union of Entrepreneurs in Nicolskii Street, opposite the Kremlin. The entrance faced that of the GUM department store. There was no obvious connection between any activity of his and the Union of Entrepreneurs. His card said he was Chief of the International Bureau, but the Union was dormant. It had no international activities. That was why, Benin told Zidra, he was at her disposal. He spoke to her in flawless mid-Atlantic English. He had worked for fifteen years as a diplomat at the United Nations in New York. That, he explained, was where he had acquired the polish which she was kind enough to call charming.

Misha Benin was an unusual Russian. Sure, he liked vodka, got drunk too soon and then became aggressive, yapping like a dog, as small men often do. But the rest of the time he had *manners*. Opened doors for ladies, fluttered like a footman at their elbows, made small-talk, actually listened to what other people said, was modest, unassuming, witty, well informed, clever.

He had no future, but his past lived on in a network of connections which still functioned: the KGB, now called something else but still much the same; and MID, the Russian foreign ministry.

Benin's office was the width of a desk plus half a metre. It was a mouldering mass of time-blackened papers, a flickering lamp, a kettle and a telephone.

'Minakov said I should trust you completely,' he said, making curd-thick coffee in two stained glasses. 'But Minakov is an amateur, of course. You are not, I suppose.' He smiled at her.

'We have a lot to do very quickly, because things are boiling up. So let's begin,' she said. 'I need to check up on some things. That's where you can help. Maybe the Union of Entrepreneurs has files on Russian companies?'

'Sure.' He passed her the coffee. Old lipstick adhered to the rim of the glass.

'I want to find out whatever I can about a Russian oil company called Arctic Star. Who's behind it, the PR, the dirt. I met its president in London recently. He's called Ivanov.'

Benin found a sheet of paper and began to scribble. 'OK. What else?'

'There's a British businessman called Harvey Goldman. He may have an office in Moscow. He has a Dubai-registered company. I'd like to know about him.'

'OK. Next?'

'A man called Dubok. Heads up some construction outfit – Spetzatommontazh, a branch of Minatom. They built Chernobyl.'

'In Bolshaya Ordynka Street? The headquarters of Minatom?'

'Probably.'

'They have a huge satellite town, place called Elektrostahl. Could be there.' He sipped his coffee noisily. 'I'll find something out, don't worry.'

Zidra looked pleased. She'd bombarded him with tasks. He seemed to relish them.

'Anything more?'

'A bank. Called Mosinterbank.'

'It's pure mafia. Very dangerous people. I know about them.'

'There's a man called Almazov. I know he ties in somehow.' She hesitated for a moment, then told Benin the story of her late-night call from the phone booth outside the Mountbatten Hotel. 'He's close to whoever abducted my husband. He might be the key to everything.'

Benin scowled at her. 'Very, very dangerous to go to him. It's a snake pit. Be warned.'

'I want to oil him up a bit. I've laid on a little distraction for him. But I'll tell you later about that. I think you've got enough to go on for now.' She stopped, looked enquiringly at him. 'Are all of these names new, apart from Almazov's bank?'

'I don't want to seem mysterious,' he said, 'but I'd rather think

133

about it before we talk. Arctic Star I've heard of.'

They arranged to meet again at his office the next day, after her visit to Almazov.

Zidra waited outside Mosinterbank's flashy offices until Almazov left for lunch in a convoy of cars. Then she went inside. A mincing platinum blonde met her in the pretentious foyer. *Gospodin* Almazov, she was told, had left for the day. He would not be back. For form's sake, Zidra protested that she had an appointment with him at two o'clock. The girl yawned. Zidra did not argue, but asked for paper and an envelope. The girl pouted, went to a desk and came back with a sheet of the bank's lilac-coloured letterhead. Zidra wrote a few words on the paper, sealed it in a lilac envelope, gave it to Almazov's secretary, and left.

Outside, she found a *taksofon* and called Vinogradov, who panted like a puppy while he told his story. It sounded good – better than she'd hoped – although it was short on specifics because they were talking by phone.

'It'll be tonight, then,' she told him when he'd finished, heard him agree and rang off.

Next she called Benito. 'Can you talk?'

'Yeah, I'm parked up, I'm alone.'

'You ready to do as we decided?'

There was no hesitation in his voice. 'Yeah, I'm ready.'

'Tonight, then,' she told him and disconnected.

She did not trust either of them. Benito was probably straighter than Vinogradov, but the latter had the most to lose from what was about to happen – if it went wrong. Although the Lyubertsi inhabited the wilder shores of the new Russia, they had their limits like everyone else. There were rules, even in that world. Territoriality, for one thing. The country was carved up not just geographically but according to spheres of business. And the rule said that if you planned to muscle into someone else's territory do it hard enough to annihilate them totally – or face annihilation yourself.

Zidra was moving against Mosinterbank, and she was sure she would win the first round. Banks were soft targets and having colourful goons hang around the front door didn't prove much. She would win through surprise, ferocity, determination.

But then would come the inevitable counter-stroke. Because

behind Mosinterbank was the whole vast nexus of plutonium, oil and Caucasian *realpolitik*. The counter-stroke could be devastating. Could sweep everything before it.

She counted on dragging more forces into the struggle. Meanwhile she intended to concentrate on one question only: find Renard. She would run before the storm, to get him back, free him. If he still lived. She swore it.

Zidra called Misha Benin. It was early, but maybe he had begun to dig.

Benin took the receiver on the first ring. On the telephone, he had style. The little shabby man sitting in a three-by-four still sounded like a New York chargé, cool, elegant. He asked her how her meeting had gone. It hadn't, she told him.

'Good, because I have things to tell you beforehand. Things you need to know.'

'You've made progress already?'

'Yes. How long will you be?'

'Twenty minutes – say thirty, now the traffic around Dzherzhinsky's been reorganized.'

It took more than forty minutes, crawling bumper to bumper round Revolution Square, before she found her way back to Benin's office.

The little man was trembling with excitement. His cool telephone manner was just a front. Now they were face to face and it was safe to talk he could hardly get the words out.

'First of all, about your British businessman, Goldman. A very interesting chap. I'll find out more about him tonight. There's a big file on him at Dzherzhinsky. He's got an office in Moscow and he spends half his time here. Lives with a Russian woman.' He broke off and his eyes revolved upward. 'Ooh, la la, Zidra, Zidra, this is big, big stuff. My, my, my.'

She laughed. 'What, tell me?'

'No, no, first, let's drink. I need my hundred grams. Come on.'

He bustled her out of the office and over Nikolskii Street to GUM, running up three flights of stairs, half pushing her through the public areas into a staff canteen. There he bought them each a bowl of thin soup, a slice of rye bread and two hundred grams of brandy imported from Delhi. It smelt of phenol.

'Zidra, here's to you, to your clever head, to Peter Minakov, to

135

us.' He pursed his lips and drank the brandy, then slurped soup.

'This is a dangerous business, more so than I thought,' he said. 'When Minakov came to me with his stories about stolen plutonium, I decided it was a swindle dreamed up by the Astrakhan caviar mafia. But it's much more than that. Something serious.' He shook his head, staring at the floor. 'Rascals, rascals. What have they done to the country?'

'Well, what *have* they done?'

'They are very clever. The whole thing is organized from here, from Moscow. Arctic Star is the key to everything.'

'But how does Arctic Star connect up with Mosinterbank?

'I investigated Sergei Ivanov, the man who set up Arctic Star. Five years ago Ivanov was just another Soviet functionary earning a thousand rubles a month. Now he's a dollar billionaire with a huge investment portfolio, all hidden behind shell companies set up in tax havens like Luxembourg, Switzerland and Cyprus. I haven't uncovered even a fraction of the whole story. But it doesn't matter, the principle is clear. I know how he did it. Nothing was ever written down, of course. It was all done through personal contact. He created the first privately owned Russian oil corporation. Using his connections, he pieced the tapestry together, a geological institute here, some pipelines there, chunks of Urals heavy industry converted from making tanks to drilling rigs. It was a paper exercise until the great Soviet collapse happened, but then he was ready. He had registered Arctic Star. It was just a brass plate in Moscow, a tiny company with no visible assets. But his pals – who were the general directors of the enterprises he wanted to take over – became directors of Arctic Star's board. And then by bribery, coercion and corruption they arranged for the state to sell for peanuts whatever they needed. The whole scam was the organized theft of state property. Then one day people realized that a new industrial giant had come to life in in their midst – Arctic Star.'

'I understand that, in principle. I don't see how it connects with the plutonium, though.'

'Like all great ideas, Ivanov's was simple. When he set up Arctic Star, he canvassed his friends to see what each of them could bring to the party. Soviet defence industry was not high on most people's list of desirable assets, but Ivanov signed up a big Perm-based enterprise. It manufactured power engineering stuff for the Soviet nuclear industry. It operated reactors. Theoretically it was owned by Minatom, the Ministry of Atomic Energy. In practice, Minatom would love to close, sell, forget about all those gigantic Soviet factories which produced nothing anyone wants. They were happy to let the place go to Arctic Star. With whatever was left in the factory backyard.'

'And you think that included thirty tonnes of plutonium?'

'Not quite. But the Perm factory built the fast-breeder reactor at Shevchenko. They built the plutonium storage facility there, too. And Ivanov had them build another, secret facility in Astrakhan. That was part of the price for letting them join Arctic Star. And he got them to bring the thirty tonnes of plutonium out. It was then stored at the Raketa plant in Astrakhan.'

'I heard about that from Minakov.'

'You did? And did you hear that Raketa is also now a member of the Arctic Star conglomerate? From missile electronics to oil company at the stroke of a pen.'

'Signing up Raketa might prove to be their biggest mistake. It's a direct link to the plutonium.'

'Certainly they have made plenty of mistakes. The question, as Lenin used to say, is whether they've made fatal ones.'

'So how does this link with Mosinterbank?'

'Mosinterbank provided the billion dollars which Arctic Star paid to join the Azeri oil consortium. These are dangerous people, Zidra. They are connected to the Chechens. Worse, they are backed by the Moscow city administration.'

'You mean the mayor's office?'

Ilya 'Spats' Almazov was not a violent man. He was soft-spoken, even kindly. He had spent time in the West and been educated partly in America (six weeks at Harvard Business School, and several summers in California). Spats Almazov had learnt the art of patronage – the deference which the great show their inferiors, which marks the former as responsible, solid citizens, the bearers of the national destiny.

Twenty-nine years old, Almazov was not big physically, about five feet eight inches, slightly too plump, with fine expressive hands, twinkling brown eyes and the clear complexion of someone who lives well, sleeps well, vacations in the right places. The gilded child of party bigwigs. In former times he would have been a Komsomolist, a servant of the people. Now he was a banker. Spats Almazov was a powerful member of the Moscow establishment. He had no enemies that he knew of. He could afford to be soft-spoken.

He liked to wear two-tone Italian shoes. He also favoured a homburg and a blue cashmere overcoat, which made him look like a rabbi. But it was the shoes which defined him. He wore them because they proved he never had to step into the mire of Moscow's streets. It was a form of narcissism.

He dealt in futures, played the budding Moscow securities market, had made money in London and on the Chicago derivatives markets. He looked the type who could easily become a central banker one day. He had friends at the IMF, was an architect of systems, understood technology, visualized the New Russia as leapfrogging over the antiquated, hard-wired West straight into an etherealized, networked future. One of Almazov's cleverest moves had been to acquire an interest for Mosinterbank in the old Soviet Army's *Iskra* fibre optic system, which had once connected Russia to Army Group West's former German garrisons. Now it was destined to become the spine of a future telecoms giant, linking old Europe with New Russia.

In private meetings in his remote lakeside resort, held with an eminent Western businessman, he had learnt of a secret which he at once became obsessive about: *Nostradamus*. He discussed it with no one, but it was the clue to his plans for penetrating Bison Oil. When he first understood the significance of *Nostradamus*, Almazov developed Napoleonic visions of ruling the world's capital markets. First he would plunder the intellectual legacy of the GRAT team and then put to work on it the battalions of hungry software geniuses culled from the former Soviet defence industry. He would grip international finance in electronic tentacles of the West's own devising.

Almazov believed the greatness of his vision justified the necessary sacrifices which building the New Russia entailed. After all, it was Dale Carnegie, was it not, who said that behind every fortune lies a crime? And if there were crimes, there could always be atonement. Expiation.

Perhaps that was why Spats Almazov, in common with many others, took an interest in restoring the former glory of the Orthodox Church. He personally had sponsored the renovation of one (small) place of worship in south Moscow.

In recent days a cloud had appeared over Almazov's horizon. His biggest coup yet was fraying at the edges. The wrong people had found out too much. He had had to take dangerous counter-measures. What kept him awake nights was the discovery that the CIA had got involved. It had never occurred to him that the CIA would investigate British matters. Had the English no shame?

His friends had organized drastic steps to cut them out again. But that only increased the danger of an uncontrollable escalation into major scandal.

Worse, within hours of the CIA cell being taken out, a woman had called him in Moscow. Said in clear text that she knew he'd organized it.

Almazov had not slept again that night.

Now this woman had returned to haunt him. And Almazov knew he must deal with her alone, or risk jeopardizing his whole position. Because rolling on that CIA group had been his initiative. If things got out of hand as a result his partners would sacrifice him without qualms.

He had spoken in panic to the people who had dealt with the matter in London. They told him the woman was the wife of the CIA man they were holding. And they'd accused him of greed, because he was the one who'd wanted the man alive. But he knew what the agent Renard was worth as a hostage; they did not. Now they were afraid to kill him and the woman had disappeared.

His friends had taken steps to involve the British police. They assured him she was a loose cannon, alone, without support. They had made her the chief suspect for the killing of the second CIA man and in doing so had kept themselves entirely out of it. The matter had been made to look as if a visiting American businessman had been murdered in his hotel by his wife for some private reason. Now Scotland Yard had issued an all-points bulletin for her arrest – so they said.

All that was fine. Disaster clawed back. But just when he started to relax the woman arrived in Moscow. Called him, even turned up at the bank.

Suddenly things were spinning away. It left him feeling hollow, evacuated.

And the worst was, she'd left a six-word note which had seared his hand when he touched it, which had blacked out his whole day.

The note read: *I know where the collateral is.*

When the Latvian woman had called him with her nonsensical story about Baltic dried milk he recognized her at once as the same person who had called him after the hit. Almazov had immediately checked with his friends in London. They gave him several possible aliases she might use. Katya Springels was one of them. Then there was nothing to do but wait.

She knew where the collateral was.

That thought was unbelievable, impermissible.

And the woman was good. Within a day of her arriving in Moscow he'd got the first sign that something was happening when his personal bodyguard had disappeared to the polyclinic complaining of stomach cramps.

For Spats that was the main purpose of the big boys with hard eyes. They were like an early warning system. When they disappeared you knew someone was about to roll on you.

The bank operated a pool of driver/guards for its senior personnel. That morning he had rejected the first three who were offered in place of his own, accepted the fourth, let the man drive him to the office but took another guard and a back-up car with him. Later he'd switched drivers and guards once more. He'd made sure he was away from the bank by two.

She would have to find another way to nail him. It was more or less impossible for the woman to bribe the whole car pool and even if she did, it was impossible to update each one of them to take account of his constant changes of plan.

For the next couple of days he would be elusive. He'd had his secretary tear up his appointments and start again. There was one particularly precious date he'd had lined up for a while: with the Patriarch himself. That would be when she'd try to take him, of course, assuming she knew his itinerary by now. He cancelled it, donating another hundred thousand dollars to the church to make up for it.

Chapter 13

Now that his diary was empty, Almazov had time to do some of the small but necessary things he'd been putting off for months. He looked over his tax affairs, phoned his mother in Voronezh, called his dentist. The line was bad; it took a few goes to get through. Then he discovered that his dentist had moved to a better location, had gone even more upmarket, but yes, the dentist's new partner told him, he'd find time for him, early that evening, no problem.

Satisfied, Almazov went to Fyodorov's little place in Kropotkinskaya for a late lunch. It was off his usual list, but that was why he chose the spot, taking five guards with him and three cars.

What did it mean, *I know where the collateral is*? It must be a wild stab in the dark – it must be. The words meant something to him, meant the dark secret at the heart of his universe in fact, but she was not to know that. Maybe the whole thing was just nonsense. He had allowed himself to get jittery for no reason. Almazov relaxed. He would take it all in his stride, as always.

Probably the worst punishment he would take for this CIA business would be a few more fillings in a bad molar.

That evening he called for a car to take him to his dentist. Naturally, he changed the first driver who appeared, and took three guards with him.

His dentist had certainly moved up in the world. His new surgery was palatial, magnificent. The receptionist told him he would see him straight away. She introduced the new partner, who was charm itself. Almazov told his guards to wait in reception and was led away by a gorgeous dental nurse whose uniform left just enough to the imagination. In the treatment room, Almazov looked around, admiring the new set-up. The dentist showed him the equipment – a new Siemens X-ray machine, a new furnace for making the most exquisite porcelain crowns on the premises – and

141

led Almazov to one of the new horizontal stomatological couches, probed about in his mouth a bit, made notes which his stunning nurse wrote down.

Almazov looked at the girl and she smiled into his throat. He decided he was about to be rewarded for the hundred thousand dollars. When the dentist stepped into the adjoining laboratory for a moment he took the opportunity to ask her name.

'Nina,' she told him, smiling bashfully. She obviously knew her VIPs, because when her boss was away her uniform became even more engagingly revealing, and Almazov was so busy looking he didn't notice that a new dentist had appeared and had begun to strap his arms to the couch, and when he turned his head and a question began to form someone jammed lint wedges into his gums so he couldn't speak. But the girl's expression changed and then he knew who she was and why she was strapping his other flailing arm down. He let out a strangled cry, but he no longer expected his three guards to appear. The cry died away and Almazov closed his eyes and lay back, offering his throat like a rabbit to a predator when the end has come. There was no point in screaming any more. No one notices at a Russian dentist's, do they?

A large damp stain appeared round his flies and spread down his legs.

'We're going to give you some cavities,' Almazov heard the girl say as if in a dream. He felt no pain as yet, and for a while he watched in silence as the girl and the newcomer moved purposefully around, clinking instruments. 'Then maybe we'll fill them in again,' the girl continued. Her voice was ice. 'But first, I want to thank you for visiting with us today. You arranged everything so helpfully.'

Almazov glared at her and began to gurgle but just then he heard the drill start, right by his ear. 'We've rewired it a bit,' he heard her say, her voice remote, hallucinatory, 'so now you get electric shocks as well as cavities. Just like in *Marathon Man*.' Her face swam closer into view. 'Remember that movie?' He gargled at her. Her skin was white, smooth, flawless like the surface of cream, and when she smiled she revealed the most perfect, pearlescent set of teeth he'd ever seen and he knew that she'd never been to a dentist. Her eyes were big, almond-shaped. He wanted to tell her that he could fall in love with her and make her the queen of his nights if she promised not to hurt him but the drill was very close now and he felt the myriad splashes its tiny turbine was throwing out. He began to weep.

And then the universe imploded and burst right out again, as if his head was inside a shrapnel bomb going off.

Almazov realized that he had never, ever, felt pain before. This was the first time.

It did not go on for long.

It went on for ever.

When it stopped they took the bungs out and he began to gabble, begging her to ask him any questions she liked, starting with the least important things like the numbers of all his Swiss accounts. At the same time, Almazov was surprised to discover he'd acquired a lisp and that he could stick his tongue right through his front teeth.

The girl took a towel and wiped blood from her hands, smiling brightly at him.

'I do hope you haven't got AIDS,' she said.

The questions went on for a long time.

At the end of them, there wasn't much the dental nurse didn't know about Spats Almazov, or about Mosinterbank and its connections with the business world.

They patched his teeth up. Then they discussed what to do with him.

Vinogradov wanted to get rid of him. 'We don't need him any more. He's just nuisance value now.' He looked across Almazov's supine form at Zidra, awe in his eyes. What they'd just heard would change his life, he knew. 'We can dump him in the river. It's just starting to freeze over for the winter.'

The river was nearby. She thought about it for a moment. 'But he's useful to *me*,' she said. 'I need him to keep my husband alive.'

They sat facing each other over Almazov, ignoring him. One of her problems was that Vinogradov now knew everything she knew, and soon the Lyubertsi chief would know it all too. It complicated matters. 'Besides,' she went on, 'you can't dispose of him without talking to your colleagues first. Think about it. What you've got on him now can make him an asset to your organization in the future.'

Vinogradov thought about it, and nodded. She had a point, as usual. 'I think you suffer from a kind heart,' he said. 'But if you insist. Then I'll call my bosses. They'll want to see him.'

'But first he must make that call. I have to safeguard the life of my husband.'

'Sure, no problem.'

Zidra felt vertiginous. She knew now that Renard was still in England. They hadn't been able to move him far because they'd damaged him too much. But at least he was alive. It had taken the utmost self-control not to break off the interrogation as soon as she heard that news, but she'd pressed on to the end. She wanted the whole picture, as far as Almazov knew it – and he knew most of it, she decided. And the story was big.

She needed Almazov to call his contact in Britain, to give the necessary instruction. Renard was not to be moved. Then Almazov would find out exactly where they were holding him. And she would be on the next flight back.

Almazov would not dare have Renard killed as long as she was still alive because she knew too much. From now on, Almazov was her property – hers and the Lyubertsi's, unless she could get rid of Vinogradov at once. Maybe it had occurred to him that she might decide he was disposable, because she noticed he no longer turned his back on her.

Would *he* kill *her*? She doubted it; not immediately, anyway. The man was head over heels in love with her, for one thing. But in the long run that meant nothing. There were just too many imponderables in the game. Whatever they decided now, life could overturn in hours.

All she wanted to do was to get out of Moscow and out of Russia. Get back to Renard.

They wheeled Almazov's couch to a phone and dialled a London number, one he knew by heart. The telephone was the hands-free variety, presumably so that the dentist could chat and operate at the same time.

She gave Almazov her terrifying smile. 'If Renard is dead, you will die. If you don't tell me exactly where he is I'll kill you anyway.' She showed him a disposable scalpel. 'Got it?'

Almazov nodded. His face was the colour of cucumber face mask. Vinogradov had dialled and now they heard the number ring, heard a man's voice answer. He spoke in English, but with a Russian accent.

Almazov asked him how the American was.

'Who is this?' the Russian repeated, irritable with suspicion. 'Doesn't sound like you.'

'Of course it's me,' Almazov squeaked.

'You sound different.'

'I've been to the dentist.'

The Russian was silent for a moment, then he started to laugh. 'Good.'

'So, how is he – the American?'

'Weak.'

'Well, is he *alive*?' Almazov panted.

'Yeah, alive. Just.'

'Ask what's wrong with him,' Zidra whispered fiercely.

Almazov asked.

'Nothing, just lost blood. He's OK, not too damaged. I already said.'

'Where is he?'

'The clinic still.' The Russian sounded surprised. 'Where you told us to put him.'

'Well, I know that, but what's the address of the clinic, Sasha?'

'I dunno, do I? You need to ask that English guy.'

'Where is the Englishman, then?'

There was another silence. For a moment they thought the Russian had rung off. 'You're stupid,' he said sourly. Then: 'He left for Moscow yesterday, that's what I heard. So he must be there, with you.'

'Fuck, fuck and double fuck,' Almazov squawked, seeing the look on Zidra's face. 'If he's here then why the fuck hasn't he called me?'

'Well, what's to shout about?' Sasha yelled. 'How the fuck should I know why the fuck he called or didn't fucking call? You're in Moscow, not me.'

'OK, calm down, Sasha. Stay where you are. I'll be in touch.'

'OK, fuckhead,' Sasha mumbled. They disconnected.

'Now what?' Zidra growled.

'I got to call my bosses,' Vinogradov said.

'Call, then.'

She watched him dial a number, then turned away, prowled up and down, thinking, listening to him make an appointment with someone called Gyorgy. Then he listened for a while, shouted at someone, listened again, slammed the phone down. She shrugged and went next door to change into jeans and jumper. When she came back out, Vinogradov had already let Almazov up. Now he handcuffed the banker, taped his eyes shut and covered them with Ray-bans, put his cashmere overcoat round his shoulders. Then they led him downstairs to the rear entrance and Vinogradov drove them to the Lyubertsi headquarters, forty kilometres south of Moscow.

'I think we made a bad mistake,' he said to her. After that he didn't speak at all and they drove in silence. Zidra anyway did not wish to start a discussion about the politics of the Lyubertsi in front of Almazov.

She was in a quandary. It was dangerous to go with Vinogradov, but even more dangerous not to. She had to find common ground with the Lyubertsi bosses.

Otherwise she would never leave Moscow alive.

They were not received like heroes. The Lyubertsi had assembled a council of war in a private room in a run-down Palace of Culture. A long table, where a decade ago bureaucrats had faced down meetings of collective farm workers, fronted an empty room. Rows of folding chairs were stacked at the back; three had been brought forward for Vinogradov, Zidra and Almazov.

Zidra didn't like it. They were staging it like a show-trial and someone had even placed a big, ostentatious tape recorder on the long table. Almazov sat down disconsolately, mewling with pain because the analgesic they'd given him was wearing off. Zidra paced around the room conscious of the absurdity of it all and wondering if she'd ever find out who the performance was really being staged for, if they decided after all to kill her.

The council filed in. There were four of them. Vinogradov was given a chair at the end of the table, side on to the others. The ambiguity was clear; he could end up either back with her, or opposite her in the rank of judges. It depended on what he said, presumably.

Zidra wanted to laugh. She sat down facing them and crossed her legs.

They all looked at her. No one bothered with Almazov. A fat waitress from the restaurant downstairs appeared with a dirty cup of water and a pill for him. Almazov wasn't satisfied; his moaning grew louder and he began clutching his chest. This drew looks of surprise. He was told to stop bothering them and after that he sat very still and didn't make a sound.

The members of the council didn't introduce themselves. One of them, a squat, broad-shouldered Ukrainian with a face like a misshapen potato, whose name seemed to be Milyenko, told Zidra and Almazov they'd be given equal rights to prove their cases, and that Vinogradov was now in the role of witness who would corroborate or otherwise their stories.

'What, actually, do I need to explain?' Zidra asked.

'Everything. Who you are. Why you're here. Why you involved us in this business with Mosinterbank, with whom we have only good business relations.'

'I'm not going to say anything in front of this shit Almazov.'

Vinogradov tried to argue that indeed it made poor sense to ask her to reveal everything in front of the banker, if what she had was useful to the Lyubertsi. 'And I know it is. So why can't we listen to them one at a time?'

The Lyubertsi who seemed to head up the council, whom the others referred to only as Meshkin, agreed. 'It's obvious she's not going to talk in front of him, so why waste time? Let him wait outside.'

'Let me speak!' Almazov lisped.

'Maybe I can give a general idea of the issue without being too specific,' Vinogradov offered hastily. But he blew his presentation, waffling incomprehensibly about oil and caviar mafias and nukes, and the meeting soon degenerated into a slanging match with council members shouting amongst themselves, and with Vinogradov scattering precious secrets like confetti, to Zidra's dismay.

She'd been watching the one called Rudolf, who was obviously the youngest – he was in his late twenties and probably a soldier, she judged.

He was serious, intelligent, good-humoured, and he looked sympathetically at her.

It was mostly him she appealed to when she stood and walked across to the table, standing in front of them. She insisted on a private meeting with them, even if the price was a similar private meeting between them and Almazov. 'It won't make things worse, anyway. We're just delaying now, and we have to resolve it. I want to share it with you, but not with him—' She turned and pointed at

147

Almazov. 'There is blood between us. My husband's blood. That's all I care about. He's got my husband, the sonofabitch, and I want him back. I don't give a damn about anything else, and if anything I've got is useful to you you're welcome to it. As for Vinogradov, in my opinion he always acted with your interests in mind, and he made no mistakes that I'm aware of.'

They heard her out, and she added that, yes, there were big issues involved, even international political questions. But there was also a clear way forward for them to exploit the possibilities which she and Vinogradov had brought them.

Rudolf said quietly: 'We're not afraid of anyone, don't misunderstand us. Especially people like Almazov. Our problem is that Vinogradov did not have our agreement to do this. I have to admit this now, in front of Almazov. I have to apologize to him and tell him that if it turns he's been wronged you and Vinogradov will take the consequences. And you'll be compensated,' he said to Almazov. 'OK?'

Almazov nodded weakly. On that basis, he was taken to another room so they could discuss the matter alone with Zidra.

'The options are simple,' Milyenko told her: 'Either we give the banker your head and send him on his way, or we kill him now.'

'You don't need to do either. You can use the situation. Almazov has over-reached himself. Not in Moscow, not even in Russia, but by meddling in bigger things altogether. He's over-reached himself and he and his bank are going to be taken down. That's already certain. So there *will* be a change. It's up to you how you react to it, but you can't alter it.'

'If you mean all this plutonium shit,' Milyenko shouted, 'I can sell you any missiles or warheads you want, right now. But that's just Interpol shit, just chicken-shit in fact, and there's nothing in it for us.'

'This isn't about a few warheads,' she told him. 'Almazov has got himself at the centre of the biggest oil deal since Saudi Arabia was invented, and he's done it through fraud, extortion and now the murder of CIA agents.'

'So what?' Rudolf said, grinning. 'That's how we always do things.'

She laughed. 'Maybe, here, but not in the real world. No one will forgive him or his Mosinterbank for that. The game is just too big for them; they're going to come unstuck. So whoever is playing papa to Almazov is going to come unstuck too. Or is going to dump him as soon as he sees what's happening. All of which means that Mosinterbank, and whatever else Almazov has got going, is yours for the taking. Because if you don't take him someone else will.'

Meshkin told her: 'The problem is that you don't know who's behind Almazov and we do.'

Rudolf said, 'We can't throw away an opportunity. The girl is right; trouble is coming and we all know it. Maybe this gives us a chance to get in first.'

'Meaning?' Meshkin demanded.

'Look, what can this sonofabitch Almazov do to us? OK, so he got more dental work than he expected, so what? Even if he blabs around, it's not enough to start anything. But he won't blab, will he? Because he's left his footprints all over the place, and anyone who digs hard enough will uncover them. We can do it ourselves.'

'Maybe we'll send Vinogradov to Astrakhan, let him bring us back some caviar,' Meshkin joked. 'Check out the girl's story.'

'We can keep this clown here for a couple of days, enough to worry them.'

'Too risky,' Milyenko said emphatically. 'What we need to do is pull facts and figures out of him, then take him back to his bank and get the paperwork too. Then he's ours.'

'What about the girl? We don't need her, do we?'

The three of them looked at her.

'You were right first time,' she told Meshkin. 'Send Vinogradov to Astrakhan. I'm going there with the owner of the Hanseatic Hotel, Hans Uhlaf, tomorrow. He's also in on the Azeri oil deal. But from what I heard from Almazov today, Hans Uhlaf may not be the owner much longer. Maybe that's another business opportunity for you to look at. Let Vinogradov go with me. I can hire him as a high-class bodyguard.'

Rudolf leaned towards her and said: 'Hans Uhlaf isn't the owner of the Hanseatic. Maybe he has a piece of paper which says he is. But someone else owns Uhlaf, and that's the real owner of the Hanseatic. Believe me, I know.'

'If "someone else" is Yura Pryapov, then I know too. I know that the mayor of Moscow thinks he's the most powerful man in Russia after Yeltsin and that even the Lyubertsi think he's untouchable. I know he plans to be the next president of Russia, but I also know he's about to get rolled on.' She said it very quietly. 'It's going to happen. Pryapov will be destroyed.'

The meeting was over. They would keep Almazov for a while, but she wasn't worried. For one thing, she knew anything he said willingly or otherwise would only confirm her story, because it was true. For another, they liked her, and that counted for much.

For the first time she began to hope a little.

The strike against Mosinterbank had been a success.

Chapter 14

They let her go, if only because, as she rightly anticipated, they could not unravel her connections with Yura Pryapov and they were afraid of him still.

On the way back to Moscow, in a car driven by a taciturn Lyubertsi who had been warned not to talk to her, Zidra went through Almazov's story again. Like any banker obsessed with the minutiae of a deal, Spats Almazov had talked in technicalities which were difficult for a lay person to follow. But she understood a number of things, the most important of which was very simple: Azerbaijan was a battleground. At stake was the oil wealth under the Caspian. The Russians were determined to remain the dominant power in the region. The British and the Americans were eager to deny them this position. Against all of them was the rising tide of Islam, stoked by Iran.

To buy the Russians off, Hans Uhlaf had persuaded Bison to let a Russian company participate in the Azeri oil consortium: Arctic Star. What Zidra now knew was where Arctic Star's billion-dollar investment came from: selling plutonium to Iran. And she knew who was laundering the transaction: Uhlaf through the British Plate River Corporation, in which his Hanse group had acquired a controlling interest. And, according to Almazov, Plate River was nothing but a mafia front.

There was more. Mosinterbank worked closely with an old, discreet and highly respected British merchant bank, Palfrey & Griblock. As far as the outside world was concerned, Palfrey & Griblock was a senior partner showing a brand new Russian bank the ropes. The reality was entirely different. Palfrey & Griblock had suffered badly in the recession of the early 1990s. When it got into difficulties it was saved from collapse largely by its participation in Hans Uhlaf's highly successful leveraged takeover of Plate River Corporation. A second stroke of good fortune had been its burgeoning involvement in the London metals market, in particular its successful participation in non-ferrous trading. It had, in short, made a killing in aluminium, mainly because of the insider knowledge gained from its mafia contacts.

It was clear that if the Russians pulled out of Plate River Corporation it might go down, and if PRC collapsed then Palfrey & Griblock would follow and the dominoes would start falling all over the place. There might be a run on Britain's secondary banks, as there had been once before, in 1974, when a payments failure by a minor bank threatened to bring down the entire British banking system. Only Bank of England intervention had saved it. The following year the Conservatives lost a General Election. The same thing could happen again.

Almazov was hot on specifics but weak on the big political picture. Zidra had to fill that in for herself. But one specific which Almazov was sure of was that a senior British politician was taking payoffs from Plate River in return for various kinds of tacit assistance.

Now Zidra understood what Renard was up to, why the game was so big, and why the CIA were involved.

Zidra watched the silent land slip by. Misha Benin was right: it was big stuff. She was tired. It was time to sink silently to the bottom while the sharks bloodied the water overhead.

The Lyubertsi left her at the Mezh. She took her car and drove back to the Hanseatic for the night. As she headed towards the Square of the Year 1905, a Moskvich fired its engine and slithered after her.

It was four a.m. By four-fifteen she was pulling into the hotel's pretentious esplanade.

The night porter wore the same regalia as his day-time counterparts: royal blue greatcoat, epaulettes the size of lavatory brushes, more scambled egg on his chest than a Russian general. But he didn't look the part. His eyes were ferocious and they tracked her as she clicked across the marble foyer.

She thought of going to the night bar for a drink, thought better of it and took the lift to her room. The vast hotel was cloaked in sepulchral silence, the silence that is really the mutterings and broken dreams and creaking beds of a thousand guilty consciences. It made her feel lonely.

She double-locked the door, threw off her shoes and overcoat, took two miniatures of Glenfiddich from the minibar and emptied them both into a cut-crystal glass.

She looked more closely at the glass. It was pressed lead crystal, not cut.

Everything about Hans Uhlaf and his hotels was the same. Falseness, sham glitter, empty charades. Better than it ought to be but still not good enough. Insecurity run riot, disguised as over-confidence.

No, she did not like Uhlaf. In this city of scoundrels, she thought, it did not pay to be so obvious. People developed a sixth sense for this kind of thing. Russia, after all, was the homeland of *pokazukha*, of the Potemkin-village, the false show of power, success, wealth, which hid only a pathological uncertainty. She was having second thoughts about accompanying him to Astrakhan the next day.

She took her clothes off and stood looking in the mirror. Her face was grey with fatigue. She sighed, and the stud glinted dully. *Fuck this life.* Nothing would be the same afterwards, if there was an afterwards.

But what if she couldn't find him? If they killed him and hid the story so deep that nothing was left? For once, she allowed the thought to crawl out of the lizard-brain where fears hide.

If Renard was killed, and she was still free to act – who would she take with her?

Of the long list of candidates, one name stood out: Yura Pryapov, the mayor of Moscow.

He was the grey eminence behind Hans Uhlaf. That connected him not only to corrupt Moscow real estate deals, but to oil, to the arms trade and even to Great Power politics in the Caspian. Mosinterbank was his personal money-laundry. And it was Pryapov's Chechen soldiers who'd taken Renard.

And yes, she could reach him. Mobilize some old connections. Cut the head off the whole beast.

She could kill him, but it wouldn't bring Renard back.

She swilled the whisky down, rinsing it round her mouth. Then she went over to the picture window. It overlooked the Moskva river that lay like a lead sheet between the hotel and the Kremlin opposite. A few cars crawled along the embankment. The Kremlin's anachronistic ruby stars, proposed for its spires by

Leon Trotsky long ago, glowed for no one. She drew the curtains and the last faint murmur of Moscow was eliminated.

Down below in the car park, a man climbed from the Moskvich and paid off the night porter.

One thing was sure, Zidra decided as she showered. Vinogradov had done well. For instance, it had cost ten thousand dollars to persuade the technical controller at the telephone exchange serving Almazov's number at the bank to divert his calls through Vinogradov's office at the Mezh. Vinogradov had found that cash, had told her that it was his investment in her. That was astonishing. The man was a street-fighter at one remove, but he had a streak of honour a yard across.

Vinogradov had listened to Almazov's calls, had decided the call to his dentist was the one to intercept, and then improvised and bluffed his way successfully through the conversation, putting his neck further on the line by evicting the Mezh dentist for the evening and helping Zidra to deal with Almazov. It was reckless bravery, motivated by Lyubertsi bravado and a desire to impress her after their encounter the previous evening.

Benito the driver had also played his part, sending that first premonitory warning to Almazov by frightening his own bodyguard into absence.

The stroke against Mosinterbank was a coup. And Zidra had no doubt she would be made to pay for it.

Back in the Lyubertsi headquarters, pandemonium broke out after Zidra left. Vinogradov's bosses understood they had been drawn into a different kind of street-fight: a brawl between Western intelligence services and big corporations, which the intrigues of the Russian mafia had stirred up. Things were spinning out of control, and that is the kind of situation gangs like the Lyubertsi exist to exploit.

They put a twenty-four-hour watch on the girl. Rudolf organized the line taps, cars, watchers and shadows, while Meshkin and Milyenko and members of their war council gave thought to strategy. They kept Vinogradov around for the time time being. He was their link to her.

Milyenko insisted, and Meshkin agreed, that damage-limitation must be one categorical imperative. At all costs, the Lyubertsi must avoid appearing to head for open conflict with Yura Pryapov.

The accommodation they had reached with the City Hall mafia had been painfully negotiated and rigorously policed by both sides since the street wars of the early 1990s.

They divided up Moscow's retail trade between them. This new business produced a torrent of money. Now Mayor Pryapov was too powerful to attack directly. Nevertheless, the Lyubertsi were sworn to destroy him. And this shaped the second categorical imperative: Pryapov must not be allowed to become stronger.

Pryapov had friends in the army, but enemies in the mafia which controlled the oil and gas industry. That mafia had already installed their own prime minister and meant to chose the next president. Only the Chechens stood in the way, and that was why Pryapov became their ally. A gigantic power struggle was starting to unfold, triggered by events in the Caucasus, and the Lyubertsi leaders had no illusions about Yura Pryapov.

Any peace with him was temporary.

When he could move against them, he would.

And Pryapov did not believe in Geneva rules. There were no wounded left to nurse grievances when he won a battle. There were only corpses.

Zidra Renard had arrived amongst the Lyubertsi like a stormy petrel, in the nick of time. They would not allow her to know it, but overnight she had become the gang's single most precious asset.

She was a beautiful flower, as Rudolf said, adding, 'We'll carry this bloom in our hands, and not one petal must drop.'

The telephone exchange controller who took ten thousand dollars from Vinogradov betrayed him the same day, selling the story back to Almazov for another ten thousand. He told the banker the whereabouts of Zidra Renard, informing him she had rooms at the Mezh and the Hanseatic, even giving him the numbers she'd dialled. Vinogradov's calls from the Mezh to the Lyubertsi, made under stress, gave away enough for Almazov to piece together all the remaining connections.

Two days later, when the Lyubertsi belatedly realized the danger, the exchange manager had disappeared. By then the damage was done.

Releasing Almazov was an error Meshkin would soon regret. Meshkin was too confident in the strength of his organization, too sure that Almazov, cowed and desperate, would stay in line. The Lyubertsi leader had planned to watch secretly over Zidra. Within forty-eight hours he would have difficulty protecting his own life.

Almazov did not intend to compound his betrayal of his partners and backers. The knowledge that his captors were aware of the exact nature of the vast scandal now forming over the heads of powerful Russian persons and institutions meant the Lyubertsi would have to be destroyed; there was no other way. Meantime, he continued as before with Arctic Star's investment in the Azeri oil consortium. The deal could not be allowed to collapse.

Suddenly the vast web of interlocking interests which the banker had worked to build looked more like a band of wolves howling beyond a bonfire. His British associates could not allow the deal to fail either, because the success of the consortium's plans for Caspian offshore oil was now a major policy aim for the British government. They were locked in.

Almazov had no alternative but to initiate decisive steps. He could not do this without his chief backer, Yura Pryapov, mayor of Moscow and the man he feared most. Pryapov was personally interested in the success of the scheme, which accorded with his own long-term ambitions. But Almazov had no doubt he would pay the price for the mistakes which necessitated a war with the Lyubertsi.

It was now doubly necessary to find Zidra and eliminate her, thus clearing the way for the killing of the remaining CIA hostage, Renard. The morning after his ordeal Spats Almazov went straight to City Hall. At eleven he was received by one of Mayor Pryapov's aides. Thirty minutes later he was in conference with Pryapov himself.

The mayor was boiling with rage. He fumed that in a couple of weeks he and President Yeltsin were due to receive the Queen of England on the first official state visit by a British monarch since before the Revolution. The visit would confer respectability on the regime, add a touch of authenticity to their attempts to renovate the tsarist regalia of the past – if fools like Almazov didn't destroy everything first.

Chapter 15

While Almazov was meeting Mayor Pryapov, Zidra went to Misha Benin's office in Nicolskii Street. She planned to tell him what had happened the previous day, to seek his advice – and to warn him.

Zidra had been followed from the Hanseatic that morning. It had taken time and a few changes of scenery to lose the tail because they were professionals. She guessed they were Lyubertsi – but what if they were not?

Benin was bubbling as usual. He had much to tell her, but she cut him off.

'We need to change offices and telephone numbers for a while, and to do it right away,' she told him. 'And I also suggest that if your family are in Moscow – and I know you've got a young wife, and a daughter studying at the Bolshoi school because Minakov told me – you'd better send them to your dacha for a few days.'

Benin sat down at once, looking anguished. 'If you say so.' He knew she was a professional and he was not disposed to argue – he'd been under surveillance before. 'So, then, what has happened?'

'Misha, let's have a good talk, but not here.'

They went without phoning first to a friend with a couple of spare desks in an office fifty yards higher up Nicolskii Street. When they were settled, she told him what had happened the previous day. Benin was an old soldier; he thoroughly approved of pulling the teeth of young bankers. But the business with the telephone exchange worried him. He considered that to be a simple error, and no amount of expediency justified it because it compromised everyone's security. That bit of adventurism took them forward a pace but would surely send them two more steps back. And it was completely unnecessary, he told her. He would certainly have found a way to get to Almazov without leaving clues everywhere, like an Agatha Christie novel.

'That may be,' she told him, 'but Vinogradov was right to be in

157

a hurry. And when such big forces are in play this sort of thing is bound to happen. There is pushing and shoving on all sides, and the only way to avoid risk is to stay home in bed.'

'Perhaps,' Benin said, 'but it is exactly my plan to die in bed with my boots off. Well, OK, I need to make a couple of calls.'

'Don't – there will be intercepts on your home and on Minakov's numbers by now.'

'You're right, of course.' He stood up. 'There is no alternative. We'll have to go in person.'

They went first to Varvarka Street, but as the cab pulled over to the kerb Benin told the driver to carry on round the block.

'Watchers?'

'Yes.' He looked worried. 'I need to be getting home. I'm worried about my wife's safety. I was going to tell you when we met Minakov, but maybe there won't be time.' He handed her a slip of paper. 'You asked me to find someone called Goldman. I have his Moscow address: it's in Maly Gruzinski Street. It's quite a good area; nice apartments. I called there yesterday evening and a woman answered, very cagey. She wouldn't say, but I think he's here.'

'There's no office address?'

'That's it. He lives over the store. One more thing – see, I wrote down another number.' He pointed it out to her on the torn fragment of paper. 'That's Dubok at Minatom.' He looked at her. 'This guy is very high up, very controversial. He's a high-profile hardware salesman. He's been trying to sell reactors to the Saudis, the North Koreans, you name it. He thinks he has a right. He wants to defend his employees. He's a strong nationalist. I was going to suggest we set up a meeting, but I have to go and see that my family is OK.'

She nodded. The car had gone a full circle. The driver would be happy to do that until his gas ran out, at thirty dollars an hour. They had him cruise slowly past the entrance to Minakov's premises again, and she saw for herself the unmarked white Lada with two men sitting inside.

Opposite was a small store selling video trash and souvenirs. Its door was open, passers-by were lounging about.

'There must be a back way.'

'It'll be covered.' Benin was getting desperate. Minakov had told her how he doted on his twenty-eight-year-old wife and their love-child, unexpected gifts of the Lord for a man his age.

She left the car a hundred yards lower down and let him go. They arranged three fall-back meeting places, in case he was unable to come to them at Varvarka Street.

She was on her own, starting to flounder.

She guessed that the first bunch of watchers who had been waiting for her outside the Hanseatic were Lyubertsi, and she now somewhat regretted losing them, because this lot could only be the enemy. But she had no wish to be in at the birth of what was bound to be one of Moscow's bloodiest gang wars. She would find the rear entrance to the offices of the Astrakhan Limnological Institute (Moscow Branch) and see who had found it first.

She retraced her route around the huge block in which the Institute's offices were embedded. There was a big inner courtyard, typical in such cases, but she did not want to walk openly into it. Much better to come through someone else's backyard.

On the far side of the block there was a small co-operative shop selling a meagre range of imported clothes and tinned meats. Two young girls were visible inside, sitting forlornly behind a brightly lit counter. Zidra went in, smiled at the girls, asked them about the price of Dutch ham. They were young, pretty in a cheap kind of way. She told them in a gushing, gossipy voice that she wanted to get to see her lover but the man's wife was waiting in a car by the rear entrance to the courtyard, and his wife's boyfriend was sitting at the front.

The girls grinned and giggled.

'I need to find a discreet way through,' she told them. 'I don't want to get shot at!'

The girls sympathized at once. If she'd let them they'd have become instant allies, but all she wanted was to use their back door.

But there was a problem with that, the elder of the two said. She looked upset. 'Our boss will kill us if we let anyone we don't know through the back. Won't he, Irichka?' she said to the other. 'Otarik will kill us.'

Masha flung open the barred and bolted back door and let her out.

Zidra had already spotted the Volga with two men inside, engine running. Almost certainly there were more men inside the institute.

159

The inner courtyard was a tangle of rubbish skips half covered in snow, of broken street furniture, abandoned truck tyres, and a vast jumble of cars, mostly deep in snow, left by their owners until the spring.

If the car used by the watchers was a Volga then it was probably official. The police sometimes used BMWs and Mercedes, but the mafia did not use Russian cars at all.

It meant that Almazov had squealed, as she had known he would.

She pulled the Makarov out and shoved it inside her unbuttoned coat, then walked slowly over to the Volga.

The hell with it.

She tapped on the driver's window. 'Hi, guys.'

They had watched her come towards them. Watched without seeing. It wasn't predictable behaviour, unless their target was completely stupid, which they'd been told she definitely wasn't.

The driver wound the window down. 'Yes?' He was fed up and not interested in telling someone where the nearest Metro was.

'Hi,' she repeated, giving them time.

The look on the driver's face changed. The man beside him sat bolt upright, then went very still.

'Take the keys out and just drop them on the snow,' she told him. The Makarov's muzzle was pointing at the driver's forehead. 'In case you were wondering, I have done this sort of thing before.'

The driver took out the ignition keys, dropped them through the window.

The other man had begun to shuffle so she fired the gun. The bullet went through the passenger window about one inch from his nose. The report was deafening.

'Jesus Christ,' the driver hissed.

'I told you, I've done this before.'

She calmly wrapped her head scarf around the gun. Anyone who ran to a window would see a woman talking to a car driver. People don't draw the obvious conclusions in situations like this.

'Put your hands flat on the dash,' she told the passenger. 'You, hands on the wheel and keep them there. Now, I know where you keep your artillery, gentlemen, over your hearts. And where do you keep your cuffs?' She smiled at the driver.

'Over my bum,' he grinned.

160

'Good boy. So take your right hand and pull your pal's cuff out. But keep your other hand on the wheel.'

She was not happy about this. These two also looked as if they had been here before, and the passenger seemed more angry than tamed.

'Cuff your pal's right hand to the wheel,' she told the driver when he'd freed the handcuffs from the other's back pocket.

'Tighter,' she said. 'So he feels it.' The driver ratcheted the cuffs a notch tighter. 'Hands on the wheel again.' She held the gun close to his head, now – close enough for him to grab. But he had already made up his mind. Nothing in his terms of employment said anything about heroics. With her left hand she pulled open his jacket and twitched the gun out of his shoulder holster. It was a Makarov 9mm, like hers, but newer. And it was silenced.

She stood back and put the gun in her pocket. 'Now,' she said, 'take your own cuffs out with your right hand, but do it very, very slowly, and don't touch your pal.'

She knew it was going to happen the moment it did, but she'd left it too late. The driver grinned at her, and then the door exploded open, hurling her back into the snow, and she saw the driver coming at her with his partner's sidearm in hand. The Makarov had been flung from her by the impact.

As the driver threw her on to her stomach, she saw other men running – presumably the team at the front, which had heard gunfire and come to check. She felt cuffs bite deep on her wrists and the driver was telling her to get up, had one rough hand under her upper arm, wrenching her to her feet, when he collapsed, silently, like a sack of flour that leaked red into the snow.

A car came racing backwards through the courtyard, wheels whining as they spun through the snow. Two men grabbed her and dragged her over to it, flinging her into the back seat, and the car shot out of the courtyard and away towards Varvarka Street. She felt hands pull her arms out backwards, and the man to her left had wrenched the cuffs off. On her right, the other man was shouting instructions to the driver, yelling at him to slow down, to head towards Leninskii Prospekt.

She sat back, felt a cold wind on her face from the car's open windows, watched the two men beside her, both now lunging forward, yelling at the driver, ignoring her.

*

They took her to an apartment block in Leninskii. It had once been a prestigious location, but it was moving downmarket as the process of building suburbs gathered pace in Russia. The place was a stop-off occasionally used by Lyubertsi bosses, crowded now with shouting, sweaty men, with Rudolf, the Lyubertsi soldier, dangerous, beautiful, at their silent centre, waiting for her.

After Rudolf's men explained what had happened at Varvarka Street, he asked: 'You were going to see your biologist pal, Minakov?'

'Yes.'

'And now we've killed a cop.' It was said without anger.

'So what? Anyway, I didn't ask you to get involved.'

'The fact is, angel, like it or not, we *are* involved now. So we have a right to be consulted from here on. I require it, in fact.'

Zidra paused to look at him. In his dog-tooth, baggy jacket and silk slacks, Rudolf was wiry, fair complexioned, with curly blond hair. He had clever eyes. He spoke with authority. 'Take us into your confidence,' he told her. 'Then we can avoid upsets.'

'OK, I accept that I need something from you and I'm ready to help you in return. But don't expect me to strew roses in your path, Rudolf.'

Rudolf grinned. 'Let's not waste time. Begin.'

'I still need to talk to Minakov,' she reminded him.

'You'll have a problem with that.' He waved her to a long table set near a window, and sat facing her. 'Minakov left his offices at midday. We tracked him to Domodedovo, where he bought a ticket on the first flight to Astrakhan.'

'You don't know why?'

'I was going to ask you that. There were no phone calls, not that we picked up on, at any rate. He left Moscow at the speed of sound.'

She looked puzzled.

'What was he to you, anyway?' Rudolf asked.

'It's a long story and I'm not sure I know the ending. But—' She broke off, wondering why Misha Benin hadn't known of Minakov's decision to leave for Astrakhan.

'You need to level with me,' Rudolf said. 'Meshkin is worried. He didn't wait for the shit to start flying. He tried to reach Pryapov through intermediaries first thing this morning, and got nowhere. Pryapov was unavailable. And if Pryapov doesn't talk now, it means he's not going to talk to us, period. We're in a new situation

– and that's why Meshkin is worried. We weren't ready for it.'

'Maybe war is still avoidable.'

'I don't think so, frankly.'

'Why not?'

'Because we would have to give ground.' Rudolf crushed a cigarette stub underfoot. 'But it's too early for public disputes in any case. Pryapov can't move yet – he has important unfinished business. In a couple of weeks he's got the Queen of England coming here. Yeltsin is off his head with drink, no one else counts for shit, so Pryapov will be the main man to receive her, in Moscow at least. There'll be no war just yet, if only because of that.'

'Perhaps now's the time to nail the bastard, then.'

'We're thinking about it. But it would help me greatly if you told me what I need to know, lady.'

One of Rudolf's lieutenants came in with coffee and hard biscuits. Rudolf took a biscuit and shunted the plate over to her. 'So tell me, about this thirty tonnes of plutonium bullshit. Is it real? Where is the stuff hidden?'

'In Astrakhan, if it *is* real.'

'There's a lot of caviar in Astrakhan, and a big caviar mafia. But I never heard about plutonium.'

'I think the plutonium does exist. Which means you can cut through all the cloudy theories about whether it can be collateralized or used to blackmail the USA or whatever. In the end it will be sold to the highest bidder. The only alternative outcome would be if it were returned to the Russian government in daylight with the US Marines for an honour guard, just to make sure the government doesn't lose it again.'

She paused.

'Go on, I'm listening.' Rudolf crunched a biscuit.

'If the Lyubertsi turn it in, you'll get Brownie points. If you can also prove that Mosinterbank was involved, then it's bad news for Pryapov.'

'As I understand it, you want the Lyubertsi to do voluntary work for Interpol and the UN now, is that the idea?' He smirked across the table at her. 'You've got balls, to make that kind of proposal to someone like me.'

'The answer is yes, you should do it.'

Rudolf started to laugh. 'You want me to be respectable, like Pryapov is dreaming about? He wants to be the first man to be ennobled by the first tsar since 1917. Some hope.'

'It will pay off,' Zidra insisted. 'You'll find a lot of doors opening. What else can you do? If you try to steal the stuff first, even killing me won't keep it a secret. Too many people already know the Lyubertsi are involved. The only thing you can do is use the episode to nail Pryapov.'

'And what do you need from this?'

'An address in England. But I'll help you fix Pryapov first. I won't just bale out when I get what I want.' She looked him squarely in the eye. 'Deal?'

Rudolf had been leaning back on his chair, balancing on two legs. He paused for a moment, thinking, then jerked forward. 'OK, deal. Tell me what help you need, and why.'

'First I need to talk to a British businessman, a crook, who has a place here in Moscow. He's a small fish, but he's the one who makes a lot of loose ends meet.'

'Thrill me with the details.'

'Here's his name and address.' She gave Rudolf the slip of paper from Misha Benin. 'We couldn't get him to the phone. Maybe he's in England. But it would be best to meet him here, because it's also his office. He keeps his files there. We need contracts, stuff like that.'

'So tell me how he fits in?'

'I don't know yet. That's why we need to talk to him. But the general idea is clear enough. There are big boys on both sides of the divide who want to deal with each other. They're afraid to do it openly, so they use businessmen-adventurers, small fish who swim around the sharks, feeding off scraps. The idea is to use so many of these intermediaries that no one can discover who really are the end buyers or sellers. That's what someone like Goldman organizes. The problem both sides share is that half the intermediaries are actually fronts for intelligence services testing each other out, looking for scams and trying to uncover fraud or contraband or illegal exports of aluminum or embargoed Iraqi oil being channelled through Russia, or plutonium or heroin or whatever. Goldman is a fraudster and a smuggler, but he's got mixed up with the KGB and with MI6. They use him, he tries to use them. He must know a lot about the mechanics of the deal.'

'So you think he can prove Pryapov's involvement?'

'Maybe.'

Rudolf called in one of his lieutenants, gave him the details Zidra had provided and tasked him to find Goldman.

'Another thing,' Zidra said. 'There's a guy called Dubok. He's a director of a state-owned company called Spetzatommontazh.'

'I know them. They make reactors and stuff. We do business with them.'

'Right. Dubok is up to his neck in all this.'

Rudolf gave another subordinate instructions to try to set up a meeting with Dubok.

'I need to make a call,' Zidra said when the man left.

'Where?'

'The Hanseatic.'

'Too dangerous from here. We'll go for lunch and find a *taksofon*.'

'I also have an appointment with a hairdresser. I want to change my appearance.'

'If you could grow a beard that would be good, too. Which reminds me: as of eleven-forty this morning, there's an Interpol warrant out for your arrest on a murder charge. Apparently you killed some American businessman in London last week. You're a busy gal.'

'How do you know it's me? What name are they looking for?'

'Wait. I'll check.' Rudolf dialled a number, spoke briefly to someone, then rang off. 'Sandra Davies. Same name you registered at the Hanseatic. So you can't go back there.'

'Check where this warrant came from. Is it from Britain, or did it come from some bribed person in Interpol's Moscow office?'

Rudolf stared at her, grinned, and left the room. He was gone for a long while and she began to worry. Eventually, he returned.

'You were right. It's Moscow. It's been done to gee up the Russian police to find you. But it cost someone fifty thousand dollars to arrange. They are *very* keen to get their hands on you. Another thing. We've found your pal Goldman. Let's go!'

Chapter 16

Goldman's woman was out somewhere and he would not answer the door, which was armoured steel, unbreachable. So Rudolf's men roused a neighbour two floors above, abseiled over the balcony and went in by the French windows. They'd already cut the phone wires. They found Goldman hiding behind the false wall in the bathroom which contained the sewage pipes.

Rudolf invited Zidra into the kitchen and closed the door. He put the kettle on. She was beginning to speak when a thin, shrill cry reached up into a falsetto scream and was suddenly cut off. 'What was that? You haven't killed him?'

Rudolf laughed. "No. He thought we were cutting his balls off. But we weren't. Yet.'

Also found in the bathroom by Rudolf's boys was an aerosol Fruits of the Forest room freshener. Its propane propellant produced a flame several feet long when they lit it. They'd attached the canister to a spray tube from a bottle of his girlfriend's perfume, then tied Goldman on the bed and made a small incision in his scrotum with her nail scissors. That was when he began to scream. They blew in propellant and when Goldman's scrotum was as big as a tennis ball they taped it shut.

Goldman was in shock and it took a while to calm him, but he felt surprisingly little pain. He had once been offered similar treatment by a whore in Bangkok. She said blowing air in and letting it out again at the appropriate moment enhances enjoyment. But propane is different and it takes a harder person than Goldman to live with the thought of his balls being detonated.

Goldman cried somewhat. Experience had taught Rudolf that an atmosphere of quiet is needed in this sort of situation. They gave him tea laced with distilled valerian, which his girlfriend used to calm her nerves. After a while Goldman became fatalistic. He was ready to talk, he said, but – conscious of the indignity of his position – he asked them to cover him with a blanket before they let Zidra in the room.

'We won't do anything worse to you,' Zidra told him, 'if you're helpful. It's your friends you'll have to worry about.' The little bump in the blanket made her want to laugh.

'Thank you,' Goldman said. He was perspiring.

Zidra poured tea. She had them untie a hand for him to drink it. 'Tell us about your dealings with Julian Benderby,' she said.

He told her he knew Benderby worked at Palfrey & Griblock and had heard of but never met the bank's chairman, Henry Carter-Allis. He'd first met Benderby in 1990, when he was involved in exporting Russian aluminium. He needed a banker to underwrite his first deal and found Benderby.

The aluminium was exported via Riga. The price was low, because the metal was being smuggled out of Russia by airframe manufacturers whose directors were amassing their first fortunes. They bribed or frightened customs officers, the ministry officials who provided phoney export licences, and anyone else they had to, using Chechen muscle to do it. Goldman made and lost a fortune. Benderby collected around five million dollars personally, and Carter-Allis another ten. And the landed price of the metal still undercut the world market by nearly half.

Goldman could not explain what happened to the money afterwards. The proceeds were split different ways. How much? Zidra asked. He didn't know. Two or three hundred million dollars.

When she told this to Rudolf, the frost on his face thawed for a while.

Goldman had been squeezed out of the alu game. The big boys didn't need him once the business got established, and, as he said, no one gives you five per cent of something just for the colour of your eyes.

So Goldman was in the doldrums. He still visited Moscow, got involved in the dried milk scam, when bent Russian officials persuaded the West that famine was imminent and convoys of lorries appeared, loaded with European Community aid: surplus milk, rapeseed oil, soap, you name it. A lot of money was made then, off-loading it on to the black market.

Then one day one of his Russian contacts, Mikhail, phoned him. Mikhail had a dirty office off Gorky Street and a company called Mega Corporation Inc. A man from Samara who knew Mikhail's second cousin had called one day and said he had five million tonnes of oil to sell, which Mikhail obviously didn't believe, but the man from Samara kept on about it and in the end Mikhail got off his bum and called Goldman.

Then followed, from Goldman's point of view, a great deal of wasted time.

But in the end, Mikhail found the right people to talk to, and they weren't in Samara at all, they were in Perm.

'*Perm?*' Zidra repeated. 'In the Urals?'

She knitted her brow. The face of Humphries, the Bison Oil expert, flashed before her eyes. Now everything was starting to connect. Oil, plutonium, Great Power games in the Caspian, corruption in the Russian government, corruption in Britain.

And Goldman was at the centre, like a worm in an apple. That was why he was hiding in his girlfriend's flat.

'Yes. Perm in the Urals,' he answered her wearily.

'What was the name of that company?'

'Astro Trading Corporation. As far as I could see, it was a two-men-and-a-dog outfit occupying two rooms in a defence enterprise.'

Sasha Leven, president of Astro Trading, was co-signatory of a contract with Harvey Goldman for a general amount of five million tonnes of oil, worth around half a billion dollars. The deal was like the good old alu days, Goldman said: the oil was cheap and the rake-offs they all took were huge.

'Where did the oil come from?' Zidra asked.

'That's what's odd. It isn't Russian oil at all. The oil is shipped from Novorossysk, but it definitely isn't Urals blend. It's Iranian.'

'And what was the name of the Perm defence plant?'

As far as Goldman could remember, it was called Permmontazh. The sort of stupid name you forget at once or remember for ever. It used to make nuclear reactors, he thought, but now it was owned by somebody else, he didn't know who. In any case, Astro Trading had closed down almost the day the deal was struck and promptly disappeared. And no, he didn't know or care who'd taken over the contract as long as everything continued smoothly, two seventy-thousand-tonne oil tankers left Novorossysk each month and the money flowed.

Goldman was growing restless. He thought he might be getting an air embolism, or a propane embolism, which sounded worse. Rudolf told him he was lucky they hadn't used his girlfriend's hair lacquer.

There was just one other thing Zidra wanted to know before they let the gas out of him and let him find all the contracts and related papers.

'Does the name Dubok mean anything to you?'

Goldman seemed to start at the name. He subsided into thought, made strenuous, visible efforts at recollection. Then he remembered. He'd met him at a Russian defence industry exhibition held in Birmingham in 1993. They'd exchanged cards and Dubok had invited him to visit his offices at Minatom. But nothing came of their talks, Goldman told her. No one wanted to buy Dubok's mini-reactors and water desalination plants. In any case, he didn't think Dubok worked for Minatom any more. He'd gone off to work for an oil company.

'What oil company? Can you remember?'

'I might have his new card, if you let me up.'

They let him up. Someone went to find his girlfriend's needle-case and the dental floss Goldman said was in the bathroom. Zidra went to the kitchen and drank more tea. When they called her back, Goldman was upright but ashen-faced.

It took a while to go through the papers.

In the end they just cleaned out all the cupboards, piled hundreds of trade proposals and papers into carrier bags. Goldman didn't care. A more beloved thing had been restored to him. He even reminded Zidra about Dubok's visiting card.

It was canary yellow with a golden oak emblazoned on the front, because his name was derived from the Russian word for oak tree. *Michael P. Dubok*, it said in English. *Construction Manager, Arctic Star Corporation, Perm Branch*.

'What it means,' Zidra said as they drove back down Bolshoi Gruzinski, answering a question of Rudolf's, 'is that the Iranians have bought plutonium and paid for it with oil. At least half a billion dollars' worth, although that's just for starters, I'm sure. So we know the stuff exists, and we know more or less how the deal was set up. Arctic Star sells the oil on the world market and keeps the proceeds.'

Rudolf sniffed. 'Who gives a fuck?' He'd left two boys to look after the Englishman. They'd have thrown him from his French windows by now. He didn't tell her that. 'I have more important news. Pryapov was behind the Interpol warrant, as you suspected. Now he's given us an ultimatum. He wants you. Today.'

Zidra took a breath and held it.

Rudolf grinned. 'Don't say I said it, but fuck him. But you'll have to leave town, right away. We can stall him for an hour or two, that's all.'

'Then stop the car and let me out now.'

'Can't do that. You'll have to come back to Leninskii and then we'll decide.'

'Then let's have something to eat first. I'm starving.'

They stopped at a restaurant called the Hunter, which specialized in game dishes, and talked more while Zidra riffled through Goldman's archive, taking the most likely things out and sorting them into a small pile in the centre of the table.

Zidra was at Rudolf's mercy, dependent on his good intentions. She couldn't stay in Moscow. Even showing her face in the street was dangerous. Benin had disappeared – she'd tried to call both his home and office numbers from a *taksofon*. No answer at either. She could not hope to catch a plane or a train undetected. She was trapped and Pryapov was closing in.

From the restaurant she put a call through to Hans Uhlaf at the Hanseatic, and spoke to his secretary, who sounded flustered.

'Oh, Mrs Renard! He was trying to call you all morning. He's already left for the airport. He's going to Astrakhan this afternoon, and he understood you meant to join his party.'

'I know. I'm so sorry. When he calls, please tell him I had to go back to England unexpectedly.'

She put the phone down and joined Rudolf at the table. 'If we're about to be shot by Pryapov, let's have a drink with the *pelmeniye*,' she said.

Rudolf grinned, ordered Smirnoff from the freezer. They drank the first hundred grams and ate wild boar *pelmeniye*, the little envelopes of dough floating in a strong broth. It was good.

'I need to go to Astrakhan, today,' she told him.

'Take me with you,' he joked. 'I need a holiday.'

'Why not? I'll need a friend.'

Rudolf put his spoon down and looked at her. It was one of

those moments that decide lives. 'OK, maybe I will go with you.'

While Zidra finished the Smirnoff, Rudolf went to call his 'friends in the air force'. He came back a while later, looking pleased, saying he'd not only found a plane, but also found Dubok at his Arctic Star office in the Minatom headquarters in Bolshaya Ordynka Street.

Dubok had agreed to meet. But he was leaving the office in thirty minutes so they had to hurry.

They hurried.

Chapter 17

The headquarters of Minatom is a gigantic reactor-shaped cube of a building set amongst the trees of Bolshaya Ordynka.

Its offices are big and pretentious in the solid, old-fashioned Soviet way. They mostly have grandfather clocks in the corners. The clocks are all German-made. They were brought to Russia after the war, on the same train as Germany's rocket scientists and nuclear engineers.

The Dubok who was watching his world fall apart from a Moscow office was a different person from the genial, bluff character Renard had met in Baku. Dubok was in the mould of a traditional Soviet bureaucrat, big, aggressive, a heavy drinker who had functioned for years in that condition. The team he led had once built Chernobyl. He lived through that and survived. They knew when they saw him he would not break.

Zidra began.

'I don't expect you to confirm anything of what I'm going to say, but I do expect you to listen. I want to talk to you about Harvey Goldman.'

Dubok looked at Rudolf in surprise. 'Who is this woman? I thought you came here to discuss Lyubertsi business?'

'This is Lyubertsi business.'

'You started in the wrong way, friends. I expected to discuss your investment plans for Elektrostahl. You better leave.'

'Mrs Davies is an American,' Rudolf said. 'You need to understand. They are not polite like us.'

'I met many Americans. Mostly they were polite. She's a shit.' He picked up a few Minatom promotional catalogues lying on his desk, threw them to the floor. 'Fucking bimbo.'

'Goldman has told us everything. We met him today. He told us all about the thirty tonnes of plutonium which you personally stole from Shevchenko and hid in Astrakhan, while you were still works director there. About your association with Sergei Ivanov and his Arctic Star. About your dealings with Iran. Your alliance with certain dubious Western companies.'

'What?'

'I said, Harvey Goldman,' Zidra said. 'Remember him?'

Dubok sat like a monolith. Even the eyes, squeezed between scabrous lids like gobs of grease, did not move. Aggression disappeared behind his slab of a face. This was the man known to his colleagues as *Zhelyezniye*, *Iron-arse*.

'I see you do,' Zidra went on.

When he began to speak it was to Rudolf, slowly at first, almost reproachfully: 'What we did was for the country. I won't discuss it with scum like her.' His eyes still did not move from Zidra. 'You should not mix with this sort of person. I am disappointed with you.'

Rudolf protested. 'You sold nukes to the fucking Ayatollahs! You crazy?'

Dubok said, 'This is not an issue. We were scientists, not politicians. The ministry set us tasks. The question was, would we carry them out?' He slammed a log-shaped fist on the desk. 'We did. We built the best reactors in the world. In theory they were fool-proof. Some mistakes were made, we did not organize some things properly. That is the Russian nature. We are not like Germans. But in general we did what was necessary, and we always met our norms. Now I have to hear this shit from young girls. I say you should get out of here, Rudolf. There is Jewish blood in you, for sure.' He wiped his lips with the back of his hand. 'Russia is a big country,' he said more quietly. 'It is not like America – just a soup of different races. Who would have thought in 1945 that one day Japanese people would own the Rockefeller Center? But it's true. So anything can happen. But now you come to me and you speak like that in this place? That is unforgivable.'

Zidra and Rudolf looked at each other.

'Let's go,' she said.

They stood up together.

'Remember this, Dubok,' Zidra said. 'We won't let this deal go forward. Tell your friends at Arctic Star to forget it.'

'The deal already happened,' Dubok said, barely mouthing the words, which came out as though at gunpoint, as though forced. He did not crow. What was the point? He just announced flatly: 'In two days the plutonium will be delivered. So you were wrong to interfere, chicken-brained American.'

The only thing faster than a Mig-29 that still obeys gravity is a Sukhoi, but they don't have room for passengers.

Anyway, Rudolf had trained on Migs before he became a Lyubertsi soldier, and he still had friends in that part of the air force.

They arrived at Mgalov airbase, thirty kilometres north of Moscow, when dusk was creeping off the endless forests.

Giant steel doors with rusting red stars in their centres ground open and the big BMW swept on to the perimeter road. It was twenty-five kilometres long. At last ragged buildings came into view. They stopped by a hangar, so big that fog clouded its extremities. They walked across the hardstand, Zidra's heels clicking in the enormous silence around them. A sleepy Siberian crow came to look, made its mocking cry and left.

A Russian military jeep, roof-strobes flashing, raced from behind the hangar. The jeep braked and an air force officer came from it at a run.

It was the comrade-in-arms Rudolf had called from the Hunter. He shook their hands and Rudolf introduced Zidra vaguely as 'Miss York, *Amerikanka*'. The officer was effusive, deferential. He gave her his card. It read in English: 'Col. P. Ivanov. President. Mgalov Pilot Training Firm Limited.'

They drove to his office on the ground floor of the control tower. It had wood-panelled walls decorated with dusty portraits of Soviet aviators. A big desk supported a pink plastic globe circled by a metal Mig towing a plastic banner which read 'Mgalov Defenders of the Motherland Air Training School'.

There was a bottle of Azeri cognac and some curling squares of bread sprinkled with dusty pink caviar. Ivanov poured cognac and they drank. He talked for a while about life and business and showed them a framed Learjet dealership certificate and a photograph of himself shaking hands with the president of Learjet.

'Is the plane prepared?' Rudolf asked.

'Sure it is.' Ivanov grinned at Zidra. 'You ready for a big thrill, Miss York?'

'I'm struggling with the idea,' she told him.

Ivanov showed them through to a preparation room, where

technicians were waiting. She went to the changing room and put on the flying clothes provided, putting her blue suit in a plastic bag. Ivanov looked disappointed when she took the bag with her to the plane.

Outside, they climbed back into the jeep which bucked its way round the hangar on to a wide concrete apron. The Mig was waiting. In the amber sunlight it looked like a steel shark. A spume of condensed gases shimmered from valves on its grey flanks. Motors whirred. Technicians walked around plugging and unplugging diagnostic kit.

'The rubber band is fully wound,' Ivanov joked. Rudolf looked serious. He wandered around the plane, talking to a technician. They seemed to be making a deal. From the corner of her eye Zidra saw the technician race back to the hangar and return in a service truck. When he began bolting reserve fuel tanks and fitting weapons on the wing, Ivanov rushed off at once to argue with Rudolf.

It was too late – everything was decided. They went back to the office while the changes were made. On the way, Rudolf said he wanted the plane until tomorrow, and that was that. Eventually, Ivanov cheered up again.

An hour later, Zidra was strapped to a parachute and wired into the plane. The lid slid shut and then she could hear the rustle of machinery and Rudolf speaking in her ear.

There was a lot of talk between him and the control tower while the engine whined into life and the plane trundled on to the runway. The Mig lurched suddenly and then shot forward. Engine noise spread horizon to horizon, pitted concrete jarred through to her spine; then the whine became a roar and the whole surface of the world disappeared behind her.

The Mig arrowed upwards and Zidra's face began to swell as G-forces multiplied. Her eyeballs distended and she could not see; when they were ready to explode she tried to reach up to her face but every finger weighed a kilo and each hand a tonne. The engine note went up an octave and a giant fist stuffed itself into her throat and began dragging the flesh of her face after it, pulling it down on to her chest. She suffocated, speechless, pinioned.

Just as suddenly, the pressure lifted and she was a feather floating up in an elevator that was falling at the rate of ten Empire State Buildings a minute. And then the engine blast died to a murmur. The vibration stopped, the plane lunged through the cloud layer and a million silent suns spread over the world. Then Rudolf's voice insinuated itself in her ear: 'We're going in a straight line now.'

'Where are we?' she asked in a whisper that filled the universe.

'Halfway to Astrakhan. We'll be there in thirty minutes.'

'How fast are we going?'

'Fast.'

After a while, she heard him say, 'You got friends in Astrakhan?'

'Yeah,' she whispered. 'Peter Minakov, the biologist. Who do you know?'

Outside it was glider-quiet, with no sound but a silken wind.

'The mayor of Astrakhan. A few businessmen.'

They planed slowly down as gradually the light died, and then the engine roared and the giant hand punched her in the back again as the Mig spun through 360 degrees. The world capsized and Russia spilled its bleak brown farms and fields all over the sky, so close she covered her face. The Mig spun right side round and they seared back into the clouds, sudden turbulence throwing them around the sky like spaghetti in a sieve. Then they burst through, the Mig shuddering out of the clouds and coasting into the glow of violet that is the canopy on the world.

'Sorry about the Jeager loop,' Rudolf whispered. 'Someone's radar was tracking me and I wanted to lose it. Hope you didn't spill *pelmeniye* on the cockpit lid.'

'No, not yet.'

She watched the violet deepen into the indigo shoreline of space. The tumult outside died into the hiss of a thin wind across the airfoils.

'Fucking hell,' she breathed. Beneath them, the Volga sprawled under riven clouds, south to the Caspian Sea. Behind, stars paraded their mockery of men. The Mig leapt like a fish into the sunlight below.

The deputy mayor met them at the airport. He had been sent to collect Uhlaf's party as well, but Uhlaf was late and Zidra didn't want to meet him, so they decided to leave at once. Rudolf commandeered the official black Volga. The deputy mayor looked around the empty sky, turned and left with them.

Rudolf's boys would follow the next day, on a scheduled flight.

Astrakhan.

From here armed merchants once travelled the Silk Route, in caravans laden with silver, gold and diamonds, with mink, sable and fox and with the precious astrakhan, fleece of an unborn lamb. And with barrels of caviar, worth more than gold.

'The British kept a consulate here until the Revolution,' Dmitrov, the deputy mayor, a small, cheerful man with shining, bird-like eyes, told them. 'There's a rumour they might come back.'

The Volga entered the city boundary, sweeping past huge cantonments of dimly lit Soviet-era tenements. But when they neared the centre the highway petered out into a rutted lane that snaked through sprawls of ancient, half-capsized tied log and clapboard dwellings.

They stopped outside a high-walled enclosure. Guards appeared, checked papers and swung open the wrought-iron gates. They drove down a wooded drive, stopping at wide steps which led to a house. Lights began to come on. They saw that the house was big, with four storeys, and built of pink-painted clapboard.

'This was Nikita Khrushchev's dacha,' Dmitrov told them. 'The General Secretary loved to fish, and where better than here at the mouth of the Volga?'

The place was a well-staffed, exclusive hotel for official guests of the city. Dmitrov showed them to their rooms, gave them supper, and left to meet Hans Uhlaf, who would take his party to the still more palatial premises recently opened in Astrakhan by the Plate River Corporation.

Zidra went to her room with a scratch supper, stripped, showered and crawled into bed. She lay awake a long while, replaying Moscow; no ends met. She was no further forward but she was another thousand miles from Renard. At last she began to drift. Downstairs billiard balls clicked and snapped, and the last thing she heard was girlish laughter when Rudolf finished the game he was playing with one of the guards and took to bed a maid he'd had his eye on over supper.

Zidra slept late. When she awoke she knew it was already mid-morning. A deep silence prevailed in Khrushchev's dacha. It was the sunlight streaming in past the ill-fitting curtains, flooding over the bed, dazzling her sleep-filled eyes, that had roused her. She went to the triple-glazed balcony doors, threw back the curtains and was astonished by what she saw.

She began tugging at the rusty bolts. It took a while but she opened them and then the doors suddenly flew apart and there was a noise like an express train as a mile of grey water roared past the window. The dacha had been built on a concrete embankment hard by the Volga. It was the time of the autumn floods, when Siberia's rains empty into the Caspian. The water was grey, turgid, viscous with cold. The river was so wide she had trouble seeing where the grey waters ended and the grey shore opposite began.

Zidra walked the length of the balcony, sucking in the cold air. There was nothing else but the Volga as far as the eye could see, drenched in brilliant sunshine. She balled her fists and jumped on the spot. There had been a frost overnight. Her toes squeezed small clots of ice congealed on the planks.

She watched the water for a while, wondering why she had not heard the noise the previous evening. The Volga was the biggest thing in the world. Then she dressed and went downstairs to find breakfast. Rudolf had left hours before, the watchman told her. But breakfast would be served.

She went into the dining room. There were no other guests. While she waited she walked over to the giant map of the Soviet Union which hung on the far wall, looking again at the Caspian Sea and its hinterland. It was the same map as in Minakov's office in Varvarka Street.

She turned back to the room when she heard a door open behind her. A woman had entered and stood motionless, watching her.

The woman was an attractive blonde, in her late thirties. Before Zidra could speak, she introduced herself as Irina Belinskaya, chair of the Astrakhan trade planning committee. Looking after foreign visitors was one of her duties. The deputy mayor had assigned her to look after Zidra and she had come to take her to the Plate River Corporation building.

'Thank you, but I need to see Professor Minakov at the Limnological Institute first.'

'I had no idea that he was in Astrakhan. OK, I can arrange that. Be seated, please; I'll do it while you have breakfast.'

'I was looking at the map,' Zidra said. 'At ferry routes.' She drew her finger down the Volga, which even more than the Urals is the great divide between European Russia and the east.

'Yes, the river boats still function,' Irina glanced at the map. 'Surprisingly enough, given that Astrakhan is in the middle of the Volga wetlands, a region which is the epicentre of catastrophe.' Her finger circled the huge tract lying between Moscow and the Lower Volga.

'This is a zone of deepening anarchy. From Kuibyshev down to Saratov there are Cossack bands roaming loose. To the east are empty steppelands. West is Kalmykia, a hotbed of unrest. Behind Kalmykia is the Caucasus: Chechnya, Abkhazia, Georgia. Only Stalin knew how to rule *them*. Here is Grozny' – she stabbed the map – 'a word which means "terrible" in Russian. Before Yeltsin flattened the place, it was the mafia capital of Eastern Europe. There were charter flights to Bogota and Palermo. You could buy anything – a guided missile, a tank, a million rifles, some fresh boys or girls? No problem, and American Express would do nicely. No one in the Kremlin cared, until Dodaev's mafia made the mistake of trying to grab a percentage of the Caspian oil flowing through Chechnya. That's when Yeltsin got mad.'

They looked at the map in silence.

'Look south,' Irina said, 'and you see an arc of states all riven with ethnic conflict: Iran, Afghanistan, Turkey. Azerbaijan is sandwiched between them, but a lot of Azeris also live in Turkey and Iran. One day there will be war in the region.' She smiled at Zidra. 'Geopolitics. I think I'll retire to St Petersburg.'

Zidra laughed. 'Is that how you encourage Western companies to come here?'

'Of course not, but you are different. Rudolf called me this morning to tell me about you.'

'I should prefer to have heard that from him.'

'You will. But now he's gone to City Hall to meet with the mayor. Perhaps you'd like to go there first?'

'I don't mind.'

Zidra ate eggs for breakfast and when Irina Belinskaya came back from phoning she'd arranged a meeting with Minakov, that afternoon.

They went by car to the vast building which housed the provincial administration. Irina led Zidra to a large conference room, whose wood-panelled walls were covered with framed photographs of pre-revolutionary Astrakhan. Young men in boaters punted their girls up and down the river. Huge bearded merchants plied their trade in the streets. A bear danced before onlookers at a funfair. It was 1916.

Most of the room was occupied by a circular table sixty feet in diameter. Rudolf was sitting on the far side talking with Dmitrov and another man, a colossus, six foot four tall, about two hundred pounds. This was Yurin, the mayor of Astrakhan.

Yurin proposed taking them somewhere informal, and they left at once. They walked through quiet streets to an imposing square whose centrepiece was a statue of an officer in 1930s uniform.

'It is the monument to Sergei Mironovich Kirov,' Dmitrov told them. Zidra read the inscription: *While one communist lives, there shall be Soviet power in the Caucasus.*

The little restaurant faced the statue of Kirov. The manager showed them up a flight of stairs to a private room, brought coffee and Stravropol cognac, ice cream, fruit and biscuits.

'Caviar is a two-billion-dollar business,' Yurin said to Zidra when they were settled and the pleasantries were over. 'But if it was organized properly, with an end to poaching, less pollution, capital invested in the fisheries, it could be twenty billion. That is what Hans Uhlaf has promised us, with British government help. We need new feed mills, new fishery protection teams, water bailiffs, boats, helicopters, new processing plants, you name it. At the moment the caviar industry is being destroyed by poachers who dynamite the fish out of the water.'

'When you arrived, *gospodin* Yurin was explaining to me how grateful they are to Uhlaf and the Plate River Corporation,' Rudolf put in.

Zidra had been studying Yurin, wondering what he knew. She decided to find out.

'You've got thirty tonnes of hijacked plutonium stored in the Raketa works,' she told the mayor bluntly, 'and that's Uhlaf's business too.'

'You're crazy. There's no plutonium at Raketa. It's an electronics plant.' Yurin's response was pure aggression. 'Anyway, so what if there is? This country's full of plutonium. Isotopes are all around, in the water, the air. That was Beria's fault, not Uhlaf's.' The words came tumbling out. 'I don't know who told you such a crazy story, but in any case you're mad to mention it.'

180

He ran a finger round his collar. 'Look, we need Plate River Corporation here. They bring capital with them. And I know Hans Uhlaf. He's a serious man.'

'Serious or not, he's shipping plutonium to Iran in two days.'

'What?' Yurin did a double take. 'Where are you getting this from?' He opened his palms at Rudolf. 'You told me this woman was connected with Plate River Corporation, and I believed you. I even heard from Uhlaf personally this morning that he was expecting her to come. So why this crap about plutonium now?'

'You're way out of line, Yurin,' Rudolf said. 'You act as if it was true. She's just pulling your leg, that's all. There's no plutonium. Take it easy.'

Zidra pursed her lips, told Yurin, 'OK, I don't need all this. Get Uhlaf on the phone now, and I'll talk to him.'

Yurin shook his head, but he called the waiter over and gave him a number to dial. The waiter got through at once and called Yurin to the bar. Zidra and the others watched him talk. He began to gesticulate, then to shout, defending himself somehow. Then he beckoned Zidra over.

'There's been a mix-up,' Uhlaf's voice said, slick as oil. 'You were taken to the wrong place – a very suspect establishment, that old Khrushchev dacha. I'm sending a car for you at once.'

'It won't be necessary. The mayor has provided me with a Volga. I'm going to look at the kremlin here, and go to an art gallery.'

This was absurd. No one was listening; they were play-acting for each other's benefit. But she kept up the pretence. He had to be reassured that she would not do anything drastic before they met. 'I've never been to Astrakhan before. Apparently there's also a fur factory.'

'As you wish, of course. Come for dinner, anyway. I'll send someone to the dacha for you.'

'Really, it's not necessary. I fully intend to join you later.' She emphasized *intend*.

The charade had gone on long enough. They said goodbye and she hung up.

Zidra went back to the others. Irina had translated her conversation with relish.

'Rudolf was right,' she told Yurin flatly. 'I was pulling your leg. You over-reacted. But you'll put yourself in jeopardy if you attack

181

me. I'm an American citizen with high-ranking connections.'

'OK, I understand.' Yurin was sweating.

'Good. Now all you have to do is organize a car. I need to meet with Uhlaf.'

'OK.' Yurin was defeated. Zidra, Rudolf and Irina bade him a frosty farewell, took his own official black Volga and left.

'You ever worry that one day your kamikaze negotiating style will get you killed?' Rudolf asked Zidra as they bounced over the city's rutted roads.

'This is the endgame, Rudolf. I'm just pissed with all this hole-in-the-corner stuff.' She punched his arm, more or less playfully. 'You refuelled that bucket of bolts of yours? I have a feeling we'll be needing it.'

'Funny, I had the same feeling. Yeah, it's juiced up.'

'What's it armed with?'

Rudolf looked at the driver. He was inscrutable. Rudolf didn't want to say much in his hearing.

'Plenty of bang. Don't worry. Vinogradov will arrive this morning with the boys. And I'll have a couple of guys sit on it and keep it warm.'

'That won't be enough,' Zidra whispered. 'You can't leave it standing on the tarmac. We need to put it somewhere else.'

Rudolf looked thoughtful, nodded. 'You're right. Too many people already know about it.' He prodded the driver, asked him to pull over.

'I need to go back to the dacha,' he told Irina, who was sitting in the front. 'I forgot something.'

The car lurched round and sped back into the city. They sat in silence for a while, thinking. Zidra motioned with her eyes to Irina: *Can this woman be trusted?*

Rudolf shrugged. Who knew? She was a Russian, at least, and not a Kazakh or any of the other hell-knows-what mixtures of Turkic, Caucasian and Mongol strains that sprawl over Central Asia.

Zidra tapped her on the shoulder. 'Why do you want to go and live in St Petersburg?' she asked.

'My daughter lives there. Katya. She's twelve.' Irina turned and gave them her open smile. 'She lives with her Babulya. I miss her. Terribly. But there's nothing for her in this place. And nothing for me there.'

'I could get you out of this life. Katya too.'

The women looked hard into each other's eyes.

'Trust me?' Zidra said.

'I've known you for an hour and a half. Sure, I trust you.' Her cheeks coloured up and she glanced at Rudolf.

'Help us, Irina,' he said. 'You know why we're here.'

'Sure. Looking for windmills.' She glanced from one to the other, wondering whether to admit what was on her mind. They waited. In a while she said, 'I have ten thousand dollars. That's the sum total of my life. I take small bribes from a German who's building a brick factory – we have special clay here in Astrakhan. And I dabble in caviar, like everyone else. Once a month I go to Petersburg and give Babulya the money. She keeps it under the floor. When we say goodbye it always feels like it's for ever.'

Rudolf dug into his baggy silk slacks and pulled out a big roll of thousand-dollar bills. He peeled off ten of them, low down where the driver couldn't see. 'I need somewhere to put something.' He finished counting, looked into Irina's eyes, smiled. 'Something hangar-sized.' He took her hand, pushed the roll into it. 'Today, like now.' He met her gaze, saw that she understood. She raised a warning finger, for him not to say more.

She squinted at the size of the roll and caught her breath. 'OK.' She smiled ruefully. 'I didn't need all this.' She took the money, anyway, stuffing it in her raincoat pocket. 'I know just the place.'

Chapter 18

They couldn't trust the driver. When they arrived at the dacha Irina invented a story and sent him to a town fifty kilometres away, taking documents to someone. They would use another car.

'Let Uhlaf's people follow him for the day,' Rudolf said. 'But we need something inconspicuous, not the Volvo I hired.'

It took Irina almost an hour to find a car and a driver who knew the region inside out. The little Lada was driven by an Armenian, grizzled, cheerful, in his early fifties, who introduced himself as Hachinyan.

They left the city again and in twenty minutes were speeding along the crest of a ridge which ran long and straight up to the horizon. Zidra looked down and saw that the ridge was actually a dike. The seething Volga raced by on either side.

She asked the driver to stop the car.

They climbed out and the three of them walked a little way down the road. Apart from the network of dikes, some of which joined the one they were on, some with roads on top, some not, there was nothing but water.

'I have to put the Mig somewhere,' Rudolf told Irina.

'I guessed what you were after, and I know of a place. Near here.'

Rudolf said: 'It's a plane. It flies. Not swims.'

'Don't worry, it's dry land. There's even a landmark for you to find it from the air.'

They went back to the car, and Irina gave the driver new directions. He turned off the main road down one of the dikes that ran from each side like the feathers of an arrow.

'I never saw the Volga delta before,' Zidra remarked.

'In summer when the floods recede it's a mass of tiny islands floating in lotus-blooms, and the breeze rustles through the bulrush beds,' Irina said. 'Then people come and picnic. They light fires and eat fish and drink beer. And there are so many fish

184

you can hardly see the water. Millions of carp mating in the shallows. And pop-cheeked frogs – hundreds of varieties of aquatic life, in fact. The whole river goes sex-crazy. Not only the river, because there's a tumult of birds too.'

They came to a fork. The car slewed off the endless, straight asphalt and sped down a side road. Ahead of them a thin column of black smoke rose vertically like a stick of charcoal into the motionless air. Sunlight had brought mist off the river, creating hallucinatory optical effects. A giant Lenin, cap clenched in his fist, seemed to rise from the water, the eyes glittering at the emptiness around. They drove straight towards the apparition, swerving on to an area of raised cinder-covered infill. A sprawl of low buildings lay on this higher ground. A rusty metal sign beside the vast mosaic of Lenin, which covered the side of a building, read: *Astrakhan Poultry Combine. Hatchery and Broiler House No. 5.*

'Please wait here,' Irina said. She ran into the building.

The driver stopped the engine. Zidra and Rudolf explored. Behind the administration block were four or five long, low sheds. They could hear the cheeping of thousands of birds. Next door was a boiler house, from which the column of black smoke belched. On the far side of the boiler house was an unfinished construction – the concrete shell of a much larger shed.

There were no other buildings as far as the eye could see in any direction.

'Perfect,' Rudolf said at once, pointing at the big shed. 'Clever girl.'

'Can you land on these roads?'

'It's brilliant. I'll go back to Astrakhan now and bring it here.'

'Do it. The sooner the better.'

'Have to square up these guys, though.'

They watched Irina and a man come crunching over the cinder track. Irina introduced them to the director of the poultry house, Gennady Izumov.

'He's desolated by the fact that they haven't had time to arrange a proper reception for you.' She grinned. 'This is Russia. You can't avoid hospitality.'

It was decided that Rudolf and Izumov would do their business while the two women made an honorary tour of inspection. Izumov's deputies gave them white coats, hats and over-shoes and took them round the poultry house. The hens went crazy. The place was immaculately clean. A manager explained why it had been built in such a remote spot. There never had been and never would be any outbreaks of salmonella in their chickens, he told them proudly.

'You can make mayonnaise with our eggs, no problem. Even though we ran out of antibiotics two years ago.'

The eggs were huge.

The last thing they saw as they left was the sick bay. Two tired Rhode Island Reds squawked bleakly at Zidra and Irina.

In his office, Izumov toasted the international solidarity of poultry producers with Russian champagne. Pink spots had appeared in his cheeks; he was wild with barely controlled excitement. A table was set and women served egg mayonnaise and chicken liver pâté. They drank cognac and the next course, egg soufflé on a bed of fried eggs, was brought. There were more toasts and then the main course arrived: fried chicken *tabak*. Izumov's men watched them eating with intense, silent interest.

'Why don't they eat?' Rudolf asked.

'They say they are not hungry.'

'Strange, lunch is really good.'

After lunch Rudolf returned to Astrakhan. They would meet later at the dacha. Zidra and Irina went to meet Minakov.

The Limnological Institute had premises in different parts of Astrakhan province. Irina had tracked Minakov to a research station upriver, where the famous Nobel prizewinner spent much of his time.

'This is where he lives,' Irina told Zidra. 'I'll take you to him, and then you'll have to excuse me – I have to fulfil another task for your Rudolf.'

They found an ancient caretaker who led Zidra to Minakov's private quarters. She waited alone in the professor's dilapidated office, which smelt faintly of fish-oil and formaldehyde, while his assistant fetched him.

As in Moscow, a large sturgeon was displayed in a glass case, and the room was filled with dusty relics of a life in science.

But there was also something different: a huge, elaborately framed painting depicting a gloomy forest. The boles of giant oaks extended in all directions. Nothing grew in their shadow.

Feeble sunlight barely penetrated the canopy. The trees were cleverly arranged to look random but in fact there was rigorous order. Zidra measured the two outer trees between her thumb and forefinger, then worked inwards. The distance between the trees reduced geometrically. The painter had plotted the romantic scene as a Fibonacci series. The effect drew the viewer's eye to the two trees at the centre. A hammock was strung between them, pierced by a solitary shaft of sunlight. A young girl reclined in the hammock, one dainty foot touching the ground, to swing to and fro. She wore Victorian clothing, with a buttoned bodice and a flowing dress of purple velvet under which the frilly ends of pantalets were visible at her ankles.

The girl's face, seraphic, untouched by life, was framed in a mass of coiffeured ringlets. One pale, exquisite hand carelessly entwined the hammock ropes above her head. The other held the book of poetry she was reading. The girl, alone in this vast, brooding forest, was smiling. Where her skin was visible, it was the luminescent highlight of the painting.

Zidra stood back to see it better. One detail made the picture work: the top four buttons of the girl's dress were undone. The impression was of innocence alone. She had loosened her clothing because of the stifling heat in that secluded place. The girl was wearing a gossamer-thin camisole under the dress. Her breasts were visible through the camisole, firm, young, with pink virginal nipples, like rosebuds.

'It's a copy of a Courbet,' Zidra heard Minakov say. She spun round. She had not heard him enter. 'I think the original is in the Prado. This was a gift from Misha Benin.'

She went to him and they shook hands. She saw at once that something had changed. He was tall, steely, with the same piercing eyes as before. But the expression was different. He looked as if something had broken inside.

Minakov was glad to see her. He poured coffee and they talked while he absent-mindedly crumbled stale cake on the coffee table.

She commented on the sturgeon in its glass case and he said: 'In dreams fish symbolize sexuality, as Hieronymus Bosch and many others knew. There are murals at Pompeii which dwell on the phallic suggestiveness of fish. But maybe there is a more physical basis for such correspondences. The most primitive parts of the human brain are inherited from reptiles. We share more with them than we know. The sturgeon seems utterly strange with its sinuous body, marvellous sensors, the purpose of which we do not understand, and phosphorescent eyes glimmering through the murk. It's a living fossil from the dawn of the Cenozoic period we are now bringing to an end. Yet the difference between the sturgeon and the girl in the painting is small. Both are creatures of instinct, both roe-bearing vertebrates. Both inhabit a mental world inconceivable to the rest of us.'

'You're teasing me,' she said, smiling.

He placed a big folder on the table in front of her, his long, beak-like nose twitching, his gaze stark and invasive as ever, as if there were some devastating secret he was forever on the point of sharing and never doing so. 'Let's get down to business, shall we? I've made an important discovery. I know where the plutonium is hidden. The exact location, here in Astrakhan, from where they plan to ship it to Iran tomorrow.'

'If so, then we will stop them.'

He opened the folder. A mass of 8x10 photographs fell out, some monochrome, some colour. Most were thermal imaging or other forms of remote sensing.

'We are able to see a great many things by satellite surveillance. Unfortunately the intentions of the mafia are not among them. These pictures are very recent; it was Misha's achievement to procure them.'

Minakov shuffled the pictures. 'Remote sensing has shown us the growing salinity of the Caspian Sea, and the effects of the increase in recent years, the mechanisms for which are not well understood.' He pointed to yellow and red whorls. 'Most of the ecological problems have arisen from two causes: the great changes resulting from the dams of the 1930s; and massive industrial pollution in the post-war period. Now there is a new danger.' He pulled out one of the pictures covered with green whorls. They all looked like expressionist paintings to Zidra; she hadn't yet worked out which was sea and which was land. 'Of course, there's still life in the Caspian. However, I'm afraid that the development of a vast new oil and gas industry will complete the achievements of our forefathers.'

Zidra watched his expressive hands moving. They reminded her of someone, but who?

'In its seventh year the sturgeon swims up the Volga to spawn and die. Unfortunately it cannot swim through concrete. When the way is blocked by a dam, it thrashes against it until it dies from exhaustion. No one thought of this when the dams were built. Now we have to fly sturgeon fry north in airborne tanks. I do not believe the sturgeon will survive another sixty million years courtesy of Aeroflot,' he said. 'Ah – here it is. The one I was looking for.'

He showed her the photograph. It was a high-resolution monochrome picture of Astrakhan.

'This was taken from the Mir space station twelve months ago.' He showed her a segment two centimetres square highlighted in red. 'The Raketa works.' The picture was the first of a series. He produced another. Fuzzy outlines of a big works, with workers' housing, service roads and a railway branch line. 'Now look.' He showed her another picture. The railway line which in the previous picture had run into the works now stopped just inside the factory perimeter. 'This was taken three weeks ago.'

'What happened?'

'It looks as though they tore up the track. But they didn't. In fact they dug out a gigantic trench and lined it with concrete.'

'And that's where they're keeping the plutonium?'

'Yes. It's utter madness, of course. In ten or fifteen years the whole area could be underneath the Caspian Sea. The water table's already risen to danger level.' He replaced the photographs in the folder. 'It is a sinister coincidence that *Homo sapiens* evolved twenty-five thousand years ago, and that is also the half-life of plutonium-239, our most enduring creation.'

'You're preaching to the converted, professor,' she told him.

'I know. Come to my office. I'll show you some maps.'

'Have you heard from Misha Benin since he sent you those photographs?' she asked him as he led the way.

He stopped, looked at her in surprise. 'You don't know?'

'What?'

'Misha Benin is dead.'

She stopped in her tracks. 'How did he die?'

'He suffered a massive coronary thrombosis, apparently.' Minakov stood in the doorway looking at her. 'His wife found him. In the toilet. He'd been dead for some time, at least six hours. She'd been visiting friends. I'd been trying to call him before I left Moscow, but there was no reply from any of his numbers.'

She stared at him. 'Misha was coming to see you. I was with him. He didn't know you'd already left for Astrakhan.' She scrutinized his eyes. Something was hidden there, some veiled truth about Benin. 'I don't believe he had a heart attack,' she said. 'He was killed.'

Minakov blinked, turned away. 'Who knows?'

'How close were you?' she asked his retreating back.

'We were friends.'

More than that, she thought, but it was impossible to say what. Minakov did not want to talk.

In his office Minakov unlocked a fire safe and pulled out a thick file which contained detailed scale drawings of the Raketa works. The railway spur joined a spaghetti of lines which led north, to the Moscow main line, west to Grozny, east to Turyev and Shevchenko, and south to the waterfront. Other pictures showed the scene in Astrakhan port: a Russian chaos of cranes, barges, lighters and tugs. 'There's berthing room for deep-draught vessels,' he told her. 'I know that one ten-thousand-tonne Iranian cargo boat is in port today; another is waiting in the Astrakhan roads.'

'I need details; pictures of the boats, profile and top-down.'

'I have no more recent satellite pictures, I'm afraid. I have acquired some snapshots of the Iranian boat *Isfahan*, though.' He showed them to her. They were murky black and white photographs taken from a distance and in poor visibility while the *Isfahan* was still at sea. They would have to do.

'Where is the plutonium now?' she asked.

'Still in the bunkers. They've slipped a day in their schedule. They'll shunt the flat cars carrying the containers tomorrow night under cover of darkness. The loading may take several nights, I suspect.'

'The only guard is the Chechens?'

'No. The factory has its own security, strengthened by a detachment of OMON Interior Ministry troops. There is also a garrison in Astrakhan. The conscripts are demoralized and likely to run away from gunfire, but the officers may not. There are several thousand men.'

'What were you planning to do?'

'I've had a meeting with the Armenians. They're disorganized and demoralized too; the Chechens have rolled on them. There isn't much they can do except cheer us on. But I have contacts among the traditional Astrakhan fishing community, as well. We might get some help from them. I was going to try to get them to dynamite the railway line. I couldn't think of anything else.'

Zidra grinned at him. 'That's not so bad – don't be modest. I suppose there's no point in doing the obvious thing and telling someone in the government?'

'No, of course not. No one in Moscow will do anything except pass your name on to the Chechens.'

'How well guarded is Uhlaf's headquarters?'

'You mean the Plate River building? It's a big former merchant's house, pre-revolutionary, in a stockade. It's very secure.'

'I've been invited there. Uhlaf is expecting me for dinner this evening.'

'How much does he know of your recent activities?'

Zidra told him about her involvement with the Lyubertsi, which horrified him, but she made him understand the inevitability of it. She described what they had learnt from the banker, Almazov. It was hard to say how much of this had got back to Uhlaf. It depended on how his business was organized. It looked as if he went to some trouble to distance himself from the criminality which underpinned his success, the way big magnates often do. Maybe he chose not to hear about some things.

Minakov looked cynical. 'Of course people like Uhlaf know everything that's being done in their name. The mask of innocence is just that: a mask. Uhlaf is the prime mover in all his affairs.'

'Except perhaps when his own people are hiding something, which is what happens when things start to go wrong. But I agree with you in principle. I'm sure he knows what's been going on in Moscow.'

'In that case, he'll certainly want you killed. You can hardly go and share his supper.'

'Why not? I'll test his ability to play charades. To begin with, he has to talk to me, find out what I know. And he has the appearance of respectability to maintain. He won't shoot me down over the canapés, in front of an eminent journalist, will he?'

'You've already said he knows of your involvement with the Lyubertsi. I'm sure he sees everything, as they say, seven metres under the ground. If you go, it's going to look like unconditional surrender.'

'I don't think so. I'll frighten him enough to let me come away again, and – what's more important – to make sure Renard stays alive. Look, you say we've got until tomorrow evening to do something. Let's go back into town now, meet these Lyubertsi friends of mine and make our final decisions. There's one thing you've forgotten: I'm mostly concerned with finding my husband, and there might be someone in Uhlaf's party who knows where he is. So I *have* to go.'

Minakov could not persuade her to stay at the Research Station, so they left together.

It was six in the evening when they arrived back at the Khrushchev dacha. Vinogradov was waiting, standing at the head of the wide stone steps leading to the threshold, hands on hips, looking triumphant, and pleased as a puppy to see her.

Chapter 19

The message Hachinyan brought to Zidra, scrawled in Russian and with no signature, was unambiguous: be at the PRC building that evening with the Goldman papers or Renard would pay the price.

Zidra insisted she would go, even though the papers were in Moscow. She had no choice. And if anything happened to her it would have no bearing on tomorrow's operation. From now on, hers was a purely private matter.

They were sitting in Irina's apartment, the discussion had dragged on and they were all tired. Minakov didn't like Vinogradov and Rudolf and didn't hide the fact. Zidra herself was bone-weary, with no appetite for Vinogradov's animal spirits. But time was short and they had to decide the details of the next day's strike at Raketa.

'There won't be a problem,' Rudolf said when he'd looked over the photographs of the port. 'We'll sink the outer one where it sits, and let the Iranians and the Russians argue about what happened afterwards. We can make the docks unusable too. They won't make any shipments tomorrow. Not that route.'

'But we should also blow up the spur line. We need to make sure the stuff stays where it is until we can get the world to sit up and take notice,' Minakov suggested.

'That's more dangerous,' Rudolf said. 'The closer we get to the plutonium, the more likely we are to hit the wrong thing.'

They were still arguing when Zidra left. Vinogradov drove her back to the dacha and was going to take her on from there to the Plate River building.

The Khrushchev dacha, with its dusty chandeliers, orange wallpaper and sagging rose-coloured curtains, was silent. The staff had disappeared for the night, apart from one old porter. Zidra showered and changed then came downstairs to find

Vinogradov. She put her big shoulder-bag on a table in the dining room. The Makarov was inside: not the one she'd bought in the car park of the Mezh, but the newer, silenced version she'd collected from a detective outside Varvarka Street.

A cue slapped down on the billiard table next door, and she heard voices. Then the door opened and a stranger walked into the room.

Four others followed him. One went to the outer door and locked it. Another padded soundlessly around the room, going behind Zidra to the French windows, from where he could see most of the entrance area to the dacha.

The man by the door, who had the dead eyes and even the callused knuckles that were the Chechen trade marks, motioned to someone else, standing in the shadow, who came and pulled the shoulder-bag away from her, then motioned her to sit.

She sat.

No one spoke. A constriction gripped Zidra's throat. She tried to stop her hands from shaking.

The Chechen wore blue Levi's, perfectly pressed, Camel boots and a blue polo-neck sweater with 'Southampton Polo Club' emblazoned on it. The one by the window had the same hard eyes and crew-cut hair. All of them wore the same clothes. It was a uniform.

Two more men came into the room and sat opposite Zidra. These were different – motley, scavenging *biznismeni*. One of them was unusually tall and thin, with a polished, domed forehead. He was wearing an old dog-tooth tweed jacket and grey flannels. The other was short and also thin. He was a Mongol, and now his half-moon face puckered in a smile.

'Where is my colleague?' Zidra asked.

'He gone for walk. Come back later,' the short one said in bad English.

'I don't know who you are, but—'

'It's OK, lady, everything OK,' he said. 'Maybe you weren't expecting us? OK, no problem.'

'My name is Ivanov,' the tall one said. 'I am Cossack. These are my friends. This is Ankha. He is from Yakutia, now the Sakha Republic. Maybe you been there?'

'Not really, no. Has anybody?'

Ankha grinned. 'Yakutia is nice place. Lots of girls. Lots of

194

diamonds. You don't worry, lady. We take you there. You like it there.'

He laughed. The Chechens watched in silence.

Then Ivanov leaned across the table so that his face was close to Zidra's. 'We make you nice proposal,' he whispered. He unzipped a leather document case and pulled out a gold-trimmed, leather bound Filofax. 'My card.'

Zidra took it. *East-west Invest Corp. Ltd. Astrakhan, Tehran, Paris*, it read in English. *Ivanov, Vladimir. First vice-president.*

'Mr Ivanov, thank you,' she said in Russian. 'But I have to go. If you have some business with me, I will try to meet you tomorrow.'

Ivanov relaxed. 'You speak good Russian. I speak good English. You saw it. But it's better for everyone to use Russian. But no. We can't meet tomorrow. Ankha flies home. We have to talk now.'

'What about?'

'What about? Diamonds, of course. Oil, gas. We invite you to Yakutia.'

Zidra looked incredulous. 'On whose behalf?'

'The President of the Sakha Republic, who else? Ankha is his second nephew. You are an important American businesswoman, and you will come to Yakutia. As the guest of the President. Ankha has a nice private plane, a Boeing. You cannot refuse. It would be seen as an insult.'

'Now I show you my credentials,' Ankha smiled. All his teeth were gold.

He opened a small velvet pouch, spilled the contents on the tablecloth.

'This is just a technical sample,' Ivanov said. 'See for yourself. The colour is good, blue, no flaws, no internal carbon. Check for yourself.' He handed her a jeweller's eyeglass.

Zidra looked down at the heap of diamonds, enough to fill an egg cup. Ankha pushed his small brown index finger into the pile and pushed the gems around, selecting one.

'We don't cut them so good,' he said. 'That's our main problem. We get lots of Israeli help. But we still don't cut so good.' He pushed the diamond towards her. 'You see, this one is three and a half, maybe four carats, flawless. Worth maybe fifty thousand US, wholesale. Maybe more.' Ankha laughed. 'De Beers got a monopoly now, that's the trouble. But this gem needs to be cut again.' Zidra held it up to the light, inspected it through the eyeglass. As Ankha said, it was flawless. No defects marred its deep blue fire.

She handed it back. 'Thank you for showing me. But I am not a jeweller—'

'We know that,' Ivanov said. 'That's why we chose you. Like Ankha says, de Beers got a monopoly on Russian rocks. They've strangled the market. Look, these are unofficial stones. They're not doped with isotopes, so they won't show up at airports. That's why we want to trade with you. This is just a small sample. Later we can do more.'

'How do you know you can trust me?'

'Ankha heard about you, we know you're connected with the CIA, maybe we can make a deal?'

'You heard wrong,' Zidra said. 'I'm a private American citizen. I'm here as a guest of the city, with a private party from a Western corporation. And I'm late for a meeting. They'll send people to find me if I don't go soon.'

Ivanov, who was volatile, irascible, waved dismissively. 'We know all that. The German, Uhlaf. The main thing is, you come from Latvia, right?'

She boggled.

'You got family, there, one or two relatives, right? I checked all this. That's good; family is the main thing in life. We know where yours is. So we can trust you.'

'What's your proposal?'

'Simple. You take these stones to Rotterdam or Hatton Garden, sell them, and you keep ten per cent.'

Ankha scooped up the glittering heap and dropped them back into the velvet pouch. He pulled the drawstring tight and pushed the pouch across the table.

'Twenty-four stones, around one hundred carats. I'd say it's worth around one million US. All you got to do is take the rocks out and sell them.'

'Maybe we can deal,' Zidra said. 'But I need to know more. Where are you from?' she asked Ankha.

'Pardon me, madam, here's my card.'

She read it: *Yakutsk Gemmology Joint Stock Research Enterprise. Director, V. I. Ankha*. There were Yakutsk and

Moscow telephone numbers.

'How will I contact you in future? Can I call these numbers?'

'No, absolutely not,' Ivanov said. He scrawled another number on Ankha's card. 'This is in Paris.'

'You have a network in Paris, right?'

Ivanov nodded.

'Then why do you need me?'

'We've been looking for something better. Paris is too expensive. Who is the tail, who is the dog, anyway?' Ivanov was nervous, his beady eyes darting.

Zidra said: 'OK, I understand. You want to loosen your collars a little, you're here doing all the dirty work while the fat cats are sitting in Paris milking the trade.'

They both grinned. She understood everything. They just wanted a compliant courier, without all the overheads the business was carrying.

'But one thing still worries me,' she told Ivanov. 'You're a Cossack, so why are you working with the Chechens? This is a problem for me. I don't mix with Chechens. And I think maybe you're just a Chechen front.'

Ivanov shook his head violently, and both men began to shout. She was wrong; they hired these guys as protection, because Chechens controlled Astrakhan and there was no other way. But it was all arm's-length business.

Zidra was unconvinced. 'Who's giving you a roof?' she'd started to ask, when they suddenly heard the sound of fighting in the corridor outside. There was shouting and a body crashed to the floor, then the door burst open and Vinogradov came flying in, blood streaming from one eye. Two Chechens rushed after him, but Zidra was on her feet and at the door in three strides.

'This man is my colleague,' she shouted. 'Leave him!'

It was Ankha who came between them, ordering the Chechens out.

Vinogradov grinned at her. 'You OK? I was worried, but they had a gun in my neck. It was hard to shake them.'

She smiled back at him. Order was restored and they sat down again, and Zidra told them at once that she'd take the diamonds but only after she'd talked to the Chechens. Alone. They didn't like it, but she insisted, so they brought the Chechen leader in and left them together.

The leader's name was Soss, and he had a lieutenant, Goga, with him. Soss refused to talk to her on her own so she called Vinogradov back in to even up the numbers.

Soss was tall, well made, extremely strong, in his late twenties. Dark and swarthy, like all *yuzhniki* – southerners – he had a broken nose and he told her at once that he and his colleagues were criminals, and had no time to waste with business talk. He was intelligent and had presence but Zidra found it was like talking to someone through a glass wall. Chechens generally reserved their feelings for their own kind.

As she'd guessed, they were calling the shots. Soss didn't mince words. Ivanov was just shit and would do as he was told. Ankha was different because he provided a flow of diamonds. They looked after him.

They would look after her, Soss offered, if she became part of the business. But if she ever crossed them, and he excused himself for saying it, they would shoot her. Soss hoped she would try to understand. It was not personal. But no one could be in business without protection. Otherwise everyone would try. It was a principle, therefore.

Zidra was unsmiling and unfrightened. 'If we ever fall out, I won't be sitting waiting for you. But in any case, I accept the arrangement. If we agree terms.'

'Sure, I understand,' he said. 'We're reasonable people, we'll reach an understanding.' He was like a sympathetic surgeon about to carry out a difficult operation, explaining the procedure. They talked more, and began to warm to each other. There was no side to Soss, none of the sexual fascism of the average Russian male. Even when he threatened her, he did it with courtesy. He respected her because she was powerful, and because she showed respect for him.

He told her he hoped they would meet later, after she'd seen Hans Uhlaf.

Zidra was growing accustomed to her appointments' being public knowledge, and anyway this gave her the opening she was looking for. She wanted to know what the Chechens thought about Uhlaf – and why, intriguingly, they had formed the idea that she was his business associate.

Uhlaf was a clever German, Soss said. They were in big business with him.

198

But who, in this context, did Soss mean by 'they'?

Soss looked askance. Who did she suppose? Papa, of course. The big Chechen Papa, who wasn't in Grozny at all, but in Moscow.

While they'd been talking, a couple more Chechens had entered the room. Zidra watched them stiffen now, but Soss didn't blink.

So was this Chechen Godfather selling plutonium to Iran? she asked, and it was as if somebody had opened a window and let the frozen air from the Volga inside.

Soss looked at his fingers, then at her. Some people, he said after a while, thought something like that. But nothing was what it seemed, so they'd better not talk about it. He spoke so softly it was hard to catch the words. 'We know you are CIA-connected. That makes Astrakhan a dangerous place for you. Better keep out of the big stuff. There's plenty of good money to be made without all that.'

'OK, then let's get back to basics,' she said and watched life flow back into the room as Soss told her what she needed to know about Astrakhan.

There had been caviar wars for three years now. The Chechens were winning, taking over the trade. Anyone who opposed them was shot – policemen, politicians (there were several honest ones, they'd been surprised to discover), Armenian rivals, anybody who tried to stop the privatization of the fisheries, the processing factories, the whole distribution set-up, which was passing into the hands of Chechen-controlled fronts, their bigwig Moscow allies and their foreign friends.

Like Uhlaf's company?

Exactly.

Throughout the conversation, Soss and Goga had never exchanged looks, never smiled, rarely shown any kind of emotion at all. The chemistry between them was all in the mind. Now they both stood up at the same moment. Goga said goodbye at once and left, offering Vinogradov an ironic handshake first. There were no hard feelings.

Soss nodded to Zidra. She walked him to the door. 'We're the third generation, already,' he told her. 'Our fathers taught us when they came back from exile. We can't be stopped. Not everyone understands that.'

Goga came back with Ivanov and Ankha. They seemed

subdued, especially Ivanov. In front of the Chechens, Ankha handed over the little pouch of Yakut stones to Zidra. They shook hands, drank Georgian cognac, and left, and Zidra headed for Hans Uhlaf's palatial offices.

This conversation had shown one thing: as she had said to Minakov, sometimes subordinates don't tell their boss the bad news. Obviously, no one wanted to tell it to the Chechens, even Hans Uhlaf. He'd had to pretend that Zidra was on his team.

And that explained why Uhlaf was sitting quietly, waiting for her to show up, knowing she'd come because she wanted Renard back.

It was past nine when they arrived at Plate River's offices. Zidra had Vinogradov drive them slowly around the mesh of tiny alleys and rutted, dank, ill-lit streets in which the PRC building was embedded, to give them a good look at the lay-out. The area was silent and deserted. She told Vinogradov to wait in a quiet side road, near the PRC perimeter wall.

Then they drove round to the main entrance and Zidra left the car and walked through the gates, announcing herself to the guard. In a few minutes, the big entrance door was thrown open and Uhlaf himself appeared. Adjusting to the gloom on the path from the gates to the house, he didn't see her at first. Instead he stopped and looked round, like a fox sniffing the dogs above its lair. Then he spotted her, raised an arm in greeting and came down the balustraded steps to meet her.

Outside the arc-lit compound, thick fog curdled over the town and the unsleeping Volga.

He needed to decide about Zidra.

Even when he had met her in Moscow a couple of days before, he had not realized how she fitted in. Had still thought or hoped she was the trophy wife of a superannuated CIA man. His associates had even then not relayed to him important details, like a murder, an abduction, and the real history of this fearsome woman. Appalled, he'd only begun to hear the truth when they were already in the Learjet on the way to Astrakhan.

Benderby, as usual, exuded confidence. But what Uhlaf saw was events spinning out of control. That the woman should have homed in on a key link in the whole business was not just worrisome. It was a bonfire of all his ambitions.

His only hope of salvation was the embarrassment of Western governments.

The paid-off politicians fearing exposure. The corrupt merchant bankers facing ruin. The hubristic central bank officials confronting nemesis as national currencies unravelled. A servile press shamed by the revelation of its wilful blindness would shield him.

The solidarity of all that self-interest would enfold him. Its agents would protect him.

Julian Benderby would save him. *Had* to save him.

Uhlaf stared down at the woman standing in the spill from an arc light, while the mist that crept off the Volga shrouded everything else. He gave silent thanks for it and glanced upwards. No stars were visible. The fog swirling over Astrakhan defeated every form of surveillance.

He had given the orders. The loading was to be brought forward.

Tonight the first ship would be readied. Tomorrow, with no one to witness it, the boat would sail south to Moallem Kelaieh.

While he'd been watching her, he'd made his mind up.

They would kill her. Tonight.

Chapter 20

At least now there was no argument in Renard's mind about where the leak had sprung.

It was the Irish Republicans and their leader Sean McMahon who'd betrayed his mission.

Within a day, two at the most, they'd take delivery of the plutonium for real. Maybe they already had – Renard was missing at least a day by his reckoning, when he'd been unconscious in a clinic somewhere.

He still couldn't walk. When they decided he'd live they'd trussed him on a stretcher and put him in the back of a van. The drive was a long one. When it ended, they took him blindfolded from the van, and carried him through narrow doorways that were hard to negotiate and down a steep set of stairs into a cellar of some kind. Dank air that smelled of sour fruit and rot. And there was something else – an acid tang which he could not place for a while and then identified: it was printer's ink, the old-fashioned kind. The place was a printer's shop.

When they removed the blindfold, before the lights were turned out, he glimpsed the cellar. There was an ancient stone sink where servants or poachers had once prepared game. Then the door slammed shut and bolts were rammed home. He was in darkness and silence. Entombed.

But he knew the place. This was the cellar of the antiquarian bookstore he and Zidra had been watching for weeks. The Eden Castle bookstore that was used as a safe house by the IRA Active Service Unit who'd set up base in the area.

The bookseller, life-long closet Nazi, was an old man, shuddering with decrepitude, driven only by the embers of a dying malice, but still making himself serviceable to any cause no matter how perverse which declared itself the enemy of queen and country.

Hitchens was a very English kind of fascist. An eccentric who had shown personal bravery during his service in a tank battalion in the last year of the war, only to become caught up in the last post-war writhings of fascism, supporting with an eccentric's mad energy the pitiful lost causes of the right throughout the 1950s and 1960s, and finally retreating, broken, to one of the remotest towns in England. And here his prolonged retirement had suddenly, unexpectedly flickered into life for the last time.

Besides selling books, Hitchens worked as a jobbing printer on an ancient Dana printing press, making up stationery, parish newsletters, and agendas for the Women's Institute, the British Legion, the Conservative and Unionist Club. He was a recidivist political intriguer who meant to keep his grimy fingers stuck into the byways of local life. He knew everything and everybody for fifteen miles around Eden Castle, and his spider's brain hoarded the dried husks of other people's lives.

And one day a young man had come to his shop to browse, stayed to chat and left promising to return. The man was pleasant, educated, in his early thirties, a well-spoken Irishman who was a banker or broker, by the name of Jenkins. He was thinking of settling in the area. He had relatives nearby. Like himself, he said, they came from an old Galway-based Anglo-Irish clan.

Hitchens would serve. With the utmost discretion he would help Jenkins find a remote farmhouse in the hills, would point him at a bent local lawyer, would give him the dirt he needed to keep the lawyer quiet when he bought the property for cash under an assumed name.

Hitchens would help Jenkins cultivate the Eden Castle constabulary, which consisted of two constables and a part-timer, all of whom could be bought in their own way.

Above all, he would give Jenkins a social route map, an indispensable guide to remaining anonymous in a small, gossipy market town.

Jenkins had done his homework, knew enough of Hitchens' past to know he could be used. He did not discuss his mission, operating strictly on a need-to-know basis. But Hitchens soon worked out what was afoot, and was pleased to be a part of it. Was pleased to volunteer – without waiting to be asked – all the compromising information about himself which his new master needed to be sure he could be trusted. All the perverted disciplines of a fascist past came flooding back at the prospect of inflicting carnage and mayhem on innocent lives.

*

Renard had plenty of time to think in Hitchens' cellar. His thoughts were not comforting. First of all, Hitchens had recognized him as the American who'd been staying locally.

There were more serious worries. President Morgan had believed Irish republican claims of good intent, but now their peaceful talk was shown to be a crude lie. They meant to carry on their military campaign to force the British out of Ireland.

The whole charade of co-operation between McMahon and the CIA was a device to hook President Morgan and cynically use his good intentions. Sinn Fein's secret, unofficial meetings with the President's representatives, in Dublin and Washington, had created a groundswell of opinion in the Administration that the IRA was serious about wanting a negotiated settlement. Insistently, they had told him they wanted peace. But they were lying – that was clear now. If nothing else, Renard's disappearance would be its own warning to the President to act accordingly.

Renard assumed that the republican plan was to put new pressure on the British by keeping all their assets in place, maintaining readiness to resume and intensify their mainland campaign, while persuading the gullible Americans to forcefully intercede on their behalf with Whitehall. They took advantage of the American President's known dislike for the British Conservative government, who had even sent political advisers to help the Republicans in the last presidential campaign. President Morgan's dislike of the British Prime Minister was personal – he called the PM a sonofabitch, told his Secretary of State the man was a 'hypocritical, sanctimonious, snot-nosed bastard', and swore there would be no Special Relationship with the British during his tenancy of the White House – except on his terms, and they included a new deal for Ireland. 'They need us more than we need them,' he'd said in Renard's hearing, 'and we'll show them just how much.'

The Irish republican leadership knew all this, knew that they'd been dealt a potential ace and planned to use it.

Unless the President could be warned, he would end up humiliated, exposed as a tool of Irish extremism. Sooner or later someone would even notice that the President's Irish ancestors were probably not Catholics at all – he was descended from good Scottish Presbyterian stock, which had settled for generations in Ulster before finally emigrating to the States.

Preventing all that presidential embarrassment was a priority in itself. Either way, whatever happened now, any result short of an amicable settlement in Ireland, one acceptable to all parties, was likely to do lasting damage to America's relations with Britain, its oldest, proudest ally. The stakes had been dramatically raised. And Renard was out of the game.

He had spent an agonizing night cramped on the stone sink, his waist chained to a heavy ring which from the look of it had only recently been set in the wall. Medieval methods had their uses.

Next morning, it was Hitchens who came to see him.

After prolonged darkness, even the miserable glow from a weak lamp in the passage outside the cellar was enough to dazzle Renard at first, but he recognized the old man.

Hitchens slid the bolts back on the cellar door, left a paper plate with sandwiches and a jug of water, and was leaving without a word when Renard called out his name.

'I know who you are,' Renard said. 'I know all about you, Hitchens.'

The man slammed the door shut and Renard heard him scuttle away.

He came back an hour later to remove the slop-bucket.

'I need medical treatment,' Renard said. 'I have septicaemia in my right foot. If I die you will be held responsible.'

Hitchens stared at him, shone a feeble torch at his feet.

They were bandaged, but the bandages needed changing. Renard's feet had been torn apart by the barbed wire, and he still couldn't place any weight on them. The pain had grown worse, apart from an ominous numbing of the toes of one foot.

'You can see it's serious,' Renard insisted.

'What can I do?' Hitchens said, his laugh a nervous cackle. 'I'm not a doctor.'

'You can change these dressings, or give me clean water and fresh dressings and I'll do it myself. Or tell your bosses. Otherwise you'll be blamed.'

'No one will blame me,' Hitchens said. 'I'm doing my job.'

'Do you know who I am?' Renard asked.

'You're the American traitor,' Hitchens said. 'I know they plan to shoot you, so you won't be needing your feet, will you?'

'You're a fool. I'm a US diplomat on official business. I've been kidnapped unlawfully, and if you've been left alone with me then it's you who'll go down.'

Hitchens shook his head. 'I'm not alone,' he said 'You are.'

He locked the door, disappeared up the steps again. But this time he left the passage light on and Renard had the benefit of a faint glimmering through the cracks around the door.

Hitchens returned a little later with a bottle of strong antiseptic, a bowl of clean warm water and new bandages and lint. He left Renard to dress his wounds.

'I need scissors,' Renard said.

Hitchens thought for a while, then refused. 'You'll manage,' he told him. 'You're a big boy.'

'But I can't see in this light. Be reasonable. I'm chained, I can't escape. Either bring a light here or leave the door ajar.'

Hitchens repeated, 'You'll manage,' bolted the door and went upstairs.

He did not return that day, but maybe Renard's words had some effect because next morning he had visitors.

Pete was the first to appear, Pete the girl-segmenter, and his arrival did not encourage feelings of confidence in the prisoner. He hauled Renard from the cellar, ignoring the gasps of pain when his torn, inflamed feet fell on the broken step-ladder. As they emerged into a filthy back room, which smelt of printer's ink and unwashed clothes, Renard glimpsed himself in the broken mirror on Hitchens' wall. He looked like a portrait by El Greco, his unshaven face somehow elongated, bleached by gloom, the eyes hollow.

When he'd got used to the light, he saw that two other men were present. Hitchens was not one of them.

Pete, never placid, this morning was incandescent with rage. The malevolence barely contained within his frigid exterior had burst out. Now he shoved Renard in the back, catapulting him across the room. 'Take it easy!' one of the others snapped. 'There's no need for that.' The speaker smiled bleakly at Renard. 'Perhaps we'd better go upstairs and talk. Follow me, please.'

Renard looked at Pete's seething back as he complied and wondered what kind of conflict required the services of such a dysfunctional thug. Every kind, he realized, from Ireland to Somalia to Yugoslavia.

'Come on,' the one who'd smiled said softly. 'We're near the end, let's relax. Colm, help Mr Renard upstairs. Pete, go and get some bandages. Antiseptic and stuff. Please.'

Pete glared, opened his mouth to speak, thought again and left. 'You'll reimburse me,' Renard heard him mumble as he pushed through the rickety door which led to the front of the shop.

The outer door slammed and the tension left the room at once. The soft-spoken one said, 'My name's Jenkins, Paul Jenkins.' He waved to the other man, who already had a hand under Renard's elbow to help him up the stairs. 'This is Colm.'

'Pleased I'm sure,' Colm said. He was Irish as the day is long.

They led Renard upstairs to Hitchens' living quarters, which were even more squalid than the business premises below. Tattered linoleum, curled at the edges, browned with age and incrusted with years of neglected filth, lay under a few broken chairs and a narrow bed heaped with grey sheets and soiled blankets.

Jenkins went to the sink in the corner and filled a kettle. 'A nice cup of tea will do the trick.'

Colm fetched hot water from a hissing, creaking geyser and gave Renard soap and a towel, then silently left the room.

When he'd cleaned them up, Renard saw that his feet, though inflamed and discharging from several puncture wounds, were healing better then he'd hoped.

Jenkins brought tea in big chipped mugs and gave one to Renard. Hitchens had not been near him for nearly twenty-four hours and his thirst was raging.

'We're going to Ireland tonight, Mr Renard.' Jenkins drank his tea, looking troubled, even scared. Not the image of a hardened IRA Active Service Unit commander. 'Our leaders want to talk to you. They don't understand some events which have occurred in the last few days. There are two ways to do it. We can smuggle you over, which wouldn't be at all comfortable for you, and might be difficult for us. The British watch who's coming and going very carefully. The alternative is for you to come voluntarily.'

Renard grimaced. 'And Pete doesn't like anything voluntary.'

'Yes. That's why he's bitching. He doesn't agree with how I'd like to do it. But the way I see it, there's nothing to be gained from treating each other like children. You need to talk to our people. They're anxious to meet you. No one needs to be forced into it, do they?'

'You're full of surprises, Jenkins.'

'Yeah.'

'Look, I do plan to meet your leadership. So I agree to go voluntarily to Ireland with you.' Jenkins instantly grinned with relief. 'Only—'

'Only what?' The grin disappeared.

'Only no changes of plan without prior discussion. That's my condition. If something comes up unexpectedly, tell me about it before you start to go ballistic. OK?'

Jenkins capitulated. 'OK, Mr Renard. I would like your undertaking that you won't try and contact anyone or to leave us for any reason until we get where we're going. I'd be satisfied with that. I don't doubt you're an honourable man.'

'And what happens afterwards?'

'That's not for me to say.'

Renard opened his mouth to speak, but just then a door slammed downstairs. Jenkins raised a finger to his lips. He took two strides to the stairwell. It was Colm. They exchanged words which Renard couldn't hear and then Jenkins came back, looking in more of a hurry then before. Leather-soled shoes slapping the bare wood of the steps followed him, and Colm re-entered. He looked round in surprise. 'Pete not back yet?'

'He'll be holding up the bar in the Lamb and Lion, the sod. Leave him there. We don't need him.'

'I didn't credit him with being so trusting.'

'He isn't. He's watching out the window, don't worry.'

'I'm not worried at all,' Colm blurted. 'I'll have his fucking guts for garters one of these fine days.'

'Why do you keep him around? Renard asked.

'We don't keep him around,' Colm spat with anger. 'It's others who wished him on us.'

Jenkins raised a warning hand and the Irishman shut up. 'What Colm means is, we inherited him and he makes himself useful from time to time.'

'Is he coming with us?' Renard asked.

'No. Of course not. He's not one of ours. We don't even want him here.'

'That clarifies things, anyway.' He looked from one to the other. 'And now, if you don't object, I'd like to use the bathroom. I need to clean up.'

'Show him,' Jenkins told Colm. 'I'll be downstairs.'

'Sure. I might even have a disposable razor you can use,' Colm offered. He led the way to a long and narrow bathroom, checked that Renard had the necessaries and left him.

The bathroom jutted out from the rear of the house, over an extended kitchen. An old-fashioned sashed window opened easily but there was a thirty-foot drop to the ground. Big old-fashioned cast-iron pipes ran down the wall, and there was an unkempt garden backing on to the narrow street at the rear.

Renard closed the window, filled the sink and began to wash his face. The bathroom was squalid, but the water from the geyser was hot. Renard took his time to freshen up.

After a while he heard a sound like mice scuffling behind plaster. He concentrated and the mice became voices, whispering. The sound came from a small grille set in the wall near the ceiling, above the sink.

He knew what it was – a Victorian ventilation pipe, installed to carry smells away. The grille evidently opened into one of the acoustically resonant cast-iron pipes he'd seen outside, rising from the kitchen below. Painfully, Renard climbed on the toilet seat, gripping the ceiling-high cistern by its rusty edge, and put his ear to the grille. Now he could clearly make out Pete's voice, talking in a hissing whisper to Jenkins in the room below.

'We'll do it like I say,' Pete said. 'We'll hit them on the day.'

'I need to get new instructions,' Jenkins whispered, urgent, compelling. 'Too many things have changed, and now we've got the Yanks on our backs, so I've got to talk to McMahon—'

'Fuck McMahon!' Pete shouted, then hissed again: '*Fuck them!* It doesn't change anything! In any case, the Yank will try to persuade McMahon himself, that's the only reason he's here, you fuck, because otherwise I'd have killed the sod.'

'Why should he do that?'

'Because otherwise he'll lose his whore-wife. Don't you understand *anything*?'

'Even so, I can't do anything without fresh orders,' Jenkins said doggedly.

'We're going to do it, you fuck, no argument. She'll give you the money. You bring it to me, like we decided.'

'But suppose McMahon decides not to continue with it? Suppose the Yank blocks them despite his wife?'

'He can't block anybody,' Pete sneered. 'He can't stop the

delivery, because *the delivery already happened. The stuff is already in Wales.* Understand me?'

There was a silence and then a shuffling sound. Then Jenkins again, this time incredulous. 'I don't believe you.'

'You don't believe me,' Pete mimicked, sneering. 'Asshole! We're not playing some kind of game, you stupid Mick bastard. *It's been here for a week already.* And the Russians are here too, so now I need the money to pay them off. It's a whole fucking warhead, Jenkins, primed and ready to go. And I'll detonate the bastard myself, just for the fuck of it, if I don't get what I want.'

'You're mad. Anyway, you couldn't do it.'

'Oh, yeah? Well, you're wrong. This is kid's stuff. I know the priming sequences and launch codes, and if I don't they'll show me. If we don't get the money we'll do it, and that's what you can tell McMahon, asshole.'

'So you've got the warhead?' Jenkins asked in a queer voice.

'That's what I said.'

'It changes things.'

'It changes everything. So what do you say? It's your own wife, for chrissake. What's the problem?'

Mystified, Renard listened as Jenkins began to speak again, but just then Colm knocked at the bathroom door and yelled: 'Are you all right, Mr Renard?'

Renard abandoned his perch and went close to the door. 'I'll be right with you, Colm. Give me a couple of minutes.' He crept back to the lavatory, craned up to the ornate vent to listen.

Silence.

Jenkins and Pete had finished their talk.

He grabbed a towel and left, limping down the passage and almost colliding with Hitchens who was stumbling up the stairs.

He'd brought the phone with him, an ancient Bakelite instrument with its leads knotted like intestines and dragging behind. 'It's for you,' he said to Renard, holding out the handset.

It was Zidra.

Chapter 21

Hans Uhlaf led Zidra into the Plate River Corporation building, handling her with exaggerated politeness as if she was so fragile she might break. They entered a large lobby and the first thing she saw was Henrietta Broughton coming toward them. She'd just emerged from what must be the dining room, at the lobby's far end.

'Zidra! Is it really you?' she said, hurrying to meet her, embracing her, squeezing her tight, whispering, '*I've been so worried*,' then springing back to gaze at her. 'But how are you? How did you get here? Hans said you were in Astrakhan, but we only said goodbye in London last week!'

Zidra was speechless. This was the last thing she'd expected. She struggled to find words. 'Hans invited me,' she said at last.

Her friend took her hand and led her slowly back down the hall to the dining room. There was something so touching in her obvious, barely concealed concern, in the warmth of her physical closeness and the solidarity of the hand holding hers, that Zidra wanted to cry. Lady Broughton ushered her upstairs to the bathroom, shooing Uhlaf away with the promise to be down again in five minutes.

It was nearer half an hour. Zidra literally cried on Henrietta's shoulder, and took time to steel herself again, while Henrietta talked, trying to comfort her and showing obvious and real affection.

'My God, you poor girl. Derek told me the awful things that have happened, some of them anyway. No doubt he kept the worst bits back. But he said you were also attacked, just after we said goodbye. A Kalmyk assassin, in the middle of London! You must still be in shock!'

'That doesn't matter – I'm just desperately worried about Douglas.'

'And poor Bob Hill! Does he leave a wife?'

'Yes.'

Lady Broughton shook her head with dismay. 'Dreadful. For something like that to happen in England!'

'I know, but we knew the risks. And let's face it, it could have happened anywhere.'

'Of course, but it doesn't diminish one's outrage. Do you know what the kidnappers want, yet?' She shook her head, biting her lip. 'It's impossible to understand or even work with these people. You cannot imagine the stories Hans has told me about the mafia here in Astrakhan.'

'I was terribly surprised to see you here.'

'I'm a trifle surprised to be here myself. It was Derek's idea to send me. He was pencilled in to come and inaugurate the Know-How Fund's fisheries protection project, which Hans is supporting. But the Queen's impending visit put paid to that, so here I am in *locum tenens* as it were. Twenty-four hours of delicious peace and quiet with only one ghastly civic reception to worry about, before going back to the madness of Moscow. That was the idea. Completely spoilt, now, of course, by what's happened to you. Actually, I have a suspicion Derek stayed in Moscow on your account.' Henrietta opened her mouth to say more, and hesitated.

'You want to know why I'm here?' Zidra asked gently.

'I didn't want to ask, and you'd probably better not tell me anyway.'

'We haven't any secrets, Henrietta, you know that. It's because of Professor Minakov.'

'Him!'

Zidra laughed ruefully. 'He seems to know something about what's happened to Douglas,' she said, 'and I came here to talk to him about it. Bit of a wild goose chase, I expect. But you never know.'

'There's a big reception tomorrow evening.'

'I know, and I know he'll be there.'

'I hope you'll come too. I'll die without you.'

They stood up. In the miraculous way of an English diplomat's wife, Lady Broughton had created an atmosphere of normality. It was inconceivable that anything untoward would happen while she was around. Zidra decided to say nothing about Hans Uhlaf. Lady Broughton might cease to be an asset and become a semihysterical liability. That had to be avoided.

They were ready to go back down. Lady Broughton was magnificent in a dazzling while cocktail dress, covered in white beads and natural pearls. She smoothed it down; like the pass of a magician's hands, it changed her. Suddenly the ambassador's wife, brittle as Bohemian glass, was back. 'I'm sure everything will be all right. I'm sure you'll get him back, he's so clever and strong anyway,' she said. 'He's a survivor, like you.' They touched hands and then Lady Broughton leant towards Zidra, so that the diamond necklace she wore over a plunging neckline swung free, leaving tiny powder marks on her throat. 'I'll be praying for you,' she whispered.

There were four guests seated at the table. Uhlaf introduced them: David Gour-Hemmings, a jejune red-cheeked banker from Palfrey & Griblock, bowing and stuttering compliments as if it were a Hunt Ball; Heidi, Uhlaf's personal assistant, a willowy blonde from Bavaria, whose iceberg smile sucked heat from the air; Jack Reid, from the *Financial Daily*; and Julian Benderby, Gour-Hemmings senior colleague, who nodded and said nothing.

Lady Broughton sat next to Uhlaf. She rested her hand on his. 'Hans is such a generous host, my dear. I'm sure he'll strive his utmost to accommodate you, if you'll allow him to.'

'Thanks. And thank you, Hans,' Zidra said. 'I don't want to inconvenience you, though. I know how busy you must be just now.'

'With the caviar project. Yes, of course.'

'And all the other deliveries you have to make.'

He smiled bleakly at her. A waiter fussed with chicken terrine, then helped her to caviar. She took two thick slices of Borodinsky bread, plastered them with butter, piled them with caviar, and pressed them into a doorstep sandwich. 'Excuse me, I'm hungry,' she announced, then said to Uhlaf through a mouthful: 'Speaking of which, how are your Iranian deliveries going?'

He blinked. 'I'm sorry?'

'Aren't you delivering thirty tonnes of caviar to Iran tomorrow? So I heard.'

He laughed. 'Hardly. That's about the entire annual catch. If I had three tonnes I'd be pleased as punch. Who on earth is spreading such rumours? Only poachers have access to such quantities.'

213

A few of the others laughed politely with him. 'I am so pleased to see you here, really. We shall have to have a private talk,' Uhlaf said. 'I mean, if you are really interested in these things. Are you?'

'In the caviar trade? I eat the stuff.'

'So we see!'

'I don't have any commercial interest in it. I think of caviar as something beyond all that. It's priceless the way a human being is. No one has the right to deal in people. No one should mess with the poor sturgeon either. Because you never know what will happen.'

Uhlaf smiled broadly. 'We definitely must discuss your eccentric theories, Zidra. But not now – they are too dangerous for public consumption.'

'Why's that?' Reid asked. He'd been watching Zidra, and following her example had made himself a matching sandwich.

'Zidra is a romantic, and she wants to subvert you all with theories which could only result in death by starvation if she pursued them to extremes.'

She chewed in silence; Reid grunted something non-committal.

Zidra looked around the table for someone else to talk to, while waiters brought the main course – chicken *tabak* and wild boar. She felt the weight of Benderby's presence beside her. He was turned slightly toward her, silently eyeing her up, judging her. There was mockery in his face.

Gour-Hemmings, the boy-banker from Palfrey & Griblock, who seemed to notice nothing, asked if it was true she had arrived in a Mig, and told her about the time he went up in one – Julian Benderby had arranged a flight. He'd be interested to compare notes with her. Who was her pilot?

Someone from the air training school, she told him.

Uhlaf said he'd stayed at the Khrushchev dacha once, hadn't slept because of the sound of the river. He'd send a car over to collect her things. She wouldn't spend another night there.

A waiter brought more wine, and the conversation flowed back into its original channel, almost as if she was not present. But the slightest move she made silenced everyone, so that the talk didn't rush as swift and straight as a navigation between dikes; it stuttered and gushed and meandered.

Gour-Hemmings explained to them his plans for privatizing the Astrakhan poultry industry, which he would buy with not much

214

more than a business plan and a few containers of antibiotics and chicken-feed. It would be a kind of hobby, not a big deal like the caviar business, of course, but a steady earner. Heidi listened without hearing. She was riveted to Zidra. Finally Uhlaf sent her away on some pretext. Gour-Hemmings went with her, his ruddy face flushing. Reid looked indecisive, then muttered some kind of farewell and left as well. When Lady Broughton stood, everyone else did too. 'Come with me, Zidra,' she said, extending a hand.

Zidra made as if to go, but Uhlaf said: 'Lady Broughton, I wonder if I might spend ten minutes with our charming guest. She had a meeting with Professor Minakov today, so my spies tell me, and I'm quite anxious to find out what the old devil is going to say at the reception tomorrow night. I don't want any surprises.'

'Don't keep her long,' Henrietta said in a severe voice. 'She's tired, poor girl.' Then she relented, let him bow dutifully and told him she knew he meant well.

Waiters came and cleared the table. They offered drinks. Uhlaf had whisky and soda. Benderby took port. Zidra didn't take anything.

The waiters left, closing the double doors behind them.

They were alone: Zidra, Benderby, Uhlaf.

Benderby sat close to her, their knees almost touching. When he reached over and placed his drink on the table, they did touch. During dinner, he had not spoken to her. But she had not seen him speak to anybody else either.

Uhlaf sat to her left, at the head of the table. He did not offer to adjourn to more comfortable chairs. He sipped his whisky in a troubled silence.

Zidra was half turned to Uhlaf, so she was facing away from Benderby. She held Uhlaf's gaze, but when she spoke the words were for Benderby.

'I know that you are responsible for the abduction of my husband, Mr Benderby. And I want you to tell me where you are holding him.'

Benderby guffawed, and slopped his glass back on the table. 'I heard you were direct,' he said, exchanging looks with Uhlaf who got up and left the room without a word. Benderby went to the door and locked it.

When he came back he put a hand in his pocket and with theatrical slowness pulled out his exerciser. 'It's a mad world, isn't it?' He squeezed the exerciser, making its springs squeak. He was jocular, good-humoured. He walked about the room, his black patent shoes kicking at the carpet. He went to a humidor on the sideboard and took a Havana cigar, lit it with a cast-zinc lighter shaped like a 1940s Buick roadster.

'I like you,' he said. 'You've got more balls than most people. Harvey Goldman for example. You got to him before me. That was clever, too.'

'You found time to look for him, then?' she asked. 'I thought you'd already left for Astrakhan.'

'I've been looking for him for two weeks. People in Moscow I thought were serious were looking for him. They couldn't find him. We were already strapped into the Learjet when we got Dubok's frantic little message that you'd got to him first. That's why we were late getting here.'

The thought of Benderby's mad scramble back into Moscow to try to limit the damage she'd done was compelling. It meant the Goldman archive was just as important as she'd thought. 'How did you find him?' she asked.

'The Moscow police found him, lying on the pavement outside his flat. His neck was broken. You didn't know?'

'No. That wasn't my idea.' But Rudolf had been right not to ask her – and right to do it. 'You were running like hell, then,' she said. 'You must be more desperate than you look.'

'What do you expect? That's why it's so convenient your dropping in here tonight. We checked in Goldman's flat. We know you stole his papers. That was clever. But I need to know who has them now.'

'Where is Renard?'

Benderby hawked derisively. 'Not much of a conversationalist, are you? Just the one thought. I want to discuss Goldman's papers, if you don't mind.'

'Where is Renard?'

'Tell me about Goldman's papers.'

'It's all coming apart, isn't it?'

'You haven't been the most helpful elemental force I've met recently.'

'It's worse than you think. You don't know who I've talked to. Or how I've insured myself.' She laughed at him. 'You don't know where I've put my *In the event of my death* missives.

Perhaps you'll find it in your electronic mail one Monday morning. Probably the whole Internet will be reading it. It's a nightmare, isn't it?'

Benderby stared at her. 'Tell me what else you've been up to.'

'What do you want to know?'

'Who you've been talking to.'

'The CIA.'

'Really?' Benderby looked sceptical 'Not the important CIA. Not the real CIA. Or I'd have heard about it. What about the Defence Intelligence Agency? Rung them yet? No?'

She was silent.

'But that's where your Renard comes from.'

There was a flicker of an eyelid at that.

'You didn't know?' He noticed everything. 'That he was DIA? So he strung you along all this time.'

'You're talking crap.'

He watched her in silence for a while.

'I know you haven't talked to Broughton,' he said eventually. 'But that's because you sussed something was wrong there. That was clever; I'd have been on the *qui vive* a bit there, too.'

'You're fishing. You don't know anything.'

He gave her a long look, pulled out a pack of Marlboros, offered her one – she refused – and lit one himself.

'Let's see, then. You haven't talked to any of us Brits. That's understandable. We're shifty and unreliable. The coolies of the Anglo-Saxon world.'

He went on staring. His eyes made Soss look warm.

The stare grew, began to fill her mind. He'd started to see the truth, much as she blocked it.

He straightened up. 'You haven't talked to *anyone*, have you?' It was a kind of epiphany. 'You *haven't* insured yourself. You had no time. You came from England like a cork from a champagne bottle.'

She didn't answer.

He stretched, yawned a little. She watched his pale tongue lick his lips. Benderby wore a silk suit which had been sculpted to fit his stoop. It was expensive, but it was over-used. Benderby sat down too much. Smoked and ate too much.

'So all I have to worry about is the Goldman papers. Maybe that won't be a problem either. You left Moscow in a hurry, too. You couldn't have organized much. So the papers are with Minakov. Or they're being held by the Lyubertsi.'

He was clever. Didn't leave many stones unturned.

'How will you get them back?

'Pryapov will do it for us.'

'You trust Pryapov, then?'

Benderby grinned. 'The mayor of Moscow wants to send his obese little child to an English school. One day, when he has to leave Russia in a hurry, it's us he'll come to.'

'Then he'd have reason to keep the papers if he found them. As a guarantee of your good reception.'

Zidra watched him break a *Romeo y Julieta* in pieces and crumble the tobacco, sniffing it.

'You can trust me as much as you trust Pryapov,' she said. 'I'll swap the papers for Renard.'

'Which means, the Lyubertsi do have them.'

'I'm making you an offer.'

He sighed, crossed his legs, flicked ash away. There was a long silence while he thought about it. 'Very well, I agree. But unless you take me straight to the Goldman papers, I shall have to kill you.'

She laughed. 'What guarantee do I have that you'll let Renard go after I give you the papers?'

He thought, then said, 'As they say in insurance, I'll give you an illustration. I'm a banker. Sort of. When a client wants to buy something from a foreign country and he's afraid to pay cash up front, we arrange a Letter of Credit. It's between two banks, the buyer's and the seller's. We take the buyer's money, irrevocably. That's the seller's guarantee. And when the seller proves to his bank that the goods have crossed the frontier, his bank pays him the equivalent amount. That's the buyer's guarantee – his money is safe in his bank till he gets the goods. The banks take the risk, but they trust each other.'

'Thanks for the lesson. So who's going to stand surety in this transaction?'

'You will give the papers to someone in Moscow whom we both trust to do what is necessary. I will hand Renard over to some equivalent person in England. Renard will be freed when the papers are passed safely to me.'

'Who do you nominate in Moscow?'

'Yura Pryapov.'

'If he gets the papers, he'll keep them.'

'No, I've already told you, he needs us. Anyway, that'll be my problem, won't it?'

'Then I suggest James Wilshman in England.'

'The Foreign Secretary?'

'Yes.'

He looked at her in silence. 'Assuming it's even remotely possible, and it seems like fantasy, why him?'

'Renard will agree to it, for one thing. Renard would therefore be a voluntary hostage in his hands, so no one will be able to accuse Wilshman of false arrest later.'

'Why should Renard agree to voluntary imprisonment?'

'To free me, of course. You're holding me, remember?'

She watched him think it over.

Even if Benderby accepted the idea, would Wilshman agree? There was plenty of reason why he should. Goldman's archive contained a scandal that could blow his government away and perhaps destroy the Conservative party for ever. That would be reason enough. It still left Wilshman free to clean the MI5 stables later, discreetly. And having custody over Renard would not compromise him later – it would be presented as securing his release from his present captors.

But she didn't believe Benderby would agree, for fear of being purged afterwards. Unless he had been acting under orders all this time. In which case British Intelligence was conniving at the supply of plutonium to the IRA, amongst other crimes. Was *that* possible? No, of course not, so he wouldn't buy her proposal.

'OK, I agree,' he said, and watched her slowly expel breath. 'You look surprised. Are you?'

'Yes, I am. OK, good.' She frowned, still thinking it through. 'A deal is a deal.'

Then Benderby surprised her by suddenly offering to let her talk to Renard. Now. By phone. 'What could be better evidence of my good intentions than that?' he said.

'Obviously, I'd be delighted.'

'Wait here.'

She watched him walk into the next room. He was heavy, like a big cat.

Why had he agreed so easily? An idea that seemed absurd – particularly since it involved Pryapov – had suddenly got serious.

He was gone for a while. She could hear him talking on the phone, first in Russian, then in English.

Then she heard him say hello to Renard.

Suddenly Zidra felt she was suffocating. The room revolved slowly; she was afraid of fainting. She could hear her heartbeat. The pounding slowed but didn't stop. She wondered if death was like that: a hovering in some final moment of expectation without end.

Benderby was back, standing before her. She hadn't seen him enter.

'Come on.'

She followed him into the drawing room beyond the double doors. There was a high-backed, shiny leather chair. It was new, like everything else; you could smell the leather. Next to it stood an imitation Louis XIV table, with a retro-style white telephone, the kind with a separate extension. Benderby spoke into it first. 'You hear me, Renard? OK, I'm saying this to both of you. The rules: speak normally. Nothing I can't understand. No subtexts. Plain English. I'm keeping my finger on the crossbar.'

'OK, Benderby,' Renard said. Zidra nodded her agreement.

She grasped the handset, said hello. It was a digital line. There was no background noise. That meant a satellite link, because Astrakhan's public service was ancient analogue.

So Renard wasn't in Russia.

She said hello again.

Renard answered. 'Are you well?' he whispered. She was tongue-tied. Idiotic silence beamed thirty-six thousand miles into space and back again. 'Zidra?' She still could not speak. 'Zidra?'

'Renard?'

He began to repeat a verse: '*Stay me with flagons, comfort me with apples: for I am sick of love.*'

'I love you, Renard.'

'I love you too.'

She said more, but Benderby had already disconnected.

She turned round and the room and Benderby and the city slowly came back.

'I didn't get the verse,' Benderby said, his face black with anger. 'And I told you both: no messages. No open codes.'

'It's from *The Song of Solomon.*' She struggled to speak. '*My beloved is mine, and I am his: he feedeth among the lilies. Until the day break and the shadows flee away.*' She gave him a tight little smile. 'You were too quick to cut us off. It was harmless. It has no hidden significance, don't worry. It's just a beautiful sentiment.' There were tears in her eyes now. 'Thank you for letting me speak to him, anyway.'

Benderby seemed to relax a little. Maybe the poetry was innocuous. Almost certainly it was, but he didn't let go until she touched his arm.

He relented. 'It was my pleasure. For what it's worth, what happened to him was not my idea. I presume you know that.' He leant close, stared intently in her eyes, and whispered, astonishingly: 'I face the same danger, believe me. I did my best for him.'

She stared back. 'You can tell me now. Where he is.'

Benderby laughed. 'I'll give you a clue. Keep going long enough, and you'll come back to him. Hypothetically.'

'I don't understand.'

He shrugged, led her back through the dining room and on into the lobby, pushing her gently towards the door.

Uhlaf was waiting for them.

'You're taking her to the boat-house?' he said in a nervous croak.

Benderby didn't answer, but she saw the look in his eye and then everything was clear. They were going to kill her after all.

'I don't understand why you need to do this,' she whispered.

'You're some kind of fool, Uhlaf,' Benderby hissed. The gun he'd produced seemed to come from nowhere. It was small, chrome-plated, flashy, the sort of prize they give away in some Los Angeles gaming rooms. He held it to her neck with his left hand, locking her wrist with his right.

'You created the situation yourself, Zidra,' Uhlaf told her. 'You didn't leave us much alternative.'

'Can it, Hans!' Benderby said, furious. He pushed her to the main door.

'I'm glad I saw you again, Hans,' she said over her shoulder. 'Because you didn't ask me about tomorrow, and I wanted to tell you.'

'What about tomorrow?' Uhlaf looked angry too, now.

'I know your boat won't sail.'

Uhlaf's eyes gleamed like a nocturnal rodent's in the subdued light of the hall. 'What boat, Zidra?'

'The sailing to Iran,' she said. 'The first plutonium shipment.'

Benderby reacted first. '*Fucking* Minakov knows about Moallem Kelaieh. It has to be him.'

'Don't worry about it,' Uhlaf said in a voice suddenly as smooth as snake-oil, staring venomously at her. 'I've already made arrangements. The Chechens will deal with them. Tonight we'll close down both him and the Moscow gang she brought with her. There won't be a problem.' He smiled at Zidra. 'Goodbye. I don't believe we'll meet again.'

Benderby glared at Uhlaf. 'I'll take her to the boat-house. But I'll be back. Be waiting, Hans. I want some answers.'

The three of them suddenly froze. One of the PRC's robotic staff had appeared from nowhere to answer the doorbell that none of them had heard. Zidra wondered how long he'd been standing there, listening.

The caller was Vinogradov.

He sized everything up at once.

Benderby was a big man, slow-moving, unfit, but solid.

Vinogradov had him on the floor like tossing a pillow. The little chrome gun sailed through the air and landed on the drive somewhere beyond the front door.

Zidra stepped over Benderby and retrieved it.

Uhlaf had pressed an alarm bell, and the noise was shattering. People were running from all over. Vinogradov held a gun to Uhlaf's head.

'You need me alive, Hans, not dead. I'm more dangerous to you dead. Tell him,' Zidra said to Benderby, shouting over the howl of the alarm, as the banker struggled to his feet.

'She's right, Hans. We need her,' Benderby said. 'I wouldn't have killed you,' he shouted to her. 'You know that. And we still have a deal.'

'What deal?' Uhlaf cried. 'What deal?'

Armed men had formed a ring around them. But Zidra had the little gun and it too was pointed at Uhlaf's head.

'Amateur,' she whispered. 'And one more thing, Mr Benderby. *You will have to release Renard.* Whatever happens to me. Because if you don't, or if I don't return to Moscow to collect them, the Goldman papers will be sent to the NSA. In four days' time. Think about it.'

Benderby shook his head. 'No papers, no Renard. This changes nothing. You will have to come back to me.'

Zidra stepped out of the house and walked towards the gates. Vinogradov pushed Uhlaf in front of them and the circle of guards slowly gave ground. 'Don't anybody use a weapon! No firing!' Uhlaf was yelling as they pushed him down the drive. Vinogradov's boys appeared at the gates. A car backed in, then another.

More of Uhlaf's guards piled out of their quarters. The compound filled with men. It was a stand-off.

Dogs barked. Cold air off the steppes filled the city. The fog was thickening.

Somewhere a riverboat honked its foghorn and another boat answered.

Chapter 22

Back at Khrushchev's dacha, there was mayhem.

Rudolf and his boys were having a party. When Zidra arrived, a big and blowsy woman called Leonora was curled awkwardly into Rudolf's side. She was like a raspberry torte, the kind you want to put your fingers into. When she sashayed around it made Zidra laugh.

'I can't stay here,' she said. 'You've turned it into a brothel.'

Rudolf grinned, blew a kiss at her, and said, 'Your limnologist is an all-right guy. He's cute with maps and stuff. We worked out a few nice moves for tomorrow.' Rudolf hiccuped.

Zidra looked over to where Vinogradov was standing. 'Take your boss somewhere quiet and talk to him. *Now.*'

'No problem. The cars are waiting. But so is Soss, upstairs.'

'OK, I'll find him. But get Rudolf organized. We're out of here in five minutes.'

She ran upstairs to meet the Chechen leader, Soss.

'Thank you for coming,' she said. 'I wanted to get our lines straight. So teach me the rules.'

'Like I said, you must pay your protection, like everybody else.'

'How much?'

'Five per cent.'

'How much is that?'

'How many gems did you receive?'

'Twenty-four.'

'So give me one.'

'OK.' She pulled out the pouch. 'But then I want something from you.'

'I'm listening.'

'I want you to look out for Professor Minakov, the biologist.'

Soss gave her his watery smile. 'What for? No one will harm him. He's irrelevant.'

'I know for sure that the PRC people will go after him.' She handed him a three- or four-carat cut stone. He looked at it critically in the light, then pocketed it. Zidra watched him, suppressing impatience. Outside, she could hear car engines firing up. Uhlaf's men could arrive any time.

'OK, I'll see to it. He'll be in good hands.'

Soss stood up. They said goodbye, shook hands and she walked him to the door. As he was leaving, he said, 'Don't stay here tonight.'

She studied his face. 'I heard there would be trouble. I wasn't sure you were involved.'

'Leave Astrakhan. Go tonight.'

'No, that wouldn't do. I can't leave yet.'

He shrugged. 'OK. It's your decision. We finished our business, I think.'

A few minutes later, Zidra, Vinogradov and a sobered-up Rudolf left the dacha by the back door, avoiding the local KGB who would report any movement to Uhlaf.

Vinogradov led them to where an old, inconspicuous Volga was concealed in a stand of scrubby birches, and in a remarkably short space of time they were coasting through the empty city squares. No one followed.

'Where to?' Vinogradov asked.

'Irina Belinskaya's. We'll be OK there. Rudolf, you'd better go straight on to your other henhouse.'

Rudolf laughed. 'Not so much fun there.'

'You can polish your plane. Stay with him,' she told Vinogradov.

A great weight had been lifted from her that evening. She knew where Renard was. He had told her, and Benderby had confirmed it. *Keep going long enough, and you'll come back to him.*

Keep going long enough in a straight line and you'll come back to where you started.

Eden Castle.

She would find him, but where in the town had they placed him?

The lines gave no clue to that. Or did they?

Whatever, she only knew she wanted Renard. Wanted to sleep with him, to feel his hard body, to nuzzle him and smell his smell.

It was late when they reached Irina's place. She was in a shift, had been in bed, and her eyes were crinkly with sleep, but she embraced Zidra warmly.

They sent Vinogradov and Rudolf away and Zidra crawled into Irina's big bed with her and they nestled up like sisters in a dreaming forest.

Zidra dreamt she was a Chinese girl, with bound feet. She wore silk socks like small bags, tied at the ankles with red ribbons, and apart from a heavily embroidered kimono that divided loosely like a cape, from the throat down, she was naked. She was on a swing in a rose-garden, with fountains and lotus-blossoms, not sitting straight but with her knees hooked round the bar, her hands holding the ropes, while two girls pushed.

A mynah bird sang. The trapeze rose and fell. The kimono fluttered out behind.

Renard stood in front of her. He was naked, and he was aroused. The girls were pushing her back and forth, back and forth, on to him.

It was six-thirty when the crackle of gunfire in the city woke them.

They lay still, listening. 'It happens often enough,' Irina said. A mortar went off. The blast was deafening. She sat up suddenly. 'But not like that. Usually it's just kids in the street.' She looked worried. 'I'll make tea and call for a car.'

'Don't rush,' Zidra told her. 'We're safe enough here.'

As she spoke an enormous rumbling boom came up from the city, followed by a thunderclap that echoed hollowly around the tallest buildings. Then they could hear the rattle of small arms fire.

They leapt out of bed.

From the balcony of Irina's fourteenth-floor studio flat they had a panoramic view of Astrakhan. It was grey dawn. Here and there high buildings like their own shone like sapphires in the first sunlight. It was cold.

Nothing moved. There were no sounds of people, cars, sirens.

Only gunfire and, in the heart of the city, a black pall of smoke.

'It's the docks,' Zidra said at once.

'It isn't.' Irina went indoors, came back with a pair of Tento 40x60 binoculars. She scanned the city.

'It's the Khrushchev dacha,' she said with finality. She passed the glasses to Zidra. 'You can clearly see it.'

Zidra had different eyes, it took a while to focus each lens. Her fingers trembled. When she finished, all she could see was the pall of smoke, and occasional orange tongues of flame.

She swung the glasses left. The river and the docks were in full view. Cranes hung motionless like the beaks of birds. Ships were double, triple berthed. To the right, back past the column of smoke, was Astrakhan's white kremlin.

They watched for a while – ten, fifteen minutes. The chatter of AK-47s continued, but the intensity grew less.

The wind that came off the steppes was biting. Snow was forecast, and the climatic peculiarity of Astrakhan, with temperature drops of twenty or thirty degrees overnight as winter clamped down, was making itself felt. Irina went for blankets. In a few minutes she went for tea.

They began to hear the far-off sound of sirens – a few. A very few.

Zidra looked around the vast colony of tenement-blocks where Irina lived. Here and there, lights had come on. People readied for work and school. A few inhabitants appeared briefly to see what was going on and went back indoors.

Then Zidra saw the flash and the vapour trail of a missile.

'It's near the Raketa works,' Irina said.

The missile wrote crazy curlicues over the sky and faded like a spent firework. Another, then a third, traced fire over the azure morning.

'They're nervous, they were too quick,' Zidra muttered, and then the whole building shook in the vast roar of the Mig as it shot almost directly overhead.

They watched the big jet weave like a fish through the tenements, then catapult at telegraph-pole height down the main drag into the city.

'*Rudolf!*' Zidra shouted. 'My God, he must be going at six hundred miles an hour!'

The Mig banked over the Astrakhan kremlin and rose sheer in the air, howling like a banshee, then looped back down.

Zidra danced a jig, shouted *Go for it, Rudolf!*

They watched the Mig tumble around the sky over the city centre, watched tracer come up from somewhere, and then the Mig began dumping decoy foils and they saw a fusillade of Stingers swirl up from around Raketa. But the decoy flares foiled the Stingers' infra-red detectors, and the Mig leapt away out over the Caspian, its afterburners glowing white.

'What happened? Did they shoot him down?' Irina yelled.

'Not yet they didn't.'

Now the two sides had squared off. Each knew where the other was. It had begun.

The Mig must have had a stand-off weapon because the next thing they saw was the blast of a bomb out of an empty sky directly hitting the docks. The plane was high, out of sight, and the Chechens had no answers. Then came another direct hit.

Then silence for four, five, six minutes. At last they heard the far-off drone of a jet.

'He's waiting to see,' Zidra said. 'He's good. He's really good.'

'To see *what*? I don't understand.'

'You will. It isn't over.'

After a while another blast shook the Raketa works.

'That wasn't airborne,' Zidra said at once. 'Maybe the Armenians did something. I hope so. They'd be crazy not to – the track runs straight from Astrakhan to Grozny—'

She stopped. The Mig appeared, falling like a star from way up.

More Stingers erupted, maybe half a dozen. 'Christ, they've cornered the world market,' Irina muttered. It looked overwhelming.

They watched the Mig fall with teasing slowness. There was a muffled double boom. 'Sound barrier,' Zidra commented. Rudolf bottomed out a thousand feet over the city, barrelled down the river, ducking through the Stingers.

'Don't wait, Rudolf, get out of it!'

Through the glasses Zidra watched the splatter of rockets over the water, saw ships berthed in the harbour convulse and sag; amid the vast plumes of water a waterfront crane started to keel over.

There was a shattering explosion in the port. Another plume of smoke began to billow. A ship was on fire. Maybe another had settled on the berth bottom, Zidra couldn't tell. She slowly scanned the waterfront. Visibility was worsening; smoke and haze were clogging the air.

Irina was shouting, tearing at her arm. Zidra put the glasses aside, looked up and saw the Mig harried by a shoal of Stingers, saw the blast as one got near Rudolf's tailpipe, watched the Mig start to spin crazily.

'*Bale out, Rudolf!*'

Suddenly the plane levelled off, then cruised like a roller coaster out over the Caspian, billowing smoke.

They didn't see it fall, didn't see a parachute either. But they heard the sound as it hit the water.

Zidra and Irina stared out at the empty immensity of the Caspian for a long time. When they turned back to the town, the port was burning fiercely. Now there were many more sirens, and more neighbours grandstanding in nearby apartments.

They went back inside. Zidra sat down and poured the tea. In a while Irina stopped shaking. Then Zidra said: 'It was a nice *son et lumière*, Irichka, but after this I need to leave Astrakhan.'

Irina stared blankly at her.

'You better come with me, Irichka.'

Irina went to the window. 'Is Rudolf dead?' The city centre was shrouded in smoke.

'Maybe. Maybe he baled out.' Zidra stood, went over to the other woman. 'Irichka, we should call Minakov.'

'Minakov is not the person we need now,' Irina said mechanically. 'We need to think. They'll be looking for you; me too if I don't show at the office. Unless they think you're dead.'

'Why should they?'

'We don't know what happened at the dacha. But as far as anyone but Vinogradov knows, you spent the night there.'

'It makes no difference. I have to go. Maybe you too.'

'We cannot go direct to Moscow. They'll be watching the airport. And there won't be any ferries after today.'

'But the way out by road is too dangerous. Think, Irina. We need to get a long way away.'

Irina put an irresolute hand to the phone. 'It's too risky to make calls,' Zidra said at once.

'A businessman I know sells fish and caviar to a company in Almaty. He flies there once a week, on Thursdays.' She looked at Zidra. 'Today is Thursday.'

Zidra bit her lip. 'There are daily flights to Heathrow from Almaty. Maybe that is a way.' She looked at Irina. 'What will you do?'

'Go to Petersburg. I'll sit in Kazakhstan if I need to, first, until it dies down. Everything gets forgotten in this country, in time.'

'You're right. No one will chase you there.'

'I need to call Babulya.'

'Later. First phone your friend, but call from a neighbour's, not from here.'

Irina put on a coat, was about to leave when they heard the doorbell. She crept across the room and peered through the peephole. She opened the door at once.

It was Vinogradov, and he was wounded. A metal splinter had passed through his arm. Irina found bandages, left Zidra to dress it while she went to a friend's house to make calls.

'So – tell me your story,' Zidra said, dabbing iodine on the wound.

'I drove Rudolf to the chicken farm. We spent an hour and a half trying to start the plane. I thought it wouldn't wind up, but it did in the end. Then some guy came running out and told us there'd been a phone call. Someone in the city, warning us. Next thing, there was a convoy of cars coming to the poultry farm. Rudolf got the Mig up before they arrived, and strafed them.' Vinogradov's eyes lit up. 'There were wrecks all over the place. Mostly in the water. Then he set off for town and I followed.'

'You went to the dacha?'

'Yes. But the place went up before I arrived. I don't know what happened. There was a fire-fight, and then the whole place suddenly went up like there was a tonne of Semtex in the basement.' He shook his head in wonder. 'There was nothing left, just matchwood.'

'There were no roadblocks?'

'Of course. That was what delayed me. I had to go kilometres upriver and then double back to the spot where I brought you out last night.'

'How did you get injured?'

'I was trying to get close to see if there were any of our boys left, which was stupid because there weren't. Then a grenade went off. After that I came here.'

'In the same car?'

Vinogradov grinned. 'No, of course not. Don't worry! And guess who's downstairs? Professor Minakov.'

'Minakov?' Zidra was amazed. 'Why is he here?'

'He turned up at the chicken farm just before I left. He'd heard something.' Vinogradov grimaced. 'He was frightened by the shooting, but he didn't show it.'

She tied off the bandage and let him up.

'Minakov has his ecology mafia, that's how he hears things,' Vinogradov said. 'Everyone is in a mafia.'

'No, they aren't. How's that feel?'

'Not good. How bad is it?'

'You'll live.' She went to the samovar, poured tea. 'What happened at the docks?'

'I don't know.' Vinogradov went to the window. 'Whole place is on fire, looks like.'

'Why did you leave Minakov downstairs? He must be exhausted. He's not as young as you.'

'I wanted to check the place first.' He stood up. 'Fucking *yuzhniki*,' he said. 'They got Rudolf.'

'Maybe.'

'Yeah, maybe.' Vinogradov shook his head. 'I'll go get Minakov.'

'Hurry. We need to be going.'

Irina returned before Vinogradov. She hadn't been able to reach her pilot, probably because he was already at the airstrip at Narimanov, a settlement thirty kilometres north of Astrakhan.

'But if we go there we might find we've missed him,' Irina said. 'Or he might refuse to take us. And there'll be roadblocks.'

'Fuck the roadblocks. And if he's there, he'll take us. If not, we'll find another way.'

Minakov arrived, looking grim. 'You've managed to sink one of the Iranian boats,' he told Zidra. 'But the plutonium was loaded last night. *It was on that boat*. So we've engineered the catastrophe we tried to prevent.'

'Don't be so sure. Which boat?'

'The one that's berthed in the port. It's sitting on the bottom now, so it won't sink deeper. But it's burning. Theoretically, the containers are fire- and bomb-proof, but we shall see. I don't have any faith in Spetzatommontazh technology.'

Zidra said, 'We did what we came for. No plutonium will go to Iran. And the vessel wasn't sunk at sea. I presume a port can be cleaned up.'

Minakov looked sour. She wondered if he had a stake in the perpetuation of eco-nightmares. The thought annoyed her. 'Someone died for this. Let's remember that.'

'Heroic folly!' Minakov raked his fingers through his hair,

paced the room. 'I need to call Moscow. If these local fools try to organize the clear-up themselves, they'll make disaster inevitable.'

'If they plan to hush things up, then maybe you better *not* call from here. They'll kill you first.'

He stopped at that. 'You're right, of course. But it's inconceivable that they'd kill me—'

'Why? A lot of heads will roll now.'

He sat down opposite Zidra. 'What do you advise?'

'We're leaving, I hope. Come with us.'

'How are you going?'

'We need to get to—' She'd forgotten the place. She looked at Irina.

'Narimanov.'

'Thanks. There's an airstrip there, and—'

She stopped. Minakov and Irina were glaring at each other. Zidra had never seen Minakov look so angry.

Chapter 23

Minakov paced to the window of Irina's flat. The pall of smoke over the docks had thickened at its apex, like the cap of a poisonous mushroom. When he turned to face the others he was beside himself with rage, and when he spoke he almost screamed the words: 'So you're in the caviar game, eh, Belinskaya?'

There was a long silence before he glared silently at Zidra instead, barely containing his anger. 'Your friend here is a *kontrabandistka*. She's involved with Armenian smugglers.'

'That's a lie,' Irina said at last. She looked miserable.

'Narimanov airstrip – I know what that is. A patch of grass used by an Armenian caviar mafia.'

'If you know a better way—'

Minakov was livid. 'They take fresh-caught caviar, out of season, to European Russia—'

'Kazakhstan, actually,' Irina spat. 'What do you know about it? It's been a way of life for centuries—'

'Wait a minute. You said Kazakhstan? And you want to go with them?'

'Yes.'

'Why not fly to Moscow?'

'We don't have any choice, Peter,' Zidra said appeasingly.

'But where in Kazakhstan?'

'Not far from Almaty,' Irina said.

'Where, exactly?' Minakov insisted.

'The plane lands at a place called Cholpon Ata.'

'That's nowhere near Almaty. It's not even Kazakhstan, for heaven's sake. It's Kyrgyzstan.'

'It's an hour's drive from Almaty. Why should you worry?'

'Because I'm a member of Yeltsin's cabinet, remember? I can't just arrive somewhere unannounced.'

'You have to decide, Peter,' Zidra told him. 'Now. Because we need to be going.' She looked at Irina. 'Frankly, I don't give a fuck where, so long as it's out.'

'How do we get to Narimanov without being stopped?' Vinogradov demanded.

Minakov said slowly, 'That's no problem, I know a way.' They looked at him with surprise. 'I'll show you,' he said. He'd decided.

The others made ready to go, but Irina sat helpless. Zidra packed a few things for her and made her find her essential documents. 'It's still your flat, you'll be back,' she told her. 'You won't lose anything.'

'Wait.' Irina went to the kitchen, found a bottle of Malinovka – brandy made from Caucasian mountain raspberries. '*Na pasashok*, for the journey,' she said.

It was sweet, aromatic, but strong. She poured a thimbleful each, and they drank a hasty toast, and left.

'It's a helluva long way to Almaty,' Vinogradov complained in the lift. 'Further than Moscow.'

'Nowhere is further than Moscow. It's a different planet,' Zidra said. All she wanted was to get out of Astrakhan, out of Russia, and back to England.

Because if they thought she was dead it might mean they wouldn't be looking for her.

But it also meant they could kill Renard at last. Because they had only kept him alive to guarantee her silence.

Minakov took them to a small jetty with buildings and a boatyard operated by the Limnological Institute.

Amidst a jumble of hawsers and sailing debris, parked on a slipway above a berth crammed with small boats, was Minakov's air-cushion craft.

It took a while to start the motor. It hadn't been used for months. Minakov was no technician, and his maintenance staff were not around. It was still before nine.

The craft was designed to take two men and a dog. There were four of them, and it took them two hours to get upriver to Narimanov. Once they were away from the main waterway and locked in a maze of shallows known only to Minakov, they saw no one until they were almost in the small settlement.

It was nearly noon before they'd made their way to the airstrip, concealed behind tall trees and collective farm buildings.

The plane was still there. They could see a truck parked nearby, and men loading boxes.

Irina had called up one of her local associates, and it was his white Volga which took them to the airstrip. Even so, the unexpected sight of a car brought armed men running. One of them was the plane's owner and operator, Timur Ter-Sarayan, a gangly, weary-looking Armenian with several gold teeth and chocolate-brown eyes, who began shouting at Irina as soon as he saw Minakov.

It took a while to explain what had happened, but when the Armenians got the idea that the hated Chechens who were infesting Astrakhan had taken a dent, their attitude changed for the better. And Minakov was in so much of a hurry to stop the possible discharge of plutonium isotopes into the Volga delta that he was placatory. Enmities fomented in decades-long caviar wars were settled in half an hour, while Ter-Sarayan's men reorganized the plane.

What finally proved decisive was the private conversation between Zidra and Ter-Sarayan. She paid him with four of the Yakutian diamonds – one for each passenger.

They took off at nine in the evening.

The plane was a small, twin-engine Yak turboprop, designed to carry three or four passengers and a tonne or so of cargo. Ter-Sarayan had not sacrificed much to the comfort of his unexpected passengers: only two of its seats had been put back on the plane. Minakov sat up front in the second pilot's seat. Behind him, the cramped hold of the plane was stuffed with cardboard boxes containing tins of caviar: one tonne of state-certified Grade Nine, superior quality osetrina, worth at least a quarter of a million dollars in the fashionable new restaurants and hotels of Tashkent and Almaty, with their many foreign visitors. The rest of the space was filled with boxes of dried *vobla* fish that filled the cabin with their smell.

Vobla is hard-dried fish, best dissected at leisure with a sharp knife, then swallowed with plenty of beer. Ter-Sarayan had packed a few crates of strong German lager and Vinogradov cracked the first while the shimmering ribbon that was the Volga was still visible behind them.

The Yak touched down just after midnight at Kzil-Orda, a steppe town several thousand kilometres from anywhere. Half the

235

cargo was unloaded, to be taken by road to Tashkent, the capital of Uzbekistan. The plane was refuelled and ready to take off only after three in the morning.

For the last leg of the flight, Minakov changed places with Irina, who'd been sitting in the cabin talking to Zidra. Irina had wanted to sit by Vinogradov and tend his wounded arm, and now they shared the second pilot's seat. She was, Zidra decided, a charming but lonely woman. Minakov was surprisingly cheerful. He told Zidra that he'd learnt more about caviar mafias in the past two hours than the previous twenty years. He sat facing her across the small table strewn with *vobla* chippings, and told her that they would clean up the plutonium. They would clean the moral decay in Astrakhan. They would even clean up Russia. He offered her a beer.

Zidra looked forward: Ter-Sarayan was telling Vinogradov about Nestorian Christianity. The plane was on auto-pilot. Irina was giggling. It meant that she and Minakov could talk.

While he carved up another *vobla*, she told him she knew who he was. And Misha Benin. She said she didn't know why the discovery had shocked her so much, but it had. 'He was your brother, wasn't he?'

Minakov froze. Then he leant across the table. 'You are the first person to guess that. I congratulate you.'

'He was a very charming, funny, good man,' she said. 'A good Russian – like you, although you're so different.'

'How?'

'You're not charming. You are terrible, austere.'

Minakov grinned. 'I am the presidential adviser for ecology. That means I am Cassandra on the walls. Would you want that burden? To announce apocalypse to the room full of drunks which happens to be the current government of Russia?'

She drank the beer. 'You know how I guessed?'

He shook his head.

'Your hands. They're expressive, like his.' She leaned forward. 'I have another theory. You were twins.'

'Also true. Again, I congratulate you.'

'So what happened to make it a secret?'

'Our father was a senior diplomat, and our family was based in Paris until Misha and I were six or seven. Then our father was accused of cosmopolitanism. It was 1950 and Zhdanov's cultural

236

purge was at its height. Our parents disappeared in the camps. Misha was sent to a KGB orphanage and I was despatched to a special school run by the Academy of Sciences in Odessa. I don't know why it was done like that.'

'But you found each other, later?'

'Twelve years later. I was a student at Moscow State University and he was a KGB cadet. Misha decided that we should reveal to *no one* the truth about our relationship. He considered this would make it easier for him to assist me in my future life, and I was in no position to doubt his judgement. So that was how we began.'

'I should say you are a most unusual member of the Russian government.'

He laughed. 'Something which will soon be rectified, no doubt.' He stared at her. 'It's a long way to Almaty. I never realized how hard our *kontrabandisti* have to work.'

Zidra smiled. After a while she dozed.

Minakov was sleepless. For him, procrastination and delay were finished. He would begin the battle the instant he reached Almaty.

Irina slept, curled in Vinogradov's lap, his good hand snuggled round her breast. She dreamt of coral reefs in the sunlight.

Vinogradov looked at the unwinking green and orange dials and listened to the motors. Whatever happened he would not go back. Would not return to the life of a *thief-within-the-code*, to a silence which was not honour after all but just anticipation of death.

Ter-Sarayan held up stiff in his seat, staring ahead.

Outside, the steppes without end – sand, scrub and grass empty but for pipelines and nomads and occasional townships – unwound into another day.

The uplands reached into hills.

Stars faded. A rim of light appeared in the east, stuck through with the dark jagged teeth of a mountain range. Ter-Sarayan turned and said: 'Not much farther. That is Tien-Shan, the mountains of Heavenly Peace.'

Daylight came.

The plane left Kazakhstan and entered Kyrgyzstan, the border republic that stretches across the swath of mountains fronting China. The steppes had begun to undulate, now they broke apart.

Ter-Sarayan woke the others as the Yak coasted down towards Lake Issyk-Kul, visible as a splash of white, brilliant on the smoky landscape. For a time it disappeared as they rounded a hillside. Then suddenly they saw it again, shining like a star, impossibly high in Tien-Shan's thousand-kilometre crumpled vastness of abyss and cloud-wreathed peak that sweeps north towards the Gobi desert and south towards to the Himalayas.

Irina sucked in breath when she saw it first. 'That's Issyk-Kul? My God, what Russia gave up when we abandoned Central Asia.'

'Beautiful, isn't it?'

Zidra crawled from a fastness of sleep as Irina and Vinogradov shouted at her to look. She hoisted herself up and peered over Ter-Sarayan's shoulder. The lake was now only a mile or two distant. On either side of them, valley sides reared up to heights which were impossible to see from inside the plane; then suddenly the Yak was free, swooping down in the final descent over Issyk-Kul. The iridescent green and gold shores of the lake stretched out of sight fifty kilometres south and east. The intense milky-turquoise blue of the water looked opaque as opal but as they shot over an outlier Ter-Sarayan shouted: 'Genghis Khan!' and they could see, a hundred feet through the water, the bleached bones of towers and city streets. 'Six hundred years ago the Golden Horde built a city here,' he told them. 'Right here, on the shores of the world's highest lake. Then the waters advanced and swallowed the city.'

He yanked the stick and the Yak reared nose-up. Ahead lay the sprawling feet of the Celestial Mountains, their summits invisible behind coral-pink cloud, their sides home to a hundred glaciers that still sometimes disgorge the frozen remains of Genghis Khan's warriors.

'We're flying in a straight line to the base of Pik Pobyeda,' Ter-Sarayan shouted, referring to Victory Peak, Tien-Shan's twenty-four-thousand-feet-high crowning glory. Its coral-pink immensity crowded out the sky.

As the far shore of Issyk-Kul swept under them the Yak soared briefly then plummeted on to one of the great stone toes that jut from the rock-filled ravines. They glided through spume and a spray of rainbows, and roared to a halt amid the files of old cedars and emerald-green pines that march up Pobyeda's riven sides.

Zidra was the last to emerge from the plane. During the flight she had realized that she would have to return to Moscow. She could not go direct to England. It meant losing a day, maybe two, but she needed Goldman's archive. There was no other guarantee of Renard's safety.

If Benderby had decided she was dead, killed in the shoot-out at the Khrushchev dacha, and if he believed her story that the Goldman file would be in the hands of someone at the US National Security Agency in a few days' time, he would run like hell to Moscow in order to try to retrieve the papers from the Lyubertsi. When they were in his hands, he would have Renard killed.

She went in search of Vinogradov.

'How's the arm?'

'Better.'

'Good. Look, I'll have to come back to Moscow with you. I can't leave for England yet. I need to get Harvey Goldman's papers.'

Vinogradov nodded. 'I wondered about that. They'll be in Rudolf's Leninskii place.'

'Who else can access them?'

'It's hard to say – especially if Rudolf is dead. But in principle no one was allowed in there without his explicit say-so.'

'Who can you call, to find out what's going on? Whether it's safe for us in Moscow?'

'I've been thinking about that, too. Until we know what we achieved in Astrakhan, we don't know whether we're heroes or the damned. So I don't know who it's safe to call, yet.'

'But you must make a start. Minakov is in a hurry – he's worried about plutonium leaking into the Caspian. And if Minakov starts calling before you, and we're only villains and not yet heroes, then we're going to get Moscow KGB on our heads in twenty-four hours, even here in Kyrgyzstan.'

'Twenty-four hours or less.' Vinogradov stamped his foot in the sand. 'I think you should hole up here for a day, while I take Minakov to Almaty and find out. It'll be safer if we make calls from there.'

'OK. Minakov's lost his best KGB contact, by the way – Pryapov's people killed him.' She took him by both arms, kissed his cheeks. 'Go! And I'll wait for you here.'

Somehow the idea of her waiting, for whatever reason, was enough motivation. He agreed at once.

*

They walked back to the plane, watching a pair of red-legged falcons wheel slowly overhead. A small truck had arrived. It was Ter-Sarayan's partner, a swarthy Uzbek with a mouth full of gold teeth, come to collect the caviar destined for Almaty's night-spots. Vinogradov and Minakov went back with him.

Zidra and Irina went a few miles down the coast to Zvezda, a Soviet-era resort, now a forgotten relic on the fringes of China, where doctors and masseuses still attended their empty clinics.

At Zvezda, pedalos rusted on the empty, endless beach.

A ski-lift grumbled up and down, without skiers.

Pleasure boats cruised the lake, their discos blaring lambada into crystalline nights where no one danced.

Kirgiz tribesmen rode their horses over the rusty placards announcing the dawn of Communism.

Up in the hills wolves haunted pastures where they had not been seen since war and revolution.

In the neighbouring villages old women went back to their flocks. Islam had returned on the same night wind that swept the old order away, consigning their daughters three at a time to the stomach and sex of Kirgiz men.

The lucky ones got jobs in Almaty, helping Western oilmen and computer specialists relax.

In Kyrgyzstan the *bish-barmak* ruled – the five-fingered feast that is the heart of Kirgiz life, so much so that even the capital, Bishkek, is named for it.

Like a disconnected wheel spinning in a broken machine, Zvezda spun inertially on, its skeleton staff mechanically performing duties which had scant meaning in the absence of paying guests. The arrival of Zidra's party was a sensation. The director, a squat, swarthy Uzbek, fawned and wrung his hands. He was a cone of expectation, of tedious, unremitting ingratiation. He attended them constantly. He took them on a grand tour of inspection and encouraged Zidra and Irina to make use of the facilities. There was some point in that. They bathed in the mud baths, massaged, relaxed, sauna'd and steamed and Zidra was reminded of some forgotten and highly beneficial features of the old world, with its sanatoria and rest-camps.

It was twenty-four hours before Vinogradov returned. He found the women relaxing on sunbeds in the warm autumnal sun which filtered through the foliage inside a giant solarium. A samovar hissed on an enamel table loaded with Turkish delight, a pot of Turkish coffee, and a bottle of Nastoika Balzam herbal vodka. The Zvezda director told them it was effective against eczema and impotence. Irina filled their glasses anyway.

Minakov, Vinogradov told them, had installed himself in the Kazakh Academy of Sciences and would not be back.

The Iranian vessel which Rudolf had sunk had been fully loaded with plutonium. None of the massive titanium-clad containers had leaked and the scandal had been hushed up. But a team from Moscow had arrived to investigate. The ripples were starting to spread.

The Plate River Corporation delegation visiting Astrakhan had left for Moscow.

Rudolf was dead. His body had not been recovered.

And Vinogradov had spoken to Meshkin, the Lyubertsi leader. The conversation was short and energetic. He'd told Vinogradov to get on the next plane and return to Moscow at once. And to bring with him the Goldman papers.

And the woman.

Chapter 24

'Your wife is here,' Benderby had told Renard when he called him from Uhlaf's place. 'And I can tell you she's worth a million dollars. Ten million dollars, in fact. That's what your meddling has cost us.'

'I know what she's worth, Benderby,' Renard had said, cradling the handset. 'Let me speak to her.'

'In a moment. First we have business.'

'What business?'

'You must persuade my Irish clients there with you that the deal is still on. Nothing has changed.'

When Zidra came on the line, it was a beautiful moment, but Renard didn't know how long it would last so he gave her the lines from *The Song of Solomon* at once. Benderby had warned them to use plain text, but she had to know where he was.

Then it was over. He handed the phone back to Hitchens and had to sit down; his knees were jelly.

Not just because he'd heard her.

But because for the first time he'd started to believe that Benderby's crazy scheme had a chance of success. So what if whole regiments of marines surrounded the IRA's headquarters in Dublin, if by then they had a couple of warheads aimed at London? The marines could sit there for ever. All that would come of it would be a united Ireland and the first all-Irish government – which would be headed by the present leaders of the IRA.

Crazy? Not any more.

Jenkins drove the eighty miles from Eden Castle to Holyhead in three hours. Renard sat in the back with Colm. The crossing was on time and they were in Dun Laoghaire before six a.m.

They drove straight through Dublin, cleared the city while it was still waking up, and continued west along the N6, stopping only once, at Maynooth.

After Maynooth, Jenkins told Renard where the meeting was to be: in Galway.

'How long till we get there?' Renard asked.

'Four hours.'

'Ever been to Galway?' Colm asked.

'No.'

'It's the last stop in Ireland. The next town after that is New York, and many an Irishman has gone that way.'

Outside, rain drove down on a potholed, bumpy highway. By two-thirty they were passing through Loughrea, with the Slieve Aughty mountains a black smudge to the south. At four they swept round Oranmore Bay and down into Galway city.

It was dusk when the Mercedes nosed into a quiet cul-de-sac off William Street, conveniently near to the old walled city. Gracious slate-sided mid-Victorian houses lined the street, their storeyed elegance bespeaking the self-confidence of Empire. The car stopped outside a smaller, privet-shrouded residence towards the more secluded end of the street. Jenkins threw open the door and Renard emerged to find himself on a private drive.

He looked around. To the right of the house a dirt alley led round to the rear. There was woodland behind the row of buildings. He could see sycamores and birches, mostly leaning drunkenly to the right, pushed over by incessant Atlantic storms.

Colm locked the Mercedes and stood watching Renard, then pulled out the Marlboros which Jenkins had forbidden in the car and lit one. Renard saw a ground-floor curtain twitch and the front door opened. Jenkins went in first, alone. They waited while street lamps flared, spilling garish light over them.

Then Jenkins came back. 'They're waiting for you,' he told Renard. 'Let's go.'

They were met on the threshold by a young woman, a redhead. 'This him?' she asked Jenkins.

'Yeah.' He turned to Renard. 'This is Maire O'Connell.'

They shook hands. Hers were slender and cool, and the backs were freckled. Her mouth was wide and uncomplicated, painted with kitsch pink lipstick. 'Come in, please.'

They went into a dingy entrance hall lit by one bulb. Renard was tired and for the moment off balance. He looked gloomily round. There were no special security measures that he could see.

It was a safe house, but not another prison.

The girl helped Renard off with his coat and showed him upstairs into an office. It had a bay window looking out on the street and dilapidated but serviceable furnishings. There was a small iron fireplace, but the fire wasn't lit and a vase with dried flowers had been placed in the grate. She gestured him to a big old-fashioned high-backed armchair and sat down opposite.

Maire was young, younger than Zidra, and her manner was open and direct.

'Is Renard your real name?' she enquired. 'Not something out of *Aesop's Fables*?'

He laughed. 'Yes, it's my real name. Is O'Connell yours? Sounds straight out of the Hollywood version of Irish history.'

She laughed too. 'If you mean that *the* O'Connell's story was a political romance, I'd agree with you.'

'Why are we meeting in Galway?' he asked her. 'It's a centre of Irish Protestantism, isn't it?'

'Well, it was once, but that's not a reason for avoiding the place. We have no sectarian enemies here. Galway people rub along together. And that's despite the six centuries Galway was an English outpost, for most of which a sign hung on the town walls banning anyone with an Irish surname from entering the place. But that's the English for you, Mr Renard. They built fine squares and parks from Shanghai to Nairobi, but there was always a sign somewhere saying *Dogs and Natives Forbidden.*'

She paused, because Jenkins had come into the room. He apologized to Renard for the interruption but he needed to talk to Maire. She stood up to go. 'I'll bring you some tea when I come back, Mr Renard. Or would you prefer something stronger?'

'Tea will be fine.'

After ten minutes Maire O'Connell came back, carrying a tray of food. 'I made Earl Grey tea,' she told him. 'There are crumpets, toast and anchovy spread – and a bottle of Bushmills.'

'Good. The cuisine in your Eden Castle dungeon wasn't what I'm used to.'

'It isn't our dungeon, Mr Renard,' she said hotly.

Renard opened the whiskey, poured for himself. She said she wouldn't drink, but then changed her mind and he poured her a glass too. She perched on the edge of her seat, jumpy as a kitten.

'Who's more nervous, you or me?' he wondered aloud.

'I think we both have reason to be. Mr Renard, there's someone I'd like you to meet.'

'You mean, you want me to hear your side of the story first?'

'If you want to put it like that. We don't want any more misunderstandings.'

'Like the misunderstanding about Bob Hill, whom no one admits to murdering?'

'I understand why you're angry, but I must tell you categorically that we had no part at all in that. I just hope you're conscious of the risks *we* are all taking,' she told him. Her voice was trembling now. He wondered what she'd just heard that had so unbalanced her. 'Until now we've shown great trust in the good faith of the American Administration. Just my being here and meeting you here openly – it's . . .' Her voice trailed off.

'I know what you want to say – that the British SAS are no respecters of youth or gender.'

'Exactly. I won't even tell you how many comrades we've lost to their assassins in the past five years alone. This is a real war, Mr Renard, make no mistake about it.'

'Things have given me that impression.'

'I can only repeat that what happened to you and your colleague wasn't our doing. I've only just heard that your colleagues in America – in Langley – do blame us for it.'

So that was why she was jumpy.

'And they're shaking your tree right now, I guess.'

The look in her eyes said it all.

Renard could well imagine that the reaction from Langley would be vertiginous.

'I could accept your disclaimers about Bob Hill more easily if I knew who you think *is* responsible. Because from here I can only see you in the frame. And I don't even know whether you really are IRA. You could be something else altogether.'

'I know you need to meet a recognized spokesperson, but that's a terrible risk for us. We would simply be unravelling our organization for your benefit, with no guarantees at all that we wouldn't be destroyed tomorrow, and the cause set back two decades. That's why I wanted to meet you first, despite the urgency of the situation. I'd like to get whatever assurances of good faith I can from you.'

'I'm hardly in a position to give you any guarantees. You need to go elsewhere for that.' He stared at her. 'So you *are* a representative of the IRA?'

'Isn't it obvious?'

'Not until I hear it from your own mouth. I want to know who I'm dealing with.'

'It was never our intention to mistreat you, Mr Renard. Or hold you against your will.'

Third time. They were desperate. Renard wondered what was coming down the wires from Washington on his account. 'I hear what you say,' he told her. 'But you haven't convinced me.'

'I'll try to. For one thing, our quarrel isn't with you. For another, we are in the middle of our most successful bombing campaign on the British mainland. We don't need any red herrings like this. And it's also a matter of policy. We always target property. When people are killed it's almost always either an accident or a British provocation.'

'You mean the British are blowing up their own people to make you unpopular?'

'Do you think nothing like that has ever happened?'

'I'd need some persuading.' He buttered some toast and ate it. 'I think if you really believe that then you're living in the wilderness of mirrors that all terrorist organizations inhabit. You're collectively in the grip of a paranoid delusional system.'

'You're wrong. Even here in the Republic our organization is illegal, our cadres hunted down and imprisoned or even shot. That's not delusion, it happens.'

'And that's why you think that having your own nuclear deterrent would even up the ante a little?'

'We don't think anything of the kind. We could have acquired black-market nuclear weapons at any time in the past five years, Mr Renard. We had the chance long before the Soviet Union collapsed. And we never did. Why should we now, when our armed struggle is entering its most successful stage? We leave nuclear weapons to big countries like yours or the United Kingdom, which seem to need them more than the rest of us.'

Renard laughed. Maybe he was too hard on her. The Irish had their grievances, after all. 'OK, that's enough debate. Let's not talk like students.'

She leant closer. 'This is a very critical time for us. Help us understand American intentions, if you can.'

'I'm out of touch. And anyway, I have no remit to help you in your struggle. I don't agree with your methods, and neither does my government.'

'Maybe so, but you can agree that we are approaching the end-game in Ireland. In a few years no one will care about the Troubles or even remember they existed. But now the struggle is hotter than ever.'

Renard looked sceptical. '*Are* you approaching the end-game?'

'Yes. Apart from anything else, the plutonium black market makes it too dangerous for everyone. The British government know that while mainstream republicanism places limits on the weapons it uses, others are not so squeamish. And it's no secret that the Russians offer whatever people want.' She ran her fingers round the glass until it whistled. 'Whatever people think, the IRA is a responsible organization. It's not a branch of organized crime. We know there are limits to the military struggle. In the end there must be an agreed peace and we won't get that using nuclear weapons. But the British must also see the need to negotiate.'

Renard looked cynical. 'So you want to warn them, in a neighbourly way – without threatening them, of course.'

'What would you prefer? Wait until some loony lets off a nuclear weapon and then say *we told you so*?'

There was a knock at the door and Jenkins appeared. 'The others have arrived,' he told Maire. 'They're coming up now.'

She stood up as the door opened again and three men entered. Two of them were guards, the kind with dead eyes and bored faces. They motioned Renard to his feet and frisked him. Then they turned and nodded to the third man, who told them to wait outside.

Renard recognized him. This was Sean McMahon, the IRA leader.

Chapter 25

Meshkin, in the Lyubertsi headquarters near Moscow, had sounded more angry than frightened when Vinogradov called from Almaty, but behind the anger was something else: frustration, perhaps, because the Lyubertsi were now so close to a triumph. They had done something right for a change: stopped a massive plutonium scam, saved the environment. They ought to get the Nobel prize, he told Vinogradov, but they were just as likely to be annihilated by Pryapov's dragoons. Moscow was hovering on a knife-edge.

'We have to get hold of the papers,' Zidra said. 'At least we know that Meshkin hasn't found them.'

'Its strange, though,' Vinogradov said. 'He'd have searched the Leninskii flat straight away, I should have thought. Rudolf must have put them in the fire safe, which only he has the keys to, but it wouldn't take long to open it. What's the matter?'

Zidra was sitting open-mouthed, the colour leached from her face.

'The fucking papers – oh, Christ!'

Small wires were snapping inside her, one by one, the wires that had held her together since she had opened a minibar door in a London hotel.

Snap. The Goldman papers were the only guarantee he would live, and she'd lost them. The only insurance policy on Renard's life. Lost in the stupidest way imaginable.

Snap. The scene at the Hunter came crowding back. By wilful carelessness, she had destroyed him.

'On the last day in Moscow,' she whispered, 'Rudolf took me to a restaurant. Then we found Dubok, and we had to go in a hurry, because he was leaving his office early.' Tears were falling now. She stopped. Wasn't it obvious how she'd betrayed Renard?

Suddenly Vinogradov slammed his hand down on the table. *'You left them in the restaurant?'*

248

Zidra could only nod.

'Tell me exactly what happened,' he ordered.

'The papers were in two carrier bags. I remember they were stuffed between my chair and Rudolf's.' She saw it all now – the sudden flurry of shouted orders as the restaurateur bustled around them, then the smack of cold air on her cheeks as she scrambled into the back of Rudolf's staff car. 'I was sure *he'd* got them,' she whispered. 'I just didn't think about it. Because he was the one who carried them in. But of course he didn't – he couldn't have, or they'd have ended up in Astrakhan.' She leant back. 'Fuck, fuck, fuck.'

Vinogradov stood and walked round behind her, putting both hands on her shoulders. 'That restaurant – that's our place – the Hunter. They wouldn't throw away anything belonging to Rudolf. The papers are still there, I'd stake my life on it.' He leant and whispered to her. 'In fact, it's miraculous. That's the one place where they're safe from *everybody*.'

She sighed heavily. 'OK, so how are we going to Moscow?'

'By air, of course. Tomorrow I'll fix you up with a Kazakh passport. No one will be expecting us to fly in from Almaty. It's a cinch.'

'Tomorrow's too late. I need to go today.'

'It's impossible. Minakov wants to meet you and—'

'Fuck Minakov! Just get me on a plane, will you!'

They drove to Almaty early the following morning. Vinogradov had had someone take photographs of Zidra, and a passport was promised before their midday flight. It cost a thousand dollars.

Then they called Minakov. Zidra would not go to the Academy of Sciences; it was too dangerous. They met in a gloomy Kazakh eatery.

Minakov had already begun to create a stir. He'd agreed not to cause any bad publicity, but the *quid pro quo* was the Russian government's agreement to take massive steps to remove all possible danger of plutonium contamination in the Astrakhan region.

He'd suggested no connection between the plutonium discovered at Raketa and the Arctic Star group, or between Arctic Star and Plate River Corporation. Responsibility would be shuffled to some long-departed bureaucrat from Soviet times. No one presently in a position of power or responsibility would be implicated.

In any case, Minakov was not interested in the question of blame. He knew that conspiracy is the art of life, especially in countries like Russia. What concerned him was the physical danger of plutonium leakage. The cover-ups and alleged investigations he would leave for others.

He had therefore cut himself off decisively from Zidra and her concerns, which suited her as well. When he'd made this clear to her, they parted as friends. A government plane had been sent from Moscow for him, and he offered her seats, knowing she would refuse, and why.

By eleven, Zidra, Irina and Vinogradov were waiting at the airport for the next scheduled Aeroflot flight. By two o'clock Moscow time they were landing at Domodedovo airport.

They saw the busload of troops circle the plane even while it taxied to its hardstand.

By the time they emerged on to the stair, the plane was ringed by OMON troops toting submachine guns. A squad of regular militia waited at the foot of the steps. Three plainclothes men went through the documents of each disembarking passenger. In case these detectives missed anything, all the passengers were taken under escort to a police bus. They would be questioned again in the airport detention centre.

'They may not be after you,' Zidra told Vinogradov under her breath. 'It's me they want.' They were at the tail of the aircraft, amongst the last to leave. 'If you get away, don't talk to Meshkin or anyone else. Don't go anywhere regular. *Just get the papers.* There's a girl at the Mezh. Her name is Zizi.' She saw him grin. 'OK, you know her. I'll contact you at her number when I can.'

Vinogradov nodded. They were near the exit; stewardesses were watching. He moved away from her. She saw him go down the steps. He showed his documents – it took only moments. They let him through.

From the way they arrested her, Zidra knew it was serious.

They pinioned her arms and threw her face down on the filthy snow.

'Something wrong?' the gangly OMON cop said after he'd cuffed her so tightly the blood stopped flowing to her hands.

Zidra struggled to her feet, watched him smile and wouldn't

give him the pleasure. 'Why? That's how I always wear them. Asshole.'

She didn't see what happened to Irina. Someone threw a coat over her head, and they took her at a jog towards the police cars she'd seen waiting beyond the OMON ring.

She had no idea where they took her, because they kept the coat on her head and no one spoke to her even when she told them she was a US citizen.

They took the coat and the cuffs off in the holding cell.

There was no feeling in her hands. It was an hour before she could use them.

After an hour and a half, a uniformed militiaman opened the cell door, releasing her into the custody of a small, brutally clean detective with vicious eyes, who identified himself as Blinov.

Blinov led her up several flights of concrete stairs and showed her into his office.

'This isn't regular,' she said at once. 'There must be two of you to interview me. And I insist on being allowed to call my embassy.'

'Sit down.'

When she refused, Blinov had two uniformed officers come in and make her do so.

He told her she would be charged with carrying firearms on a scheduled plane; having unregistered firearms on her person, without a permit; soliciting as a prostitute at the Hanseatic hotel; theft of hotel property; fraud; possession of false passports and other documents, and other charges to be determined.

'When we've finished the paperwork and formally charged you, it will be time to call your embassy,' he said. 'They won't stop you from serving five years in a penal colony.'

It took several hours to work through Blinov's absurd list. He knew her real name was Sandra Davies, he said, and that was how he booked her.

What interested her was that Blinov had made no mention of Interpol, yet she knew from Rudolf that there was a Scotland Yard warrant out for the arrest of Sandra Davies for the alleged murder of a guest at the Mountbatten Hotel in Covent Garden.

So they meant to keep her in Russia.

She was sure it was Minakov who had unwittingly betrayed them.

If Vinogradov had got clear, it would not matter. Being arrested might even have its advantages. It was Napoleon who said that to win a battle you have to grip your enemy. The enemy right now was Mayor Pryapov, and Moscow's militia was little better than his private army. She could not have been arrested on these trumped-up charges except by his personal order. It meant she was getting close to him, and the ground was starting to smoulder under his feet. Pryapov's links with the plutonium mafia were unravelling, and in public. It had made him desperate.

But who else was involved? Maybe the Lyubertsi, if they'd cooked up a deal together, or if Pryapov had somehow brought them to heel. And now Vinogradov was loose and knew where Goldman's archive was.

But she did not believe the Lyubertsi had turned on her. Meshkin wanted her for himself. She would have been an ace-in-the-hole against Pryapov.

The obvious explanation was always the best. It could only be Benderby. He would do it indirectly, of course, through his Arctic Star connection. But it would be him.

She sat upright on a hard chair and tried not to sleep. In the morning Blinov came back, and this time he offered to let her call the embassy – if she accepted the charges laid.

'What's the point?' she asked. 'You're going to let me go anyway.'

'I don't think so. You've already been charged. You'll appear before an examining magistrate this morning. We can't release you now without a proper trial.'

'How can I take you seriously when you deny my rights under your own crappy laws? You will only allow me to call the US embassy if I agree to confess to things I haven't done.'

'You're a Latvian, aren't you? Maybe you're a Russian by origin, in which case you don't have any such rights. I'm still checking.'

'You're lying, and you know it. I have a right to call my national representative.'

Blinov thought for a while. Maybe a direct, unsubtle but not unfriendly approach was worth a try. He offered her tea. She accepted. She'd had nothing to drink since the plane from Almaty. He said, 'Some papers have gone astray. If you help us find them it might favourably incline the district magistrate.'

'Which papers?'

'Business documents. Ledgers, correspondence, contracts. That kind of thing. They were stolen from a British businessman, here in Moscow.' He leaned close enough for her to catch his bad breath. 'Actually the charges can be still more serious. The man in question died recently, apparently of natural causes. But now there's to be another post-mortem. Seems his heart attack might have been engineered.'

'So what?'

'Your fingerprints were found all over his place. You'd been having kinky sex with him. The day he died, looks like. How do you account for that?'

'I didn't have sex with any British businessman.'

'But you don't deny stealing his papers?'

'Yes. Categorically. What's more, I don't plan to continue this discussion with you. If Yura Pryapov wants to talk over old times with me, or anything else, he should invite me to his office. I'd agree to go. There's something I want to discuss with him, as a matter of fact.'

Perhaps Blinov had heard something on the grapevine, because the torrent of insults she'd expected did not materialize. Instead, he picked up the intercom and barked down it. In less than a minute a uniformed officer arrived to take her to a bare but more wholesome first-floor office, while Blinov made his calls.

They were there for a while. She made small talk with the new cop. His name was Dima. She showed him a diamond she pulled from the pouch round her neck, which no one had removed because they hadn't bothered to strip-search her. Invited him to check its authenticity. He scratched a long line on the window, came back to the table they were sitting at and returned it to her. She pushed it back to him.

'I need to make one call,' she told him. 'A brief one.'

He thought for a while, then pocketed the stone and pushed the phone that was sitting in front of him over to her.

She dialled the number Zizi had given her that first night at the Mezh.

Vinogradov answered on the first ring. He was raving. She shut him up at once. 'I'm in Central District Station Number Ten,' she told him.

'I've got them,' he shouted. 'All of them.'

'OK, then come and collect me,' she snapped and put the phone down.

'Thanks,' she told Dima.

'No problem,' he grinned.

She was about to answer when they heard Blinov coming down the corridor, shouting angrily at a desk sergeant. When he came in his manner had changed.

A mistake had been made, he told Zidra in a syrupy voice that had Dima gawping with incredulity. Heads would roll, he promised; she would get redress. His honour was at stake. He led her back upstairs to his own office, where he showed her a hastily typed disclaimer. It said that she had been properly treated by the Moscow municipal militia during her period of protective custody at her own request, after she had been threatened with physical violence by unknown third parties. She was entirely happy to be now discharged into the safekeeping of her colleague, the British citizen, Julian Benderby.

'Where is Benderby?'

'Waiting downstairs.'

'Who informed him I was here?'

'I have no idea. I called the mayor's office, as you suggested. They told me to wait. Half an hour later they called back and told me to release you but only into the custody of this *gospodin* Benderby, for your own protection. Sign, please.'

'I have not asked Julian Benderby to come here and I do not intend to leave with him.'

'You crazy?' Blinov stuttered. 'You want to go back in the tank?' He prodded the page with his pen; in a minute he would sign himself.

'Look, who told you to write such a nonsensical document?' She pointed to the disclaimer. 'Last night you formally charged me. What happened to all that paperwork?'

'The charges? Forget them. I—'

A phone rang on his desk and he snatched the handset, shouted at someone in the front office and slammed it down.

He looked up at her slowly, shook his head, deciding.

'This is how it is with us,' he said. 'Wait here.'

He left the room. Zidra rubbed her aching wrists and waited. Ten minutes later he came back. 'Someone else has arrived for you. An American lawyer.' Blinov had relaxed, as if things were too out of control to worry about any more. 'I have strict orders from City Hall, but anything can happen in that place. I could find a different person on the end of the phone in a week's time, saying an opposite thing. Then I'll be in the shit.'

'My heart is bleeding for you.'

He tossed a business card over the table. It said: *Gilbert & Reddy. Attorneys-at-Law. New York, London, Rome, Moscow. Presented by Michael P. Favours, Moscow.*

'You can be released to him,' Blinov pleaded.

She turned the card over. On the back was written the word 'Zizi'.

'I need to think,' she said.

Blinov scowled. 'Don't you want to leave? Look, you sign the disclaimer. Then we go downstairs. I'll have both these guys waiting outside in their cars. Then you choose where you want to go.'

'That's corny as hell. How will that save you?' She laughed at him.

'Well, that's what I'm going to do,' he yelled. 'Sign the damn thing!'

'Where's my bag? Personal effects?'

'Oh, shit! You want the gun back? You think I want a shoot-out on the fucking premises, or what?'

She sat back and looked at him. After a while he sighed, stood up noisily and went to a cupboard, pulled her bag out of it and dumped it on the desk. It landed with the heavy kind of sound it should do, but she broke out the Makarov anyway, right there in front of him, and checked it was loaded. She watched Blinov from the corner of her eye. He was writhing like a snake on a stove.

She took a pen, crossed out the last paragraph and signed the disclaimer.

Cursing quietly, Blinov went downstairs to make the final arrangements.

When he came back he looked relaxed again. 'You don't have to worry. Your pal, this Benderby, has left by himself. You're free to go.'

Downstairs, Blinov had assembled three militiamen to escort her off the premises, the main idea being that once she was out she stayed out. They frog-marched her down the station steps. A black Cadillac with tinted windows was waiting outside.

The door opened. A militiaman pushed her hard in the back; hands reached out and pulled her in. The door slammed shut and the Cadillac moved away.

There were three men in the rear compartment. A small Jewish-looking lawyer she assumed was Michael P. Favours. Vinogradov. And Julian Benderby.

They had Favours seated on the dickey seat facing rear. Vinogradov and Benderby made room for her to sit between them.

It was Vinogradov who gently took the shoulder bag from her.

She looked him in the eye. He shrugged, grinned feebly.

'When did you change your mind?' she asked him.

'I didn't. You made a mistake.'

Next to her, she could feel Benderby chuckle.

'What's your role in all this?' she asked Favours.

'Me? I represent my clients.'

She leant forward and put a hand on his knee. He stiffened but didn't move it. 'Who are your clients?' she said quietly.

'Elektrostahl Fabrications.'

'And who the fuck are they?'

'A subsidiary of the Arctic Star corporation.'

Zidra sat back. The limousine was big, but not big enough. She told Vinogradov to take the other dickey seat. He moved places in silence.

Benderby said, 'You must have had a difficult night. The car has a coffee-maker, perhaps you'd like a cup?'

'Thank you, yes.'

Benderby told Vinogradov in his flawless Russian to make the coffee. Zidra watched with disgust while he obeyed.

'We're going there, actually,' Benderby told her.

'Where?'

'Elektrostahl.'

'Why?'

'There are some people we want you to meet, obviously.'

'What have you done with Renard?'

'He was still alive this morning.' Benderby was relaxed. 'I must congratulate you for what you organized in Astrakhan.'

'Don't waste your breath.'

Benderby laughed. 'Difficult to the end. But Zidra, you must learn to accept praise, especially from your enemies.'

'If a brick fell on my head I wouldn't call it an enemy,' she told him. 'I choose my enemies; they don't choose me.'

'Someone should write a book about you.'

'Yeah? There has to be an ending first. Are you sure you know what it is?'

He laughed again. In an odious way, Benderby could be charming. 'I wouldn't believe any ending. If you were buried at a crossroads with a stake through your heart, I'd still eat garlic in bed. Well, we shall see what happens.'

The car was racing through flat, desolate land. It took an hour to get where they were going. At last they reached the outliers of a bleak Soviet-era company town.

'This is Elektrostahl,' Benderby told her. 'One of Ernest Dubok's plants. The Chernobyl reactors were fabricated here. Now they make dairy equipment. And pipeline flanges.'

The car swung into a vast, desolate factory yard, its walls decorated anachronistically with faded red banners exhorting comrade co-workers to surpass the plan targets.

The Cadillac pulled up by a huge Honour Wall hung with steel-framed photographs of bemedalled labour heroes. They climbed out and walked into the main entrance. Inside a vast unlit vestibule a marble bust of Lenin peered into the gloom. A small bunch of withered red carnations lay on the base of the pedestal.

Everything was covered in dust. The place seemed empty of life.

Vinogradov led the way down echoing corridors to the director's office. A huddle of people stood at one end, engaged in muted conversation. The first person she saw was Dubok.

Chapter 26

Sean McMahon was stocky, five-foot eight or nine, with a fair complexion and sharp humorous eyes. He spoke with a brogue which deepened when he grew animated and became impenetrable if he got excited.

He was a man who knew his time had come. Renard watched him and the people around him. They were experienced, dedicated fighters. They had the ease of men and women who've shared years of struggle. They were confident – but with the caution born of bitter lessons.

As McMahon put it, if they did not overestimate themselves, they did not underestimate the enemy, either. Their confidence was based on a view long enough to encompass decades of struggle. They were strong – far stronger than at any time since the Irish Free State was founded in the triumph of 1921 – but their war was not yet won, they could still be wiped out, and they knew it.

McMahon's IRA was nearing the climax of a twenty-five-year campaign. He told Renard that just as Ireland had been Britain's first colony, it would also be her last. McMahon and his colleagues would go down in history as the realizers of an old dream: Irish unity.

Yet this was still not victory, but, as Maire said, only the end-game, when a wrong move could consign the movement to more years of darkness. And there were bitter memories of the times when it had lived only in rebel songs and old men's stories. Now they were making history, but not in circumstances of their choosing – or in company of their choice either, but in a twilit world of deranged soldiers like Pete, or fraudsters, opportunists, political fanatics, simple gangsters.

Their meeting had begun at once. McMahon did not stand on ceremony.

'I think we need to talk alone,' Renard said. 'There are things only you need to know.'

McMahon agreed and asked Maire to leave the room.

'I've been trying to work out your game,' Renard told McMahon. 'And what I've realized in the past two days is that it wasn't your game but someone else's. You were being set up by the same people who set us up. The people who are behind Benderby and his stooge Goldman. I still don't know who they are. Maybe you do?'

'I assumed it was MI5, and I'm still not sure it isn't.'

'It's not. You can definitely discount the Brits. Anyway, I'm prepared to believe that you're sticking with our entrapment operation. But maybe I'm wrong and you really do want the stuff for your own purposes.'

McMahon's eyes were bulging. 'If you had any idea what's been happening here, you wouldn't suppose for a second that we plan to do anything other than keep our agreement.'

'I can imagine that you've had input from Washington.'

'Input! I've had more than that. They've given me until eight o'clock this evening to hear from you personally. After that, all bets are off. From what the US ambassador told me in a secure room in the Dublin embassy this morning, the only support we can hope for from President Morgan, after this debacle, is a rope. Believe me, no one was ever more pleased to see you alive and in one piece than I am now.'

Renard laughed. 'OK, I'll have the dogs called off, on certain conditions.'

'Name them!'

'I need your help with what to do about the delivery.'

'Delivery?' McMahon exploded. 'Surely no one's planning to make one any more? We're certainly washing our hands of the whole thing. Even we can't deal with the Russians. It's more trouble than it's worth. We'll stick to Semtex, if it comes to that.'

McMahon was a showman, and he showed it now. Renard had the feeling he was secretly half amused by what had happened. He radiated some kind of inner certainty – as if this was poker and he still expected to take the hand.

'The delivery will go ahead,' Renard told him. 'And your help is still essential. I spoke to Benderby before we came here. He told me the Russians are keen to continue.'

McMahon affected astonishment. 'Let me see if I understand this aright. Benderby the banker told you the CIA man to tell me the IRA leader to be of good cheer and strong heart because I'm about to receive my first shipment of plutonium?'

Renard laughed. 'That sums it up.'

McMahon waggled his head from side to side. 'I'm not sure my old Irish brain can circumnavigate that one. Who's pulling whose leg?'

'Benderby assumes that you will take advantage of the delivery and use it to good effect against the British. And also against us. That's what he would do, and he naturally thinks even worse of you.'

'And what do you think?'

'That you are a political leader. That you were born for this moment. That your whole life was a preparation for it. Because for the first time, you can prove everybody wrong. You can show the world – or anyway, the bits that matter, namely, Downing Street and the White House – that you are honourable. Unquestionably. That even when offered such a gift, you refused it because you wouldn't break your previously given word. I'd say it's a sacrifice which will stand you in good stead in the future. When the fighting stops and talks begin, there'll be many a rocky place along the way to peace in Ireland. But whenever things get tough and talks break down and the fighting looks set to start again because there's no trust anywhere, people will remember the day when you showed great faith. When you made a sacrifice for peace without being prompted, without promise of reward, to your own military disadvantage, and for no reason except that someone trusted your word. They'll remember that. Those who know. And they will never let your political enemies forget it, either. The Ulster Unionists will always be secret hostages to your stand on principle today.'

McMahon regarded him in silence for a while. Then he said: 'Are you sure there's no Irish blood in you?'

'The operation is on,' McMahon told Maire O'Connell. 'And you'll be going with Mr Renard to England.'

'This is news to me. When's it planned for?'

'Tomorrow.'

'In Eden Castle?'

'Yes.'

'Then we don't need to be involved, surely. Leave it to the

British police. They can handle it from now.'

'No, Maire. They won't make the delivery unless they're completely sure about who they're dealing with. In other words, they mustn't suspect a sting. That means there must be someone they know as a high IRA official at hand during the change-over. Am I right, Mr. Renard?'

'You are indeed.'

'How will it be set up?'

'The British police will be there and so will we. I'll make the arrangements with Brown, the Dublin ambassador. I'll meet him on the way back. Maire can come with me.'

'Good. As long as our interests are covered.'

'They will be. The only other matter is the money.'

'The ten million your people gave us?'

'Yes.'

'We have a problem with that,' Maire said, looking worried suddenly. 'The Russians may not accept the means of payment. I talked endlessly to the go-between, Harvey Goldman, about it.' She made a face at the memory. 'At first the Russians said they wanted cash. That was fine. It was how your people delivered it anyway – two suitcases full of thousand dollar bills. But then Goldman told me they'd changed their minds. Didn't fancy the bother of counting and checking such a huge amount in a hurry.'

'They were worried about forgeries?'

'Exactly. There's so much Iranian stuff about, almost undetectable. So I offered to pay through a nominee account in the Cayman Islands instead, but that was no good because they'd heard a story about the CIA opening their own bank in the Caymans for entrapment purposes. In the end we agreed it would be bearer bonds, drawn on a New York prime bank. And that's what I've got. They fit into one folder.'

'And they're easy to handle,' said Renard. 'They can be taken on a scheduled flight with no worries about Customs.'

'They're negotiable too.'

'Absolutely. There are restaurants near Wall Street where the waiters will do it while you eat a squid and potato salad.'

'That's what I told Goldman. But he said bonds are always a problem in this kind of transaction. He'd changed his mind again. And it was his idea in the first place!'

'These are the details that can derail a deal like this.'

'Indeed, don't I know it. Large sums are involved and because of the nature of the deal there's no possibility of legal redress. Will the goods be delivered, the payment made, the getaway be OK? Just who is setting up whom, or is the whole thing just a sting?'

Renard laughed. 'I defer to your expertise in general, Maire, but I know something about Russians. Don't worry, they won't say no to money when they see it. They'll get bearer bonds and like it. With any luck, they won't have time to spend the dosh anyway. They'll be arrested by the British police.'

'OK, then if you're sure, I'll bring the bonds with me tomorrow.'

'I'd like to check them over with you first.'

'Fine.'

McMahon took charge again. 'Then, Mr Renard, you'll take Maire, Jenkins and one of my guards — Eamonn — with you to England. We'll arrange a plane.'

'Excellent. I'd prefer to fly tonight.'

'I'll see if it's possible.'

The two men took their leave of each other. 'I'll leave Maire to work out the details with you,' McMahon said in parting.

Renard took his hand. 'See you in Washington, sometime soon.'

'Surely.'

When McMahon had left, Renard at once said, 'I'm worried about Pete. He's a worse sonofabitch than you understand, Maire. And I'm sure he followed us here from England.'

'Why didn't you say before?'

'I hadn't met Sean McMahon before.'

'You wanted to look in his eyes and see if you trust him?'

'Something like that.'

'And do you?'

'We reached an understanding.'

She laughed at that. 'How would you like some Irish hospitality, Mr Renard?'

'Greatly. I haven't eaten properly for a day or so. Where are the bonds, by the way?'

'Not here. This is just a safe house. Don't worry, Paul will bring them to us.'

'Is Jenkins a long-time associate of yours?'

She looked puzzled. 'Yes. Why?'

'Just want to know who's the back-up. He's the most senior person after you, right?'

'Yes. He's also my husband.'

'Ah. That's good. I have a prejudice in favour of husband and wife teams.' Renard smiled at her. 'Thanks. Then I'm not worried about anything.'

'All the same, I'll send Eamonn with Paul when he goes for the money.'

Renard wondered whether the hard-faced red-head would be enough, tough as he looked.

'Maybe you should send someone else as well,' he suggested.

'Don't worry. I'll warn the boys.' She smiled. 'I think they'll know what to do.'

When Maire left the room, Renard sipped whiskey and pondered Pete's whispered words, overheard in the bathroom at Hitchens' place: *It's your own wife, for chrissake. What's the problem?*

Renard was well into his second pint of Guinness. The band fiddled, strummed and drummed, making conversation impossible, so he and Marie just drank and let the rebel songs wash over them.

The ceilidh would finish in the early hours, but they didn't plan to stay till the end. They were waiting for Jenkins. He would drive them to Shannon from where they would fly in a Piper across the Irish Sea to an airstrip a few miles from Eden Castle.

By ten-thirty Jenkins hadn't shown up and Maire grew nervous. When her pager bleeped she fairly ran for the phone, came back almost at once and beckoned Renard out. Her face had changed. 'There's no one at the safe house. Our boys have been looking for Paul and Eamonn for the past hour.'

As she spoke, a Land Rover slewed to a halt and someone called her name from it. She pulled Renard over to it at a run. 'It's Eamonn! Come on!'

'Where's Paul?' she almost shouted. 'You should have stayed with him.'

'He sent me for this,' he told her, pointing to an overnight bag thrown on the back seat. 'And some papers, which I couldn't find.'

'That could have waited – you should never have left him.'

263

'Where is he? I thought he'd be here with you?'

'Where were you supposed to meet him?'

'Here if I missed him at St Nicholas's. But I was late. You didn't say there might be a problem,' Eamonn yelled, suddenly as alarmed as she was. 'Get in the car!'

They climbed in and the Land Rover roared off towards the William Street safe house.

It was as if Renard's warnings had only just sunk in. Maire went from over-confidence to blind panic with no intervening steps.

They arrived at William Street in five minutes. She went inside at a run and Renard hobbled along behind.

The place was empty. There was no sign of Colm or Jenkins, nor of Pete. But the heavy mahogany-framed mirror hanging over the fireplace, which must have made a showy centrepiece when the house was in its prime, had a skull and crossbones daubed over it. Renard walked slowly over and tested it with his finger, then rubbed finger and thumb together. It was lipstick, the kind of rose-pink colour Maire used.

Eamonn said, 'Jesus fucking Christ.' If the host of Cú Chulainn had chosen that moment to ride down William Street in ghostly splendour it wouldn't have appalled him more.

Maire went rigid. 'He's dead, isn't he?'

'Don't go to pieces yet,' Renard said softly. 'We need to think. Did Paul have the money?'

'He had the bearer bonds, if he went to the office.' Her face had gone a liverish colour which melded with the freckles. 'I knew that was a mistake.' She knew her man was dead. Without any preliminaries, she'd plunged into grief. 'St Nicholas's,' she said in a small voice. 'That's what it is. What else?'

'Then let's go!'

Galway City is a small enough place. From the cul-de-sac off William Street to St Nicholas's Collegiate Church is half a mile or so. It seemed like much more.

They found Paul Jenkins in the churchyard. Despite its location in the city centre, the place was quiet and dark. The body might have stayed undiscovered until morning if its staring eyes hadn't caught the light of Maire's lamp. Jenkins, they found, had been hanged with his own belt. When they loosed him down, they could see no sign of struggle, no marks on him other than the welt round the neck, the blackened skin and protrusive tongue and eyes.

Renard shone the lamp around. The stone window frame from which Jenkins had been hanged reared up over a carved stone plaque showing a skull and crossbones. Cut into the stone pier beneath were the words: REMEMBER DEATHE. VANITI OF VANITI & ALL IS BUT VANITI! . . . *the stern and unbending justice of the chief magistrate of this city, James Lynch Fitzstephen, elected mayor in 1493, who condemned and executed his own guilty son Walter on this spot. . .*

Behind Renard, Maire, crouched over the body, made small sobbing noises.

'Artistic sonofabitch, isn't he?' Renard breathed to no one in particular. 'You wouldn't think it, to see him.' He turned to Eamonn. 'You'll have to bring the jeep round to the wicket gate over there.' The Irishman didn't hear. He stood like one of the grisly gargoyles which festooned the ancient stonework of Saint Nicholas's, casting big shadows in the moonlight. '*Eamonn.* You hear me? We have to get the fuck out of here and find the sonofabitch.'

Maire stood up jerkily. 'He's right. We have to get Paul away from here. Fetch the Land Rover.'

Eamonn shambled off. They heard the engine fire up and stood looking at each other in silence, waiting. When the car pulled up outside the churchyard gate, Renard hitched his arms under the dead man's shoulders and dragged him over to the entrance, then into the back of the hard-top, trying not to notice the way the head flopped around. Maire was catatonic, tranced, but when the Land Rover moved off and Jenkins rolled over like a sack of potatoes in the back, she squirmed over the seat and pulled him to her, cradling him in her lap.

They carried the body into the house off William Street. Renard sent Eamonn to make the necessary calls, then poured two large tumblers of Bushmills and forced one down Maire before swallowing the other.

The consensus was that the operation had been smashed like quarks in a cyclotron. And that Pete had taken the ten million dollars' worth of bearer bonds.

That meant the handover would happen, and *that* meant that Zidra was expendable.

Unless Renard got to Pete first.

Chapter 27

Zidra walked slowly down the big meeting-room at Elektrostahl, working out who was who.

She recognized Meshkin, the Lyubertsi leader. Spats Almazov, looking more frightened than angry, had had nice porcelain crowns fitted to the remains of his front teeth. And Irina Belinskaya came over to her and embraced her tearfully.

There were two men she didn't recognize. No one introduced them.

They'd given Dubok the job of chairing the meeting. Zidra knew how Russians conducted their business. She concluded that Dubok was not the most important person in the gathering.

It was hard to say who that might be. Meshkin must be a front-ranker. It was either him or one of the two unknowns.

The purpose of the meeting – according to Dubok – was to settle an untimely conflict between friends and partners, and then to recommend a course of action to the law enforcement authorities with respect to one Zidra Renard. Dubok was calm and collected. But this was the kind of thing he'd had plenty of experience at. Finding the culprits. Exposing the guilty. Passing the buck.

It emerged that Meshkin, meaning the Lyubertsi, had made mistakes in the conduct of their relations with City Hall. On the other hand, Meshkin had acquired important documents. To return these, uncopied, would be one solution to the impasse.

One of the two unknowns was emphatic about the desirability of this outcome. Zidra looked at him closely, because it meant he was Pryapov's representative. The man was young, over-relaxed, well dressed in casual clothes, with a supercilious air. She concluded that the other unidentified person represented Arctic Star.

Dubok said that events in Astrakhan meant that certain 'international instances', as he called them, had got involved. He listed the 'instances': the International Atomic Energy Authority, the US Defence Intelligence Agency, and British Intelligence.

Meshkin, speaking for the Lyubertsi, set out their position. Zidra must be freed. No one – Dubok repeated it – *no one* – agreed with them about this. Even now, he said in his cement-mixer voice, the Procurator-General of the Russian Federation was considering pressing charges against her for wilful sabotage of strategic facilities in Astrakhan, including secret nuclear storage zones.

It was possible she might be arrested during the course of the meeting, Dubok added for effect when he still saw no sign of panic in her face. Of course, he did not want to prejudge. Such an influential body as this might have its say in shaping the authorities' attitude to her.

She tried not to laugh. Stared at the floor, hoping to look contrite.

Dubok was mad. Barking. He thought this was some kind of Party self-criticism seance, or a show trial.

Zidra Renard would be spared, Meshkin repeated doggedly. In fact, it was a decided point, so why waste time? The problem was that she also wanted some kind of assurance about her husband's welfare, and he was in England. Meshkin was at a loss to know how it concerned them, but she said it did, and therefore the papers wouldn't be handed over until she was satisfied on the point.

By this time Zidra had fallen in love with Meshkin.

The whole Lyubertsi clan, in fact. She could even forgive Vinogradov.

The supercilious young man from City Hall asked Zidra a question: would she adhere to the agreement she'd made and then immediately broken with Julian Benderby? Would she agree to the exchange of her husband for the missing papers?

'Yes, of course,' she said at once. 'And I did not break any agreement with Benderby. I was under duress. He held a gun on me. We *discussed* an agreement, but we didn't finalize it.'

'You're splitting hairs,' Dubok said.

'I don't think so.'

'Don't waste time,' the man from City Hall said, mostly to Dubok. 'Finish the business.'

Zidra looked down the table. That small, one-sided exchange

told her everything. The last piece of the puzzle fell into place. The man from City Hall was the conductor of this choir. Mayor Pryapov – an unimportant public figure in any normal country – outranked them all.

'Do you agree to the terms?' Dubok asked her.

'Who is the surety on the British side? Obviously I need to know that. Otherwise there's no guarantee.'

Everyone looked at Benderby.

'It is as we discussed,' Benderby said quietly, addressing Meshkin. Then he spoke to Zidra in English: 'We don't need to mention any names. Will you take my word?'

'Of course not. You must give me proof that the person I proposed in Astrakhan actually agrees to be guarantor.'

There was a problem, he announced in Russian. The person they'd agreed should be invited to act as guarantor was a British minister. They could not discuss the matter with him except face to face, perhaps not even then. So Zidra must take this on trust.

Meshkin said, 'Nonsense. Your word is not enough. There has to be a go-between, a third party whom she can talk to. And you must demonstrate his consent.'

How she adored Meshkin!

Benderby leant across and whispered: 'If he can find a form of words, even on the phone, would that do?'

'I would accept his word, yes,' Zidra said.

'Good. Gentlemen, I must ask for a short adjournment. We need to make a telephone call.'

Zidra and Benderby went to the Elektrostahl director's deserted secretariat. He dialled a number. It was answered at once.

'Henrietta?. . . Yes, it's me. Is Derek there?. . . Put him on. Derek. Good morning. . .Yes. . .Yes, indeed. She's here now. . .Yes, I will.'

He handed the phone to Zidra.

'Derek. What's going on? Can I trust Julian Benderby? Do you know what it's about?'

'Yes, I do. The voluntary arrangement applicable to Douglas, yes?'

'Yes.'

'I can confirm that it shall be as you decided with Julian. The name that was mentioned has agreed to act.' He sounded deathly tired. Defeated.

'Derek, all this is fine, but I'm worried about that Interpol warrant, and if the British police want to talk to me, then—'

'My dear Zidra, you can be easy about that at least. I have spoken to them. You will not be arrested at the airport.'

'Where is Douglas?'

'My last information, which I heard only an hour ago, is that he's in Ireland. This came from the Foreign Office, via the American embassy in Dublin. He's coming back to England tonight.'

'Then he's already free?'

'Yes. Yes, he is. But my advice is not to call him now. Get the evening flight to London, then try the American embassy.'

She handed the phone back to Benderby and walked back to the meeting-room. No one approached her until Benderby came back and then they all went to the big, dusty table and resumed their seats.

'Is everything decided?' Dubok asked. They nodded at him. 'Yes? Good.'

'Then it's down to practicalities now,' Dubok said. 'And fast. A lot of eyes are on us. Not only in the Kremlin, unfortunately.' He glared at Zidra.

Benderby snapped, 'You know as well as I do that you have not lost anything. If anything, you've all gained. Now the financial requirements of Arctic Star will be underwritten in full, by my bank and others, and with the support of the British government.'

The meeting broke up almost at once. There was general relief, general satisfaction. Only Zidra was excluded. It was as if a vacuum had formed around her. No one spoke to her, not even Irina. She sought out Benderby.

'You lost control,' she said to him when they were alone. 'You lost Goldman's archive.'

'Not really. Sure, they'll be copied. But that's just replicating one turd in an ocean of shit. It really doesn't matter.'

'So what happens now?'

'To you?' Benderby lit a cigarette, thought for a while. 'You can do what you like. You're free to go.'

'But Renard?'

'He'll be waiting for you when you get home. You did what you set out to do.'

'It's too easy. I don't believe it.'

'I can have you shot, if you think it adds verisimilitude.'

'Don't mess with me, Benderby. I need to understand what's going on.'

'It's over. The plutonium in Astrakhan is now in the public domain. So it's no use to anyone any more. The marines will guard it for eternity, period. One headache less. Look at the upside. And Arctic Star will still be deep into Azeri oil, so the Russians will have no grievance against the West for stealing the cherries off their plate. No one wants Arctic Star out. Everyone see the advantages in throwing the bear a spoonful of honey. So the money they lost when you zapped their collateral in Astrakhan harbour will be made up to them.'

'I don't get it. How? Who's going to pay them?'

'Taxpayers, I guess. Forget it. Concentrate on finding your man.' Benderby smiled. 'Lucky fellow. OK, so to come to the point: I have no interest in killing you. We don't want the Cousins up our nose. We still have to explain away Bob Hill.' He stubbed out his cigarette, screwing it into shreds. 'You'll do that for us. You know the truth: it was the Russians who did it. That's what you'll keep repeating. It's important to us.'

'OK, I understand.'

'Good. So everyone's content. The Cousins get Renard back, the mistake with Hill is covered, honour is satisfied, and we can all go back to whatever we like doing best.'

It was hard to believe, coming from Benderby, but it made some sort of sense. 'You'll miss your plane,' he told her. 'You need to hurry.' He gentled her towards the door.

She made up her mind, 'OK, I'm going. But remember, I don't give a shit about MI6 or any of your fucking games. If I don't get Renard back, I'm coming after you, Benderby.'

Benderby raised both arms. 'Trust me, lady. By this time tomorrow you'll be together again, sharing the same fate. That's if you scrape the five o'clock flight.' He found her coat from the pile of winter gear piled on a table and passed it to her. 'Go, go. There's nothing here for you. You're just an embarrassment now, frankly.'

'Have the car take me to the airport, then.'

They didn't say goodbye.

She reached Sheremetyevo airport before three. She had time to kill so she decided to check in early and make her way to the Irish bar.

270

She had started a second pint of Guinness and a bowl of Irish stew when Irina and Vinogradov turned up. She was pleased to see them. Sheremetyevo is a depressing kind of place. She had bought the *Financial Daily* and that hadn't cheered her up, either. John Reid's report from Astrakhan was headed 'Privatization in the Russian Provinces: the future of the poultry industry'. A long discussion about Gour-Hemmings' plans for Astrakhan's chickens followed, describing the difficulties intrepid British entrepreneurs face in such remote places, where the telephones don't work and the water is bad. At the end of the twenty-inch article a four-line Reuters postscript said that Astrakhan had returned to normal after gang fights involving a stolen Mig had been quelled by the authorities.

She put the paper aside when she saw them. 'How did you find your way back here?' Zidra asked. The Irish bar was located in the duty-free area beyond the customs and passport clearance.

'I know a man here,' Vinogradov told her.

'What was all that about, this morning?' she asked them. 'And why did it have to happen in Elektrostahl?'

'Because that's how things work. Elektrostahl caused the problem. So they had to host the settlement meeting. In the end, everyone was satisfied, so it's their success.'

'But why were the Lyubertsi involved? I thought you'd sold me to Pryapov.'

'Of course not. I was afraid you'd think that. That's why I wanted to be sure and see you one last time. That – and another thing.'

'What?'

'I know you wanted to keep those papers,' Vinogradov said. 'But you'd never have got out of Russia with them. The Lyubertsi has to have something to insure itself. And they weren't so important for you.' He pushed a big manila envelope to her. 'Irina looked through the papers. We sat up all night copying them. We brought a copy of the plutonium contract for you. Maybe it'll help.'

Zidra grinned at him. 'Thanks.' She leant across and patted his cheek. Vinogradov blushed.

'He'll miss you,' Irina told her. 'We all will.'

'Put the envelope away,' Vinogradov instructed.

'Don't worry. This time I won't leave it behind when I go. And

271

that reminds me: I have something for you.' She gave each of them three of the diamonds she'd brought from Astrakhan.

They drank cognac one last time, *na pasashok*, and then it was time to go. Vinogradov and Irina walked to the final check-in point, where passengers about to board pass through the security arch a final time and have their hand-luggage X-rayed. The departure lounge is screened off by glass walls. As Zidra queued up to go through the security point, they stood and waved to her, faithful to the last. She put her carrier bag on the conveyor. The two girls sitting by the monitors continued chatting. She went through the security arch, nothing bleeped, and the guard smiled and waved her through.

Just then Irina held out an enormous *matryoshka* doll. 'I forgot my present for you.' She handed it to the guard, who smiled and passed it round the arch to Zidra. Irina blew kisses. 'Have a nice flight!'

'Thanks! I'll send you a postcard.'

'Don't open the doll till you arrive,' Irina called to her.

'OK, I promise.' Zidra watched them leave, and felt like crying.

She put the heavy *matryoshka* under her arm and walked over to the jetty entrance. While the British Airways 767 was idling on the taxiway for take-off, curiosity overcame her and she pulled the two halves of the doll apart.

Good job no one's sitting next to me, she thought when the silenced Makarov came out. With it was a note which apocalyptically read: *Dear Zidra. Hope you had a nice flight, although not as nice as ours to Kyrgyzstan. I will always remember it! The beautiful mountains. Volodya says it isn't over yet. I am very worried for you, my dear friend. Please call your friend Irina when you can. I'll be in St Petersburg.*

So that explained why they had gone to the trouble of coming to find her at Sheremetyevo, and the double act with the guard on the departure gate.

But why hadn't Vinogradov told her what he knew?

As far as Renard could see, Pete had three options: fly from Shannon on a scheduled flight; take the ferry; or go some other way by sea.

He would not fly. Shannon was too easy to monitor.

It had to be either the ferry or some private boat.

272

Renard was starting to understand the guy. He was lazy, and his indolence was buttressed by his easy contempt for everyone around. He was not Nintendo, but something worse, cloacal. . . evil.

Pete would take the easy way. Drive back to Dun Laoghaire and take the car ferry to Holyhead, the way he'd come.

There was another alternative. He could take the money and run. Hole up in Ireland for a while then leave for some warmer climate. But Renard did not think so. Pete always acted under orders. That was another feature of his lazy nature. The only time he showed initiative was when it came to killing. He had no other real interests, and that was why he worked for Benderby. Money didn't mean anything – if he wanted any, he just took it, no problem. So he wouldn't disappear, despite the ten million. He needed Benderby too much.

And Benderby couldn't go to ground yet, either. First the two of them had to finish their business with the Russians. Benderby still had everything to play for. If he got his hands on Maire O'Connell, then he'd have the proof he needed of IRA plutonium smuggling and of CIA complicity therein, and the stage would be set for a major hiatus in Anglo-American relations. In the meantime, the huge Iran delivery would go through – not exactly unnoticed, but not in the forefront of people's attention either.

What would he do with Zidra? He would have to bring her back to England to make use of her, but that wouldn't be difficult.

All those were reasons why Pete would now be going back to Eden Castle.

In a hurried meeting with Sean McMahon, Renard explained why it was now more necessary than ever to go after him, and McMahon agreed at once.

Maire wanted to go too. She was under control now. She would be useful. She had nothing to lose.

They left at once, Renard and Maire heading south towards Shannon, Eamonn going east, to Dublin. He would look for Pete on the ferry, and try to keep him under observation.

Fifty miles east of Galway, Pete's silver Fiat spun through the night.

As always after a kill, he felt good. Refreshed, relaxed. The feeling he got from a workout or good sex. He wasn't tired, and

273

wouldn't stop until he reached Dublin. Then he would eat a good breakfast and make his way on to the ferry. While he drove, he whistled tunelessly and sometimes he laughed. Jenkins had been asking for it; with great pleasure he'd given it to him. He particularly liked the little touches of melodrama he'd been able to add, like going back to the Micks' place and daubing the mirror. He was going to get a bollocking from Benders for that, but what the fuck?

He had to laugh. The location was glorious; it satisfied his sense of the gothic. Dead people are absurd, all awkward poses and surprised looks, until you start to separate them. It is rare to be able to do justice to all the comic possibilities of death and its effects, but the ancient churchyard at St Nicholas's had been perfect.

His only regret was that he hadn't had a camcorder and some lighting. Jenkins had squirmed for a while, and Pete had liked that. But time was short. He'd had to finish it off, yanking a couple of times on Jenkins' feet to break the neck.

Chapter 28

At Heathrow passport control Zidra produced a Latvian passport issued in the name of Karla Lutautas, complete with the right of abode seals issued by the Home Office Immigration Department. The official – a young woman in her early twenties – spent an age trawling through the list of names in her wanted persons book, smiled, stamped the passport, took her entry certificate and she was through. Until that moment she had wondered about Sir Derek Broughton's promise, and she would not feel sure that the British police were no longer interested in her until she was well away from the airport. She went to the Avis desk and hired a white two-litre Mondeo, using a credit card in the Lutautas name, then caught the courtesy bus to the Avis depot and collected her car.

It was not much after six, London time. England was grey.

It was past ten when she came into Eden Castle's High Street. She'd tried to call the farmhouse; there was no reply. She didn't want to face the place alone. She decided to stop for a few groceries first, so she pulled over near the town's late night shop.

She looked around carefully, as she had done since Heathrow.

The road to Eden Castle is long and straight in places, with very little traffic. She knew she had not been followed. And no one was waiting for her, either. She crossed the road, walking in front of a red Volkswagen with two men inside, and went into the shop.

She paid for her purchases and returned to the car. When she set off up the narrow hill which leads to the church, the red car followed.

She pulled over without warning and stopped.

The red Volkswagen crawled past and went on up the hill.

She waited five minutes and set off again, making a U-turn by the church and heading back down into the town.

Because Eden Castle's High Street is a loop, it doesn't matter in which direction you leave town; vehicles returning the way they came don't need to double back, they just keep going.

You would only double back if you were following someone.

Zidra pulled abruptly into the car park of the Lamb and Lion pub at the bottom of the hill, doused the lights and waited. In a couple of minutes the same red Volkswagen nosed past the car park. It must have made a circuit of the town – looking for her. As it drew level with the Mondeo the VW stopped. She ducked; let them think she was in the bar having a drink. The car crept on and she saw the reflection of its tail-lights glow red on her windscreen, then fade. She peered over the dash to see. They'd stopped fifty yards further on, where the High Street bends round to the left and runs on down to the main road which connects Eden Castle with the world.

She sat for a while making up her mind. The Volkswagen had doused its lights. They'd seen the white Mondeo. They were waiting for her.

Amateurs. She'd seen them in five minutes. But they'd been expecting her, so they could only be Benderby's irregulars.

Pete could smell opposition, and he smelt it now. He'd seen the Merc following him, and as the Stena Sealink ferry described a big arc in Dun Laoghaire harbour, reversing into open water, and Dublin opened out ahead, glittering in the lemon sunlight filtering through lowering clouds, he saw him. Pete clucked with disgust. It was the one he'd got near enough to hear Jenkins call Eamonn. A stupid young Mick not worth the time of day.

In an hour it would start to get dark. He'd find the moment and lug the Mick over the side. Meantime, he went below to the restaurant and ordered *fruits de mer* and a sixteen-ounce T-bone, with a bottle of Jacob's Creek to wash it down.

There was plenty of time.

And Pete felt sure he'd find Renard too. That would be a bonus.

He'd finished with the starter – told the waiter to take it away because the little grey gobs of mollusc and prawn, all lying on their backs with their eyes staring up, made him feel sick, and it had obviously been frozen and then microwaved.

He was reading the restaurant's complimentary copy of the *Daily Mail* when Eamonn came and sat quietly next to him.

'What do you want, Carrot-top?' Pete asked him.

'A word with you, sunshine. Only not here.'

'A word with me.' Pete mimicked. 'Go and chew a razor-blade, Paddy, and get a mouthful of blood that way. Save me the bother.'

Eamonn said, 'I'll be waiting for you. By your wheels.' He stood up. 'You should get a car with an alarm if you want to leave valuables inside. Enjoy your steak.'

Pete watched him leave.

So, the Mick had taken back the bearer bonds. What the hell; he wasn't going to swim back with them in his buck teeth, was he?

Pete's steak arrived. He cut it carefully into one-inch cubes and ate them one by one. Then he ordered ice cream with pralines and coffee.

After that he went to find Eamonn.

The Irishman was nowhere around when he went to Car Deck G where his Fiat stood. Perhaps it was a mistake not to have gone straight after him. He hadn't realized how many car decks there were, and all full.

He wandered back to one of the saloon decks, went to the men's room, then to a gaming room and fed slot machines for half an hour, then cruised around the bars.

Finally he went out on deck.

It was a cloudless, starlit night. The boat was making good passage and its twenty-five knots cruising speed created a stiff breeze. Pete went aft and stared at the phosphorescent wake for a while.

Where the fuck was the Mick?

Pete was getting seriously displeased.

The after deck was deserted; it was too cold to hang about. He turned round, meaning to walk forwards, but there the Mick was, standing about eighteen inches away and just staring at him, his big hands clasped like two crossed spades, a stupid smile on his face.

Pete reacted at the level he knew best – below conscious thought. The scream of rage that erupted from him was entirely spontaneous, and it was fierce enough to make Eamonn step back a pace. It didn't save him from Pete's drop-kick, of course, which caught him right in the solar plexus. Eamonn catapulted into a stanchion which drove into his kidney and sent him sprawling in agony. Pete was on him like a big cat pouncing on wounded prey, and his first kick ruptured the Irishman's spleen. The second cannoned into his chin like a cue into a ruck of balls.

It should have been enough, and he stood back for a second

277

instead of crashing with the full weight of his body projecting through his knees through the Mick's skull into the deck-plating beneath, which definitely would have been enough.

After all, he still didn't know where the bearer bonds were.

But the Irishman surprised him. Staggered slowly to his feet, shaking his head, sucking air noisily, coughing out the first blood, and producing a fist which came from nowhere and ended in Pete's guts the way big trucks sometimes end in the piers of motorway bridges.

Pete didn't gasp, but he looked surprised. His eyes bulged. His knees sagged a millimetre, and he sighed.

But the Irishman's next effort was even better. It caught Pete under the diaphragm and lifted him off his feet and this time all his breath came out at once, even the last half-litre that isn't supposed to, and then he subsided on to the deck gasping and sobbing and if Eamonn's last throw hadn't also forced a long, fatal gout of blood from the Irishman Pete might have been in trouble.

But he wasn't.

By the time Pete got his breath back Eamonn was staring out his last stars.

Pete searched the body and found the car keys, which conveniently had a tag with a registration number on. There was nothing else.

He hefted the body over the stern and staggered forward.

The men in the Volkswagen were still there. They were watching, waiting to see what she'd do.

It was dangerous to drive to the farmhouse, so she walked into the pub and booked a room for the night. The landlord remembered her. She asked if the four-poster suite was available. It was, and she took it.

The room overlooked the High Street. It was accessible only from the landing. If they came for her they would have to come through the pub, deal with the landlord and his dogs. That was possible. But it was more likely that they'd wait until morning.

Zidra trundled the room's oak dresser across the door and put the Makarov on the pillow, showered and went straight to bed, planning to rise early and take a look around outside as soon as the landlord stirred.

She slept well, plunged straight into a deep and dreamless sleep.

When she woke up it was midday on a bright, noisy Wednesday.

The landlord's wife was knocking at the door: would she like breakfast?

Zidra sat bolt upright, wondered where she was, remembered and collapsed back.

Renard hadn't arrived.

Yes, she told the landlady. She would like the works, with coffee.

She'd decided in her sleep: she would go to Hawtree and take what came. She was the bait. They would lead her to Renard. She tumbled out of bed, peered through the net curtains, saw no red Volkswagens, stumbled into the bathroom and stood under the shower.

She fell on the English breakfast the landlady had prepared, then readied to go.

If they meant to kill her, why hadn't they done it the night before? Contract killers do their work and leave. It meant they had unfinished business, here in Eden Castle.

An old, inconspicuous Land Rover trailed her from the town, but when she turned the Mondeo up the gravel track which wound the length of the valley to the house it didn't follow.

It didn't need to. There was no other way out. The place was shielded to the left and right by scree slopes and to the rear by the vast black cliff, formed of fractured and fissured basaltic rock, which reared up to Hawtree Fell. Zidra had scrambled up this ruptured cliff, explored every split and ledge, each stubborn hawthorn and ancient buzzard nest. Had basked in the sun, smelt the acrid earth by the pool, swum with Renard under the white roaring of the cascade and in the dark silence of the deep pool which had formed where the cliff had faulted and ledged. Had flexed in his hands in a coquetry of surrender offered and withheld in the same sinuous instant, until he seized her at last as she sank through the water.

Zidra parked the car and went round the back of the farmhouse, through the kitchen garden. According to ancient Welsh custom, the front door was only used for funerals and weddings. Its bolts were rusted solid. Inhabitants used the back door. She found the key where they had hidden it: behind a loose brick in the garden wall.

The house was as they had left it two weeks before, except that it had been dismantled and reassembled, millimetre by millimetre. Even bars of soap had had their wrappers unpeeled. Toothpaste tubes had been replaced. The linen cupboard had been gone through; so had all the bedroom drawers.

She went to the window and looked out again. The sunlight hurt her eyes. Nothing moved.

Renard kept a shotgun, a fine Purdey fowling piece. He stored it under a loose floorboard in the hall. She went downstairs and prised the board up. The gun had gone. A box of cartridges was left and she took that out.

She went back upstairs, opened a bedside cupboard, took out the auto-focus binoculars Renard kept there, pulled on his Barbour waterproof, collected the Makarov and went outside.

She sat on the drystone wall in front of the house, scanning the road into the valley and the hills all around. Even the sheep that flecked the daleside like puffs of cotton were immobile. It was early evening. The shadows were already long in the spinney.

She watched for a while until a breeze sprang up, flapping a loose corrugated sheet on the outhouse roof. The sound was loud as a gunshot. She stood, went to the Mondeo and climbed in. She would leave the car in the spinney whose tall larch and spruce trees were a windbreak for the house, and then climb the path which led up through a few scrubby paddocks and sheep folds on to the moor. She drove a quarter of a mile before a bullet-hole appeared in the Mondeo's hood and the engine stopped.

She threw herself from the car and rolled to the ditch at the roadside, clutching the Makarov. She was out in the open, pinned down, and when she moved more bullets spattered around her. They came from a silenced gun. Someone else had had the same idea – the watchers were already up above. She wondered how many. She lay still, listening. At first she heard nothing, then the sound of someone running down the path, dislodging stones as they came.

Twilight was thickening and the wind freshened, beginning to gust. There would be a storm that night; clouds tumbled into the valley off the moor, dousing the early stars one by one. Small zephyrs of cold thrilled up her back.

The spinney was fifty yards away, all open ground.

Fifty yards. Eight seconds to zigzag over.

Time for him to get off a hundred shells.

She did a breathing exercise for thirty seconds, saturating blood and muscles with oxygen. Snapped the safety on the Makarov. Unscrewed the silencer and left it on the ground.

Then she launched herself straight at the spinney.

He hadn't expected it because she covered twenty yards, made fifteen, sixteen strides, before the first plumes of dust started fountaining around her feet. Five seconds. Six. Eight. She cannoned into a fragile young birch tree and threw herself into a shallow depression.

He'd stopped.

She was up at once, racing for the path which was visible as a line of lighter ground ascending left to right only thirty feet overhead, but they were thirty feet of thick bramble. She scrambled through in what seemed like minutes but was four seconds or less. Now she could hear him, running up the path. A small shower of stones and grit came down. She even saw him for a second. A small, slim-looking figure sprinting back up the hill.

She went after him, without much hope of finding him, bursting through the undergrowth and lunging straight up a few yards of scree separating two halves of a dog-leg in the path.

Now they were both out of the copse and on to moorlands. A few bullets whistled around, but he hadn't aimed, was firing wild. She could even see the Land Rover, dumped under a rocky outcrop. He was almost there, and when he turned to loose off another volley she threw herself to the ground, landing headlong in a brackish bit of bog so that when she crawled out she was muddy from head to foot. He was in the car, churning the engine. She crouched down and began to shoot, saw the windscreen shatter, and then the starter motor stopped turning and it went quiet.

She went right round the vehicle, keeping her distance and working her way on to the outcrop above the Land Rover. One of her shots had hit him in the left shoulder and he was lying across the seat, staring up at her, his face pale and sweaty.

She swung down on to the bonnet, reached inside and pulled out his weapon. When she opened the door, she had to prop him against the pillar. He mumbled a few words of Russian while she cushioned his head.

'Where've you come from?' she asked.

He mumbled something that sounded like *Volgograd*, as if she

281

was curious to know his birthplace. He was losing blood. She'd hit him in the lung.

'You need help,' she told him.

He tried to laugh and flecks of foam appeared round his mouth.

'I'll take you to a doctor. But I have to move you first.'

He nodded, and she went round to the other side and levered him across to the passenger seat.

She started the car and drove it back down the little path leading to the house. It was rough going, and by the time she yanked to a stop at the foot of the hill, the brakes had given out completely; the hydraulic reservoir, punctured by one of her shells, had drained away.

He hadn't uttered a sound and was already much worse, his eyes starting to cloud over.

'I'll call for an ambulance,' she told him.

He shook his head. 'Keep me here,' he managed to croak. 'I want to tell you something.'

Renard had piloted the Piper, though they'd lost their departure slot at Shannon and had to wait six hours for another. During that time he'd had an exchange of messages with Ambassador Brown in Dublin. The upshot was that they were on their own, because State didn't believe enough in Benderby's spurious warheads to risk a major breach in Anglo-American relations by asking the British to help out at this stage.

They touched down at Halfpenny Green early in the evening. By that time Zidra was already at the farmhouse and Pete was sitting down to a big supper in a pub five miles from Eden Castle.

Maire had slept most of the flight. Now she looked crumpled, ashen-faced. There didn't seem to be any fight left in her; he'd had to prise her from the plane and half carry her to the airfield huts, where the Hertz they'd booked was already waiting. They set off at once; it was an hour's drive to Eden Castle.

Pete was less and less pleased by what he heard. He'd spent the afternoon visiting his clients, checking the final arrangements for the handover next day. He'd been to see Hitchens, and knew Renard's wife was back. What annoyed him was the bungling by the helpers, which meant the bitch had been unnecessarily alerted and was now holed up in the farmhouse – a place he'd gone through personally a few days before. He wanted to dispose of both of them at the same time, not separately. Renard was one of the very few serious professionals he'd met, and Pete wanted to have every advantage when he dealt with him. Having a wife as hostage was an advantage. Having killed her was definitely not. Yet they couldn't leave her to her own devices, which meant Pete had had to divide his forces.

Even he could see that everything hung on a knife-edge now. As a matter of fact, it was miraculous that the whole territory was not crawling with SAS and specialist police. His two assistants could see it too, and they were nervous. He'd calmed them down, but the difficult part was still to come.

He decided to go and talk to Hitchens. He might need the old man's basement again. They needed to prepare. Hitchens was very willing, and Pete went to the basement to check everything and had been there only minutes when he was astonished to hear Renard's voice in the shop overhead. He heard a woman too, and after listening for a while decided it was Maire O'Connell. His luck was in!

When he heard the American order Hitchens down into the basement, Pete ducked into the store cupboard opposite the door to the cellar they used for a dungeon.

It was just too easy. When Renard pushed Hitchens, Pete pushed Renard, catapulting both men into a heap, slamming and bolting the door behind them. Then he went for the wooden steps, leapt up them in two strides, and caught O'Connell by the front door. She swung round, a gun already in her hands. It was a small-calibre lady's automatic. She fired point-blank at him. He was two metres away but he didn't hurry, just quietly stepped over to her with his hand outstretched as if he was offering her a prize draw ticket, and smiled at her and said, 'That's not the way you do it,' and when she fired again he didn't even blink, just reached out and took her by the wrist so that the little gun went flying across the room and she cannoned into him.

He had her in a kind of embrace, squeezing one arm up her back and then the other too, both hands gripped in his paw. She looked up at him and there was loathing and fascination and fear on her face. He dragged her through the room like a bundle of clothes, picked up the small pistol and held it an inch from her forehead, saying '*This* is what you do', and the noise was slight, like corn popping. She slid over backwards, slowly, her head tipping back, the red hair tumbling down, a little pink rivulet leaking from the hole above the bridge of her nose. He let her go and she fluttered to the ground. Then Pete put the gun in his pocket and bent to rip open her blouse, inspecting the torso, which was marble white and freckled, especially around the neck and breasts, which were small, with pink nipples the size of tiny Caucasian mountain strawberries. He dropped her and went over to Hitchens' printing press. Somewhere amongst all the filthy little boxes he knew there was a tear-gas aerosol he'd given Hitchens once, just in case. He found it, grabbed the inspection lamp and went back down the steps to the cellar.

'You there, Yank?' he called out. 'You'd better let Hitchens out, or I'll shoot both of you now.'

Renard swore at him.

'Let him out.' Pete laughed. He threw open the door and zapped them both in one movement with the gas. Renard hadn't been ready for that. The stink was unbearable. Pete grabbed Hitchens by the collar, yanked him out, bolted the door again and hoisted him up the steps. He dragged the girl out into the yard at the rear and went back inside. Hitchens had more or less stopped coughing, but they could hear Renard gagging his lungs up for a while afterwards. Pete put the kettle on and brewed some tea while they waited. Then, when the coughing subsided, which meant the air was clear, he went back downstairs. He was there for a while – ten minutes or so. It didn't sound pretty.

Chapter 29

O my dove, that art in the clefts of the rock, in the secret places of the stairs, let me see thy countenance, let me hear thy voice.

The Song of Solomon

Zidra's face was unsmiling, leached of colour like a mask.

The loft was tomb-dark except for chinks of light where tiles had slipped. But Zidra had explored here once and her memory was eidetic. She crawled over dusty laths to squat on a joist in the eaves at the front of the house.

There were bat droppings everywhere and she could hear the tiny animals fluttering as she passed by. She ignored them, levering slates apart until she could see the road down the valley.

Now every nerve strained to the world outside. While she watched she tried to recollect the route up the cliff behind the house. It was impassable – occasionally climbers had come with ropes and equipment to scale it. She and Renard had done it but not in darkness.

Zidra heard noises outside and peered through the broken tiles. Shapes moved but they were not human: a family of badgers sniffling for food; rabbits playing on the grass, their tails a ghostly phosphorescence in the growing gloom.

The loft was warm but she had chilled. Her legs were beginning to cramp. A few drops of rain spattered on the tiles overhead. Soon the storm would begin in earnest and it would be time to leave.

Where was Renard?

She pushed angrily at a slate and it broke free suddenly and clattered down the roof, thudding into the flower-bed below. She peered at the valley top, etched like eyeliner under the darkening sky. She knew they would not come for her yet. They were waiting for night and reinforcements. The scent of phlox and jasmine came on the evening air flowing through the aperture.

Five-thirty next morning, at Staple Cross. She even mouthed the words: *Staple Cross.*

That was what the little man had told her, before he died.

The time and place.

A refrigerated container vehicle, with *Seatransco* blazoned on the side, registration number N875 HGF.

Outside a sudden wind whipped up the tarp on the outhouse roof, where she'd put the Land Rover out of sight. Another watcher would soon arrive on the tops; he'd said so.

Staple Cross was a village on the A5 near to Eden Castle. The sort of place you pass through a thousand times and don't see. She thought on this, and then the whole thing was obvious.

Trucks carrying freight to and from Ireland used that road. They drove to Holyhead and went by ferry to Dublin. Seatransco was one of the companies involved and she had often seen its trucks. There was a filling station with a Little Chef café at Staple Cross. That was where they sometimes stopped.

It was a sleepy, inconspicuous place. Ideal for making discreet deliveries.

It was time to prepare. Zidra squirmed out of the eaves, crawled to the far end of the loft, feeling her way in the darkness. This was the side of the house facing the cliff behind. You could hear the waterfall from here. The joists had been boarded over to make a storage space but it was empty. She took off her tracksuit and wrapped it and her trainers inside her cagoule, rolling it in a tight bundle. That way there was a chance the warm clothes would stay dry when she swam the pool. She would take nothing else apart from her wallet, torch and the Makarov, all zipped into the cagoule's waterproof front pocket.

She tied the cagoule to her wrist by its strings. Naked, she moved like a ghost to the small door set under the eaves. From here she could climb on to the roof and out over the extended kitchen.

It was pitch black now. The moon had disappeared behind the cloud that was clotting over the tops and more rain spattered down, but it did not last. A screech-owl she'd heard earlier made a final pass over the outbuildings and she caught the premonitory thump of its wings overhead, the rush of air a foot or so on the other side of the tiles.

Despite the dark, she could see herself. Human skin is luminescent – she'd heard that somewhere and it was true. She imagined Renard's hand flat on her belly, warm, requiring, and ground the thought away in her teeth.

She brushed her palm against her right breast and the stud that was set there, cupped her hand round it, felt the hard little nugget with its bright diamond.

There was a light on the tops. When she looked through the broken tile again the lights were back, inching up the road. It should have taken another ten minutes to come that far, but they were here!

Sudden rain drummed on the roof. Soon the bluff would be shrouded in pluvial mist. Then she would leave.

For a moment panic rose like nausea. She stifled the feeling, forced herself to take deep breaths. She would swim across the pool beneath the moor and rake the clouds sweeping over it. The watchers would not touch her. Not on this moor. Not this night.

She would find him.

Down below: the sound of someone moving. She looked into the gloom. The car she had seen had not arrived, but a man was standing below, sweeping a torch beam round the house. He looked straight up, but missed her.

A roll of thunder crashed over the hills. The storm was gathering force. Curtains of rain slashed over the valley. She saw lightning reflected on the tops, but then it persisted too long and yellowed into headlights. She leaned out again and as the rain poured on her head she heard the squeal of brakes and voices shouting as the man below ran back to the car.

This was the moment. She scrambled convulsively to the end of the roof where the ground behind the house rose up so sharply that a leap of a metre and a half was enough to take her out on to the infill. She scrambled down to level ground as a vast sheet of lightning lit the valley. Men in fatigues and balaclavas were scattering around the house from the front.

She ran over the thick grass and entered the coppice. The black cliff rose up sheer in front of her. It would take them time to search the house, more to check the grounds. Then they would start back down the valley, because it was clear no one would attempt the cliff in this numbing rain. It was as though a new tectonic shift had plunged the valley back into the seabed it had once been.

She felt her way until she struck against the rock at the foot of the cliff. The place was heart-achingly familiar.

Inching sideways, Zidra turned when she came to the tall cedar that was the start-point. When her hand touched it, exultation flowed like sudden fire in her and she stopped shivering. Her toes dug into mud, fingers exploring for holds as she readied to launch up. She climbed like a cat for twenty feet, then swung out for a toehold on an outcrop extending from the bluff. She reached across to the rock face, seized a briar root, swung into space then crashed into the cliff, tumbling amid rocks that chafed her back and sides. From here she crawled back to the edge. Nothing showed of her except that faint luminescence of the skin, like the sheen of candle wax. But the bluff was visible from below and as lightning flashed she saw that one of the watchers had followed.

Now she climbed in a passion of calculation and instinct, thrusting up from ledge to under-crack hold to briar root swirling in mist and rain, climbing fifty feet then traversing a ledge where a fissure rose vertically another forty feet up to the pool. The chimney ran parallel to the cascade and its mind-numbing roaring filled her ears. She braced herself inside it, her back against one face and her feet on the other, the cagoule clenched between her teeth.

It took thirty minutes to climb. The rain had not abated, but she was more protected here. The fissure opened wider at the top and she could not brace herself within it. She tiptoed to the right on a ledge three inches wide, supporting herself with her left hand in a waist-high crack while her right reached for a grip on the flat surface above. Suddenly she lost the toehold and hung, her left arm shaking with the strain. She toed back again and stood flat against the rock on tiptoe. Then she edged to the right again and this time her right hand found a finger-hold just below the top surface. She gripped it and let go with her left hand. Her feet slipped at once and she hung by the fingers of her right hand and scrabbled again for a toe-hold, but the ledge disappeared to the right. She had to swing herself up and trust to luck. As her left knee came up it struck an extrusion on which she could balance if she could get her foot to it, but by now her right arm, in agony, was giving way and she was sliding right off the rock face. There was nothing below but emptiness and the razor rocks at the foot of the cliff. She fought her knee up on to the extrusion, pressing against it with her breast-bone, and propelled herself to seize the top surface. Rough moor grass grew along it, but she knew it would tear out under her weight and then she would fall. Chippings,

288

pebbles and wet, sweet-smelling earth cascaded on to her face as she scrabbled for a solid purchase. She was still balancing on her left knee and her upper thigh began convulsing with cramp. As she slid off the cliff her right leg swung useless and with a spasmodic final thrust of her left knee she lunged up. This time her right hand found something – a twisted root – which held. For five agonizing seconds she hung on, her feet swinging in space, her left hand lunging for a hold, and then slowly she inched up over the edge, collapsing on the grass verge.

He had followed her. She had heard him at intervals, through the hiss and spatter of rain and the roar of the cascade, as he scrambled in fell boots among the rocks and sent small avalanches flying, his lamp flickering in the gloom.

She peered over the grassy edge, waited for a while, and then at last caught sight of him, only fifteen or so yards below. He must have seen her leave the house. She wondered why he had not opened fire on her. She looked around for a rock or sharp slate. She found a stone that had been polished smooth in the stream and turned back to see him already halfway up on the edge. She saw his black shape solidify in the gloom and without thinking rushed to him and struck his skull with all her force.

The man went limp and slid over the edge. She dropped the stone and grabbed at him, catching the balaclava which came off in her hands so that she had a clear view of the man's face as he fell on to the rocks beneath.

Despair gripped her. She was halfway up the cliff, exhausted, and if she made it to the top this was only a prelude. She had a long way to go yet. And first she had to swim the pool and get behind the cascade, because that was where the path was. Zidra sat up but the pulled muscles of her stomach stabbed like a knife and bile flooded her throat. The cagoule was still tied to her waist, but she could not unpick the knot. Her nails were torn and her hands trembled so violently that she gave up twice before the nylon cord finally slipped apart. She stood up and looked around. The rain was now just a fine drizzle, but the cliff was shrouded with mist and she could see nothing. Good. It meant the watchers were also blind.

She shook her arms and legs and turned to the pool. She was drunk with fatigue and cold but she could not pause. It would be fatal to give her limbs time to stiffen. Zidra grasped the cagoule and plunged into the water. It was deathly cold, worse than she'd imagined, and the cagoule slipped from her frozen fingers immediately. She dived for it but the gouging undertow at the pool bottom sucked her down, and she knew she had to break for it or she would drown. She lunged back to the surface and struck out for the rear of the pool, sucking in lungfuls of air and then diving again to pass under the waterfall, which crashed around her head and threatened to throw her to the bottom again. At last she pulled clear and hurled herself at the small ledge of flat rock which jutted out behind the cascade. It was a familiar place for her. She hauled herself from the pool and threw herself on the ledge, gasping for breath, choking and crying. Then she sat for a while, head in hands. This was the final absurdity. Naked, hunted, alone, at least she would have no encumbrances on the final climb. She turned to face the cliff. The roaring cascade filled her mind; its spume soaked the air.

No lights moved on the tops. Soon she would be there. And if they had seen her they would walk or drive off the moor down to the waterhead, and be waiting for her. She had not yet escaped.

She turned back into the funnel of rock and began to haul herself up.

The fissure narrowed above her head and an outcrop of crumbling rock blocked it. It would be necessary to feel her way outwards to the cliff face, then find a handhold she could hang from. Searching for handholds she inched out, dug fingernails in the crevices at the edge of the outcrop and then swung free. Now she was hanging by her fingernails, swinging to get the momentum she needed to throw her left leg out and up over the outcrop. Her finger-hold seemed solid but the slaty rock suddenly sheered and her right hand lost its hold. She hung from her left and swung back in, trying desperately to find a finger-hold with the right arm while the biceps of her left tore in agony. She thrust her fingers deep into the morass of broken slate and found something smooth – an exposed root, perhaps. But as she squeezed it thrust back and then the thing happened which she had worried about when she had visualized the climb earlier, and had then forgotten completely in the wild ascent from the house. There were grass snakes and occasional adders in the woods and stony high places on this moor. They lived in hidden parts of the cliff, out of sight of hawks and buzzards and foxes. She had found an adder, and in the gloom its shiny head blinked past her eyes, the mouth opened to strike, the venom that would kill in minutes spurting on her cheek.

She fell into space with the snake, heard it hiss, but her fall was broken by a ledge she had missed in the blinding dark. She grabbed for a hold, anything, and found a bush, wrenched up on to the ledge. Now she was on the reverse side of the fissure, and when she set off again immediately found the path over the blockage.

In ten minutes more she climbed out on to Hawtree Fell, emerging on to the flat table rock at the top of the cliff from which the cascade thundered down.

In a few minutes the waterfall was just a murmur behind her. She had reached the drystone wall which kept sheep away from the cliff, crossed a stile and set off over the high moor. The path was flat, soft earth beneath her feet, and it was easy to follow except where run-off from the hills turned into bog and she missed her way and lost more time. She set off, jogging slowly, and at last she reached the bridleway which ran over the moor to the junction with the Eden Castle road near Staple Cross. By now the sky had begun to lighten and the rain had ceased completely. It was just after five.

As the dawn breeze sprang up she reached the tree line on the rim of the fell. She entered the wood at the edge of the moors and slowed to a walk. The highway to Eden Castle cut through the wood and there was still time to reach Staple Cross service station and the Little Chef café by five-thirty.

Running in loping strides through a roadside feld, she could actually see the Little Chef and the forecourt of the services. It was silent; only a night light glimmered feebly inside. The parking lot was empty apart from the service station towing truck – and one articulated truck marked *Seatransco Ireland–Europe Overnight* on its aluminium side. She could hear the buzz of its refrigeration unit. That had to be it.

Zidra decided to approach the café from behind, try to find a way in, steal a boiler suit, anything to cover her nakedness.

She walked back the length of the field and crossed the road out of sight of the services. Fifty yards further down, a tree-lined crescent curved back from the road towards Staple Cross services. She ran into it. She was now in the settlement. Houses lined the crescent on each side, all the dreaming serenity of middle-class

England. She heard the sound of an electric milk float, bottles rattling, motor whining, and watched it pull out from behind a car and stop again ten yards further down. It gave her an idea. She crept up behind the line of parked cars, watching the milkman at his work, hoping that no early riser was standing by a bedroom window watching her.

Five-thirty. Where *were* they?

The milkman jerked his float to life and it ground on another few yards. She watched him emerge from the cab, push back his peaked cap and scratch his head over a note some housewife had left. She had an urge to laugh. What had Renard called it? *A new turn in human affairs*, when something so deadly that the only way to dispose of it is to load it on rockets and shoot them into the sun becomes the plaything of the mad and the dispossessed.

She had heard him say: *When it hits the streets at last, plutonium will be the enfranchisement of terror. No government can resist it.*

Well, it had hit the streets. She knew because she was looking at it.

Zidra watched the dairyman walk down the drive of a big house, whistling tunelessly, clinking empties. He was a small man, wiry, walking with a jaunty gait. She knew he would not be a problem.

She stood by his float, smiling, waiting.

Chapter 30

Zidra parked the milk float outside the Little Chef, facing the Seatransco truck. She was dressed in the milkman's white jacket and grubby trousers, having left their owner trussed in polythene sacks behind the service bay. He didn't seem to mind. He'd never been mugged by a naked woman before. He'd dine out on it for years.

It was after five-fifty, and the place was still deserted. No one had come. The cargo doors at the rear of the truck were secured with an internal lock and a hard alloy Chubb padlock. The driver's cab was locked. She walked to the rear of the service station, intending to break in and find some tools, but the place was secure. Pulling the dairyman's peaked hat down on her head, she walked slowly back to the milk float, took money from the cash-box and went over to the forecourt telephone kiosk. She called Directory Enquiries and asked for the number of the American embassy in London. It took a while; there was a variety of numbers. The operator was bored, irritated, but Zidra forced her to go on, and the girl at last produced the one she wanted just as a car pulled up outside the services. She was dialling Bryce, the CIA man, as the big beige Mercedes drove in a slow circle round the Seatransco truck and then stopped twenty yards away. The phone had stopped ringing and a recorded voice told her to *please wait*, while people climbed out of the car and walked across the forecourt towards her. The redirect cut in and the phone began ringing again. By the fourth ring they were less than twenty yards away and she could see the Seatransco logo – two fishes circling each other like an astrological sign – emblazoned on the blue overalls they wore. One of the men turned and walked round to the far side of the truck but the other came right on, while the answer-phone clicked and whirred and then Bryce's voice began telling her what to do after the tone. The one walking towards her was carrying a small attaché case; he laid it on the ground and opened it and while she told Bryce to get out of bed and get help round to Staple Cross services because worse things were changing hands than changed hands even in Grozny bazaar, she watched him pull out what looked like a silenced Uzi – right in front of her, without concealment. She put the phone down, pushed open the door and walked by him back to the float, saying 'Good morning'. He didn't answer, just followed her with his eyes, tracking past her to where the second car she'd just seen was traversing the parking lot. He'd left it too late to finish her, because this was when the vendor arrived and he had to deal with the handover first, so he slammed the Uzi back in the case.

Zidra was busy around the float, clinked bottles, carried a crate to the door of the Little Chef, whistled tunelessly. Two men climbed from the second car, waved and shouted something. The man with the Uzi looked back a last time at the milk float, shrugged and went to meet them.

Zidra put down the milk crate, pulled out a pint bottle and walked over to the beige Mercedes, tapping on the driver's window. He was young, bored, uninterested. She tapped harder, the window slid down and the bottle hit him between the eyes and exploded. She yanked the door open and pulled him to the ground, on the side away from the truck and the four men who were standing by it talking.

Zidra searched the driver. He was unarmed. She pocketed his wallet, still watching the others through the Mercedes' windows. One of them had opened the big rear doors of the container. The man with the attaché case had laid it on the ground and was opening it. The two newcomers were standing in front of him, arms folded, watching. They must be the Russians who were making the delivery. The attaché case came open – it had taken a while to set the combinations – but the man with the Uzi didn't shoot them at once. Instead, he waved them to the rear of the services. They began shouting, expostulating, but when he fired a few rounds over their heads both men set off at a run, disappearing behind the building. Moments later Zidra heard the characteristic, muted chatter of the Uzi. The man in Seatransco uniform sauntered slowly back, alone.

His partner had started the truck and it began reversing slowly, the rear coming round towards her, the tractor unit pulling away. The second man must have climbed into the cab, because the truck did not stop; it ground out of the filling station forecourt and set off back down the A5, away from Eden Castle. Zidra climbed in the Mercedes and set off after it.

The truck gathered speed, and she followed it for several miles, swinging through s-bends while she opened the glove compartment, flipped down sun-visors and checked other likely places for a gun. There wasn't one. She watched the truck sway from side to side a dozen yards in front of her when several things happened at once. The truck slammed to a halt, the door opened and the man with the Uzi leapt out and ran back towards her, while a police car shot through the bend behind them, strobes and siren working as it swept past the Mercedes and pulled in behind the truck. A second police car came after it, swerving broadside on to block the road, in the same way that police vehicles she couldn't see were blocking the road ahead of the truck. Two uniformed policemen came out of the car in front at a run. Both were armed and wore body armour. More piled from the other vehicles.

The man came leaping round the back of the truck over to the driver's door of the Mercedes, firing over his shoulder at the first two policemen, one of whom fell at once, shouting at Zidra to drive, flinging the attaché case on the rear seat and piling in beside her, the Uzi to her neck.

'*Turn it round now, or I'll kill you now*,' he yelled. The man crouched in the seat-well, his gun over his head, firing random bursts through the rear of the car. She could see in the mirror, before answering fire took it away, police scattering in all directions, and again he was shrieking at her to *Move! Move!*, ramming the gun in her neck.

Zidra slewed the car round, watching a policeman in front scream as the truck suddenly jerked forward, crushing him against a police car. Another policeman loosed off a volley of shots at the cab and the truck stopped again, this time for good.

The Mercedes was now facing the way it had come, and two, then three, policemen were firing at it, the noise intense through the vehicle's shattered windows.

She slammed the shift in gear and the far shot forward. In half a mile a side turning took a hedged lane off the highway to the left. 'Get down there!' the man with the Uzi yelled. 'Turn into the lane.' Sensing refusal, he jammed the snout of the gun in the side of her head. 'Don't think for a second I won't use this, bitch,' he hissed. 'Be sensible.'

The Mercedes screamed down into the lane. Two miles of twisting bends brought them into woods and he made her pull into a picnic area, ordering her to give him the keys. Then he went to the boot, pulled out a length of nylon tow-rope. He opened the driver's door and yanked her out, threw her on the ground and tied her hands to her ankles, behind her back.

She could hear a helicopter circling. It flew overhead once and carried on.

'You've got no chance,' she said. 'They'll be here in five minutes.'

He kicked her. 'Shut up, bitch'. Then he hit her on the side of the head, so hard that without any transition she was suddenly lying on her back staring up at treetops and at his unsmiling face. She didn't even notice being knocked out. She tried to sit up, and couldn't. He was squatting in front of her, quietly smoking a cigarette.

'Who the fuck are you?' he said.

She shook her head. She had not realized how big this man was. His frame was massive, but he moved so easily you could not notice. While she was thinking about that he slapped her face, hard so that blood trickled from her lip. 'Bitch. I asked you. A question.' He spoke very quietly, almost in a whisper.

His face was broad, somewhat pock-marked as if acne had troubled him when he was a teenager. The nose was squat, pitted like a nutmeg. Tiny beads of sweat adhered to the moustache below.

His brow furrowed and he said something which included 'bimbo' but it was hard to know what because he hit her again, filling her ears with a chainsaw racket while trees revolved and turned to mud that filled her mouth.

He grabbed her by the hair and swung her back round to face him. She spat soil and blood out, wiped her lips with the sleeve of the milkman's grubby jacket. She was panting but the man was glacial. She thought his pulse was no more than sixty-five to seventy.

'Need to knock the wax out, do we?' he said and slapped her again, but when she came up she stared into his dead eyes without flinching. He squatted down on her legs.

'Fuck you,' she told him so this time he balled his fist, grabbed her hair to steady her and smashed her forehead. He watched her eyes revolve up into her head, shook her a few times like a rag doll and dropped her.

Then he lit another cigarette and sat on a tree stump, waiting for her to come round.

It was fifteen minutes before she began to move again. He swore under his breath, stood up and pulled a lock-knife from his trouser pocket. It was a Puma, forged from Rockwell-tested steel – the kind favoured by deer hunters.

The place was deathly quiet, the sun had risen and autumnal warmth filtered through the trees, sucking vapour larded with musty smells from the hollows. The police sirens had faded. It would be a while, half an hour and probably much more, before they came back with a properly organized search party.

The man's brows furrowed. When she began to stir and retch he stood over her. 'You made me act stupid,' he told her. 'That's naughty.'

He towed her by the hair over to the stump and propped her against it. Then he squatted down on her knees and looked at her. She avoided his eyes and he chucked her under the chin and moved her head around. Supernovas sparked and died in her head. Double vision resolved and dissolved his impassive, reptilian face.

'Talk to me,' he told her softly. 'I need to know who you are.'

When she still didn't speak the man grabbed the milkman's shabby white jacket by the lapels, ripped it open and pulled it down to her waist, revealing her breasts.

He tossed the knife from hand to hand. 'Make it easy on yourself. You can't change anything now.'

'I don't know anything,' she whispered.

He worked on her for a while until she began to cry but when she still didn't tell him anything he unbound her ankles and took her trousers off as well.

When he beat her, and the sound was like dry branches cracking, she fainted but didn't break. He tried again, this time with the cigarette, and the noise she made roused the rooks in the trees nearby. At last, she told him her name, yelled it out: *Karla Lutautas.*

'What kind of name is that? Your real one?'

'Yes.'

He nestled her head in his lap and stroked her cheek. Then he hit her a few times and each time she yelled out her name.

'Who are you?'

'Latvian Intelligence.'

The man laughed. '*Latvian* fucking *intelligence*? What the fuck is that?'

She began to beg.

He told her to shut up, then asked her why she'd come to Eden Castle.

'With MI6. It's a joint operation.'

'Who – *what* – in MI6? Name a name.'

'Sir Derek Broughton,' she said at once. 'Mikhail Pankin. Sir Nigel Bolton.'

'I know Bolton, but who's Broughton? And who's the Russian?'

'Pankin is a Latvian. He's my controller. Broughton is the British ambassador to Moscow.'

'This is no good, baby. I don't know who the fuck you are or why you've been sent. I don't know these people.' He spoke quietly, leaning close to her face. 'Maybe I'll feel better if I find out what you *don't* know. I'll give you a few names. Tell me if you know them. First one: Douglas Renard.'

She shook her head, but it was too late. He'd seen the recognition in her eyes, and then all at once he knew her.

'*You're his wife!*'

He repeated the name and she wanted to ask him if Renard was alive. He could see it in her eyes. But she didn't.

'Well, well. So you're the famous Mrs Renard. It's true what I heard about you.' He squeezed her almost absent-mindedly, as if he was testing fruit, watching her squirm and gasp. He was curious about her.

She saw it and asked him to untie her hands.

'Why?'

'I'll show you.'

'Yeah?' He thought she was offering herself to him. She was going to pleasure him and be whatever he wanted.

He toyed with the knife, sat back. Why not? He'd kill her anyway, before he left. And another hour made no difference. He leant over and cut through the ropes, freeing her hands.

'*Where is he?*'

'Where I put him. Don't worry about him.'

She shook her head, trying to push away a rush of nausea. 'He's not dead, then,' she said.

'Not yet. He will be.'

He sat her down cross-legged, facing him, to his right, and stroked her face and throat, watching her eyes. When he'd hurt her he'd found he didn't enjoy it like before, and he wondered why. Something had changed. It was a discovery: pain isn't the same thing as power. Power is what *they* give *you*. The Austrian knew that, but she had nothing to give. This woman was different.

He licked blood from his fingers, bent to her and kissed her body.

'Shit, you're beautiful.'

There was a long silence. She drew her legs up under her chin and he allowed it. She rested her head on her knees, circling her legs with her arms. He gave her a cigarette and they smoked. He stared at her feet. Threw the cigarette away and pushed his index finger between her toes.

'I boiled someone's feet, once, just for a laugh,' he told her. 'They made a sort of glue.'

She remembered the Mountbatten Hotel and Bob Hill, and she knew who he was.

He traced his finger up her calf. The nails were clean, manicured. Sharp. She could feel them scratching the inside of her knee. This monotonous scratching suddenly was more real than anything else.

He was going to take her and she was willing him on, because the alternative was to die, screaming and fighting, but for nothing.

She discovered she was open the same moment he did. This shocked her because it meant she was no longer a person. She was falling like an opened parachute, and with the same inevitability.

'Why do you shave?' he asked.

'Because—' She swallowed, couldn't say, couldn't speak, even though it didn't matter any more what he knew because only one of them would be leaving here alive.

Her eyes widened again, but they never left his. She was waiting, feeling the coolness in her loins, the dryness in her throat, her tongue clicking like leather on her teeth.

He worked on her for what seemed a long time. When the tautness left her it was sudden as a string snapping and then she was so open it could have been he who had reached abruptly up into her throat and pushed out the sob which suddenly emerged. Her eyes were wide, expressionless.

He was drunk with her.

He would keep her for ever. Maybe alive, for a while.

He wanted to take her completely by surprise.

It took judgement. He gazed intently at her, at the great unblinking eyes that distracted him, at the heart-stopping mouth, at the pulse flickering in her throat, and a kind of swooning madness came over him; it was impossibly hard to concentrate. She was panting, stertorous, and it made her tremble.

Zidra scrutinized him back, caught his stare, its intrusive, clinical curiosity, until the moment when bolts from some dark spot of unreason cannoned through her like the steel balls in an arcade machine and she was lost.

He watched her and exulted.

No woman had ever surrendered before.

Facsimiles of surrender there had been.

Broken bodies, pleading, crawling in terror.

Stupid masochism.

But never this.

He told her that, his voice thick, joyous even: 'Every which way, we'll do it.'

When he stripped she saw his body was hard, at a peak of fitness, the forearms and chest matted with thick blond hair. Now the frenzy would begin. But he was in no hurry, he had control. He took his clothes and walked slowly to the car, threw them on the front seat. On the way back he paused under an old holm oak, one huge outstretched branch only inches above his head. She watched him hoist himself chin high five, six, a dozen times, single-handed. Then he stalked across to where she knelt, primal, arrogant, ready.

This kneeling – what was it?

Surrender?

Supplication?

It wasn't either. It was a coiling that burst into a vaulting cartwheel that became a ram that screamed like tearing metal as it ploughed through the man's solar plexus, bending him almost double, planting the knife in him.

He fell like a stone and she catapulted for the car, but he was strong, unsubdued, and he came roaring from the ground while she still fumbled at the door, and as she scrabbled for the Uzi she could feel him leaping, his hand touching her as the dead metal swung round like a boom and detonation filled the world, once, twice. The recoil threw her backwards; she crashed agonizingly on the gear-stick.

But she had scotched him.

The man slipped suddenly to his knees, his eyes blank, the mouth opening. She fired again, the blast scorching her belly, his head snapping back as the bullet entered the cheek, exiting behind the ear. She watched his eyes blacken, distend, blood bubbling from his mouth on to her belly. Watched him capsize, his scream turning to falsetto shreds that drowned in blood as she pulled herself free.

Outside, Zidra stood over him, the gun outstretched while his twitching grew galvanic, aimless.

Then she turned back to the car but her legs gave way and she stumbled over it, retching uncontrollably. She shook and the shaking was so violent she knew this was concussion or the beginnings of a seizure, and then she blacked out.

Chapter 31

When she came round the woods were silent. The man's body was already stiffening. She was frozen, one arm cramped under her where she'd fallen on it. It had begun to rain; the ground was saturated, and big drops spattered on her face off overhanging branches. That was what brought her round, but it was a while after she was awake before she was able to open her eyes or move a hand. She lay in a delirium of paralysis and panic until control came back from some deep place, spoking slowly out into her limbs. Then, without any transition at all, she was awake.

It was the scream which woke her – a blood-freezing yell of fright and dismay.

She snapped up straight, understood the cry was hers, and fell back against the car, shaking.

He lay very near her. She could see the body from the corner of her eye.

Astonishingly, her assailant had dragged himself a few more yards before the convulsive end. The trail of blood and clotted flesh behind him was a yard wide. The rainwashed face was remarkably undamaged. The startling china blue eyes stared unblinking as in life, the whites filmed with red. There was little blood around the entry wound under the cheekbone. A viscid trickle about the mouth. The lips were drawn apart to reveal the small yellow incisors. The face seemed to be relishing a secret. It was hard to say what.

The back of the head had been blown off. Islands of pink and grey brain matter lay in the grass amid a coil of thick gore, of bright blood mixed with green and yellow. The nature of the head wound made it all the more astonishing that he had revived enough to crawl towards her in some last spasm of malice and revenge.

She looked over the body. The first bullet she had fired had struck the thigh, causing massive bleeding and subcutaneous haematoma. The second had hit him in the groin. What she saw there made her pick up the gun, crack it open and spill out shells.

They were flattened and grooved. It was an assassin's weapon, good for extermination close up, useless for anything else. That was why his lower abdomen was torn away.

Zidra snapped the gun closed and turned away. She was shaking with icy cold and fatigue. She started the car and switched the air-conditioning to full heat.

There was nothing to wear, except the milkman's trousers. She found a tartan travel rug in the back of the Mercedes, cut a hole in the centre with Pete's hunting knife, and wore it like a poncho. She dragged the corpse into the undergrowth and scattered leaves and fallen wood on it, went to the Mercedes and found the black attaché case. Inside the case a plain A4-size manila envelope contained a sheaf of heavy, high-grade papers. They were all the same: bearer bonds drawn on the First Bronx Bank, New York.

Where was Renard? Where had they taken him?

It took an hour and a half to find her way back to Eden Castle. She left the Mercedes in a secluded lay-by outside the town. It was riddled with bullet-holes.

She would go to the police, soon, because she was near the end of her strength, but there was one more place to check first.

She walked over to the shop and could see Hitchens through the window, wearing his usual brown overall, rubbing printer's ink from his fingers while he talked to a customer. Zidra crossed the road and stared in the window of a run-down hardware shop while the customer completed her purchase and left.

Zidra had no time left. Hitchens would have to give her the answers, and if he couldn't then someone else would have to find them because she could do no more.

Hitchens had recognized her, she saw it in his eyes. Maybe he recognized something else too.

This old man, who wore the translucent skin of terminal age round his temples, whose palsied hands crept like intruders around fixtures and fittings, *knew who she was*. She saw it in the way he backed uncertainly away from her. Zidra followed him, pushed him into a chair and when his mouth opened put the gun to his khaki teeth.

'Imagine this,' she said, 'a line drawn from a bullet to your mouth, like a rubber band. Stretch it too far and your whole fucking head will come off.' She put the gun down on a pile of remaindered Bosnian war stories and meshed her fingers. Smiled. 'Got it?'

She pulled a chair up and sat next to him so their knees were touching.

'I'm pissed off, Mr Hitchens,' she told him. 'I want my man back and I want him now, so I can have a pleasant night's sleep at last. *Shut up*. I want all the answers immediately with no games or discussions, none of your fucking polite English talks, because like I said I'm pissed off and if I don't soon know all you know I shall beat you to death.'

Flecks of spittle appeared on his lips and he tried again to speak but now he couldn't, and the rotating of his hands grew more exaggerated and spastic.

And then she understood.

They weren't rotating, they were *pointing*.

She looked down. Right below his feet was a small square trapdoor. An iron ring was set in the frame. And now the clicking sound in his throat resolved itself into the word *cellar*.

'Open it,' she told him.

He was an old man greedy for the last days or hours of life. Maybe he was the mastermind behind the whole thing, whatever it was, maybe he was really Adolf Hitler, but he did not want to die. He lifted the iron ring with the kind of hook on a stick people use to open high windows, and pulled.

The trapdoor creaked open and fell back on its hinges. It was massively constructed, and acoustic baffles had been nailed to the underside. Zidra could see wooden steps extending down. She waved him in with the gun, and slowly, unwillingly, he climbed backwards down the steps. She peered after him. Stone flags were visible in the little pool of light, and a grating of some kind. She could hear water running. She waved him over to the grating, and jumped down in two steps.

The old man sidled around the wall, and beyond the grating she saw a metal door with an eye-level grille. Hitchens had a dungeon in his cellar! The door was secured by three heavy iron bolts; they were oiled and slid open easily. There was a modern Chubb lock; he found the keys on a string around his neck. The door swung open and she pushed Hitchens through. The air inside was so foul it made her gag, and the darkness was total, but even before he spoke she knew he was there.

They'd dumped Maire O'Connell's body in with him.

'Over here,' she heard him whisper.

He was chained and there was a single padlock which the old man unfastened. She stood in the doorway and watched and when he came to her she touched his cheek with her fingers.

'Renard. How are you?'

'I'll be OK. You?'

'Surviving. Do we leave Hitchens?' she asked.

'Leave him.'

They pushed him in the cell, slammed the door and bolted it, climbed the steps, and shut the trapdoor on a world neither wanted to see again.

It was dawn before they got back to the farmhouse, and not because they'd finished with the police, but because Zidra couldn't stand it any more.

It took Zidra a while to explain what had happened to her. She'd never seen him so angry. Or so remorseful.

As the days passed, it was Zidra who stayed in bed a lot, while Renard made calls and people came visiting – Bryce, the CIA Resident in London, among them. No one stayed long the first day, and no one disturbed Zidra. Renard wouldn't let them.

They put up at the Lamb and Lion and thereafter appeared each day very quietly at the farmhouse so that half the time she didn't know they were there. She couldn't sleep at night and only drifted into slumbers and bad dreams as dawn broke and the million birds in the valley woke up the world. But if she crawled out of bed early in the afternoon and plodded sleepily into the kitchen, she'd find them all sitting there: Bryce, crew-cut and squeaky-clean in a magnolia short-sleeved shirt. Two double-barrelled young men with angular bodies and faces blank as shovels, from the Foreign Office. Zidra, with her mirror-inverse background, trained at IMEMO, the Soviet diplomat's alma mater, was fascinated enough to be rescued from herself, temporarily. She could not imagine the schooling which could produce this combination of self-deprecation and a sense of historical consequence. This painful need to put people at ease, like embryonic versions of Sir Derek Broughton. She did not envy them.

They were tended by a policeman called Hewitt, a large-framed, unhappy-looking superintendent with beetling brows and slicked-back hair, who chain-smoked (in the garden) and sought out Zidra's company, as if the others made him uncomfortable. He was a servant, he seemed to be saying, and she a woman, so they could be left alone to talk.

Hewitt was a gardener. He showed her how to graft cherry and apple trees and what to do with hyacinths on this soil, and brought her pomegranate cuttings from his own garden. They meandered about the garden while the big boys did the heavy stuff in the kitchen, and Hewitt extracted what he needed from her.

He had more brains than the rest of the gang and in fact was the star of the performance, which was mostly staged to debrief her.

'Why didn't Uhlaf and Benderby just abort the IRA deal?' he asked her one morning as they sat on a stone bench facing the valley. 'I mean, they couldn't have wanted the ten million?'

'No, of course not. To begin with, it was just a nice little earner that Goldman and Dubok cooked up together. Goldman approached the IRA. Later Uhlaf, who likes to think big, leveraged the deal up from one ten-million-dollar warhead for the IRA to a two-billion-dollar deal with Iran. But they didn't drop the IRA deal. They used it for a smoke screen to cover the big Iranian sale. And they did succeed in muddying the waters. So many people were worrying about the IRA that the other deal almost slipped through.'

'Would have done, if not for you,' Hewitt said.

'After the incident with Bob Hill, which was a bungle, Benderby went in a hurry to Moscow to eliminate Goldman, who held a thread into the heart of the maze, but then he got embroiled with me.'

Hewitt grinned at her. 'Unfortunately for him. How did they bring the stuff here?'

'Surely you know that, Mr Hewitt?'

'I'm interested to hear what you think.'

'I can only repeat what I heard, mostly from my husband. It didn't come from Iran, as expected. The Russians had a fall-back plan to container it via Rotterdam, which is an intelligence nightmare, apparently, because the Dutch customs are useless and only search six out of the six thousand containers offloaded there every day. That's why Rotterdam is the narcotics capital of

Europe, Douglas says. Even so, your people were ready for this shipment. But the Russians didn't make it, they changed the arrangements, and loaded the warhead on to an Antonov and flew it to Lübeck, of all places. There isn't even a customs post.'

'That's more or less what we heard. Alarm bells which should have rung didn't and inquiries as to what happened are, as they say, *ongoing*. So Dubok and Benderby foxed a joint operation between the secret services of three countries.'

'Yes. Just goes to show what can happen when you get one bad apple.'

'Meaning Benderby?' Hewitt asked.

'Exactly. He single-handedly set the CIA against MI5, jeopardized the President's Irish policy and nearly made Iran a nuclear power.'

'Oh, Benderby was impressive all right.' Hewitt sat like a gantry, with his elbows on his knees. 'But now the main unanswered question left is, who betrayed you in the first place? It wasn't the Irish. It couldn't have been anyone in Russia. So who was it?'

'I have no idea at all. It's a mystery and will remain so, I expect.'

Hewitt nodded slowly. It was over. He had got what he came for, and seen there was nothing else to get.

He shook hands with her. 'Put it behind you now, Mrs Renard. That's the best thing.' And then he and the whole party left for ever and the Renards were alone.

'What did Hewitt really want?' Douglas asked her. 'You didn't have anything new to tell him, did you?'

'He wanted me to tell him who I thought had betrayed us. It was Henrietta Broughton, of course. But I didn't say.'

Renard stared at her. 'You're kidding.'

'No, I'm not. It was her. Sir Derek was indiscreet, and she used everything he told her. She was very serious about Uhlaf. It wasn't just an affair. She was going to leave Derek for him.'

'How involved was she in what happened?'

'Totally. It was her idea to kill Bob. I'm sure she meant to kill you too, but Benderby must have had second thoughts. She knew we were about to expose the connection between Hans Uhlaf and Dubok. That's why they did it.'

'But you were with her when Bob was killed.'

'Yes. The day it happened she kept me packing her bags for her. It wasn't to preserve me from the same fate. It was for an alibi. She couldn't be sure the story wouldn't emerge one day. Then people would remember about her liaison with Uhlaf – you know how it is. Be one ever so discreet, the truth will out. At least this would muddy the waters enough for her to argue that if she was involved, she wouldn't have saved me, would she? She relied on me to defend her! I feel insulted by that.'

'When did you discover this?'

'In Astrakhan. It was when she commiserated with me at Uhlaf's place. She told me Sir Derek had said I was brave to have defended myself against a Kalmyk assassin. That was when I knew for sure.'

'Why?'

'Because I never told Sir Derek that the phoney waiter who came to our room that night was a Kalmyk. I never told anybody. She could only have known if she was involved to the point where she knew individual gang members.'

At first they were embarrassed to be alone together.

She drew circles in the brown sugar he'd spilled on the pine table, then poured herself more coffee. 'You?'

'Yes.'

When she lifted the jug he could see the burn-marks on her hands. *How are you*, he was afraid to ask, *in your heart, in your wounded beauty, your pride, how are you?*

I love you, he wanted to say, and realized he hadn't said it since it happened.

'You never wanted me to get into all that stuff,' he told her instead.

'I was trying to prise you free, but you wouldn't let me.' Her voice trembled.

She was doodling in the sugar and he was too and their fingers met. 'I love you,' he said. 'I fucking adore you, in fact.'

'Dubok's a foxy old bureaucrat,' she said, ignoring his words but not moving her finger. 'He didn't believe all the talk about billion-dollar deals, but he reckoned his share of the ten million dollars would be enough for his retirement.' She looked steadily at Renard, then stood up and walked across the kitchen. She rummaged in a drawer and pulled out a bulky object wrapped in a bin-liner.

'Is that ten million connected with this, by the way?' She unfolded the bin-liner and the sheaf of heavy 120-gsm watermarked paper fell on the table. It was the contents of the envelope she'd found in Pete's attaché case.

'That *is* the ten million,' Renard said.

Sir James Wilshman had drawn up a balance sheet and was pleased to see almost no red ink anywhere. All outcomes were satisfactory. The IRA had performed a service, which did not atone for everything, but certainly earned them Brownie points. The result would be an IRA ceasefire and then peace in Ireland; and the Ulstermen, anachronistic irritants, would one day soon sit in the Irish Dáil and be tedious there. Ireland would at last take its proper place in the world: obscurity. And the nightmare alternative – that the IRA might have actually bought plutonium when it was first offered, might have begun waving it under Westminster's nose – had been avoided.

Decency had prevailed.

Nor had the risks been great. Even if the Iranians had managed to get their hands on the stuff, was that a more threatening outcome than having plutonium stored secretly by gangsters in southern Russia? Kept in a trench like so much contraband, at the end of a branch line to Grozny, at the mercy of Chechen irredentists? Russia was the worst option of all. Some might fret about the revival of nineteenth-century Great Power politics in the Caspian region, but the nettle would have to be grasped sooner or later. Russian disarray had left a power vacuum waiting to be filled. The future of the Caspian, like the past of the Persian Gulf, would lie in clever, sympathetic, discreet, accommodating, ineluctable Western hands. Not the paws of the bear.

That was not all: the pluses on the geopolitical balance sheet went on adding up. Because of what had happened, the future Caspian pipelines would feed the West. It could have been different: the oil might have flowed east.

And what of all that hot Russian money, siphoned through the City's vast and anonymous cooling system? Sir James might not share the view that money doesn't need to wash its face, the cynicism which said Britain was an old whore with a perennial need for new blood, which allows itself to be blackmailed into the bedroom, knowing who will rule whom in the end. But there was no moral dilemma involved in bad money put to good use.

Julian Benderby had gone bad, but someone always tended to. It didn't signify. The foulness would stay deep in its well-guarded pits, because they'd won. That was what mattered.

Others had also benefited from the adventure.

Plate River Corporation began a new chapter. Hans Uhlaf, lionized in the City, converted PRC's billion-dollar debt into equity. Everyone was a winner.

In Russia, Mayor Pryapov, the guarantor of market reforms, paraded in Red Square arm-in-arm with the Queen of England, his subjects carefully corralled out of the way, the coast clear for his presidential bid. And Professor Minakov remained at his post, his presence a salve to someone's conscience. The Volga would be saved, and the Caspian too. Maybe.

Julian Benderby disappeared.

Rumours circulated in the Square Mile that old Jules had done a runner, gone to Russia and hidden there, escaping from British justice which sought his help in its inquiries into an alleged fraudulent bond conversion.

Renard drew a different conclusion: word was that Benderby had gone to the Big Apple, like a crab scuttling between shells. It was said he ran a brokerage from a two-room dive in Brighton Beach with a couple of hungry young Russians. Maybe that too was legend because there was talk of a Malibu condo; or a ranch in some West Texas town of the walking undead, where he lived quietly in a well-guarded adobe-style compound.

Renard was in no hurry. He planned to call him up some time, when the dust had settled and even Benderby's seventeen senses of paranoia had gone to sleep. Then he would kill him, slowly.

But maybe Benderby was dead already, for there was a story borne on a different wind about a shoot-out in an office in Minatom.

Renard and Zidra stayed for a while at the farmhouse.

They made one visit to London. Zidra went shopping. Renard went to see Foreign Secretary Wilshman and told him about the night when a Lyubertsi gangster photocopied Goldman's archive so that a woman he respected could go free. Explained what would happen to the archive if anything ever happened to Zidra. Wilshman listened, patrician, indulgent, and when Renard finished agreed that there could be no recompense for Zidra's pain.

'But you and I know that there are more difficult burdens than that,' he told Renard pompously. 'The weight of secrets so important they can never be revealed, whatever the consequences may be for us personally.'

Renard couldn't help grinning, although he knew he should have punched him in the nose for that. 'Sounds like special pleading,' he said mildly, 'but I presume you are referring to *Nostradamus*?'

'Of course.'

'I don't think anyone is going to call you to account anyway, James, so the secret can sleep. And it won't worry me, either. I'm out of it, thank God.'

'Enjoy retirement, Mr Renard. I envy you, really. Plutonium, oil – they are twentieth century icons. Future wars will be fought over such things as *Nostradamus*.'

'Yeah, *Nostradamus* will be big,' Renard agreed. 'Until Bill Gates begins to sell it by mail order for fifty bucks a throw.'

Wilshman grinned. They said goodbye, and as Renard was leaving the Foreign Secretary recalled a detail, one of the loose ends which are always left at the end of any operation. 'Some bearer bonds disappeared,' he said, 'and the Treasury are chasing me for the money.'

'Really?'

'Yes. Ten million dollars' worth. It was budgeted for the Irish end of the business. You wouldn't have any idea. . .?' Sir James's bushy eyebrows flagged like semaphores.

Renard squinted at him cheerfully. 'Absolutely none.'

Zidra and Renard went back to the Borders and the house that was home. She loved his battered face more than before, was intoxicated with the hard, foxed, scarred body that he shared with her.

She was the things he could not conjecture: scents and savours, folds, curves, warmth and texture. Other.

They walked in the moonlit hills or in the damp, fog-larded mornings and talked.

They made love in bed, in the kitchen, out of doors. They waylaid each other in the midst of everything else, stalked and pounced and took, in the outhouses amid tumble-down crimson walls and sagging beams, among piles of hemp sacking and planks, wooden rakes and heaps of orchard apples. The huge lemon light filled the whole air, kindling the silent fields with citrus flame, the light that streamed off their fingers' ends.

Also available in Vista paperback

Black Lightning

MARK JONES

A stunning technothriller in the bestselling tradition of Tom Clancy.

The cold war may be over but the Russian giant is far from sleeping, and the sinister forces now in charge have developed a terrifying new weapon hidden on the Arctic sea bed – a weapon that can totally paralyse the world's electronics and neutralize all defence systems.

Renard is an experienced agent – but not so experienced that he avoids adopting the identity of a man who's in so much trouble that Renard himself may not survive.

And if Renard fails, the Russians will turn off every light, every computer and every weapon in the Western world . . .

ISBN 0 575 60009 8

Looking for the Mahdi

N. LEE WOOD

Kay Munadi had a glittering career feeding smart lines to bubbleheads who presented the TV news to the masses. Too plain to be a star, but too human not to care, she thought she had her compromises just where she wanted them – until Halton came along.

Halton was a humanoid fabricant, built with the genius of American technology and the morality of the Intelligence Service to be a bodyguard in the Middle East. Now he had to be delivered – and Kay's Arab background made her the obvious courier.

But the last time she'd been to Halton's destination she'd barely escaped with her sanity. This time she's walked into a set-up – and the only one she can trust, the only one who hasn't betrayed her, is the android himself.

Blade Runner meets *The Fist of God* in a devastating new thriller from a startling new voice.

'Wood delivers fast-paced adventure in a hybrid sci-fi/spy thriller that also connects on a personal level' *Publishers Weekly*

ISBN 0 575 60109 4
A Vista Paperback Original

Eye of the Beholder

BRIAN LYSAGHT

Vargo is back.

It was impossible, unthinkable. Four years ago Robert Vargo had fled the US with millions, leaving three dead witnesses behind him. Now he's back on American soil – and the one man who can lead Assistant Attorney Julie Beck to him is behind bars. Where she put him.

Bobby Lee Baker: the man who tipped Vargo off. And Beck's ex-lover. They'd had a passion to set the world on fire. This time they're going to have to settle for southern California. And this time the flames are going to be real.

Eye of the Beholder is a hot, tough, slick thriller.

'Mr Lysaght has just shouldered his way into the first rank of thriller writers' Peter Straub

ISBN 0 575 60097 7
A Vista Paperback Original

Coming soon in Vista paperback

The Profiler

HARRY ASHER

The Profiler – the toughest job in European crime-fighting. Across fifteen nations, beheaded and dismembered bodies are turning up, gruesomely displayed. Claudine Carter, Britain's foremost psychological profiler, is assigned by Europol – to track down the killers.

Against a background of personal tragedy that could destroy her career, and facing threats from within the organization as deadly as those without, Claudine Carter joins with a brilliant forensic pathologist and a maverick computer wizard to build a picture of people committing the worst atrocities in the EU's criminal history.

Panic – and the pressure on Claudine – rises throughout Europe as the killings continue. And when the mass-murderers discover Claudine is hunting them, she joins the list of intended victims. At the top.

ISBN 0 575 60163 9
A Vista Paperback Original

Faraday's Orphans

N. LEE WOOD

A taut, uncompromising thriller of survival in a world turned upside down.

Succeeding where all Man's efforts have failed, the Earth has created its own massive eco-holocaust by way of a geomagnetic reversal of the poles. Now, nature is beginning to heal itself – but humanity has a long way to go.

Berk Neilsen is a helicopter pilot from the domed city of Pittsburgh who spends his life monitoring the wild and dealing with the scattered settlements that still exist. But when Neilsen's helicopter is disabled he finds himself facing a world he's never even dreamed of, a jungle where survival favours not only the fittest, but the nastiest, most cunning and the most homicidal. His only ally is a psychopathic young girl who can't be trusted for an eyeblink – unless it's to tear his throat out. In her company, and with all hands turned against him, Neilsen faces a long journey home.

Faraday's Orphans, a tough post-holocaust story with the pace, colour and tension of King's *The Stand* and Zelazny's *Damnation Alley*, more than confirms the promise of Wood's acclaimed first novel, *Looking for the Mahdi*.

ISBN 0 575 60130 2

Moonblood

ALASTAIR MACNEILL

Deep in the Amazon jungle, Donald Brennan has uncovered a secret to die for. Unfortunately for him, he does.

Kelly McBride, owner and captain of the 48-foot tramp *Shamrock Girl*, has problems of her own just keeping body and soul together, and the only way she'll help Ray Brennan find out what happened to his brother is if he pays her – handsomely. Ray, a New York city cop, is accustomed to being in charge; at the mercy of Indians who knew more about his brother than he did, and having to rely on a woman who was running from her past, he couldn't feel more exposed.

Until, that is, Kelly and Ray are forced back to a domain infinitely more dangerous than the jungle: the world of politics, money – and deceit.

And Kelly learns that there are things more important than money, things more important even than the ties of blood . . .

ISBN 0 575 60198 1

VISTA books are available from all good bookshops or from:

Cassell C.S.
Book Service By Post
PO Box 29, Douglas I-O-M
IM99 1BQ
telephone: 01624 675137, fax: 01624 670923

While every effort is made to keep prices steady, it is sometimes necessary to increase prices at short notice. Cassell plc
reserves the right to show on covers and charge new retail
prices which may differ from those advertised in the text or
elsewhere.

VISTA